filters

filters

a novel

deborah ailman

filters

©2015 BY DEBORAH AILMAN

Publisher's Note:

LIBRARY OF CONGRESS CATALOGING-IN-PUBLICATION DATA
Ailman, Deborah
Filters / Deborah Ailman
p. cm.

ISBN 13: 978-1508609612   ISBN 10: 1508609616

1. Contemporary Drama—Fiction. 2. Manhattan Life—Fiction. 3. American Lifestyles—Fiction. 4. Contemporary Wealth—Fiction. 5. Plaza Hotel—Fiction
I. Title

Printed in the United States of America
Set in Palatino Linotype — Cover art by Rikke Jørgensen
Book designed by Lee McCain

10 9 8 7 6 5 4 3 2 1   FIRST EDITION

For the ones that made it possible

shton turned the collar of her coat up in a futile gesture to shield herself from the buffeting winds being channeled up Fifth Avenue. She regretted not hailing that cab; funny, she thought, in a city like New York there should have been a dozen more passing by but here she was, struggling to put one foot in front of the other. Damned wind! And it felt like knives piercing her skin. But she kept on, doggedly determined to reach her destination. What she would find there she had no idea.

Andrew Desmond stared out from the windows in his twenty-first story condo at the Plaza. Snow was starting to fall;

gently now, but soon—at least according to the weather service—New York would be blanketed with about a foot. He noticed the wind, too, now becoming a shrill whistle rattling the windows. He found it difficult to concentrate. His mind was on *her*. The power she must have; he could use that power to become even wealthier and become more powerful himself. Glancing around the room it appeared he had everything anyone could want. But Andrew was a man never satisfied. He was always reaching for the bigger, the better, and always the most exotic. And each trophy he acquired scarcely quenched his thirst. And then he was on to the next conquest. But with her, with all that power, the world could be his. But where was she?

He remembered the excitement he felt when he first heard about her, a woman who seemed to know the thoughts of others before they even spoke, from that bum who did odd jobs for him. He was annoyed that the lowlife even approached him as he exited his limo. But what he said had fascinated Desmond.

Mark Peters The Lowlife spent more time at the bars more than he did at his job as a maintenance man in one of Desmond's many buildings. And despite Desmond's building manager wanting to fire him more than once, Desmond never let him. Peters was a valuable source of information even if most of the time it was smack talk defaming others. But Desmond relished it. There were other "tasks" he carried out for Desmond as well, but they were secret and heinous. He felt he hit the jackpot with The Lowlife's latest report.

It happened as Peters downed his third whiskey and overheard a woman correctly guess what other people were thinking. Over and over again. Perfectly. And as Peters descended into the warming arms of drunkenness, he managed to file away that his boss would find such a woman valuable. He had the wherewithal to try and put himself within her sphere knowing that she'd likely never speak to a half drunk middle aged guy who, despite his best efforts to the contrary, was tripping all over himself. He extended a shaky hand, introduced himself, and asked for hers.

"Ashton Lancaster," she said, quickly moving away and obviously uncomfortable. Good, Peters thought, if she really can read minds he didn't want her to know what he was up to. He withdrew to a corner and watched as she continued her parlor trick, telling her friends their every thought.

After shaking off the hangover the next morning—what time was it, anyway?—he got himself to the Plaza. That's when he saw Desmond returning from a breakfast meeting. Desmond sighed in disgust when he heard Peters' all too familiar voice.

"Mr. Desmond, sir! Oh Mr. Desmond please wait..." Peters excitedly played back the whole night and that's when Desmond heard the name Ashton Lancaster for the first time.

IT DIDN'T TAKE TOO MUCH to find her. In fact almost no time at all, given the connections Desmond had. Ashton Lancaster, thirty-four years old, still living with her mother in an apartment on Shore Road out in Bay Ridge. Lancaster drifted from job to job, started college several times but then abruptly dropped out. Desmond pored through the information. Everywhere Lancaster went people thought she was 'strange' and 'different'. She had a small group of intimates from her high school days who lived in the same neighborhood as she, but as an adult she had apparently befriended no one. No boyfriends, either. That seemed to follow the same

9

pattern as her work history; short term relationships with the guy always leaving, saying she was "weird," and often scared away because it was reported that she could read their minds. So she had taken to drowning her sorrows at a neighborhood bar doing shots of tequila, much to the consternation of her mother and step-father.

Ashton still struggled against the howling wind and snow flakes that were becoming bigger and more intense as she walked. Where was the Plaza, she thought, and then chided herself for not knowing. After all she was a native New Yorker, and didn't everyone know where the Plaza was? With each step she took she could hear her mother's voice: *Ashton, where are you going? There's going to be a blizzard and you're wandering around New York City looking for some strange man. Honestly, I wish you'd find a nice guy and settle down with someone who can take care of you, honey.* But like always, whatever her mother said went in one ear and out the other. And, true to form, as she shut the door she heard her mother yell, "Ashton, ASHTON! It's bad out there...WHERE ARE YOU ARE GOING!?"

Ashton couldn't blame her mother. She tried so hard to support the both of them since her father walked out one night— never to return—when she was only five. And she had freaked her mother out when she said "Daddy's leaving Mommy, and he's not coming back...ever."

Her mother shook her head. Silly child, she thought, what an odd thing to say. Marian Lancaster thought she had the perfect marriage, a kind, loving husband who was a good provider for both her and little Ashton. But the little girl started saying crazy things like Daddy's got a girlfriend at work Mommy, and he wants to go live with her. Taken aback, she told her husband what the child had said. David Lancaster laughed and told her that their daughter had quite the imagination. But Marian didn't see the fear in her husband's eyes and she couldn't read his mind as he wondered how she could know?

But Ashton did know and one balmy summer night David Lancaster was gone. He left his job of over ten years and he wasn't alone. He took his pregnant administrative assistant with him. Marian searched for years trying to find him, trying to get some support for her and her little girl, but there was no trace of him. Marian had quit work when she'd married David eight years before, and she panicked—she had no marketable skills. How would she support them both?

Finally, she was able to secure a position as a cashier at a local grocery store. Thankfully, the apartment they lived in was rent controlled, meaning it could only be raised in small increments. Maybe she and Ashton could stay there after all. Marian worked hard, often overtime, and was lucky to have kind neighbors who volunteered to watch her little daughter at no charge.

As Ashton went through school Marian found herself at countless parent-teacher meetings. Her little girl was scaring the other kids in the class, telling them intimate details about their lives.

"Your mommy drinks too much and yells at you," she told one boy. "Your daddy hits your mommy and she tries to hide it," she told another.

Both children never spoke of it, so how did she know? She wasn't friends with either of the kids and had never gone to their homes or met their parents.

The situation was always the same: Marian begging the principal to keep Ashton in school; after all, she was only a child

11

and she didn't know what she was saying. She meant no harm. One chance, then two, but then Ashton was in front of the school carrying the contents of her desk, tears in her eyes, as she realized she had to find yet another school. And it was tough on Marian. Ashton had run through all of the public schools in the surrounding areas. Now there were only private schools and they could be expensive. Luckily, one of her neighbors had a son who worked in the admissions office at one of them and somehow, by some miracle, Ashton got in with some low income assistance. It was the last chance. She had to stay there or else Marian would have to home school her.

Marian would kneel in the darkness on the cold hardwood floors and pray; arms outstretched to heaven, "Please, dear God, let my Ashton get into this school. Please let us be able to afford it and please keep Ashton quiet!" Marian had her miracle.

"Be quiet, Ashton," Marian would plead with her. "Talk about happy stuff, games and what you're learning in school. What you watched on television last night."

And then Ashton would hear what she would come to hear thousands of times in her life from her mother: "Ashton, you have no filters."

IT WAS A FEW YEARS BEFORE ASHTON knew what "filters" meant—that she needed to carefully consider what she was saying to other people *before* she said it.

Somehow, Ashton managed to stay quiet. She sat at her desk, visualizing her mother saying over and over, "Filters, Ashton." She bit her tongue many times. Looking over at Larry, who sat a little to the right, she almost said, "Your dad is gay, he's just putting up a front for appearances." Or glancing to the left at Mary, it took all she had not to say, "You plan to cheat on the math test; you never study and you don't care."

Kids still thought she was weird, often sullen and withdrawn, so she had no friends. But at least she made it to eighth grade and graduated. Marian would have had a graduation party for her but there was no one to invite, at least none of her fellow classmates. The only one to show up was Marian's sister, Madeleine. Madeleine also seemed to have this "weird" ability to read people's minds. No doubt that's where Ashton got it from. The two of them would sit, giggling and whispering about it.

"Don't encourage her, Madeleine," Marian would plead. "She's got enough trouble as it is." She'd then go back to making her meatballs, clanging the heavy pots in the kitchen. And still there would be the giggling and whispering.

ndrew Desmond was a child of affluence. His parents came from nothing though, his father working hard as an investment banker (mostly junk bonds), and his mother taught kindergarten. They had a small cape cod in Massapequa, Long Island where Andrew attended the public school where his mother taught. It was a comfortable life, they were happy. Or at least Susan Desmond thought they were.

Harold Desmond was a man consumed by the flaming desires of wealth and position. He shared little of this to his wife, who seemed content with the little clapboard house and shopping at discount stores.

Yes, he was "low rent" in the banking business until one day when Andrew was about seven.

What happened was actually a blur, but Harold was in the right place at the right time—one solid investment and it skyrocketed. Within five years Harold's net worth went from zero to nearly one hundred million. Everything he touched seemed to turn to gold. The little clapboard house became a mansion in Sand's Point, the Buick morphed into a Bentley, Susan's half carat diamond ring became a ten carat honker and the clothes that hung in her closet now sported tags with names like Prada and Valentino. Half a dozen staff to care of the cleaning and the cooking. Truth be told, though, Susan Desmond was not happy. She found her joy by working with children and making a homemade dinner for her little family, not riding in a limo up and down Fifth Avenue, buying things she neither needed or wanted. Inside, she longed to go back to Massapequa.

And she didn't approve of the way Andrew was growing up. He was a happy kid, always playing and laughing, and their house was always packed with his friends. But now Andrew was growing arrogant and aloof. Even snobbish. He had few friends in that expensive private school and those he did bring to the house were just as cold as he. Soon, it was riding lessons and polo ponies, summers in Europe and winter vacations on private islands. Andrew was becoming whiney and demanding. The usual outgoing kid who would go out of his way to help an old lady carry a package was now demeaning the help.

16

"I said I wanted ice in my tea not hot; are you stupid or just deaf?" Harold seemed to revel in it, openly encouraging him by saying, "That's my boy. Those people are beneath us. Put the servants in their place!"

Susan was outraged and she felt closer to her staff then she did with all of her so-called friends at the country club. She stood by, fuming, wishing they were back in their little house and behind her desk teaching again.

And although their marriage had always been a good one, Harold had grown more than a wandering eye. All that money made him very attractive to the kind of women who would have never looked at him twice when he was still a junk bond salesman. And as the years unfolded he stopped trying to hide it from Susan; after all, she refused to embrace this fabulous life he had given her. She shied away from his business dinners and resisted his attempts to have her be friendlier to the other wives in their "circle." In his mind, Susan was an embarrassment. She even took the Long Island Rail Road into the city last week instead of using her car and driver! Yes, this annoyed Harold to no end. So he chose solace in the bed of his twenty-three-year-old "assistant." Susan became a blur. Hey, it's her loss, right?

And Harold openly shared his conquests with Andrew as he grew older.

"Your Mom is weak," he would say. "And men like us, well son, men like us have needs."

Andrew was upset at first, the idea that his father was betraying his mother. But Harold was persuasive. "She has a good life anyway now, son. All that money can buy." But Andrew still saw pain and hurt in his mother's eyes, but little by little and egged

17

on by Harold, he began to see his mother as just another piece of furniture in their opulent estate. Andrew was being groomed. Groomed to be a monster.

HAROLD STARTED TAKING HIM TO THE OFFICE when he was about fourteen, showing him off and showing him the ropes. Andrew gravitated towards making money like a fish to water; by twelve he was reading the *Wall Street Journal* and using a good portion of his sizeable allowance to invest in various enterprises. He also was a brilliant student. Okay, maybe not so brilliant, but with his aptitude and his father's generous donation he'd be off to Harvard without a second thought.

Andrew also treated the girls in his class the way his father treated his mother: as objects without feeling. Although Harold wasn't much in the looks department, only getting his women based on what he could provide them financially, Andrew was unnaturally handsome. Standing six feet tall with a well-chiseled physique courtesy of a personal trainer, he had jet-black hair and piercing gray eyes. Many girls craved to hang on the arm of Andrew Desmond, but most quickly changed their minds after experiencing his treatment. For Andrew, it was all about the quick sex; his desires were strictly carnal, he wanted no emotional ties with any of them. What he needed most was power and money, and he wouldn't be satisfied until he accumulated even more than his old man had. And he would find a way to get it.

3

There was crispness in the air as Ashton started her first day of high school. She dressed carefully, pausing in the mirror, trying to decide if she liked the way she looked in her uniform. Plaid was never her favorite, and she was looking for ways to make it, well, a bit more stylish. In the kitchen her mother was hurriedly washing the breakfast dishes, trying not to be late for work. But her mind was on Ashton. How would she do in this new school, as a freshman in high school? Marian said another silent prayer, one of many. Dear God, she said in her mind, please let Ashton know when to hold her tongue." The fact that she spent most of her summer hanging around her Aunt Madeleine didn't please Marian. Sure, Madeleine had that same strange ability to know what others were thinking, but still, she seemed more able to function with it than Ashton. Madeleine had lots of friends, a good job and a place of her own, so Marian figured that she must know how to keep her mouth shut when she had to. Hopefully Ashton would learn to do the same thing and then maybe, dear God maybe, she could have a normal life—a good life.

As Ashton bolted out the door her mother yelled, "Ashton...filters!"

"Yeah Ma, I know," she said, rolling her eyes.

It took a lot to get Ashton in this latest school—Catholic and all girls. It also was in Manhattan on Sixty-fifth Street, almost an hour away by subway from their Bay Ridge apartment. Marian wasn't sure a fourteen-year-old like Ashton should make such a long trip every day, but Madeleine assured her that it was the best thing—a fresh start with new friends. Marian asked her sister countless times during the summer about speaking to Ashton about her "special ability" and to keep it "under wraps."

"She'll be fine, I talked to her about it and she understands," Madeleine told her sister.

Ashton sat quietly on the "R" train as it made its way into Manhattan. At each stop it became more and more crowded until Ashton was shoved into a corner. In her mind she could hear cries of, "I'm so lonely, when will I meet someone who loves me?" "How will I ever get the money to send my kid to college?" "I hope my boss drops dead."

She covered her face with her hands, her head throbbing in pain. Make it stop, she thought, but finally the train screeched into the 68th Street Station and Ashton bolted off the train, up the stairs, and into the bright sunlight. Just ahead, the spires of the church next door to the school sparkled in the sun like a beacon. She ran for the school doors.

MARIAN WAS DISTRACTED ALL DAY LONG, ringing up orders wrong and being openly nervous worrying about Ashton. Thankfully, her boss was a compassionate man. "She'll be fine," he said. Of course, Marian's boss thought she was only concerned about the distance her daughter had to travel to school and not about what could possibly come out of her mouth. As she walked the ten blocks home from the store she kept glancing at the bright blue sky and prayed.

Ashton slid into a chair at the back of the classroom. This was her first experience being taught by nuns, her first day in a Catholic school. She noticed most of the girls wore their plaid skirts pretty short and they almost all seemed to be wearing high heels with their white ankle socks. Maybe she should do the same? The girl sitting next to her noticed her looking.

"They all dress like that...school hotties, the popular girls." Then she held out her hand "I'm Allison." Pumping Ashton's hand she continued, "Good ta meetcha."

Allison's uniform skirt was down to her knees just like Ashton's. She had flat shoes on just like Ashton. Ashton smiled; she had found her first friend. And Allison soon introduced her to her circle of friends, Louise, Cynthia and Carol. All were friendly but, like Ashton, were a little out of the loop. Though Ashton knew what

21

they were thinking she kept it to herself; for the first time in as long as she could remember she felt comfortable doing so. Soon she was having lunch with her little group and she was amazed to learn that all of the girls were from her same neighborhood, just a few blocks away.

"Well what are the odds," Allison remarked while inspecting her bitten fingernails, "that we all live in Bay Ridge. Now we can take the subway together every day!"

Marian breathed a sigh of relief; not only was Ashton making friends but now she didn't have to make that long trip alone.

The other girls at school made fun of what became to be known as "the funky five," the weird girls who didn't wear heels and didn't paint their nails. The ones who never talked about boys and didn't wear their skirts hiked up to their rear ends. But the "funky five" would soon have another secret—one of their members could read minds.

It was another gorgeous fall day. The leaves on the trees were turning shades of crimson and pumpkin. As the girls walked home from the subway station the sky was lit with shades of orange and pink from the setting sun. The homey smell of chimney smoke bellowed from the roofs of the old brownstones that lined the Brooklyn streets. It was then Ashton said, "I've got a secret."

IT WENT OVER BETTER THAN ASHTON could have ever hoped for. Here were four other people who thought it was wonderful that she could read their minds. On that fall afternoon, five girls cemented friendships for life.

It was another mess. Nineteen year old Andrew was involved in yet another scandal, this one his biggest yet. Harold would have to work hard covering this one up. Andrew had gotten a freshman pregnant, and then drove her to some upscale clinic to have her abort it. The girl couldn't live with the guilt she felt so she spilled the beans to her parents. Mortified, her parents raced up to the main offices at Harvard. Somehow Andrew managed to stay enrolled; how much it cost Harold no one knew, not even Susan, who spent many a night crying for the girl and her lost child. Crying for the way Andrew was turning out. Crying that Harold more often than not came home from the "office" reeking of expensive women's perfume (not her brand). Crying that the little clapboard house seemed so very far away and long ago.

Harold's voice thundered through the huge rooms of the estate. "Andrew, learn to keep it in your pants, will you?"

Andrew looked down from the second story railing, perched over the great room. He snickered. He had no remorse for any of it. She was an easy lay, and the fact that she left school, devastated, had no effect on him. He walked slowly down the spiral marble staircase to be met by his father. Harold patted his son on the back and smiled slyly. "Remember son, she's nothing. Just don't get caught next time."

From the top of the stairs, Susan Desmond couldn't believe her ears. How callous and uncaring her husband had become over the years and now he impressed all that garbage on Andrew. She retreated to her room and scanned all the obvious trappings of her wealth. She knew then that her life at the mansion had to come to an end. Harold and her son were a lost cause, as was her life in this miserable place. She would find a way to get back to the little Cape Cod. One way or another she would go back.

The heavy front door slammed shut as Andrew left to meet his friends. Harold settled in the library to read his newspaper after barking an order to one of the maids for a neat scotch. Susan padded down the stairs intent on challenging her husband about the way Andrew was turning out. She would plead with him one last time and ask his help getting their son back on track. But Harold looked at her as if she were a Martian.

"Are you kidding? What would you have him do, Susan? Become a teacher and live in a tiny little redneck town for the rest of his life? Settle down with a plain Jane who pops out lots of kids they won't be able to afford? Is that what you consider to be on track, Susan? Is that what you consider to be living? Our son has the world by the balls." he thundered.

Susan winched at his choice of words because that's exactly the word she was thinking of...*balls*. She was thinking she'd like to cut his right off about now.

"Oh, go shopping or something," Harold spewed. Susan stared hard at the man sitting in the easy chair. He was almost a stranger now. Gone were the Wednesday night spaghetti dinners with him and little Andrew, laughing and giggling as they counted their pennies to buy toys at the dollar store.

Nowadays dinners were served at a massive table by servants flitting about with only the most expensive cuts of meat. And most of them Susan ate alone—Harold at his "business meetings," and Andrew either in school, or if he was home for the weekend out with his snooty friends.

Susan turned abruptly and walked silently to the backyard where the sun was slipping below Long Island Sound. She remembered when she watched *The Great Gatsby* on television when Andrew was just a baby. How she longed to have a house like that and to live the way Gatsby did. Many years later, living in a way that would have made Gatsby proud, she hated every minute of it.

"GET OFF THE PHONE, ASHTON," Marian yelled for the sixteenth time "I'm expecting a call!"

Ashton was too busy regaling Allison with details of her upcoming date with Gary Mueller, a senior at one of the Catholic all boys schools she met at a dance. Sixteen year old Ashton was turning into quite the beauty, but somehow she had never been accepted by the hotties as Allison called them at her own school. The "funky five" was still going full steam but none of the girls seemed to make any friends outside their circle. In fact, one of the hottie girls, Mallory, was openly hostile to the group, especially to Allison. On more than one occasion Allison left school crying hysterically after Mallory had made some comment about the way she looked.

Ashton could take no more of this girl harassing her best friend. She slinked up to Mallory as she stood by her locker and hissed, "I know you got pregnant last year and I know what you did about it." It was a first for Ashton. The first time she ever said anything deliberately to hurt somebody. Up to now, she had only blurted out information because she was a kid and hadn't learned the meaning of filters. Now she was intently using her ability to strike back. It made her stomach ache and her head spin. But she had to avenge Allison.

Mallory stood in shock, her face drained of color. The only people who knew about that were her mother and father. She hadn't even told any of her friends. Not even the boy who was the father knew she was pregnant. So how did Ashton know?

"Be nice to Allison or everyone will know," were Ashton's parting words.

She rushed off leaving Mallory standing in the hallway with her mouth hanging open. But the hostility ceased right away. Now when Mallory saw Allison she just smiled and nodded. Allison was relieved but couldn't help notice that Mallory carefully averted Ashton's gaze. She made a mental note to ask Ashton about it, but by the end of the day it had slipped her mind entirely.

THE SEDAN PULLED UP TO THE APARTMENT on Shore Road and Gary Mueller got out. He was a senior at Regis High School now, and would be off to college in the fall. He met Ashton Lancaster at a school dance and although she was shy he was attracted to her piercing sea green eyes that seemed to look right through you. As he spoke with her he noticed she really was beautiful; more than even the "hot" girls, who wore tons of makeup, cracked their gum when they chewed and seemed to always travel in packs.

There was a serene innocence about Ashton. Gary wanted to get to know this girl. He was pleased when she said yes to dinner that Friday night. And now he stood in front of her building, nervous as hell. Since he went to school in Manhattan and took the subway he had no need of a car and so he borrowed his mother's. Not the sportiest thing but at least it was clean and reliable.

He took the elevator to the third floor and rang the bell; it kind of stuck and made a noise like a cat in heat. That amused him. Marian answered the door and shook his hand then scanned him head to toe. Nice kid, she thought. And then the familiar prayer formed in her mind. Please let Ashton know when to hold her tongue. Ashton appeared, this time dressed a bit edgier than her Catholic school uniform. Marian spent quite a bit on her dress, probably more than she should have, but Ashton never really asked for anything and after all it was her first date.

This first date would unfold in a pattern that became all too familiar: Ashton reading the guy's mind, knowing what he wanted to do with her, all the while his lips saying "I respect you. I want to get to know you as a friend first." Ashton knew it wasn't true and she would blurt it out...a blow-by-blow of exactly what the guy was thinking about. As she got older each relationship, if you could call it that, ended the same...making it to three or four dates at most and then ending abruptly, the guy saying something like "You're crazy! You're spooky! Stay away from me!"   When she was seventeen, she did give into one of them, just for the experience, but it left her cold. As she moved into her twenties she sometimes would sleep with the guy on the first date because she knew there probably wouldn't be another one.

GARY MUELLER DROVE HOME in his mother's sedan, hands shaking, wondering where the hell this girl came from. Ashton walked through the door looking crestfallen. Her mother knew immediately and worried about what would become of her daughter. When Gary ran into her at other dances he would nod nervously and then walk the other way...as quickly as possible. Luckily for Ashton, he never discussed the details of their date with any of his friends, he just said they "weren't compatible" and changed the subject. Gary knew his friends would never believe any of it anyway...a girl who reads minds. And besides, what if she got mad and told everybody what he really wanted to do with her? Better to keep silent...a girl like that could be dangerous.

And the other girls from the "funky five" weren't having much luck with boys either. Occasionally one of them would have a date but somehow it never grew to more. As time went on the bond between the girls grew—at least they had each other. But soon, high school would be done. Where would they go from here?

SUSAN AND HAROLD STOOD CLAPPING loudly from the front row. Andrew extended his hand to the dean to receive his diploma-an MBA from Harvard. Twenty-four year old Andrew had all eyes on him (mostly female) as he strode to his seat.

A huge party was planned at the estate with all the snobby people Susan hated, the women playing a kind of "one up" game as to who had the most expensive pair of shoes. When Marge Solis disclosed her Louboutins cost over four grand, she won. Susan, trying hard to hide her disgust walked towards the kitchen to see if she could help the servants with anything. After all these years, it was her greatest joy to sit in the huge, well equipped kitchen and talk to her staff as they cooked. She even helped them sometimes. Harold was annoyed when she did that, but he was so preoccupied with showing off Andrew's diploma he didn't notice her absence.

"He starts work next week at my firm, but first he must have a few days in Paris. Every young man needs some time in Paris don't you think?" Harold was telling his neighbor about his plans for Andrew's future. Robert, the major domo, was briskly walking past when he heard it and thought to himself "that brat needs to spend some time in a holding cell, screw Paris."

Andrew did go to Paris…but not to visit the Eiffel Tower. He frequented the seedier side of town and got drunk often. He openly sought out prostitutes…they were perfect for him. They'd do all the kinky stuff he liked and when it was over…it was over. No "when are you going to call me" or "do you love me?" Andrew loved money and power like his dear old dad. Women, well women were just playthings, good for diversion.

He started in his father's firm the next week as an executive vice president with a starting salary of a little over three hundred thousand a year. Andrew complained and wanted more, but Harold thought it might inflame his board of directors, after all, even with an MBA from Harvard he still would have started in a much lower position in the food chain had he not been the son of the Chairman. Andrew was still young and this was his first real job so he would have to work hard to show the board he was worth what he planned on asking for next.

And Andrew did work hard…he was in his element. He had a knack for knowing when to invest and when to cut loose. He also had a knack for having affairs with executive assistants and then dumping them…somehow the women were mysteriously fired after that. But there seemed to be new ones every week; Andrew's handsome face and his near perfect pecks were too much for some to resist. Others knew better: a quick roll-in-the-hay wasn't worth their job or their self esteem.

As the years went by Andrew was promoted quickly…now, as president, he was eying his father's job as CEO. And he thought to himself that it might be a good idea to add a wife to that mix. His father had never frowned on his affairs in the past, but now Harold thought that Andrew, now in his mid thirties, should take a wife. Maybe it was because he felt there should be an "heir" to pass the company to when Andrew stepped down or died. Or maybe he thought that Andrew's behavior needed to be "toned down" to protect the company's image. But it was decided…Andrew would take a wife.

Harold told Susan of his plans for Andrew one night at dinner. Susan thought it was odd; she never had dinner with Harold anymore and had taken to eating sandwiches in her bedroom while reading or knitting, a hobby she had taken up when Andrew was a baby. Since money was tight then she made many of Andrew's things to save a few dollars. Now, most of the stuff she made was either donated to a thrift store in town or given to the staff. But the rhythmic motion of it soothed her, taking her back to the little clapboard house and Andrew, just a toddler, laughing at her feet. But the call from Harold came that afternoon. "I'll be home at seven," he snapped. "Meet me in the dining room, we have to talk."

At first Susan was elated. Maybe Harold wanted a divorce and she could get out of this gold-plated hellhole. She had asked for a divorce many times over the past few years but Harold never agreed—it was bad for business, bad for appearances. No, he would not give Susan a divorce. He hardly even gave her the time of day.

She sat at the massive table as Harold strode into the room, one of the maids running behind him carrying his single malt scotch. He told her flat out: Andrew had to get married.

Susan glazed over. The thought of Andrew settling down, having a wife and children and the big Sunday dinners, and the school plays and…

"Oh stop it Susan," Harold barked. "This is not a marriage for love. This will be a marriage of appearance, of convenience. That woman he's dated a few times, yes, that Sarah Douglas, that's the one. That's the one he'll marry."

Susan was crestfallen. Sarah Douglas, though beautiful and well educated was a snob. One of these girls who "talked through

31

her nose" about how much money she spent. Her biggest accomplishment in life so far was to manage to spend more money in a week on herself than Susan had spent in ten years. She was shallow and obnoxious, not the kind of woman Susan wanted for a daughter-in-law. But nothing seemed to be about what Susan wanted anymore.

Andrew actually had been dating this girl for awhile. Wasn't it actually a few months now? But Susan had it pegged…this girl was one obnoxious snob. Susan had met her a few times when they had been guests at the Douglas estate, not far from their own in Upper Brookville. Though not quite as wealthy as the Desmonds, the Douglas family had come from old money. Sarah's father, Jonathan, was in the family business, commercial real estate started by his father, but Jonathan didn't have much interest in it…in fact he only worked a few days a week and even then they were half days.

The rest of the time he spent playing golf or riding at a nearby stable. And Sarah, though well educated, never worked a day in her life. She had a high pitched, kind of nasally whiny voice. "Oh Daddy, you're just sooooo funny," she'd comment after Jonathan made one of his lame jokes. Or she would say something like "Oh Daddy, do you really want me to wear these old things?" when she wanted to fly to Paris to pick out a new wardrobe.

Jonathan called her "his princess" as her mother idly stood by. She was so non-descript Susan couldn't even remember what she looked like. Susan saw many of those clothes…all designer, all extremely expensive and all either never or barely worn. Sarah didn't sort out her clothes to give them to the less fortunate as Susan did; she pitched them down the stairs or threw them in the garbage

32

where their staff fished them out and either kept them or gave them away. This girl was definitely going to be high maintenance. But who was she to stop it?

The wedding took place at the Waldorf-Astoria ten months later. Six hundred people attended. Sarah wore a seventy-five thousand dollar custom made gown and sported a seven carat pear shaped fancy yellow diamond from Harry Winston. The bride was luminous. The groom was making eyes at one of the bridesmaids. Harold was beaming ear-to-ear and Susan fought back tears and the only conversation she had that day was with the servers at her table. The couple took the corporate jet to some exotic island. On the second night, Andrew screwed one of the waitresses in the hot tub and stayed out all night. Sarah cried at first but then brushed back the tears, grabbed her husband's black "Am Ex" card and went into town shopping.

When she returned from town she gave her new husband a black eye from her strong left hook. He raised his hand to her but changed his mind saying, "You're just not worth it, bitch."

When the corporate jet landed back in New York, it looked like the couple had just been to a funeral instead of on their honeymoon.

They bought a twenty room colonial on Centre Island which Sarah proceeded to decorate in a frilly, feminine fashion which Andrew hated. He preferred a more modern, masculine look with sleek woods and muted colors. Sleeping in that king sized bed with the blue ruffles seemed to irritate him, and Sarah knew it. If she was not going to get a faithful loving husband then she was going to make his life as miserable for as long as she could before he divorced her, and then she would take him for everything she could as they had no pre-nup. Harold thought it would look bad in the press; he wanted the great Desmond family to appear kind and generous. She spent as much as she could. It kept her company on nights when Andrew was out being "entertained" by women other than herself.

And so the pattern was set for the new Mr. and Mrs. Desmond. He would screw who he wanted, she would spend what she wanted.

There would be no children, no big Sunday dinners. Susan rarely spoke to her daughter-in-law. At first they tried to "make nice" with Sarah dragging Susan up and down Fifth Avenue into all the most exclusive stores trying to get her to update her wardrobe. But when it became obvious that Susan was not interested, that she would rather spend the day gardening, Sarah quickly lost interest. Now there were just the occasional phone calls and the polite nods.

Andrew made CEO on his first wedding anniversary. By his third he was divorced, paying through the nose to keep Sarah in the lifestyle he had provided her during their short marriage. She kept the house; he wanted no part of it. Instead he bought a three bedroom condo on the top floor of the Plaza to be near the office.

Now that he was CEO, he really had to stop sleeping with the office staff. But, fresh from his divorce he was not interested in a relationship anyway. Sending high priced call girls to his penthouse apartment became the norm for Plaza management.

Andrew sized up this latest one, fresh off the elevator, and as he reached for her he thought how wonderfully simple this all was. He could get his rocks off with no complications and now, with the company free from his father's control, he could take it to the next level. Harold was good, no doubt, but now that he was in mid sixties he was slowing down with heart problems and high blood pressure. It was time he stepped down from the company he founded and ran for almost twenty-five years. It belonged to Andrew now.

Twenty miles away, on the north shore of Long Island his mother looked up from her gardening and thought the same thing...the company belonged to Andrew now. And then the thought "God help us all" raced through her mind.

ASHTON FOCUSED ON PUTTING ONE FOOT in front of the other as she walked to the podium to receive her high school diploma. There were so many people in the auditorium, so many thoughts in their heads and those thoughts were crowding into Ashton's mind.

"I'm so proud!"

"She barely squeaked by in school, what kind of an education will she get in community college?"

"I'll have to sell my grandmother's ring to pay for Gina's first year of college. I don't want her to know we have no money," and more were flashing through her mind.

Ashton had come to hate crowds; there was always so much going on and it often made her nauseous and dizzy. She managed to smile and shake the principal's hand, and then make her way slowly back to her seat next to Allison. The two of them had no concrete plans for their future, and both decided on Kingsborough Community College although neither knew what they wanted to study, they choose that school because it wasn't far from the McDonald's where they both got after-school jobs.

Marian sat next to Madeleine, visibly worried. Madeleine, as usual, tried to calm her sister down but this time it just wasn't working. Marian had the school program in her hand and it listed the colleges the girls were attending. Yale, Columbia, NYU…big name schools almost guaranteeing a bright future. Maybe Ashton's close friendship with Allison wasn't such a good thing…if Ashton had made other friends maybe she'd be following in their footsteps…right into the Ivy League.

She sighed heavily and shutting her eyes thought to herself that no, it wasn't right to think like that. This was Ashton's day. She made it through four years almost uneventfully; she had managed to use her "filters" and Marian figured she should be grateful for that. Ashton was only eighteen—she still had a good chance at a solid future. Yes, Marian had to believe that. At the end of the ceremony Marian hugged her, hard, and gave her that Seiko watch she had wanted so badly.

And then they were alone, the three of them: Ashton, Marian and Madeleine as they had a celebratory dinner at Peter Luger's. Ashton told them she planned to work full time at the McDonald's until school started in the fall. Madeleine was going to loan her car to her for the summer and then she would catch a ride with Allison when September came. Getting a car for Ashton just wasn't possible right now.

Thankfully, Ashton was always gracious about things like that. From the time her father left she never complained about not having what the other girls had. That was one thing that was spared Marian, although in all these years Marian never met anyone else. Sure, she was friendly with her boss, Bob; he hired her on at the store shortly after her husband took off. There were some sparks there but Marian was always more interested in spending every minute with her little girl rather than finding a date. But was it his imagination or was she growing friendlier now that Ashton was older? Bob had never married, being at the store almost from open to close each day and many times even after that. As he looked at Marian he felt a kind of sadness. Here was a woman he could care for, someone to have dinner with and laugh with. One day, one day soon he would ask Marian for a date. Maybe she would say yes. Maybe they could both be happy together...

THE MAN SKULKED UP TO THE COUNTER. "He's going to rob the place," Ashton said, eyes wide open, almost frozen in fear. "What..." the owner started but then he found them both looking down the barrel of a sawed-off shotgun. Ashton knew what the man was thinking...he had to have some cash to take his wife to the doctor. She was so sick, so weak she couldn't take care of their six month old son anymore. No one would help them. He couldn't seem to get a job anywhere. And now he was desperate.

"Your wife doesn't want you to do this," Ashton said softly, looking directly into the man's eyes. "You'll find another way. This isn't it."

The man was stunned and let his guard down, just in time for the assistant manager to grab the gun. But the man didn't even seem to notice that he was disarmed. He continued to stare at Ashton. "How did you know...?"

Contained now at a corner table, the assistant manager holding his gun over him until the police arrived the man just kept looking sadly at Ashton and repeating over and over "How did you know?"

As the police cuffed him and led him out, the owner turned to Ashton. "How DID you know? And THANK YOU!"

"Oh, it was just a feeling," she said. Better not to disclose too much information.

As she drove Madeleine's car home that night she decided not to mention it to her mother. But it wouldn't matter since the next day it was in the papers and on the news. Soon there were reporters coming into the restaurant asking to interview her. They were calling her the "girl who could read minds." Marian was appalled. Madeleine was pleased. All Allison could say was that it was only a matter of time before the whole world knew. But Ashton didn't want the whole world to know. She wished this "gift" would go away and she could be normal like everyone else.

Her boss had a new found respect for her. He gave her a raise and made her one of his assistant managers. He worked around her school schedule when fall rolled around, but that was short lived, as Ashton dropped out of college only a few months later. Sitting in the big lecture halls made her head ache, as the drama of other people's lives played out in her mind. It made it difficult to study, and besides, she was now up for manager of the restaurant. She told her mother it actually made it easier for them; she could now contribute far more to the household than she had ever done before. It would make it so much better for Marian; she could work less and maybe even enjoy a date with Bob.

Marian smiled shyly. She would like that...a date with Bob, the man that had been so kind to her all these years and a perfect gentleman to boot.

It was less than two weeks later on a cold crisp winter day that she and Bob drove up to Bear Mountain to have Sunday brunch. Now that Ashton was an assistant manager she managed to get a loan to buy a small, used car. As she drove to work that Sunday morning she had a good feeling about her mom. She knew Bob loved her and she loved him. Now would be their time.

Six months later Ashton was the picture perfect maid of honor and she watched her mother walk down the aisle towards the man she had secretly loved for so long. Little did they know that their idyllic life would eventually be torn to shreds.

ndrew woke the sleeping blonde next to him while rubbing the sleep from his eyes and trying to remember "where did she come from again? Which club did he pick her up from last night?" Oh well, it didn't matter now anyway…the sun was starting to streak through the huge bedroom windows reminding Andrew that there was a new day ahead to grab what he could…as if he didn't have enough already.

But it was a sound decision on Harold's part to make Andrew CEO; his killer instinct for making deals far exceeded Harold's ability. Under his leadership the company was making more money than ever. Andrew just seemed to have a natural ability to make money; he could smell it the way a shark could smell blood in the water. And Andrew was the "shark" that swept up bleeding companies and integrated then into his own.

Andrew was becoming annoyed with this latest "sleeping beauty" She was languishing too long in his bed and she wanted to cuddle. He pushed her hard until she fell onto the marble floor beneath her. She rose quickly, rubbing her shoulder which had obviously been injured. She moaned softly. Andrew glanced coldly at her and told her to get out, and if her shoulder was hurt the doctor bill was on him. The girl collected her belongings quickly and slid out the door, tears in her eyes and shaking her head "What a monster this guy was! Why did I ever come home with him last night?"

Andrew stood in front of the full length mirror, naked, admiring himself. Flexing his biceps he thought he looked pretty damned good for forty. He laughed to himself as he got in the shower. By the time he got out his breakfast was set on the outside terrace overlooking Central Park. He sat there, in his thick terry cloth robe, reading the "Wall Street Journal" and thinking he had the world by the balls. Well, almost anyway. He still had some work to do.

SUSAN DESMOND WAS KNEELING in the morning sun cutting fresh flowers for her dining table. Andrew was coming to dinner tonight! She was so excited, despite the fact that most of the time he spoke only with Harold and only about business, dismissing his mother rudely when she would make small talk with him about who he was dating and didn't he want to get married again and start a family? "Time's running out honey," she'd say in a loving voice. "Wouldn't it be wonderful to be a grandmother?" She'd mostly say that to herself, since the two men virtually ignored her.

As she laid the flowers carefully in the basket she saw Harold traipsing across the lawn. She knew he didn't come home last night…something that was becoming more and more common. Since semi-retiring from the company Harold had lots of time for extracurricular activities. She wasn't sure who this last one was… a brunette she thought, maybe about twenty-five?

Harold didn't even acknowledge her as he walked past. It was as if his wife didn't even exist anymore. He climbed up the heavy marble staircase towards his room. It was "his room" now because he hadn't slept with Susan in years…she still occupied the huge master bedroom. He swallowed his heart medication and drifted off to sleep knowing his son would visit tonight, his Andrew, his masterpiece.

Andrew was late and he was annoyed. That girl in his bed from last night made him late to the office…late to an important meeting. He made a mental note to himself not to bring home "guests" the night before such an important meeting again, but she was so enticing and he was so drunk.

He rode up to his office in his private elevator, his secretary nipping at his heels as he strode through its huge glass doors. Doris had been with him for years now. He handpicked her; she had originally worked for Harold. Intelligent, organized and mid forties, he would not be tempted to spend time sliding up to the side of her desk to flirt. She cornered him as he sat down in his custom leather chair and quickly went over the details of his meeting, ready to start. Doris knew the others would wait for him in the boardroom;

no matter how much each of the executives present had on their plates they couldn't start without their chairman. One of the VP's made a snide remark about Andrew's "extracurricular" activities being the reason he was late. He was quickly shushed by another one. It wouldn't be wise to have Andrew walk in and hear that. Not wise at all...

The meeting went on as most of them did, usually involving the takeover of another, smaller company. Andrew could sniff those out like a bloodhound could sniff out his master's prey, and once they were his they somehow all became profitable again, albeit after thousands of employees had lost their jobs and had been replaced with those handpicked from the Desmond Corporation, or shipped overseas for a Desmond affiliate to run. Andrew had been responsible for the closure of countless small towns, their plants being their only sustaining force and now snatched away. Danny Harper was one such employee.

He and his family lived in a little town right outside Topeka Kansas until one day the factory was gone. Now he returned just to take a look and remember what it was like—the little church and the Sunday socials, the children laughing and playing ball in the field nearby. Now the church lay in ruins along with the little houses that lined the one main street. Rotting away, rusting away.

How could so much destruction happen in just a few years? Danny himself never had steady work again, never a union paycheck or company health benefits. Nope, now he was mostly a day laborer, jumping on the big old truck that swung by in the morning when his legs could carry him. His arthritis was so bad that some days he couldn't even get out of bed. Fifty-four year old Danny was counting on a pension and not on the kindness of strangers. But Andrew Desmond changed all that, for Danny and thousands like him.

ANDREW FINISHED UP THE MEETING with his board of directors, sipping the special coffee he had imported from Kenya. His head still ached from all that partying last night, but he didn't dare show any signs of fatigue to his board. Enough of them didn't like him; although he exceeded his father in business acumen, Harold actually treated the board (and the other employees) with more kindness and respect. Although Harold Desmond would never be described as a "teddy bear" his son seemed to have a heart of stone. Those who did not march to the beat of his parade were soon discarded by the wayside.

Andrew closed the meeting, took one last sip from his cup, then turned on his heels and left the boardroom. No "thank you for being here" or "have a nice day." Nothing. As he made his way back to his office he remembered he had a dinner engagement at his parents' house that night. "Oh joy," he thought to himself. His attention was temporarily diverted by a pretty redhead in his accounting department. "Where did she come from?" he thought to himself. He'd make it a point to introduce himself later, as she watched him walk by, a bright smile on her face. He winked at her.

The rest of the day unfolded as usual for him. Papers to sign, more of that expensive coffee no one else dared try, then lunch at the club. The afternoon went by quickly as Andrew made plans to take over yet another factory somewhere in the Midwest. He scanned a handwritten letter obviously written by a small child begging him to save her mommy and daddy's jobs. "Stupid kid," he thought, and tossed the letter in the trash. That leggy redhead

45

passed by his office; he could see her through the glass. *Wonder how good she'll be in bed?* was the thought that next crossed his mind as a sly smile crept across his face.

He consoled himself with a scotch as he stared out the window of his limo, taking in the views of Long Island sound. To this day, it still took his breath away to see the mansion appear at the top of the hill. He remembered it was built by one of the barons from the "gilded age" but at this moment couldn't remember who. The car slid under the porte-cochère and his driver was quick to get his door. His mother rushed out to hug him. Andrew stiffened his body; he disapproved of any show of affection. He gently pried her arms from his shoulders and simply said, "Hello Mother." He extended his hand to his father who was beaming ear-to-ear.

Harold was anxious to hear all about the company. As his heart grew worse, his semi-retired and consultant status dwindled down to almost nothing. Months went by before he even set foot in the office and even then was barely noticed. The great man, Harold Desmond, who rose out of the ashes to build this company now had as much status as the pizza delivery boy. And Andrew did nothing to discourage it.

The dinner was tiresome, Harold going on about the old days at the office and Susan clamoring for the grandchildren she would never have. Andrew felt contempt for his parents and had begun to openly show it. Susan was used to being the "odd man out" but not Harold. He slammed his fist down on the heavy table and yelled "Boy, you have no respect for your father!" Andrew looked at him blankly and then said "I have respect for people who have value in this world, Father. I have respect for people who contribute, not for old people hanging onto past glory days. You have become useless, Father."

Harold stood, mouth hanging open in disbelief. "You little prick," he hissed. "You ungrateful little bastard, I made you what you are today! How dare you say I have no use! Get out of my house and don't *ever* come back!" Susan bolted from the table, openly sobbing, and ran into the garden. It was pitch black out now except for the illumination of the moon, which looked full. Maybe that was it...had Andrew gone crazy because it was a full moon?

Inside, Andrew was now standing as well. His composure was that of a stone figure, unlike his now sweating and visibly agitated father. "That is fine with me, Father. I will never come back here again. Never come through the doors of my company again either, Father. We are even. Goodbye."

Almost magically, his driver was at the front again. Andrew almost knocked him over getting in the back seat. "Let's get the fuck out of here!"

Inside the house, Harold clutched at his chest, one of the servants bringing him his nitroglycerin. He then took the newly installed elevator to his room. In the garden, Susan sat in silence, tears running down her face. "What happened to my little boy? What happened to my life?" She sat for hours, watching the moon's ray's dance on the inky blackness of the sound. It was morning before she went back inside, called from sleep by the chirping of robins on the great lawn.

In the morning, Andrew announced to the board that his father had permanently stepped down from his "consultant" status and wouldn't be coming into the office any longer. "His health is declining, and his doctor recommends rest," he lied. He was in a hurry to get out of the boardroom and swing by accounting, where he made a dinner date with that leggy redhead. "This is going to be a pretty good day," he thought to himself.

ALLISON WAVED BRIGHTLY AT ASHTON, who she could clearly see through the coffee shop window. Ashton looked at her blankly and thought her nursing uniform suits her, and then smiled. She was glad Allison had found her calling in life. She had been at Bellevue for awhile now, and was moving up quickly as a psychiatric nurse.

As she slid in the booth across from Ashton she said, "Even I can read your mind right now, Ashton. You're sad."

Sad was not the word for it. Ashton's life was spiraling out of control. Not too long after the incident where she foiled that robbery the appreciative owner sold the store. The new owner was leery of a store manager who, according to many people, could read your mind.

She was also becoming sullen and withdrawn again, and many new employees quit soon after being hired because they said she 'creeped them out.' One day, as she was showing a new hire how to make French fries she asked him why he cheated on his wife last night with her best friend. She regretted it right away. She could hear her mother's voice pleading, "Ashton...filters!" She felt somehow that she was losing control of her impulses.

The new hire went straight to the owner and promptly quit, saying he didn't want to work in a place with such a 'freaky' manager. It wasn't the first time the new owner had heard this...he was losing new people left and right and it was difficult to keep the store staffed properly. He found himself on many a night and weekend working behind the counter and his wife was starting to complain he was never home. Ashton was demoted to assistant manager. He brought in a new guy from one of his other stores to take her place. Just nineteen and right out of high school, Ashton felt humiliated.

THE YEARS WENT BY and of the "funky five" only Ashton seemed to be struggling. Allison was happy at her job (and happily dating as well) and the others—Cynthia, Carol and Louise all had careers, married and moved away; Cynthia to Los Angeles, where she worked as a paralegal, Carol to Chicago where she became curator of an art gallery, and Louise to Nashville, where she was an agent for the country music industry. Ashton and Allison heard from them every once and awhile but they were fast becoming a faded memory.

Allison noticed, too, as the years went by that there just seemed to be no place for Ashton. She was barely limping along at the restaurant. She had been written up countless times and even suspended. She just couldn't keep her mouth shut or use her "filters" as her mother and now her stepdad told her so many times. Allison feared she would get fired and then what?

More than a few times she had talked to Ashton about going back to school, about finding something she was interested in—something that would get her out of the Shore Road apartment she had lived in since birth. But it just fell on deaf ears. And Ashton now didn't even try to have relationships anymore; she just hung around the local bars at night and pretty much just picked someone to go home with. Maybe she just read their minds and picked the most innocuous one. Ashton was almost thirty now, and working twenty-five hours a week at that same McDonald's restaurant—no overtime ever and no benefits—since she was now only a part-time employee.

Marian and Bob were upset as well. Although Bob had come to love Ashton as his own, they both were looking forward to the day when they would finally have the apartment to themselves, or maybe even retire and leave Brooklyn altogether. Maybe Florida? But how could they leave Ashton alone- she was barely clearing two hundred dollars a week after taxes, and they both knew she was skating on thin ice at the restaurant. The rent alone on the apartment was now nearly eight hundred a month even though it remained rent controlled, so there would be no way she could continue to live there and pay all her other bills as well once they were gone.

Marian had enlisted the help of her sister Madeleine to try to reach Ashton, but now even she had given up. "Just keep your mouth shut!" Madeleine barked. Ashton was hurt, gone were the magical conversations she used to have with her aunt about how special her "gift" was. But Madeleine knew she was no longer a child, and this "gift" was now doing more harm than good.

It was only a few weeks after she met Allison for coffee that she finally was fired from the place where she had worked for almost twelve years, where she had foiled that robbery, where, for a short time she had her place of glory. She cleaned out her locker, tears in her eyes as the young manager yelled: "Freak! And don't come back here again...*ever!*"

She drowned her sorrows at a neighborhood bar and then in the arms of a young biker dude who was on his way to somewhere out west but stopped to quench his thirst. They made it on a dirty, discarded couch in a garbage heap behind the bar after it closed.

As she slinked through the door at six in the morning her mother was just getting the coffee on. One look and she knew, but she said nothing as Ashton showered and went to bed. It was time for Bob to put her on at the store; there was nothing else to do. That meant they would have to put off their plans to sell the place and retire. Marian knew the only person Ashton could work for was Bob, and with both of them in the store they could keep an eye on her.

They let Ashton sleep it off as they both went to work. That evening they all sat down in the living room. "You'll have to go to work for me Ashton, or go back to school. I don't know what else to do with you. I know you have this "gift" but when you were younger your mother said that you seemed to have more control over it. The only place you'll be safe is with us," Bob said as Marian nodded.

Ashton noticed they both looked so tired, her mother well over sixty now and Bob just over seventy. She knew they had plans to drink their morning coffee on a sandy beach and to walk that same beach at sunset with a cocktail. But all of that was going up in smoke now…and because of her.

The next week, Ashton was being trained on how to scan groceries at the cash register…by her mother. As each customer came up, they seemed to know Marian and chirped brightly "Oh, is this your daughter? What a beautiful young lady? How proud you must be to have her in the family business!"

Ashton knew what they were really thinking "are you kidding? A cashier? At her age? Where was her degree or her husband? What a loser!" She said nothing as she glanced at her mother. Marian had her "filters" look on again and Ashton knew her mother meant business. She greeted each customer pleasantly and mopped the floor at the end of the evening. That night, she sat morosely in the corner of the local bar again speaking to no one.

In her head she could hear the thoughts of the other patrons. "Wow, she's hot" thought a young man at the end of the bar. "I really gotta stop drinking but I don't know how," from a middle aged woman seated at a table chatting with her friend. After her third tequila, Ashton couldn't stand it any longer...

"SHUTUPSHUTUPSHUTUP" she screamed at the top of her lungs, slammed down her glass and bolted out the door, leaving the patrons stunned. The middle aged woman, the one who didn't know how to stop drinking belched loudly and then said to her friend "What is wrong with that girl?"

Ashton stumbled in and slammed the door, startling her mother and Bob, who were watching the late news on television before turning in. Marian looked at Bob, with a glance that said "what are we going to do with her?"

At least she was on time for her morning shift at the store. Bob came in a few minutes later, a pained look on his face. All these years he had never said anything. When he married Marian, Ashton's future looked brighter. Albeit she never went back to school but she had a good job as manager and Bob thought that if she continued on like that, maybe she would like to take over his store when he and Marian retired. He would almost give it away, as he loved Ashton as his own. Yes, one day she would have the store and a family of her own. Maybe she would keep the apartment on

Shore Road with the view of the Verrazano Bridge or maybe she and her husband would buy a house. She could visit with her kids when he and Marian retired to Florida. Palm Beach, he thought would be the perfect place or maybe Sarasota? A little condo on the beach with a balcony so they could have their morning coffee and watch the sun rise (or set, depending on the coast they chose) together.

But Bob watched Ashton deteriorate as the years progressed. Being demoted to assistant manager and then to just counter help before being fired, no college in sight. Watching all of her friends make something of themselves. Seeing her get drunk and have one night stands that made her mother cry. Maybe she couldn't live with the voices in her head. Maybe she couldn't live with all that pressure year after year.

She had been to a few therapists, but they couldn't reach her, and one actually threw her out of the office when she told him that his wife knew he was gay, that he wasn't fooling anyone. Medication didn't seem to help either. It just made her lethargic but didn't slow her mind down—she was still keenly picking up on other people's thoughts. And his damned sister-in-law Madeleine was no help either. She just shrugged her shoulders and asked him, "What do you want me to do about it?"

Bob winched; he was seventy-two years old now and these ten hour days were killing him. But if they retired and left the area what would become of Ashton? And if they stayed and retired would the people he'd sell the store to—because it was now obvious she couldn't run it—*keep Ashton on?* As those thoughts raced through his head he glanced at Ashton, who looked right at him. Her expression saddened. She knew what he was thinking.

53

She had to hang onto this job, there was nothing left. Unless, somehow, there was a miracle…a miracle that would help not only her but her parents as well get to Florida and finally get the rest they deserved. She would try to make the most of this opportunity. She would try to do a good job in the store, be responsible and use her "filters" Maybe then she could take it over. She could finally be self sufficient as were Allison and the others. She wondered what it must be like to have a career you loved and a family of your own to come home to. She longed to have "peace" in that mind of hers and not be privy to every detail of anyone who crossed her path. She did her best in the store that day. It broke her heart as each customer came up and she could hear "can't she do any better than this?" and "she's such a beautiful girl but she must be such a disappointment to her mother."

Ashton went straight home that night, no bar, no dinner. She sat upright in bed just staring at the wall in front of her until sleep finally claimed her. Her dreams that night were a jumbled mess that made her toss and turn, including one very odd dream about meeting a very handsome stranger who said he could make her rich…

As she worked the line at the store the next day she barely lifted her head up. There was nothing here for her anymore. Her "gift" had ruined so many lives…wrecked her mother's chance at happiness and ruined her own life as well. And truthfully, she hadn't been feeling all that well these last few weeks- her stomach ached and she was dizzy a lot of the time. Maybe all this "mind reading" was just too much and it seemed to be the same old stuff; Tuesday, and it was Mrs. Murkowski thinking that today would be the day she would start her diet and fit into her imaginary bikini,

Wednesday it was Mr. Sloane thinking about how he should have become a plumber instead of a dentist—it was his mother's idea, Thursday…oh, what did it matter it was the same shit all the time!

She did decide though, to make a doctor appointment that day after work but told no one, a day that would turn out to be the worst of all because as she ran the grocery items through the scanner a hand appeared with a diamond engagement ring on it— Allison—and she was getting married.

"Oh my God, congratulations," she gushed, but inside she was raging. All she could pick up from Allison was that she was so in love with Kevin she could burst. And or course Allison asked her to be her maid of honor. Allison was going to have this wonderful, perfect life and Ashton was still sleeping in the same bedroom she occupied as a baby and living with her mother.

As Marian put on the coffee the next day she noticed Ashton wasn't up yet, and she had to be at the store in half an hour. She knocked on the door but there was no answer. Opening it, she found her bed had not been slept in and there was a note on it that read "Dear Mom, don't be mad but I can't stay here anymore. I've got to make my own way or at least I have to try. I have some money saved so I'll be okay for now. Please don't try to find me."

Marian screamed and Bob came running into the room. He stood there, just staring at the note while his wife sobbed uncontrollably. A week later, they hired someone to replace her at the store. A month later Allison asked a friend from work to be her maid of honor at her wedding. Three months later a letter from Ashton saying she was doing well with no return address.

"But she had no money," Marian cried, "she couldn't have had more than a few hundred dollars."

Bob sighed. He couldn't bring himself to tell Marian that she had stolen almost ten thousand dollars from the store safe. At least he knew she would have some money; maybe she *could* make a fresh start somewhere.

Almost a year later there was a knock at the door. It was Ashton, looking tired and with tears in her eyes. She wanted to come home. Marian and Bob embraced her. She never said what she was doing in all that time. They never asked, afraid to scare her off again with their questions. Bob never mentioned the money she took from the store safe.

It was as if she never left. She was back at the store within a few days. She called Allison to apologize for missing her wedding. Allison knew that Ashton was always a tortured soul. All she said was "Ashton, if you ever want to talk about it I'm here for you." Ashton scanned her thoughts. She was sincere. The friendship stumbled along slowly at first but soon it was going at full steam again. Well as much as it could since Allison had a husband now along with her career at Bellevue, where she had just been promoted to nursing supervisor.

To all who loved her, it was as if her year away never happened. It was all still the same...it was Tuesday and Mrs. Murkowski...

At night, Ashton continued to dream about the rich, handsome man who said he could make her rich. She could see him more clearly each time...tall with raven black hair and piercing gray eyes.

ndrew shuffled off to the bathroom leaving the red head softly snoring. As he stared at his reflection in the mirror he thought to himself that this one was going to be too clingy, she might even want a relationship which would be out of the question. Not since he divorced Sarah had he been involved with anyone past the "two sexual encounters" maximum. Yes, once he had slept with them twice they were out the door. And if they worked at the company and balked at that idea they were fired, no references given. No, his three year marriage was all the commitment he would ever give, no matter what his stupid father said.

He did not have to worry about the company image anymore; he WAS the company. What he said was absolute. What he did would go unchallenged. And at least he didn't have to pay Sarah alimony anymore since she'd married again. He thought his mother might have attended her wedding. "Probably sat in the kitchen with the help," he thought to himself and laughed. And didn't Sarah pop out a rug rat already? Or did he hear her kid was adopted? He was glad he didn't have any; at least no one ever came forward to accuse him, they probably wouldn't dare.

Actually Susan ran into Sarah a few years after she remarried…at a charity event. Sarah stood, beaming ear-to-ear showing off her little girl, Jessica. She was adopted as Sarah found that she could not have children of her own. Susan remembered she was a beautiful and well behaved child and the change in Sarah was remarkable. She had married a VP from her father's company, a man who had deep ties to the community.

He was kind and generous and had been taught to help out those less fortunate. He passed these qualities onto his wife who embraced them. Long gone was the whiney, obnoxious young lady. The Sarah who stood before her now was kind and compassionate towards others and volunteered regularly for different causes. "I want my little girl to grow up respecting others," she said to Susan. Susan hugged her and thought to herself that she really would have made the perfect daughter-in-law after all…

It was funny, but now she had the relationship she wanted with Sarah. They had become good friends. They met for coffee after charity events, Sarah often bringing little Jessica who sat in Susan's lap.

"How is Andrew?" she asked.

"The same," Susan replied and shook her head. After she remarried Sarah sold the big colonial she shared with Andrew and she and her husband moved into a smaller house on the south shore of the island by the beach. After they tried unsuccessfully to conceive, they adopted Jessica, then just a baby. Sarah wanted to know all about her mother but had been told little, except that she was born to a woman in her early thirties who lived alone. There was no information available about the father, but Sarah knew even if there were she and her husband, Bill, would not be told. Little Jessica was a beautiful child, with auburn hair and sea green eyes that seemed to be able to look right into your soul. How Susan wished she were her grandchild.

AS MORNING CAME THE REDHEAD TRIED to embrace Andrew. He told her to get dressed and get to the office on time if she wanted to keep her job. She gathered her things with tears in her eyes as so many had done before her. When she got to the office her head was down. Doris noticed her through Andrew's big glass doors and walked over to her, putting her hand on the girl's shoulder. "Let it go, honey," she said softly. "If you want to keep working here you'll have to let it go."

The girl nodded gratefully and began her work. Doris looked around and thought to herself that Andrew must have slept with nearly ALL the pretty young things in the office and all of them regretted it. Each thought that they would be the one to turn him around and that they would be the next "Mrs. Andrew Desmond," Andrew never gave them a second look after their encounters. Only the strongest ones stayed on. Some quit because they were embarrassed; others were fired for opening their mouths to talk about what everybody else knew anyway...that Andrew Desmond would use each one of them and them thrown them away.

As Doris walked back to her office she saw Andrew striding in. "Bastard," she thought to herself, and then thanked God she was forty-five and married. He would never be bothering her.

"What's going on with Denise? Is she going to be cool about things or does she have to find work elsewhere?" Andrew asked Doris; she was amazed he even remembered her name.

"I spoke to her, I think she'll be fine and besides she really needs the work; her mother is having surgery and..."

"I don't give a fuck about her or her mother," he hissed back. "I had a good time with her and that's all that matters to me. I'm done with her now. She either goes back to the secretarial pool or she just goes, period."

"She's one of our accountants, Andrew, not a secretary." Doris was appalled at how little he knew or cared about his employees. She knew the Desmond Corporation had thousands of employees all over the world but he knew nothing of the people he walked past every day.

Doris then laughed to herself and thought "If Andrew could screw ALL the women in the company he'd probably have a very sore dick. Maybe it would even fall off. It would serve him right."

"Whatever, secretary or accountant, I just don't want some love sick puppy dog knocking on my door asking when we're going out again."

"Going out? Did he even take her to dinner?" Doris thought. "Or did he just ply her with drinks before he screwed her?" She knew the service staff at the Plaza must take bets as to how many women Desmond would parade through the lobby in a week on the way to his penthouse. You'd have thought he might take these women someplace else other than his own apartment but that probably would be too much trouble. He didn't want to show them too much of a good time; he just wanted to get into their pants.

Doris grabbed the stack of papers he had ready for her and walked back to her office. She had already had enough of Andrew this morning. If she wasn't paid so well, if she didn't have a son ill with leukemia and have these great benefits, well, she would have left years ago. And in all this time, all these years of service, Andrew didn't even know what her son's name was, never mind asking how he was. Sure, she got bonuses at the holidays, but even those were a check just thrown on the top of her desk- no card. No, the only "pretend caring" he did was for a new office "hottie" just before he seduced her. After that he could look right through them. It was as if they existed no longer.

Andrew sat at his desk going over the details of his next meeting and sipping that expensive coffee out of that equally expensive cup. It was given to him by his mother. Funny, it was the one thing of hers he cherished. In an odd way it made him feel close to her although he had not spoken to her since that big blow up at the mansion weeks ago.

Sometimes he actually felt bad about that...his father had been a prick most of his life but his mom...she really hadn't done anything but love him. For a moment his mind went back to when he was kid playing at her feet and they giggled together. What was he playing with again? Oh yeah, a macaroni necklace. For a moment he saddened and a single tear rolled down his face. But his composure surged back quickly and he wiped the tear away. His father had been right all these years—his mother was weak and unappreciative of all the things his great wealth could buy. She preferred to spend time in her garden or with little kids...they made her smile, but not the ten carat anniversary band that his father bought her for their twenty-fifth. How much had he spent on that? Wasn't nearly a million and she looked at it the way she would look at dust on the furniture? Andrew remembered clearly now. She cried and told his father that all she wanted was a little more time with maybe a quiet little dinner in a restaurant in town. A restaurant in town?! Andrew thought, Are you kidding? She had on her finger what most women would kill for and all she wanted was a dinner in town? Crazy bitch, he thought. They were all crazy bitches, including the redhead from last night staring at him now from her desk.]

He got up abruptly, slammed the glass doors shut and drew the blinds down. Before he sat down again he flung his mother's cup against the wall shattering it into what seemed like a hundred pieces and leaving a dark stain now making its way down the wall... from that expensive Kenyan coffee. Doris winched when she heard it but then, without missing a beat, called the cleaning staff up to take care of it. She was all too familiar with Andrew's temper tantrums.

"Doris!" he yelled at the top of his lungs.

"The cleaning crew is on their way up Mr. Desmond," she said calmly.

When Andrew was off to his next meeting she called her son to see how he was doing; at fifteen he rarely complained about how sick he felt. He did his best in school and always tried to look on the bright side of things. Her husband worked nights so that he could be home during the day in case Jeff needed him; the man always looked like he could use a good night's sleep. Doris smiled when she thought of him, too, and thought how lucky she was to have such a fine family. They didn't have much, especially with Jeff's medical bills, but she wouldn't trade places with Andrew Desmond or his family for all the money in the world.

SUSAN WAS PLANTING SOME GERANIUMS just outside the sunroom on the great lawn. There was just something about them that comforted her. So simple. So bright and beautiful. They took her back to the memories of planting them in the little backyard in Massapequa, Andrew "helping" her with his little plastic shovel and pail that he always took to the beach with him. "Good boy, Andrew," she would say, "You're Mommy's little helper."

Over the years Harold hired only the best known gardeners on Long Island who made masterpieces of hedges and trees, and planted only the most expensive and exotic flowers money could buy. Even that he tried to take from Susan, in his efforts to make her chic and sophisticated like the other wives. But ultimately he had failed, leaving Susan to her flowers and he into the arms of multiple mistresses.

Harold's health was declining quickly, exacerbated by that argument he had with Andrew. "Useless, did you hear that Susan? My boy says I'm a useless old man." And Harold was doing just that—becoming "useless." The man with the drive and motivation to keep a multi-billion dollar corporation going was winding down. In the weeks since the argument he broke off all his extra-curricular romantic activity preferring instead to stay around the house and watch Susan garden. One of the servants would set a lounge chair out in the sun and Harold would just lie there, alternately watching Susan and gazing out at the Sound. She tried to get him to swim a little in one of the pools thinking the exercise might help him but he refused.

"I'm an old man Susan and my days are nearly over," he'd tell her half a dozen times a day, his nitroglycerin spray never far from his side. Despite bringing in the best cardiologists from all over the country, Harold was starting to slip away. All the pills and all the doctors meant nothing anymore. His son had rejected him.

And Susan started to think how life could be pleasant again after Harold passed. She would sell the estate and move back to Massapequa. She had kept in touch with a few friends over the years and even managed a day trip here and there while Harold was either at the office or otherwise occupied.

She missed the simplicity of it all, and had taken to reading the real estate section of the Sunday papers, checking out the houses in the area. She had her eye on a few Cape Cods; she didn't need much—even a two bedroom would do nicely. She doubted that Andrew would ever spend the night much less ever visit. No, just a little house with a little backyard for her geraniums, and maybe a cat for company. That was one thing she missed as well—a pet. Neither Harold nor Andrew had any use for them; they both felt they were messy and unnecessary.

Yes, a little house with a nice little garden and a little black and white cat to keep her company, but for now, at least while Harold lived, she would stay in her gold plated jail. And Harold had taken to eating his meals in his room in the evening; after an hour or two outside watching Susan he would retreat inside, usually on the arm of Robert, the major domo, who helped him into the elevator and up to his room. He would watch the news on a little TV he kept on the dresser by the bed looking for any stories about Andrew and the Desmond Corporation and smiling with delight when he spied one. They were all the same- Andrew talking about how taking over a company and bankrupting a small town would somehow benefit all of mankind when everyone knew the only thing being benefitted was the Desmond Corporation.

Sometimes he would appear with Doris at his side and not one of his many bimbos; he didn't want to give the public the wrong impression. Smart boy, Harold would think to himself and smile. He still thought of Andrew as a "boy" even though he was now forty-two years old.

Harold would usually be asleep by nine and slept through to the morning. Susan knitted and sometimes watched movies on the Lifetime Channel, glancing around her huge bedroom. She thought to herself that the garish room could easily house two Cape Cods.

After she heard Harold yelling for one of the servants to bring him fresh water for his pills, she made a mental note to herself to call that realtor her friend Peggy recommended. Peggy had been her one steady friend through all of this-all these years. Though Peggy had never been to the mansion Susan visited her and her hometown as often as she could.

They had been teachers together when Andrew was little but now Peggy's health was failing. Her husband had passed s few years before and her two kids lived on the west coast and just didn't seem to take a lot of interest in their mother as their own lives blossomed. And to boot, the house where Peggy rented an apartment had just been sold and she had to move.

It didn't look like Harold would be around much longer and she wanted to be out of that house as quickly as possible after it happened. She would gladly give it all to Andrew if he wanted it but she would rather donate all its treasures for use in the community. There was no reason she couldn't purchase a home now and be ready for when the time came.

She felt bad about all this really. Harold had been the great love of her life but how much things changed when all that money came their way. She would have forgiven him his many affairs (because she knew they meant nothing to him anyway) but it was the way he treated her- and the way he spoke to Andrew about her that changed her mind. And then all those snooty women at the club- that was the icing on the cake, the fact that Harold openly encouraged her to be like them- was the final straw.

She found a house quickly, a two bedroom, two bath Cape Cod with yellow aluminum siding and blue shutters at the windows. It was not unlike the home they shared when Andrew was a baby- although now the prices were much higher, this one on the market for 695,000.00. The realtor looked at Susan. Susan just pulled her checkbook out and the realtor watched her make a check out for the full amount. She was amused actually at the price…it cost more than that just to remodel the kitchen and two of the bathrooms last year at the estate. Heck, all these years Harold encouraged her to spend money and not buy her clothes off the rack at Macy's…so now she was.

Peggy was by her side as well, and as Susan wrote the check she turned to her and said "You know, it's a shame to see it sitting here empty and I don't know how much longer Harold will live…why don't you live in it, at least for now?"

66

Peggy's mouth hung open in amazement. "I can't do that…"

"Oh yes you can, it's paid for, and I will arrange to have all the utility bills sent to me"

The realtor dropped Susan off at the Long Island Rail Road Station. She left her car and driver at home again. As the train made its way through the little towns of Long Island back to Sand's Point, Susan felt a sense of well being she hadn't felt in years.

Peggy moved into the house less than two weeks later, after the moving van that Susan sent came to pack her things for her and place them carefully in her new home. She elected to take the smaller bedroom, leaving the master for the day when Susan came.

ANDREW WAS COMING OUT OF HIS LAST meeting of the day. He walked quickly past the desk of the redhead in accounting; she smiled at him but he didn't acknowledge her at all.

As he sat behind his desk lamenting the fact that he destroyed his favorite coffee cup his thoughts suddenly shifted…south. He called the Plaza management to have a girl ready for him when he came home. He was going to stay away from the women in the office for awhile. He just wanted quick sex and then he wanted the girl to disappear and that wasn't possible when he screwed his office staff. He often had to see them the next day and the day after that and sometimes it made things …complicated. No, he'd stick to hookers, for awhile at least. They asked for nothing and he would give nothing except whatever their going rate was.

As he sipped his single malt scotch standing on his terrace he was pleased. His life was great, this apartment was great and… The doorbell rang and he opened it to a beautiful blonde wearing a dress so tight it looked like it was painted on. As he felt a stirring in his crotch he thought again that he really did have it all…almost.

The blonde worked hard that night to make him feel as if he was the most important man in the world and she was doing a good job. But in the morning she was gone and he was staring at his nakedness in the mirror again. There had to be more…

ASHTON WAS SETTING THE TABLE and placing the brightly colored streamers all around the room…it had to be perfect for Allison's baby shower. Pink, for the little girl they would name Melissa. She was seven months along now and walked like a duck, her feet were so swollen but she was happy.

She and Kevin bought a co-op in Astoria when they got married and thankfully, they settled on the two bedrooms instead of the one bedroom that Kevin wanted. It was good, because Allison got pregnant less than six months after they got married; that extra bedroom was being decorated now as the nursery. It had a view of the East River and the tram going back and forth to Roosevelt Island and thankfully, two bathrooms as well.

Originally Kevin wanted to go for the studio that was also available since they had just gotten married and wanted to save a little money, but Allison had a feeling they might need a bigger place sooner. Maybe all that time with Ashton had rubbed off on her and she had a little of that psychic ability.

Ashton wanted it all to be perfect, especially since she missed Allison's wedding…still, to this day she never said where she was and no one asked. As she carefully placed the name placards around the table she sighed…and then thought to herself

"How wonderful to be having a daughter." How lucky Allison was…how she would love to have a little girl.

They decided to have the shower at a little restaurant in Astoria not far from Allison's co-op. Ashton did not know the people who were coming, save for Allison's mother and her own mother, Marian. All the others were from Allison's work. From what she understood, Cynthia, Carol and Louise hadn't made it to the wedding. That friendship had slowly drifted away…the distance and the years passing took their toll on it. They still sent cards back and forth and the three women had sent both wedding gifts and now shower gifts to Allison. That would make her happy. Ashton was glad that their friendship stayed strong through all the ups and downs and especially since her disappearance. Maybe one day she would tell them all why, and what she did, but not for now, and maybe not ever. This day belonged to Allison and Ashton would be sure this would be one of her happiest.

Melissa Ann Crenshaw was born at New York University Hospital almost exactly two months later. She weighed 7 lbs. 11 oz, and when Ashton came to see them in the hospital she remarked that was a lucky number. Ashton looked at Allison holding her baby, a beautiful little girl with bright blue eyes just like Allison's. Kevin stood by her side beaming with pride. Ashton held the baby only for a moment and then began to cry. She gave the baby quickly back to Kevin and left the room.

"What the hell?" Allison said to her husband but then quickly turned her head. She had figured out where Ashton was that year she disappeared, now almost three years ago. Saying nothing to Kevin, she just shrugged her shoulders.

Allison took the next few months off to care for her newborn, and sometimes she would take a ride into Bay Ridge to see Ashton at the store and have lunch with her in the nearby park. It was spring and the brightly blooming flowers delighted Melissa, who reached out her chubby fingers to grab them, cooing in delight.

Ashton was always glad to see them but there was always sadness in her eyes when she looked at Melissa. Allison tried to make small talk to bring her out of her funk.

"How's business at the store"

"Okay"

"Dating anyone"

"No, same old shit. Nobody interesting ever comes into the store."

"Why not try one of those dating services, one of my friends at work met somebody she really likes...looks like it's getting pretty serious."

"Are you kidding," Ashton stood up, glaring down at Allison and the baby. "Who the hell is gonna want me, or haven't you noticed that I haven't really "met" anyone in the nearly thirty-four years I've been on this earth?"

The baby started to cry, reacting to Ashton's raised voice.

"Ashton, you're beautiful. You're the most beautiful woman I've ever met. And you're intelligent and sensitive and..."

"Oh just stop! I'm glad that you have a husband who loves you and a beautiful baby but I'm never going to have those things. Who would want a woman who knows their every thought?"

Ashton turned to go back to work. Allison gathered up the baby's things and got back into the car.

"Let's make Daddy his favorite dinner tonight," she said to Melissa. The baby laughed and smiled, grabbing at her mother's hand.

Inside the store, Ashton stood behind the register. Mrs. Clancy was yelling at her for overcharging her for grapes. As she adjusted the price to appease Mrs. Clancy she thought, When will I meet someone to take me away from all this?

That night, she had that dream again… There he was, the handsome man with the jet black hair and those piercing gray eyes. He was standing in front of a bank of windows looking over a great park covered in snow. "I will make you rich," he said again.

She sat bolt upright in bed, the sweat pouring off her. Her eyes flew open and in her head the words throbbed like angry hammers. "Who *is* he?"

SPRING SOON FADED to make way for the steaming hot summers of Brooklyn. Ninety degree temperatures made all the concrete seem unbearable, especially for Marian and Bob. They often walked back and forth from the store and the heat was getting to them. It had been years since they took a vacation. They hadn't wanted to leave Ashton running the place, especially since her disappearance a little over three years ago now. What if she did it again when they weren't there? Or what if she said the wrong thing to the wrong customer? They had to take the next step. And so it was decided…

They sat Ashton down in the living room one night after dinner. Bob was direct and spoke honestly. He told her they needed a vacation; they needed someone to run the store while they were away, and when they came back, they were going to cut back on their hours.

"I've decided to promote someone to manager and I've decided on Craig. I just can't trust you Ashton."

Craig Willis had worked at the store on and off for several years but had become full time after Ashton disappeared. Someone had to take her spot. She got along well with him actually; he was kind and funny and had a wife and two little boys. Ashton understood, but in a way she was crushed...she wanted to be the one to step up. She wanted to be the one to show her mother and Bob that she could do it; that she could take over the store...even its ownership. It would give them the rest they needed and provide a good income for her.

She stood and hugged Bob. "I understand. I'll do my best for him just like I would for you." Ashton knew she had to get along with Craig. All her mother said was "remember your filters, Ashton."

One week later Marian and Bob took off for Montauk. Bob loved to fish (though he hadn't in years) so they took a motel room for the week. It was August and the sand was hot and the weather sunny. As they sat on the terrace overlooking the Atlantic Ocean they imagined this was Florida, Palm Beach, and this was their little condo where they would walk hand-in-hand every day, no store to have to go back to. They both sat back and smiled at each other. Would that day ever come?

7

As summer gave way to fall Harold Desmond clung to life...barely. His days consisted of moving from his bedroom to the great room to a chair on the great lawn where he would watch Susan garden. "Why don't you let the landscapers do that?" he would ask, in fact, he would ask every day since he was becoming more and more senile. And Susan patiently would answer- "because I love it, because it makes me happy."

So little had made Susan happy in all these years, but she smiled at the thought of her little house in Massapequa and of being able to help her friend Peggy. Harold took long naps (okay, he slept most of the day) which enabled Susan to take the railroad out and visit Peggy, who had gotten a little black and white cat from the shelter.

"Her name is Sheena," Peggy said. She hoped Susan wouldn't mind. All Susan said, as she picked her up and stroked her in her lap was "she's perfect."

Andrew hadn't been to the house since that big blow up, so long ago now. He hadn't called either. It was as if his mother and father didn't exist anymore. Any news he got about the company Harold had to get from the TV or the newspapers, and most often, he just dozed off anyway. There were times now when he would ask Susan what time Andrew would get home from school and when did they start living in this big house?

Susan spent some of her time also with Sarah at her many charity events. She looked forward to seeing little Jessica who was going on four now. She would run up to Susan for a hug and then said, holding up four fingers "I'm this much," and then laugh. Sarah would then say "oh come on Jessica, you know you're three years old." Then Jessica would get very serious and say something like "yes, but I'm almost four."

Sarah went on to tell Susan that Jessica was truly amazing. She sometimes seemed to know what Sarah was going to do when it was still just a thought in her mind, She told Susan that Jessica said the other day "I'm happy you're making spaghetti tonight, Mommy," only seconds after she made up her mind to serve it for dinner.

Yes, Jessica was an amazing child, indeed. And those sea green eyes...such an unusual color. Susan was grateful to have this child in her life. She was the closest thing to an actual grandchild that she would ever have. As she held the child in her lap she looked up wistfully and wondered how her son was doing, she missed him so.

Doris was almost running behind Andrew…again. He was barking orders and screaming at her at the top of his lungs- "Didn't I tell you I needed this done by nine? Now I have to go into the board meeting totally unprepared. I don't want to look like an ass!"

"You always look like an ass anyway," Doris thought to herself but didn't dare say it. "I'm sorry, Andrew. This only came to my attention last night as I was leaving and I was on the way to pick up Jeff from the doctor."

"I don't care about that!" Now his face was red and half the office, including the redhead in accounting, was staring at him. "You should have stayed later until it was done. Don't I pay you through the nose? This job comes first, family second!"

Okay, she was well paid, she couldn't argue with that, but the family thing, oh hell no. No money in the world was worth her family, but she held back the tears, her hands visibly shaking. She knew that all he would do was scream at her, nothing more She was too good an assistant and besides, she knew too much about him.

Intimate details about him and the office staff and all those prostitutes going in and out of his apartment. She knew about the argument he had with his parents and that he was no longer speaking to them—Susan told her that. Over the years Doris and Susan had met on a few occasions and exchanged a friendly phone call here and there.

Maybe *he* gave up his family for money and power, but she would never do that.

Still, she apologized to him and hurriedly got the reports he needed, following him like a puppy dog into the boardroom. As she entered the room behind him she scanned the faces of the board members; there were a few women in high level positions within the company but they were always older and married, not the kind of woman Andrew would work late with and then invite to his apartment for a drink. But still, they were mostly men and now she noticed two younger men in VP positions sitting at the heavy oak table.

They looked at her and smiled, she nodded back. Maybe these two would bring new life into the company dominated by Andrew for so many years now. Not that he wasn't good; the company was making more money than ever before but she had never seen so many unhappy people. Even top board members seemed more tired than usual; every day she saw them they seemed to have more lines on their foreheads. Despite their outrageous salaries and affluent lifestyles, they didn't look happy. Nobody really wanted to work for Andrew Desmond.

Doris slipped out of the room and stopped by the break room for coffee on the way back to her office. She told herself she should have green tea, or even water; she was jittery enough and this cup of overheated black coffee wasn't helping her. She sat at one of the tables and was soon joined by that redhead from accounting. Wasn't her name Denise? she thought. *Yeah, that's it. Denise Silvestri.*

"He's a real prick, isn't he," Denise said, as she grabbed a bottle of water and sat with her. Doris smiled, "I've been with him since he first came into the company, when his father was still here. Let's see that's…eighteen years now."

"Well at least you can retire in two years," Denise replied. Doris smiled and thought that she would never do that...the pay was too good and the benefits...well, Jeff needed them. No, she would stay, twenty, thirty... Whatever it took. Family came first. She would work for this bastard for as long as she could.

Denise went on "You know, it took me awhile to get over what he did to me...use me for one night and then kick me to the curb like an old garbage pail. But I wanted to rise above that. This IS a good job and the pay is good too. I can learn a lot here, things I can use to maybe start my own accounting business in the future."

Doris smiled and thought that this girl was smart as well as pretty. She knew she would go places in life and she was glad. She knew how many budding careers Andrew ruined...how many women did not bounce back and God knows where they ended up.

This one was smart. This one stood up tall, brushed it off and kept going. Denise did not even acknowledge Andrew when she passed him in the hall now; CEO or not. And when she was in meetings with him she met his gaze and spoke firmly and knowledgeably. She had beaten him. She knew there were many after her who had done the same thing she did; given in to Andrew's looks and charm, thinking that they just might do it...they might be the next "Mrs. Andrew Desmond" only to be discarded the next morning. Most could not take it after that; the great "charmer" turned icy cold and not even gave them the time of day.

Doris glanced at her watch... she still had a ton of work to do before that prick, er, she meant Andrew, got out of his meeting. She patted Denise on the shoulder and walked the rest of the way back to her office.

Luckily for her, Andrew would be out of the office for the rest of the day. He was being fitted for a new wardrobe. "Heck," Doris thought, amused, "that might even take two days."

ANDREW WAS GROWING ANNOYED AT HIS TAILOR. How much longer was this going to take? It seemed like he was here for hours already…pinning and unpinning, measuring and then rechecking those measurements again. He came with his own team and samples of only the most expensive fabrics. But he was growing nervous as Andrew kept barking at him to hurry up and his hands began to sweat. He stood and grabbed a glass of water to calm himself but it slipped through his sweaty palms, shattering all over Andrew's Italian marble floors.

"Why are you so clumsy?" Andrew bellowed. "Look what you did to my floor!"

The glass had done nothing to the floor and it was swept away by a servant almost as soon as it happened, but Andrew, who had little patience anyway, now became downright hostile. He hated being measured for clothes, but his father taught him years ago that only poor people bought ready-to-wear. Still, he was willing to endure it.

He wanted to look good next week for his meeting just outside Omaha where another small town would die. A textile factory, which employed practically the whole town, was being shut down; the business was being shipped overseas. It was a move that would bring millions into the Desmond Corporation.

Andrew smiled at the thought of it. Truth be told, thinking about acquiring more wealth gave him almost as much of an erection as the brunette he screwed last night did. What was her

78

name again? Oh well, it didn't matter anyway...it wasn't like he was going to ever see her again. He never gave a second thought to the fate of the people of the town either; besides, wasn't there unemployment compensation? Yes, there was... See, they would all be fine.

He sat reading the *New York Times* as the corporate jet raced towards Omaha. He was annoyed that his Kenyan coffee had not been brought aboard and he had to drink this other crap. He made a mental note to himself to find out who was responsible for its absence and have them fired. And lunch wasn't any better, either. Where did they get this seafood...out of a can?

But as soon as the plane landed in Omaha he was all smiles, the steel gray color of his new suit intensifying the color of his eyes. He made some half-assed speech thanking the employees of the mill for their service, and then some bullshit about their having a bright, rosy future.

An older man, looking tired and ill, stood in the front of the crowd. He screamed at Andrew "Future, and what future will that be? I've been working here nineteen years...I would have retired with a pension next year. Now I have nothing...who is going to hire a sixty-six year old man? I hope you rot in hell you bastard!"

The rest of the crowd joined in, screaming insults and becoming more and more inflamed. No one was going to be charmed by Andrew Desmond here, not even the good looking blonde in the second row, who when he approached her with that famous smile of his, spat in his face.

Andrew grabbed a handkerchief and hissed at his driver, "Let's get the fuck out of here!"

79

As he rode back to the plane, he consoled himself with a bottle of single malt scotch, his favorite kind. As he got drunker, he almost felt sorry for them...sorry they were losing their jobs; hell, they were losing their lives. But then the voice of his father entered his mind: *Remember son, they are beneath us.*

The old Andrew came back. "Fuck 'em. Fuck 'em all!" His father was right. Harold Desmond was the rock who built this company. Harold Desmond was the man who molded him; groomed him to be who he was today. He kind of felt bad, just for a moment, about the way he spoke to his father the last time he saw him.

And at that moment, as the plane was somewhere just past Chicago, the great Harold Desmond peed his pants and then asked his wife, "When did we move into this big house?"

It was the last day of their vacation in Montauk. As they walked the beach for the last time they almost dreaded going back. Back to that little apartment on Shore Road. Sure, it had a beautiful view of the bridge but there was no terrace to sit out on to view it, unless you wanted to count the fire escape. And, as much as they both loved Ashton they had never spent any of their sixteen year marriage alone; Ashton was always in the next room, except for that year away. Marian always wondered what she did in all that time but it was clear Ashton didn't want to discuss it. She was glad her daughter was home—it was enough for her, but still, it was strange; in all this time not one mention of it? No "I went here" or "I did this?"

As they drove home they both were quiet. The time was coming when they would have to let the store go. Ashton could not run it, so they would have to sell it to a third party. Maybe Craig? Could he get a loan for all that money? They wouldn't do owner financing because if Ashton wasn't going to take it then they wanted to cut all ties with it. Take the money and run.

But the problem was, they might have to take the money and run, with Ashton. Their dreams of enjoying their morning coffee while watching the sun rise on Palm Beach might include Ashton sleeping in a second bedroom. And even then, if she went with them what would happen to her when they died? Even though selling the store would give them more than enough, would it be enough for Ashton to live on after they were gone?

Ashton worked well at the store but it was largely due to Marian or Bob being there with her most of the time and giving her that "filters" look, as Ashton called it. There had been some incidents over the years with her saying off the wall (but true) things to customers but they were quickly smoothed over with a complimentary bag of groceries. And Ashton had limited responsibilities anyway. She simply worked the register; she did no hiring or training of employees, she did no ordering or counting of inventory. And Marian openly encouraged her not to cultivate friendships with the other employees; except for her friendship with Allison, all her friendships ended badly. If she were going to have problems with people, she didn't want them to be at work where they could jeopardize her future or the store.

Ashton looked at the calendar by her register. Her mother and Bob would be coming home today. She knew they did the right thing by putting Craig in charge—he handled everything smoothly. And it made her finally realize that she could never take over the store. Without Marian (or Bob) there had been a few incidents with customers.

As a middle aged construction worker checked out with his beer and chips Ashton blurted out, "Stop thinking about what you want to do to my breasts!" The guy just stood there, mouth hanging open, wondering how the hell she could have known that. Craig pulled him aside, gave him his bag and said, "On the house." The guy just nodded, still obviously confused, and left the store. Craig said nothing to Ashton, he'd seen something like this before with her, and besides, she was the bosses' daughter.

Ashton stammered, "I'm sorry, Craig, I…" Craig just smiled and said that it was no problem and it was all taken care of now. He knew he would not tell Bob or Marian; they had their hands full with her already. And Ashton didn't want to cause problems for Craig. She knew one of his boys was autistic and he never told anyone. When asked about his children he just said they were bright kids and doing well in school.

Ashton knew the younger one, just five years old, had never spoken. She knew just last night Craig said to his son, "C'mon Bradley, Daddy loves you. Tell Daddy you love him too." And then the silence. And then the tears he cried every night for his son to say something…anything. This was a man in pain, yet he did his job cheerfully every day. Ashton wished he could buy the store. It would provide the income he really needed to take care of his family; the store had been successful for many years and had a solid customer base. There would be security there as well. She thought that if anyone deserved a break in life besides her hardworking parents, it would be this man and his family.

She busied herself in the kitchen making dinner for her mom and Bob. They called her earlier that day to let her know they'd be in about seven and she wanted to impress them. This was the first time she tried making chicken cacciatore. Cookbook wide open, she was splashing sauce all over the counters. They deserve a nice dinner, she thought. Marian had been careful not to call Ashton when they were away; she had their numbers in case of emergency and after all, Marian thought, a thirty-four year old woman should know how to take care of herself. But more than once she picked up her cell only to be thwarted in her efforts by Bob, who smiled and gently took the phone away. "Let her be," he said. "She'll be fine."

And actually, she was fine without them. She went straight home from work every night—no bars, no screwing strange men on dirty mattresses in a garbage heap. She winched when she thought of that; she wondered where he was. Did he know what she went through after that, leaving her family abruptly with no trace? Did he know how that made her feel? After all, she could only read thoughts when the person was near and he was gone, probably living in California by now with a wife and a kid. The thought of it made her sadder still.

She opened a bottle of Chianti and poured a glass. Halfway through it she abruptly set it down and stood, vowing to herself that she would not ruin this night for her parents by getting drunk. She walked back into the kitchen and started cleaning up the sauce, which had started bubbling again. She kept her mind focused on the lines in the cookbook, and for the first time successfully "filtered" her own thoughts out of her mind.

MARIAN AND BOB WERE PLEASED WITH THE DINNER and even more pleased that Ashton had come home straight from work each night instead of stopping for a few drinks which always ended in even a few more. Marian thought that maybe she went out almost every night to give them their "space" and privacy. But the truth was that she felt like a failure.

Every one of her friends from school had gone onto college and had careers. All were married; Allison was the last one of the group to do it. And all of them had children, except for Cynthia, but she had never wanted them. She was quite content living right outside of Los Angeles with her husband and their big Old English Sheep Dog. As much as she loved Allison, seeing her success was painful and baby Melissa was the icing on the cake. In fact, since the baby was born, she had pulled away from Allison.

They still saw each other, but Ashton resisted her attempts to have her over for dinner and maybe introduce her to one of Kevin's friends. Ashton didn't know why she of all people was pushing that... Hadn't there been enough disasters with her and men in the past? Allison had a bird's eye view to that. Why she would risk it with one of her husband's friends was a mystery to her.

But she did give in one Friday night. Ashton drove Bob's car over to Astoria. She looked up at Allison's building—super modern—which meant basically it didn't have the charm of the building where Ashton grew up. No crown moldings or wainscoting, no fireplace—okay it didn't work anymore but it looked nice—in the lobby. And the rooms were small and boxlike, not like the big, airy rooms with its huge windows at her place. And their condo fees were over three thousand per month (plus the price of it) and the rent controlled apartment in Bay Ridge was still only seven fifty.

New renters were coming in paying three times that much. People stayed in Ashton's building; in fact, people rarely moved out. At least the ones who had been there for many years. There was a joke going around the building that most people there died of old age and were carried out in body bags; but there was more truth to it than joke. Ashton winched when she thought she probably would be one of them. At some point Marian and Bob would either be dead or living in Palm Beach and she would be left alone; one of those crazy old ladies who collected cats and smelled of moth balls.

Maybe she could join a carnival. Yeah, that's it! She could be billed as the "woman who could read minds." And maybe she could even grow a beard so she could double as the bearded lady when she was sick or on vacation. She laughed, shook her head and walked through the lobby doors of Allison's building.

As she took the elevator to the fourth floor there was no doubt she was nervous, and her heart was pounding as she got out and knocked on Allison's door. Kevin opened it; he liked Ashton and had no idea of what she could do. Allison never told him about her "special ability." They walked into the living room. Ashton was impressed by the views of the East River and Roosevelt Island and watched the tram make its way towards the skyscrapers of Manhattan.

Allison rushed to greet her, and then mumbled in her ear "please don't fuck this up." She said her hellos to Melissa in her crib who just smiled at her with her bright blue eyes.

Then Kevin introduced her to his friend, Jim. They had gone to college together and now Jim lived upstate, somewhere called "Callicoon" and was marketing director for a resort up there. He was an avid skier and outdoorsman who built a small home for himself not far from where he worked. Ashton shook his hand and heard "Hey, this one's pretty good looking," rush through her mind. They sat and Allison handed her a glass of wine. "No tequila tonight," she whispered. Ashton nodded nervously; a shot actually would have been good right about now.

But the night went well. Allison made a prime rib and strawberry shortcake for dessert. She was becoming quite the cook who amazed Ashton because between her husband, her baby and her job where did she find the time? And this guy Jim wasn't half bad. She didn't sense anything nasty from him. But it was clear as the night wore on that there was no real chemistry between them. Besides Jim lived more than three hours away by car and Ashton wasn't much of an "outdoorsy" kind of girl.

She was glad she went. It was good to see Kevin again too, she thought. The last time was their encounter in the hospital room right after Melissa was born. But he was a nice guy and perfect for Allison.

Marian and Bob were relieved when she came home calm and sober. They knew immediately that it had been a good night so they asked about Kevin's friend. What was he like? Did she like him? Would they see each other again? Where did he live and did she blow this opportunity? Did she keep her mouth shut?

She became upset with their questions and stormed out, her mood changing, growing dark. She walked the two blocks to the corner bar and plopped herself down at one end. "You know what I want," she said to the bartender. As she downed her second shot she turned to the woman next to her and said in a loud voice, "Yes! Yes my tits are real! Now mind your own fucking business!"

The woman got up and moved to a table, mortified. She kept her back to Ashton. The bartender glanced at her sideways; he always knew there was something off about her but never could put his finger on it. He did know she screwed a lot of men who showed up here; he wondered when he would get his opportunity.

"Try never," she stared at him for a moment and then stormed out, slamming her shot glass down on the well shined bar. He stood, mouth hanging open. How the fuck did she know that?

Outside, Ashton walked slowly back home. She truly was a monster when she was drunk, but alcohol was her escape from all of this. She didn't want to be mean. She only wanted a life...a real life. One that was free of all the clutter in her brain. One that gave her peace and that would allow her to meet someone, have a real relationship; maybe even marriage and then, hopefully, a child of her own. That last part stung so much that she squeezed her eyes tight, trying to shut out the pain.

That night, she dreamt about that man again, but this time, his features were crystal clear...the last few times they were blurry as were his surroundings. But she saw him clearly, especially those steel gray eyes. And the initials "A.D" popped into her head.

She bolted upright again, sweat forming all over her. It got so bad that she raced into the shower, trying to cool off. As she leaned against the tile, she wondered when she would meet this man? Or was he even real?

ANDREW WAS WHISKED PAST THE CROWD into the lobby of the new restaurant.

Ciao Bella was the hottest Italian restaurant in town and Andrew was its major investor. On his arm was a brunette that had been his bedmate from the night before; Sylvia…yeah, that was her name. Doris had been bugging him to line up a date for the restaurant opening as she knew the paparazzi would be all over the place, and it was part of her job to make him look good, but he had forgotten until this morning.

As he was just going to send this one packing he suddenly remembered and so he said to her, "How would you like to be my date for tonight?"

The brunette grinned ear-to-ear and lunged forward to hug Andrew. He abruptly pushed her away and told her he would pick her up about eight. "Leave your address with my butler." He then handed her the clothes she had worn and said, "And now if you'll excuse me…" She took the cue and dressed quickly, scribbling her address on a piece of paper. She handed it to the butler and then took off.

Prick, she thought. But at least I'll get a free meal and maybe even get my picture in the paper. Sylvia borrowed three hundred bucks from her roommate and headed off to Saks, hoping she could find something decent to wear.

She was lucky; in the back of the store was a "sale" rack — rare for Saks, but she found a sapphire blue dress that looked perfect on her and thankfully, she had a pair of shoes home that would go perfectly with it. She wasn't sure how she would pay her roommate back. But both women were so caught up in the excitement of being Andrew Desmond's date for the evening that they didn't care. Sylvia secretly hoped it would lead to her being the next Mrs. Desmond. Sylvia would be very wrong.

He barely spoke to her the entire evening; he was too busy getting "kudos" for this latest investment, albeit a small one for him, as the place was packed and the critics were raving about the food. He moved about the crowd smiling and downing glass after glass of the expensive champagne he insisted the restaurant stock on a regular basis. And as he grew drunker he scoped out the female guests more closely.

His sight landed on another brunette, this one in a skintight gown with a slit all the way up the side. She was alone. This would be his companion for the evening. Now, if he could just figure a way to dump "what's her name?" But what happened next wasn't in his plan. Sylvia, just as drunk or maybe drunker than he was walked up to him and put his arms around him.

"Are you my baby?" she asked him, slurring her words. Andrew practically threw her across the room; she was ruining his chances with tonight's conquest. She rose quickly, which amazed everyone around her as she could barely walk before, flew back across the room and slapped Andrew—hard. Flashes went off as it was a perfect picture for the paparazzi.

"You bastard," she hissed at him. As she was escorted out she began crying "I'm sorry Andrew," realizing that her fantasy of perhaps becoming the next Mrs. Desmond had crumbled away, like a sandcastle when it meets the waves of the sea.

THE NEXT MORNING IT WAS FRONT PAGE NEWS. "Hot Pants Andrew Does It Again," read the headline. Susan frowned as she read the article; her son would never change. As she looked at his picture she realized that she almost forgot what he looked like, it had been so long since that fateful dinner. As she sipped her coffee Harold sat next to her humming the theme from *Sesame Street*. Between his heart and his senility he was driving the staff crazy.

And she had to remember to keep the guns locked up. Years ago, both she and Harold enjoyed shooting at a local range and they owned a wide array of guns, including a few hand guns. One of the maids told her she saw Harold handling one last week, pretending he was a cowboy at a gunfight. Thankfully, none of the guns was ever kept loaded but there was ammunition nearby if he had the presence of mind to figure out how to load it.

At this point in her life, Susan saw all of this as her opportunity to slip away more often; the other day she told Harold that if he was good the Easter bunny would stop by with one of his favorites, those marshmallow Peeps. He was thrilled, and was happy to take a nap in his room while he waited. Susan jumped in the car (without her driver) and drove over to Massapequa. Peggy was working, so she let herself in.

She petted Sheena, and then went to work in the little garden planting her geraniums. Sheena watched her from the window, pausing here and there to play with the cord from the blinds. Susan shook her finger at her and laughed. When she was done she put on a pot of tea and waited for Peggy to come home. As she walked in the door Susan told her,

"I've got a wonderful idea! Why don't we open a daycare?" Peggy smiled; she thought it was great. She knew Susan had spent her earlier years working with children; kindergarten kids. Peggy had the classroom across the hall and taught first graders. She knew it hurt Susan not to be with the kids anymore. She had to admit she was more than a little jealous when Susan quit her job and the whole family moved to the North Shore...what a fabulous life she would have! And never to have to worry about money again? Peggy couldn't even comprehend that.

She thought she would never see Susan again after that but she was wrong. Her good friend made countless trips back to Massapequa and helped Peggy with her husband's medical bills. She was by her side constantly when her husband passed. And now, now this house to live in and all her bills paid...what a truly wonderful friend!

And it hurt her to see that, even with all this enormous wealth, Susan was not happy. Peggy knew of Harold's many affairs and of Andrew's callousness. She was surprised that Susan stayed so long; maybe she was hoping for a miracle? Well then, this WAS that miracle. They would be together again, and working with children. Nothing could be more perfect.

Of course, it would have to wait until Harold passed. She would give the house to Andrew if he wanted it, otherwise she would sell it. She would make sure the servants were well taken care of, but she was looking forward to doing her own cooking and cleaning in the little house. There would be no need for servants, or her driver for that matter. She would auction her Bentley off and donate the money to charity, maybe that latest one Sarah was working with. She would buy a nice, mid-sized SUV. And she would drive it herself. It would be as it should be. Susan smiled; her time to be happy again was getting closer.

Andrew paced back and forth in his bedroom crumpling the morning paper in his hands. He was yelling at the top of his lungs and cursing every other word, so much so that his butler and maid were nowhere to be seen; they sat quietly in the kitchen sipping their morning coffee waiting for it to be over.

Hilda, the maid asked, "Isn't it time for him to get to work and spread all that cheeriness over there?" She winked at Donald, his butler, and laughed.

"Yeah," he responded, "and I hope it's soon. That bastard is giving me a headache."

Less than thirty minutes later, Andrew bellowed for his driver. And then there was peace and silence.

"Another cup of coffee, Hilda?" Donald asked. Hilda accepted and they both let out a collective sigh. It would be at least another ten hours before he returned, maybe more, and he seemed so upset by this latest rash of bad publicity, that he just might come back alone tonight.

His board of directors was at his throat. There had been much talk over the years about their chairman being a degenerate, and all this negative press only opened doors on the other things—mostly the callous way the corporation swallowed up other companies with little or no regard to the fate of the people who worked there.

There had been rumors—actually some of them were confirmed—of people committing suicide after the loss of their jobs. The board knew it was the high cost of doing business and it was also done by other companies, but none had such a flamboyant chairman. Brilliant in business as he was Andrew was drawing a lot of negative press and they weren't pleased.

93

His father had many affairs when he was chairman, but, being married, he was discreet. He also tended not to have affairs with the office staff, preferring instead to find his women elsewhere. Some of the older board members did remember Harold having an affair with one or two assistants, mostly in the beginning when the company first got on its feet, but after it grew larger and more powerful where he got his sex was none of the company's business. Apparently his son didn't care and also appeared to be more sexually voracious than his father.

Something had to be done, but no one dared challenge Andrew Desmond's power.

ANDREW SPENT THE NEXT FEW DAYS cocooned in his office. His mind quickly shifted from the fiasco the other night to more pressing business, one requiring the services of Mark Peters. Peters was that deadbeat handyman that he kept around for "jobs that had to be taken care of quietly."

Andrew's director of building services, Stephen Daniels, wanted to get rid of him long ago, but Andrew would never allow him to. Daniels had an inkling why, but kept silent. He could never challenge his boss. Mark Peters was a drunk and a slob; a big burly man who did half-assed repair work and whose wife and kids left him years ago.

When he flubbed a job Andrew simply had Daniels send someone else to fix it. Peters was never counseled, never suspended, no matter how many days he missed or how poor his work was. Daniels was always careful to assign an additional man on the crew that Peters was assigned to, in case he was late or too drunk to work. Other members of the crew noticed that too, but they were paid well and their jobs were steady.

Why Desmond kept this drunken sot around was none of their business; they had families to feed and children's tuitions to pay.

Mark Peters stepped out of Andrew's private elevator looking sloppy and smelling of gin. The office staff stared at this creature that looked like he crawled out of a gutter. He made his way to Andrew's huge glass doors unchallenged; older staff knew who he was; the younger ones kept quiet in case this guy was bent on robbing them; but how could he have gotten through security?

Doris nodded at him and held the glass door open for him, when he was in she grabbed a can of air freshener and blanketed the room.

"Who was that," Denise asked, but Doris just shook her head in a way that said *don't* ask.

As soon as he was in, Andrew got up to close the blinds. Once the doors were closed the office was soundproof.

"Can't you clean yourself up before you come here? Jesus, you smell like a fucking gin mill."

Peters started with his whiney litany of apologies, exactly what Andrew couldn't stand.

"Shut the fuck up and let me talk," he barked.

"We have a problem at Eleven Sutton Place. The building is ready to go condo, and most of the renters have either bought in or moved out. Except for one; Phyllis Sullivan, 4D. The old bat won't move. She's been in the building since 1965 and her rent is still only five-fifty a month. I've tried to give her cash incentives to get out but she won't take them. I've given her deadlines, but she says they don't matter. She's nearly eighty, and says she wants to die in her apartment while looking at the view of the East River. Peters, her dying in the apartment will only make more work for the cleaning crews. Make sure she dies outside of the apartment. I need her out. Do you know how much that apartment is worth? The view alone is worth a million bucks. You know what you need to do," he said, with about as much emotion as someone choosing which breakfast cereal to have.

"You know you can count on me, Mr. Desmond, sir. No problem."

"When it's done you'll receive the customary bonus."

Peters left the office quickly, aware that all eyes were on him.

Three days later Phyllis Sullivan mysteriously fell down a flight of stairs. She managed to crawl outside, desperate for someone to help her, as she bled heavily from a head wound and was on the verge of dying.

As people gathered around, she lost consciousness and passed. She bled out on the street in front of her apartment. There was very little blood in the lobby, though. Andrew was pleased.

Two months later Phyllis Sullivan's apartment sold for 7.5 million, to a couple from the U.K. who were only going to use it three months out of the year. It was the last one to be sold and the highest priced one as well. The apartment was remodeled in a sleek modern style; gone were the little knick-knacks and frilly yellow slipcovers. Her things were thrown in the trash right after the police ruled her death an accident.

Andrew knew she had family overseas somewhere that she hadn't seen in years but he contacted no one about her passing;

96

truth be told, even if he did know of someone, he wouldn't have bothered. That old bitch just wasn't worth his time. She had screwed up his plans for that building long enough. In Andrew's mind, her death was like some kind of twisted justice. But the truth was that Phyllis Sullivan didn't move just to be nasty. She stayed because Eleven Sutton Place was her home for many years. And besides, where else could she go on her limited income? The five-fifty a month that she paid was truly as much as she could afford. And Andrew wasn't offering her a fortune to move, just a few thousand dollars which would have just about paid her moving expenses and first month's rent somewhere else. She was a lonely, frightened woman and not the troublemaker that Desmond made her out to be. But it was done now, and Peters earned his "bonus."

MARK PETERS COUNTED HIS MONEY in the dimly lit room he rented for a hundred and twenty-five dollars a week just off Shore Road in Bay Ridge.

His room faced an alley, so he was denied the breathtaking view of the Verrazano Bridge and the ships passing beneath it. He gnawed on a piece of cold pizza as he pondered sending some money to his family. The thought of it brightened his mood, but then he remembered. He had not seen them in years and did not even know where they lived. Oh well, fuck it anyway, he thought. He might as well celebrate by going to that bar down the block. What was the name of it again? Oh yeah—Ovals, for the twin panes of oval leaded glass embedded in its entrance doors. It kind of made it look like an old time saloon, right out of a Wild West movie. If he had a late night tonight, so what? That pansy boss of his, Stephen Daniels, would never say a word anyway. He then thought to take a shower and change his clothes. With all that money in his pocket, he just might get lucky.

9

shton was walking the straight and narrow. She decided to take an online course on store management; she got the idea from an advertisement on the side of the bus that ran past the store each day. She didn't know how good it would be but it was something to do; it would keep her out of the bar at night and away from the shots of tequila that only made her more depressed. She was so used to passing through the doors with the leaded glass in them each night she was starting to think of it as home. She knew she was drinking too much, and when she did she had no control of her "filters" She also felt sad and lonely, especially when she thought of Allison and baby Melissa.

She tried AA, but it was too much for her, all that emotion from the others in the group pelting her right between her eyes—the terrible things they did when they were drunk, all the lies and all the heartbreak it caused. Ashton had enough of her own heartbreak. She didn't need the problems of twenty other people all at once.

She read through the material, sipping on a cup of tea. She found that when she really concentrated on it she could quiet her mind, just as she did that night that she made dinner for her mother and Bob. And Marian and Bob were pleased—pleased that their daughter was home at night and safe with them and not in some sleazy bar doing God-knows-what with God-knows-who. And a store management course to boot! Maybe there would be hope for Ashton taking over the store after all.

But they could see she was living a hollow existence. She had no spark. There was no happiness in her eyes; what did she have to look forward to? Until... the phone rang. It was Allison, saying that Cynthia was flying in from LA for some paralegal conference in Manhattan. She wanted to visit her old stomping grounds in Bay Ridge while she was here.

"Maybe we can go to Ovals and have a few drinks, after dinner of course."

Ashton had been avoiding Ovals but with Cynthia coming, well, why not? It would just be the three of them; no husbands and no babies. It would be like old times when they were just out of high school and the future belonged to them. Ashton sighed as she realized she was the only one that never got that future. But she could put that aside, at least for one night. She was pleased again; it would be a wonderful night.

Cynthia flew into LaGuardia a week later. After her conference was over, she took a taxi out to Brooklyn and dropped by the store. Ashton was thrilled to see her. She remembered Marian from their high school days but had never met Bob. Cynthia was pleased that Marian had found someone, she had been lonely for so long. But her heart went out to Ashton; obviously unhappy, like a fish out of water, she just didn't seem to belong working in a grocery store. There had to be a place for Ashton but where was it? Cynthia didn't want to dwell on that feeling too long. Ashton would pick up on it.

Cynthia told them of her life in Los Angeles; of her husband, her house on the hill, and her big Olde English Sheepdog, Jack, who seemed to shed all over everything. She joked that it was a wonder he could see with all that hair covering his eyes. Marian and Bob were happy for her, but could see Ashton become sadder and sadder as the conversation wore on. But time seemed to fly by and it was closing time; Allison pulled up and the girls embraced. After a quick dinner at the local diner only a block away the girls were off to Ovals.

Allison pulled Ashton aside. "Please watch it tonight, Ash," you've been so good these last few weeks and I…" Ashton abruptly pulled away. "I'm not a child," she whispered back, not wanting Cynthia to hear. Of course Cynthia had no idea that Ashton had been spending almost every night there getting loaded until recently.

As they entered the bar, Ashton was careful to avoid the bartender's gaze; she'd had enough trouble with him already. It was a miracle he still let her in, but she was a regular and always drank top shelf. She saw a few of the people she'd had outbursts with as well. She walked quickly past them and they settled on a table in the corner.

Cynthia and Allison ordered Bloody Marys and, thankfully, Ashton asked for a glass of white wine. Allison was relieved. She was so less volatile when there were no tequila shots involved.

They spoke of the old days; of their old plaid uniforms and the "hottie" girls with the skirts worn up to their butts. Allison remembered Mallory, who had been so mean to her for so long but then one day abruptly stopped.

She looked right at Ashton and said, "You had something to do with that, didn't you?"

Ashton dismissed her with a wave, saying, "Allison, that was a long time ago, let's just drop it, okay? The main thing was that she never bullied you again, and that's all I cared about."

Cynthia remarked that it was good to have a friend who could read minds. The women laughed and launched into a game of "tell me what I'm thinking right now," fueled by the excitement of seeing each other again and the alcohol.

Their game caught the eye of Mark Peters, sitting only a few tables away and now downing his third whiskey. He eyed Ashton up and down; she was the real beauty of the group, tall and leggy with dark auburn hair and green eyes; such an unusual color; almost the color of the sea. Man. He'd love to get her in the sack, the things he would do to her. But he shifted his thoughts quickly; if she really could read minds he wouldn't want her reading his right now. He stayed quiet and listened. The bitch knew every thought these girls were thinking. His boss could really use a woman like that. It would give him an advantage in his business dealings, and Peters was sure Desmond would be grateful. He had shown his gratefulness many times by the size of the bonuses he gave Peters.

He had to meet her. He composed himself, smoothed his hair back, and cleared his throat. He was already loaded; the only thing he'd eaten all day was that piece of cold pizza so those three whiskies hit him hard. He popped a breath mint in his mouth and stood up. He concentrated on his walk; steadied himself; he didn't want to scare her off. In a moment he was at their table introducing himself, but only to Ashton. "Mark Peters," he said, "and your name is?"

"Ashton Lancaster," she said nervously, pulling her hand away. "If you'll excuse me, I'm with my friends here."

He excused himself and went back to his table, where he ordered a fourth whiskey. "Ashton Lancaster." Wait until he told Mr. Desmond about this! He'd better not drink too much, though, since he'd want to be at corporate headquarters early. He decided to leave the whiskey untouched and went straight back to that grimy hole-in-the-wall he called home. He showered again, and set his alarm to be in before Desmond.

Back at the bar, Ashton was deep in thought about the man who just approached her. When she shook his hand she had an image of the man with the raven hair and piercing gray eyes, looking just as she had seen him in her dreams. Allison asked her what was wrong. "You look so far away."

Ashton dismissed it by saying something on the order of she was sad to see Cynthia go back to L.A.

The night was over and the women said their goodbyes. That night, Ashton couldn't get the vision of that man out of her head. Each time she fell asleep he was there again; compellingly handsome, yet there was something decidedly evil about him.

IT WAS TOUGH FOR ASHTON to get up that next morning even though she had very little to drink the night before. Cynthia was on her way back to California and Allison was already at work in Bellevue; having dropped Melissa off at the local daycare. Ashton just couldn't stop thinking about that strange man who approached her, and even stranger was that vision of that man from her dreams. Who was he?

She remembered one time when she dreamt about him he said something about "making her rich," and if that were true, if any of this was even real, then how wonderful that would be! Her parents could finally retire and go south. She could live successfully on her own without them having to worry about her. Heck, she might even meet somebody!

But then she thought, "Who am I kidding? It was just a dream. There is no tall handsome man waiting in the wings to make me rich."

She turned her attention to Mrs. Clancy. What the heck was she doing with all those grapes anyway, making wine? The old lady eyed her up carefully to make sure she made no errors on her order. "This was her life," she told herself. There was no man on a white horse riding in to save the day. That stuff was for kids.

Peters was practically at the office at the crack of dawn. The only one in was Doris, who was surprised to see him looking well, so neat. His clothes were clean and he was freshly showered. And what was this? He didn't smell of booze either.

"Where's Mr. Desmond," he asked excitedly, "I got something very important to discuss with him."

Doris could only imagine what that could be. She read about poor old Phyllis Sullivan; she knew what this man Peters was capable of doing, though she told no one. No one wanted to risk the wrath of Andrew Desmond.

"He's at a breakfast meeting downtown and then he's going back to his apartment. I don't know when he's coming in today; probably later on."

Doris was instructed by Andrew to always let Peters know where to reach him. Funny, she thought, he didn't always want his board of directors to know where he was but this handyman—he had to know?

Peters bolted out of the building and headed back uptown to the Plaza. He stood outside for quite awhile, occasionally being chased away by the doorman who couldn't quite believe that Andrew Desmond would even talk to this guy.

Finally his limo appeared and Peters raced over to it. The doorman tried to block his way but he was told by Desmond to let him through.

Desmond despised Peters. Despised his appearance and the way his voice would become whiney and high-pitched whenever he spoke to him, like now. But he was a man who could be bought; a man with no morals or scruples and a man who knew when to keep his mouth shut. Yeah, maybe he did lousy repair jobs. Maybe he was a sloppy painter who seemed to always be late to every job. But to Desmond, this man was gold.

Peters spoke excitedly as Desmond exited his limo and then turned back to bark at him, "Not here! Come upstairs with me, we'll talk there."

As they walked through the lobby towards the private elevator the desk manager thought: First, a trail of hookers and now, this? Where did Desmond get this guy from, the gutter? He thought that despite all this guy's money he must be fucking nuts. The desk manager smiled. He might be a working class stiff, but at least he still had all his marbles.

Peters had only been in the hallway of Andrew's opulent apartment once before and now he was being invited in. He sat in the wood paneled study drinking a cup of Andrew's expensive Kenyan coffee and eating a plate of eggs. In between bites, he regaled Desmond with details of the woman he met last night.

"She's amazing, Mr. Desmond, sir. She seemed to know every thought of the people around her before they even said anything! I've never seen anything like that in my life. And then I thought to myself that you might have use for someone like that."

Peters was right, there could be use for a person like that. It would be great to know what was going on in the minds of his competitors. It would be great to know what was going on in the minds of his employees. If this was really true, this could open up a whole new world to him. But of course, he'd have to check it out first. But that would be no problem.

"Okay, Mark, thank you, and here's a little something for all your trouble." Desmond gave him ten one hundred dollar bills. "Take the rest of the day off, on me," he said.

Peters took his cue, leaving the half eaten plate of eggs on Andrew's expensive mahogany desk. The desk manager looked at him strangely as he exited the lobby. Wonder what that was all about? he thought, as the rumpled Peters made for the grand entrance portico. Garbage in, garbage out, he thought.

10

It didn't take long for Desmond to gather all the information he needed about her, and what he found out, pleased him. Ashton Lancaster...thirty-four, and wow, what a beauty! He'd bed her in a minute, but then he thought, "No, not this one, I need her for more important things." As he read on, he knew she would be perfect.

Ashton Lancaster... no formal education past high school. Drifting from job to job, and now employed in her stepfather's grocery store as a cashier. The store was mid-sized and very profitable with a solid customer base. The stepfather and her mother owned the store and the land underneath it outright; they paid all their bills and taxes on time.

They wanted to give the business to Ashton but she seemed scatter brained and over emotional. And there it was, countless reports of her being able to read people's minds! Broken relationship after broken relationship; she still lived with her parents in a pre-war apartment building in Bay Ridge. He glanced at the ages of her parents; her stepfather, Robert Martin was over seventy and had owned the store for over thirty years. Her mother, Marian, was sixty-two. Both wanted to retire but were unable to.

He read the police report from the robbery she foiled all those years ago; and read the newspaper articles as well. The Girl Who Could Read Minds, it said. As he read further, the pages told the tale of a woman who felt like a failure in life; who grew into a woman who wanted to help provide for her household but was never able to. Apparently she sometimes had no control over her "ability" and blurted things out that got her into trouble. It cost her jobs, it cost her friends, and it cost her relationships. Although strikingly beautiful, she never had a steady boyfriend.

This was a woman who was uncertain in life, who pretty much was a failure. Like Peters, he thought, she could be molded to carry out his wishes; the money she would earn for her services would definitely help her family and would most likely help her to justify what she would be asked to do.

He would contact her himself. He would set up a meeting here, far from the office, far from the prying eyes of Doris and his board of directors. If she would agree, she would be his secret weapon in his bid to have it all.

110

DESMOND DROVE HIMSELF INTO BAY RIDGE only a few days later. He walked around the store, picking up a few items and putting them into one of those little baskets. He laid the items carefully at the end of the checkout counter. Ashton's line was long; so she didn't notice him at first. But then, there she was, staring right into the piercing gray eyes of the man with the raven black hair. She almost fainted. "I can make you rich," he whispered to her. Meet me here tomorrow. One o'clock. He slipped her one of his business cards. This one had his address and his private phone number written on the back of it. "Tell no one," he warned her. She was so confused that it was hard to get a read on him. But she knew one thing—she would make that meeting.

Andrew paid for his groceries and walked out. Despite the fact that there was a homeless man sitting on the curb Andrew pitched the small bag of groceries he just bought into the trash can outside the door. As he drove back to the city his mind was not on the beautiful scenery that surrounded him. His mind was focused on becoming the wealthiest man on earth.

Ashton said nothing of her meeting with, what was his name again? Oh yeah, Andrew. Thankfully, he was the last one on her line for awhile and her mother and Bob were in the office going over next week's orders. Craig was off for the day; he said he wanted to get some work done around his house but she knew he was taking his son, Bradley, to a new specialist, in a desperate attempt to get him to start speaking.

At lunch she sat on the park bench just staring at the card he gave her. The address on it read 768 Fifth Avenue. She had seen that address before. Yeah, that was the address of the Plaza Hotel. She remembered because several years ago parts of the hotel went condo. There was a big thing on TV about it.

She pulled her sweater closer to her, it was getting colder and the sky was growing darker as well. She remembered something about a snow storm tomorrow. No wonder the store had been so busy this morning; people stocking up. It was supposed to be a blizzard and a major one at that.

When she got back from lunch the store was packed again. She saw that Craig had come in—she wanted to ask about Bradley's doctor appointment but didn't dare—and had opened up another register. Customers were buzzing about the storm said to be arriving late tomorrow afternoon. Bob made an announcement over the PA system that the store would be closed tomorrow due to the coming bad weather. That seemed to spur the customers to buy even more. Ashton kept her focus on her work as best she could, but her mind was on him. She had never seen such a handsome man in all her life. So many mixed emotions running through her head. But there was one thing she heard clearly in her mind…that she must go to this meeting with him. She pushed aside the other "vibe" she got off him as well, that he was a man who could be truly evil to get what he wanted.

She looked around the store again, to see her stepfather lifting bags that were way too heavy for him now. She glimpsed her mother at the last register working to move the customers through as fast as she could, her face creased in worry. She spied Craig at the register next to her. There was sadness in his eyes.

No matter who this man was, no matter what happened, she would go tomorrow, storm be damned!

SUSAN WAS WORRIED ABOUT PEGGY with that upcoming storm. She drove out to Massapequa early, leaving Harold at the breakfast table singing One little, two little, three little Indians...

Robert, the major domo, would take care of him and make sure he got to his room and this time he needed to remember to keep that gun cabinet locked. Harold had taken yet another firearm out of it pretending to be the cowboy who shoots the "little Indians." She reminded him of that last time but really felt sorry for Robert. He had been such a conscientious worker all these years, putting up with the whims of the great Harold Desmond who pretty much treated him like dirt and now, well now, Robert was even changing his diapers. She would be sure Robert would be well taken care of when this was all over.

She got to the hardware store and picked up a generator in case Peggy lost electricity. They said they couldn't deliver it right away but quickly changed their minds when they saw the size of Susan's tip. Next stop was the grocery store where she spent over two hundred dollars. She was glad she bought that extra refrigerator that now stood in the garage, she would need the space. She made sure Sheena had everything she needed too. Plenty of food, kitty litter and a few new toys as well. Peggy was still in school so Susan went to work putting things away and covering the plants in their garden to protect them from the storm. All was in place when Peggy walked in. She was pleased to see her friend.

"Surely you didn't put that generator in the back seat of your Bentley," she joked

They laughed as Peggy helped her cover the last of the plants. The weather was colder yet, and a brisk wind was now blasting them from the west.

"I've got to go," Susan said, "before the weather kicks in."

Peggy was grateful; she would be fine. She and Sheena had everything they needed and wonderful neighbors on either side of them as well. She hugged Susan goodbye and then Susan swung the big Bentley out of the driveway and pointed it towards Sands Point.

As she drove up the winding drive she thought to herself that the mansion looked so cold, almost sad, like a lonely forgotten child although it certainly wasn't forgotten; over the years it had been remodeled and remodeled again; and even the smallest leaky faucet was repaired immediately. No, to the average person it looked like a palace but to her it was a jail. For years she wanted to leave Harold when he was at the height of his arrogance, but he would never agree to divorce. Now that he was an invalid she didn't have the heart to do it. He still had his clear days when he knew where he was and who he was; when he could read the newspaper without falling asleep and watch the news intently. But those days were few and far between now; and besides, if his senility didn't get him, his failing heart certainly would.

Harold was asleep when she got home. The staff was busy outside covering the expensive and exotic plants and landscaping; they had overlooked Susan's geraniums. She grabbed a blanket and lovingly covered them. As she looked up across the great lawn, the winds were whipping the waves up on the Sound. She never remembered waves that big before.

She sat down in the kitchen with her staff and watched the news. The weather sure didn't look good—twelve inches of snow predicted for the city alone with even more for Long Island. For a moment she thought about Andrew. Truth be told over the last few months she had called him several times and left messages, but they

114

were never returned. The only way she knew he was alright was from calling Doris. She wondered if he would be alright in the storm but then realized that Andrew was always alright. Andrew always looked after himself and put himself first. Yes, Susan knew he'd be fine. What she didn't know was that he wouldn't be alone in the storm; he was expecting a visitor.

Since Bob decided not to open the next day because of the weather, Craig would have time to spend with Bradley, who was waving his arms like a propeller while looking at the Weather Channel. He didn't understand it, but his older brother, Cooper kept telling him over and over, "Snow, say snow Bradley." But of course Bradley was silent.

Cooper, at seven, was in second grade and an 'A' student. He was patient and kind with his younger brother, and many times Craig thought that he must be a "wise, old soul." Schools would be closed tomorrow so Cooper was excited at the thought of a snow day. Evelyn, Craig's wife, was glad her husband would be home as well. It would give him an opportunity to be with his kids. He worked so much that he barely saw them. They had an ice chest and a load of candles in case the power went out. Evelyn even found one of those wind up radios in the back of a closet so they could listen to the weather reports. They would be fine.

ALLISON WOULD HAVE TO STAY AT THE HOSPITAL during the storm. The nursing supervisor always stayed on since so many of her staff lived out on the Island or in New Jersey She had to be there in case some of them couldn't make it in. She was prepared, though; her locker had two changes of clothes and she had access to a shower. The hospital of course had huge generators that would keep the lights on and the cafeteria going so she would be fine. Kevin would be off tomorrow—he was already home—so Melissa would be well taken care of.

Sarah went grocery shopping when she first heard a storm might hit, she liked to be prepared. Jessica rode in the cart smiling at the other customers who remarked at how beautiful the color of her eyes were.

"I've never seen such an unusual color of green," remarked one older lady. "It's almost like the color of the sea."

Sarah was proud of Jessica and the child was so intuitive. She often seemed to know what Sarah was going to say before she said it. She was so happy to share that with Bill. But the only thing she didn't tell him was what Jessica told her the other day: "I love you, even though you're not my real mommy." That disturbed Sarah because how could she possibly know that? They adopted her as an infant and they were the only parents she ever. They planned to tell her that she was adopted when she was older; they thought that was only fair, but Jessica wasn't even four years old yet.

At home now, Jessica looked out from the big bay windows in the family room, watching the Atlantic Ocean start to whip itself into frenzy with all that wind.

"It's going to be a big storm," she said with certainty, and Sarah nodded. "I'm sure she's right, she usually is," she thought.

BOB CLOSED THE HEAVY GATES down in front of the store and padlocked them. He had to do it quickly once the alarm was set. Marian had gone home as she had a headache, but Ashton stayed at her register, skillfully manipulating the many orders that came through. For once, she wasn't focused on anyone's thoughts. She

116

was too busy thinking about the man with the raven hair. Time flew. When she looked up again it was closing time and the shelves were nearly empty. Everyone stocking up for the coming storm. She stood next to Bob as he finished locking up and then they started the walk home. It was not snowing yet, but the wind was fierce and the temperature felt like it had dropped twenty degrees since lunchtime. As they walked home Ashton was silent. She just hoped the weather would hold out until she could get to the city tomorrow. Now she would have to come up with a good excuse for walking out of the house in the middle of a blizzard. Bob was talking but she wasn't paying attention. Every once and awhile he would say "Ashton, are you listening to me? You're a million miles away, girl."

When they arrived home Marian was making chicken soup. Her headache seemed better. Now the only thing she was worried about was losing power in the storm. Thankfully, the apartment building was heated by propane and there had been a big delivery only days before, so at least they wouldn't freeze. She served the soup and they ate in silence. Ashton excused herself and went straight to her room. She had to meet Andrew at one o'clock, and the weather might already be bad. Maybe she should leave early. She would not be able to take Bob's car—he wouldn't allow her to drive in bad weather—so she would have to take the train. Maybe her parents would both sleep late and she could sneak out before they woke up.

She finally got ready for bed. After she shut off the light she drifted quickly into sleep. The only thing she dreamt of was a pair of big, piercing, gray eyes that stared down at her.

117

DORIS WAS GLAD WHEN THE ANNOUNCEMENT was made that corporate headquarters would be closed tomorrow in anticipation of the storm. The Weather Channel said that the morning would be okay, only cold and strong winds, but by afternoon it would quickly deteriorate. People would be able to get into the office in the morning, but if mass transit shut down they would be stranded. Besides, it gave her time to spend with Jeff and her husband. She knew Jeff hadn't been feeling well these last few days so the thought of being able to be home with him, if only for a day, was comforting. She looked out onto her backyard and joked to her husband that he would have to dig out a spot for their collie, Sugar, to be able to go out. Doris's husband, Rodney, was an organized kind of guy. Having served in the military, he was totally prepared for any storm. And he was a kind man who seemed to always remain calm and look on the bright side of things. That was good for Jeff, too. So many times Jeff was ill and frightened but Rodney was able to calm him; even teaching him to meditate.

Yes, as she looked out she had to be grateful, at least a little bit, to Andrew Desmond. It was he who arranged the financing on her home; a split level in Queens with the big backyard Jeff wanted for his dog to play. Their credit wasn't great, and it looked like they would never secure financing for a home of their own, plus they had very little for a down payment.

But one phone call from Andrew to God only knew, and everything changed. All they were told was to meet at a certain title company. When they got there, seated at the head of the table was the loan officer from the bank that had turned them down. With only a five thousand dollar down payment instead of the traditional twenty percent they locked in a 30-year fixed mortgage at only two

118

percent interest. Maybe it was Andrew's way of thanking her for being at his side and covering his ass for so many years. When she thanked him he just waved her off and went about his business.

RODNEY TOOK A BIG SHOVEL out of garage and showed it to Sugar, who was wagging her tail. "See what I'll have to do for you tomorrow? If only you could learn to use the bathroom inside instead." He laughed and petted the dog; they all adored her.

ANDREW DESMOND SAT ALONE in his dining room finishing up his steak tartare. The only light in the room was the single candle positioned in the middle of the table. It was dark now and he moved towards the window. As he glanced at the street below it seemed almost deserted. He was amused by that; one of the most famous avenues in the world and there was hardly a soul out there. Normally it was packed with people at this time; people rushing home from work, grabbing cabs and tourists, yes, there were always tourists, flitting in and out of the expensive stores that lined the street. They were mostly window shoppers; most could not afford to buy in stores like Tiffany's and Bergdorf Goodman.

Andrew recalled that his father always encouraged his mother to shop there. He thought she did a few times, but then came home saying the prices were ridiculous. She shopped at the mall after that; and that annoyed his father to no end. She was never dressed as well as the other wives from the country club and honestly, she didn't care.

She never really made friends with any of these women; avoided them most of the time really. The only person she ever was friendly with was that woman Peggy from their old neighborhood.

119

She did visit her many times and that annoyed his father as well. "C'mon Susan," he would say. "Stop hanging around with that trash." That made his mother cry.

He wondered how she was for a moment; how she was holding up, as he'd heard his father was almost a total invalid now. But that was just for a moment. With the storm coming, it was impossible for the Plaza staff to find him a "companion" for the evening; even the hookers were too busy preparing for the storm to worry about work. Just as well, he thought. He would have his prize tomorrow. One o'clock.

He grabbed a brandy and settled in his bedroom, sinking into his custom made king sized bed and turned on the Weather Channel. He found it difficult to sleep since he was alone, and that very rarely happened. Finally, sleep did take him. It was deep and dreamless. His alarm clock rang at seven and he jumped up, only to realize the office was closed. He padded into his kitchen where his maid, Hilda, was having her morning coffee and watching the news about the storm. He startled her; she expected him to sleep later since she knew his office would be closed and he wasn't going to work.

She apologized and rose quickly to brew his fancy coffee and get the rest of his breakfast going. He told her to forget about that but to just have lunch set promptly at one o'clock. He wanted a big spread including lobster. Hilda couldn't imagine who his guest would be, in the daytime, and in the middle of a storm. Also, she reasoned, most of his "guests" were lucky to get a drink, much less lobster.

Andrew took a long hot shower after his sauna. Now standing in his huge closet, he carefully chose what he would wear.

He wanted something that would showcase his looks. Although he wanted her for something far more than sex, she was still beautiful and he was still vain. The thought of her made his crotch tingle. He had to remember that he needed to keep his hands to himself; he didn't want to confuse her or worse, scare her off.

He reached for that steel gray suit that made his eyes shine and showed off how fit he was. It was almost time.

11

Ashton awoke at eight and quickly jumped up to look out the window…good, no snow yet. She jumped in the shower; the steam from the hot water warmed the bathroom; the apartment was a little chilly this morning. She finished quickly and practically ran back to her room to start dressing; for a moment she thought she could get out before her mother was up but as she pulled her skirt on she heard her mother in the kitchen getting breakfast ready.

Now she would have to deal with her, but she didn't want to say where she was going. But she would do her best.

Pulling on her boots, she then grabbed her pocketbook and opened the door to her room. Thankfully, Bob was still asleep. "The poor guy must be dead tired," she thought to herself.

She tiptoed past the kitchen and almost made it out the door when her mother caught her. "Ashton! Where are you going in the middle of a blizzard?"

Ashton replied that it was not snowing yet and she was meeting a friend in the city. "What friend?" she asked.

"Oh, just a man I met. He invited me to lunch today."

Marian was not happy. This was no day for Ashton to be wandering around Manhattan, looking for some strange man. And then there was the usual lecture about her meeting some nice guy who could take care of her, and not running after strangers.

Ashton left, leaving her mother screaming after her. But she knew she had to do this. It would be for the good of all of them.

As she left the apartment building the wind coming up the alley almost knocked her over. It was freezing and the sky was almost boiling black. She walked the few blocks to the subway. As she paid her fare she heard repeated announcements over the PA system that the trains may not be running this afternoon. But they were now, and that was good enough for her.

As she boarded the 'R' train her cell phone rang. It was her mother but she chose to ignore it. The train ride was actually quite pleasant. There were fewer people on the train as most businesses shut down in preparation of the storm. That meant there were fewer voices to run through her head. She sat contently and looked out the window as the train made its way towards Manhattan. The impressive skyline loomed ahead of her. She thought she had read the map on the wall correctly but had somehow changed to the wrong train, the Flushing #7, which left her off at Fifth Avenue—but at 42nd Street. The Plaza was at 59th.

She looked at her watch—12:30, and she had seventeen blocks to walk. She looked for a cab. Usually there were plenty, but today they were few and far between and the ones that did pass by carried passengers in a hurry to leave Manhattan in anticipation of the heavy weather now advancing towards the city. The snow was coming down now—big wet flakes that were being whipped into her eyes by that fierce wind. As she fought her way up the block she could hear it howling in her ears. Maybe her mother was right. Maybe this was crazy. But there was no turning back now. One foot in front of the other fighting the wind. She could do it. Finally, an empty cab! She slid into the back seat and announced, "The Plaza."

IN HIS TOP FLOOR CONDO, Andrew stood by the huge windows in the massive living room. He could hear the wind whistling and howling; snow was falling now from a sky that looked black as coal. He realized he did not have Ashton's number; he had only given her his. Hopefully, she would be here soon. Hilda was waiting to serve lunch.

Ashton exited the cab and looked up at the Plaza. She had never been inside. She walked through the lobby doors and went straight to the desk.

"Mr. Desmond's residence please," she said, in an effort to be sophisticated. "I'm Ashton Lancaster. He's expecting me."

The desk knew she was coming so one of the clerks took her up in the private elevator. The doors opened. There he was, the man with the raven hair that had been plying her dreams for so many months.

"Hello Ashton, and welcome." He took her hand and escorted her through the foyer to the dining room where Hilda had set out lunch. "Shall we have a bite to eat?"

Ashton took in the opulent surroundings. She had never seen a home so beautiful. The aroma of the food made her realize she was hungry; she had skipped breakfast in her attempt to sneak out before her parents were up.

"Yes, I'd love something to eat, thank you."

As they sat at the table, eating and making small talk, the snow outside intensified. Looking out from the penthouse windows, all they could see now was a sea of white.

Her phone rang again. This time it was Allison. Her mother called her and hysterically told her what happened—that she was meeting some guy she had just met and that she wasn't answering her phone.

"What are you doing, are you crazy?" Allison demanded. Ashton excused herself from the table and walked back into the hallway to talk.

"This is it, Allison. This could be my big break."

"Be careful! You don't know anything about this guy and, anyway, have you noticed the weather? Mass transit stopped running fifteen minutes ago, I heard it in the radio. You're stuck there, Ashton!"

Ashton clicked off the phone without saying anything more. She glanced back at Andrew, sitting at the dining table smiling at her with a raised glass of champagne. When she got back to the table, he was all business.

"Let's have coffee in my study where we can talk."

She followed him into the wood paneled study and sat in one of the big leather chairs. He sat opposite her.

"It has been brought to my attention that you can read minds and I have a great need for someone like that in my company." Ashton didn't need to question how he knew that. She read his mind; it was that middle aged drunk from the other day that had introduced himself. Mark Peters. That was his name.

"Let's see how good you are. Can you read the thoughts in my mind?"

It all came rushing through to her so fast that at first she thought she'd pass out. All of it: the prostitutes, visions of people weeping over lost jobs, his own mother's sadness at the life she was living. The man was...*evil*. She saw Phyllis Sullivan lying on the concrete, eyes fixed and dilated as she bled to death in front of her home. She gasped and bolted from the chair. Backing up now, she stared wide eyed at him; this monster before her. Watching her reactions, Andrew Desmond knew she was the real deal.

"I'm not going to hurt you Ashton. Please, sit down and relax. I want to tell you what I know about you."

And he proceeded to tell her all of it; well, almost all of it. He didn't mention the year she went away. Surely a man so informed about all the minutia of her life would have known about that.

He told her flat out, "I know you see yourself as a failure, Ashton. I know your stepfather is getting too old to run the store and wants to retire. I know your mother feels the same but they keep going for you because they feel you can't take care of yourself. You're thirty-four now. You should be able to stand on your own

127

two feet and let your parents live their own lives. I can help you do that. I can help you be proud, Ashton."

He went on to tell her intimate details of her life but this man, this monster, or whatever he truly was, was right about her. Of course, he couldn't read minds but she guessed he had all the connections he needed to get whatever information he wanted.

He told her about her friends; how they all had gone on to become successful—careers and marriages and children, when all she had was a job her stepfather gave her, a room in her parents' apartment, and a nightly rendezvous with a bottle of Tequila which sometimes led to, shall we say, other less discreet activities?

Ashton knew that somehow, this man—however evil or twisted or whatever else she thought—could help her break free of the vicious cycle she had been in since she was a child. And more importantly, maybe, with his help, she could set her parents free. Free from their worry about her and free to finally enjoy the fruits of all those years of hard work on that beach in Florida. She knew that's what they wanted.

Over the last few years she had seen brochures about Palm Beach on the coffee table, only to be hastily picked up when either Bob or Marian thought she saw them. She had heard pieces of phone calls to realtors about properties they neither bought nor even went to see. That week in Montauk was the first vacation they'd had in years, and it was a far cry from where they really wanted to be.

"What do you need me to do?" she asked him.

Andrew knew he had to go easy on this one. She still had a conscience and morals, unlike Mark Peters, who could be counted on to do anything he wanted done. Look at Phyllis Sullivan. And she hadn't been the first, either. Mark Peters' hands were so dirty a lifetime of washing them would never make them clean again. And he was clever; he always got away with it. Andrew made a good choice in selecting him to take care of his "loose ends."

"Ashton, there are people on my board of directors that I don't believe I can trust; that I don't believe are working towards the good of the company. My company provides thousands of people with good paying jobs, and of course, they are my primary concern. I would like to bring you onboard. Your job, at this time, would be to accompany me to all my board meetings, and to get a 'feel' for what they are thinking. This way, I can weed out those who will not help us to move forward. This will make us be more profitable so we can better assist our employees."

He forced those words to the front of his mind, and with all his might, held them there, so she would "read" only those. What he really meant was "I want to get rid of anyone who will get in my way of having more. I know there are people on my board who think I am reckless and greedy and I want them out. I only want those people around me that support my dreams of more power. And those that don't can walk the unemployment line. Who cares what happens to the secretary on the third floor or the janitor. They mean nothing to me"

Ashton really wasn't sure at all about any of this, but one thing was sure...she had to take a chance. But how much of a chance would she have to take and how much would he be willing to pay her?

"We'll start you off at twenty-five hundred a week. I'll arrange for a small office for you right near mine. We'll have to make up a title for you though, some kind of employee relations consultant. That's it, that sounds about right. What do you think?"

Ashton's mouth hung so far open, she could have caught flies. Twenty-five hundred a week? It took her ten weeks working in the store to make that! And that was before taxes! And to just sit there? This was all too much. She looked at her watch. It was nearly six o'clock. Had they spent that much time talking?

"I don't know what to say, you've given me a lot to think about." And then she remembered the snow and that she had no way of getting back to Brooklyn. She expressed those thoughts to Andrew.

"No problem," he said and made a quick call to the front desk. Although the hotel was nearly full, they always set aside a suite just in case any of their high-powered guests or owners required an extra room. When he got off the phone he told her "You have a suite for the night on the fifth floor. The shops are now open in the lobby." They had been closed because of the storm but one phone call from Andrew and they were quickly re-opened.

"Go down there and get whatever you need; change of clothes or any personal items and have them charge it to me. Order whatever you want from room service. I know you have much to think about. Let's meet back here tomorrow morning, say ten o'clock, for breakfast and we can discuss all this further."

Ashton nodded and extended her hand to shake his. As she looked at him, she had to admit he was the handsomest man she'd ever seen. The private elevator whisked her back down to the lobby shops. The prices of the clothes made her wince; but the salesgirls were welcoming and helpful to her, despite the fact that they should have already gone home, but if Andrew Desmond said they needed to stay open, they stayed open. Ashton picked out a simple skirt and blouse and some undergarments. All the other things she needed were complimentary with the suite. As she opened the door, she was stunned by the opulence of the room and the huge, king sized bed. She walked to the windows and saw Central Park blanketed by snow. She ran a hot bath, then put on one of those thick, terrycloth robes with the "P" emblazoned on the front of it for the Plaza. She scanned the room service menu and ordered a steak. She studied the clothes she bought in the shop downstairs and saw the price…nine hundred dollars for the skirt and blouse. She had never spent that much on anything in her life!

She thought of her mother and dialed home. A frantic Marian answered the phone. "Ashton…where ARE you? Are you okay honey? How are you going to get home?"

"I'm not coming home tonight, Mom, I'm staying at the Plaza Hotel. I should be home tomorrow sometime. Don't worry."

Marian hung up the phone, ashen and shaking. She told Bob who just shook his head in bewilderment. "At least she's okay," he said. "We'll see her tomorrow. Don't worry Marian, she's a grown woman." Bob lied when he told her not to worry; he knew she was distraught and so was he, but he put on a brave face for his wife.

As she ate her dinner, she thought about all he told her. She knew that some of it wasn't true…that his only concern wasn't just the welfare of his employees. But all that money!

Twenty-five hundred a week, that was… *one hundred thirty thousand dollars a year!* Her parents could retire; she might even be able to help them buy their condo or help Craig buy the store. There would be so much she could do to help; when for years all she ever did was hurt. She made up her mind. She would do it. She would no longer be the girl who was pitied. She would be the one they all looked up to now.

Upstairs, in the penthouse, Andrew still sat in the study, brandy in hand. He refused Hilda's offer to make dinner. He sat, motionless, staring out the windows at the furious rate the snow was falling. He knew the Plaza had generators in case the power went; good; that meant she would be comfortable in her room and they could have their meeting tomorrow. Man, she was so beautiful! He would have loved to spend the night with her but no; they both had more important work to do.

It was after midnight when he finally went to bed. He switched on the Weather Channel and learned that over eight inches of snow had already fallen in the city; more on the island. There were widespread power outages, even here, the lights flickered and then went out. A minute later, the generators surged on.

Good, he thought, their breakfast meeting would take place as planned.

12

On Long Island, the storm continued to rage, but inside the house at Sand's Point it was business as usual. The power had gone out hours ago but the generators kicked in keeping the huge estate fully powered. Susan sat in the living room alternately watching the veracity of the snow falling and knitting; it kept her hands and mind occupied. She hadn't heard from Peggy; but she was sure she was alright. She was glad she purchased a generator for the little Cape Cod; it would mean Peggy and Sheena would be warm and have fresh food to eat. Even her cell phone wouldn't work now, and the land lines went out with the power; the generators could do nothing to help that.

Harold stood for a time at the window watching the flakes come down and then turning to Susan asked her, "Mommy, can we go play in the snow?"

Today wasn't a good day for him. Both his senility and his heart problems were at full force. Susan had the presence of mind to be sure one of the nurses who cared for him was able to stay with him through the storm; and the staff was doing their best to keep the winding driveway clear in case a hospital visit became necessary. Harold had to take his nitro spray several times that day; that wasn't a good sign, but after asking Susan if he could go play in the snow (and she telling him a little later) he fell asleep on the couch next to her.

She reached out and touched his cheek and a single tear slid down her face. For a moment he looked like the man she married so many years ago; the man that was so kind and funny, the man she would go window shopping with her "just to look" because there was little they could afford. He would tell her, "Someday I'll buy you the world," and she would smile, thinking it would never be true. But one day it would be true and she would gladly give the "world" back.

There was no power now in Massapequa, save for Peggy's house, where some of the neighbors had congregated. They brought food and their kids and their pets as well; Sheena seemed to get along with all of them; she would just sniff them and then retreat to her place on the windowsill watching that strange white stuff that seemed to keep falling from the sky. Peggy didn't mind; it was great to have company; the storm was turning into a big party.

She was especially glad that someone had brought over old Mrs. Donovan; a cold dark house was no place for a ninety-year-old woman who could barely walk. One of her neighbor's sons actually carried her across the street; the younger one pushing her walker and carried her little bag where she kept her medicine. Peggy thought to herself that Susan had picked a great house in a great neighborhood. When the time came, Peggy was sure she would love living here. She wondered how Susan was faring in the storm; being cooped up with Harold must be wearing on her.

It was chilly now too at the split level house in Queens. Rodney had it covered though; plenty of flashlights and candles, and he had multiple coolers packed with ice to save the contents of the refrigerator. Doris worried about Jeff and watched him intently; if he became ill in this storm there would be no doctor to visit and it would be tough going to get to the nearest hospital. Sugar stayed by his side as if to guard him but he seemed fine, even suggesting they play a board game by candlelight.

The only time anyone had to go out was when Sugar had to go potty but she was quick; she didn't like that white stuff falling all over her. She would run back into the house and then shake herself furiously, spraying bits of snow everywhere. Doris was glad she could settle back in her easy chair and not worry about catering to the whims of her boss today. She thought of him for a moment, was he alone? Probably not. She was sure he had found a "companion" somewhere but little did she know that "companion" would soon occupy the office next to hers.

On the South Shore, little Jessica kept looking at the snow; she wanted to go play in it. Her father explained it was too deep for such a little girl, and that she should just play with her toys or join Mommy in the kitchen, where Sarah was making beef stew. Bill had purchased a generator last year. Long Island was not immune from hurricanes and they were right on the water as well. If such a storm struck, chances were high they would lose power and he wanted his wife and baby to be safe. Little did he know they would use it in a blizzard. But Bill was a practical man and always put his family first. Over the years he had little social interaction with Sarah's parents though; only on major holidays, mostly because he felt her father, Jonathan was a lazy man who just wanted to live off the company his own father worked so hard to build. Bill hardly ever even took a sick day but noticed his boss was more out of the office than in.

But the hard work Bill did was not going unnoticed by Jonathan and Bill had moved up to president. When he promoted Bill he urged his daughter and son-in-law to move back to the more affluent North Shore, but Sarah felt she no longer needed all that "glitz." They were doing just fine where they were. She had real ties to the community now and felt that she was contributing something of value. Sure, they still had a big house and a housekeeper, but Sarah found joy in cooking for her family and even helping her housekeeper with the vacuuming when her back hurt. When she looked back at her life in her father's house she winced; she was a selfish, spoiled brat and she wasn't going back there again.

Again Bill asked his daughter to go join Mommy in the kitchen and help her cook. She answered back very matter-of-factly

136

"I will, but she's not my real mommy you know." As the little girl walked away Bill's mouth fell open. How did she ever know that?

Bradley was staring, fascinated by the snow. Cooper was egging him on "C'mon Bradley, let's go out and play! We can make a snowman or have a snowball fight!"

Bradley turned to look at his big brother and smiled but said nothing. The apartment was cold now; and the boys made "tepees" out of blankets to keep warm. Craig and Evelyn sat on the couch reading books in candlelight. The boys were getting antsy, but the snow was way too deep for them. On the wind up radio they heard the storm would be ending later tomorrow morning; by the time it was over it had dumped fourteen inches in the city and almost eighteen on Long Island.

Craig was grateful the store was closed today; he wondered how Bob and Marian were faring; they were only a few blocks away. There would be a mess when the store reopened; all that shoveling and a lot of ordering to restock the shelves. He would need help with it; he wondered if Ashton would be up to the task. It was too much for Bob and Marian. Little did he know Ashton would not be coming back to the store; she had much bigger plans now.

And a few blocks away, in the apartment on Shore Road, the propane kept the heat going, but the electricity was off. Marian sat forlornly at the kitchen table, head down, quietly sobbing. She didn't know where Ashton was; there was no phone service now, not even cell phones worked, and the last she had heard from her was that short phone call the night before. Staying at the Plaza? Where did she get the money for that or better yet was someone else paying for her? Was it that strange man she had gone to see? She just kept shaking her head, tears running down her face.

Bob did what he always did; try to comfort her. "She's a grown woman Marian. She knows what she's doing."

But Bob didn't believe the lies he was telling his wife to make her feel better. *What the hell was she doing?* he thought. He prayed silently that she would be safe and come home soon.

Allison walked quickly from the nurses' station to one of the rooms; one of the patients was trying to open a window—they were on the tenth floor—so he could jump out and land in the snow.

"It's like a cloud, it's like a cloud," the man kept saying.

The twenty-nine year old man, David was his name; was a paranoid schizophrenic who had been at Bellevue three weeks now.

He had been diagnosed at twenty-one but medication kept his symptoms under control; it enabled him to move forward in his career as a civil engineer. But a month ago he snapped in a meeting with his boss regarding the upgrading of a local bridge. The bridge needed some minor structural reinforcements but David started jumping up and down screaming at his boss that the voices in his head were telling him to dynamite the bridge.

An ambulance was called and David landed here, now intent on jumping out the window. When Allison entered the room he told her the voices in his head said it was safe and it would be fun. Allison and an aide struggled to get him under control; an injection of thorazine did the rest. As he drifted off to sleep Allison shuddered; would the "voices in her head" eventually claim Ashton as well? Where the hell was she and what did she mean about "getting her chance." But Allison didn't have much time to ponder it further; another patient in another room was acting out now. Was this damned snow making them crazier? And being short staffed didn't help either. Allison just wanted the snow to go away so she could go home to her husband and baby and make sure her best friend was alright as well.

ASHTON AWOKE, STARTLED BY THE ALARM CLOCK she set for eight o'clock. She looked around and rubbed her eyes, where was she again? Then she remembered as she scanned the room that so obviously was not her bedroom back in Bay Ridge. She sat up in bed and mentally reviewed the night before. For a moment she was just going to bolt; get the hell out of there before her breakfast meeting with Andrew. But looking out the window it was snowing still, although it appeared to be tapering off a bit. There probably would be no way to get back to Brooklyn at this point and besides, no matter what she thought of him, the money she would earn for helping him would make it easier on her parents. It would allow her to live on her own and be independent. It would be their ticket to retirement and to their sandy beach in Florida.

She took a quick shower and then dressed in the clothes that she purchased from the shops the night before. Standing in front of the full length mirror she was still amazed at the price of the clothes. Then she smiled slyly and thought that she might be able to afford these kinds of things on a regular basis if this "job" worked out. She grabbed the elevator and rode down to the lobby; quickly switching to the private one that would take her back to the penthouse. He was waiting for her, sipping his expensive Kenyan coffee. He offered her a cup. After a round of small talk, he leaned into her, becoming serious.

"Today is Thursday and I'd like you to start Monday morning. I will have my executive assistant set up the small office we use as storage now for you. It is right next to mine. Board meetings start promptly at nine o'clock, so I'd like you to be there by eight thirty. You will not speak to anyone unless you are spoken to first; and then only to say that you are here to help us find ways to make our employees more satisfied with their jobs. Carry a notebook with you in case anyone offers you suggestions. I want this to look as real as possible. And, of course, you'll need that notebook in the boardroom; I want to know what each board member really thinks about me and the things I am saying. You won't have to deal with human resources; I'll be sure to take care of all that personally; you won't have to go through Doris."

"Doris?" she asked.

"That's my executive assistant. Say as little to her as possible. No one can know what we're really doing here. And one more thing; I read in the reports that you sometimes blurt things out about people once you know what they're thinking about. Can you keep that under control, no matter what?"

"Yes, I think I can," she offered shyly.

"Well, if you want to help yourself; if you want to help your parents then you WILL keep it under control. No slip-ups."

She swallowed hard, her head spinning. She took a big gulp of the coffee and sighed. Yes, if this was going to work she would have to keep her emotions under wraps. She would do it. She owed it to her parents to finally set them free.

They spoke a little more, and then he told her he might need a great deal of her time and that maybe it would be better if he rented her a small apartment in the city; Brooklyn was at least an

140

hour away by subway. She declined; at least not right now; it would be hard enough trying to explain this new job to her parents; adding "I'm moving out" to this mix would only make it worse. How was she going to explain that she was leaving her two hundred fifty dollar a week cashier job for one that paid ten times that much? Maybe she would leave that part out for now.

As she looked out the window the snow had stopped, and the sun was peeking out from the dark clouds that held it hostage during the storm. Sanitation crews were working furiously to clear the streets; it was unclear whether mass transit service had resumed completely; the news was saying service was "spotty" at best. He told her not to worry about it; his driver would take her home. Before she left, he handed her twenty crisp one hundred dollar bills.

"Buy some decent clothes for the office over the weekend." She thanked him and shook his hand; again, all those thoughts came flooding through to her; all the evil he had done and all the heartache he had caused. But she had to learn to take it in stride; she just had to.

It would have been a struggle for any other vehicle to get through; but the custom made SUV that Andrew barely ever used was the perfect choice today. The huge tires plowed through the snow like an actual snow plow.

Ashton marveled at the bright white landscape; people just now coming out of their homes like butterflies out of a cocoon to survey the damage. Some had started digging their cars out; others walked aimlessly up and down the street; still others, small children mostly, were throwing snowballs at each other. On some streets it looked like the electricity was back on; on others... *nothing*. The driver had to take the long way home and it took nearly four hours but she made it.

The power was still out on Shore Rd so she climbed the three flights of stairs. Using her key, she startled Bob and Marian, who were half dozing off on the living room couch.

Marian jumped up as if propelled by some unseen force and ran towards Ashton; arms outstretched.

"Honey, we were so worried! Thank God you're alright! Where were you?"

Okay, Ashton thought, here it comes. How was she going to explain all this? "Let her get some rest, Marian," Bob piped up. "It'll be a big day at the store tomorrow with all that cleaning up to do."

Ashton turned to both of them and said very matter-of-factly, "Tomorrow will be my last day at the store. I have a new job starting Monday."

She didn't go into too much detail, just more or less said she was going to work as an assistant trainee at the Desmond Corporation; that she was going to learn to be a secretary. She was trying to think fast on her feet, making up some convoluted story about meeting someone at the bar who said they were hiring people who wanted to start fresh in a new career.

"I appreciate all you've done for me, keeping me on at the store, but it's time I moved on to something more lucrative so I can stand on my own two feet and you guys can finally retire."

"Well Ashton, how much does this job pay?" Her face went pale. She couldn't really tell them she'd be making well over a hundred grand a year.

"Five hundred dollars a week," she said, hoping that sounded realistic enough, but then their thoughts came racing towards her and then were plain enough. They didn't believe her. How could a woman who had virtually no skills except operating a cash register make five hundred dollars a week as a trainee? Before they had a chance to say anything further the electricity came back on. Ashton took it as her cue to say that she was really tired and wanted to go to bed. Thankfully, they really didn't ask too many questions like how did she get home when the subway wasn't running and where did she get those obviously very expensive clothes she had on, when the clothes she left wearing were in a bag emblazoned with the Plaza's 'P'.

Back in her own bed Ashton fell asleep quite quickly. She dreamt of Andrew laughing at her and saying that "she belonged to him now" while he kicked old Phyllis Sullivan down a flight of stairs.

The next day she said little as she dressed and made her way towards the store. Once there, it was a major operation just to get it shoveled out and to do a mass ordering. The store stayed open for the day but sold little from the almost bare shelves. Reluctantly, Bob asked Craig to put a help wanted ad out for Ashton's position. Craig gave him a puzzled look but Bob was in no mood to discuss it.

That night, Ashton stayed home for dinner instead of making her usual visit to Ovals. Dinner was strained. Ashton knew her parents were dying to ask her more questions about her job but they were afraid—afraid of scaring her off again. Bob took charge of the conversation.

"We both wish you luck with this new job, Ashton. We both hope it's exactly what you've always wanted."

That put her at ease, but she still had to go clothes shopping tomorrow. How would she explain where she got the money for that?

Allison called after dinner. She was finally able to leave the hospital and was now home with Kevin and Melissa. Ashton asked her if she would go shopping tomorrow with her. Allison's curiosity was peaked; not so much to see what Ashton's taste in clothing would be but to find out what exactly happened with her little trip to the city.

"Sure, I'll go with you tomorrow, I'll pick you up. We'll hit one of the malls and have lunch; it will give us a chance to catch up."

Ashton slid in the front seat of Allison's car and smiled sheepishly. She jumped right in with, "Let's go to Macy's, I've always liked the clothes there; I want to get some business attire."

"Business attire? Allison blurted out, "What for, you always wear a smock over your jeans and tee shirts."

"I've got a new job. I'm going to be training at the Desmond Corporation."

"Training for what?" Allison stopped the car and just stared at her.

"Training to be a secretary, I've always been interested in that kind of work" she lied.

"Oh, bullshit, Ashton! Why would the Desmond Corporation hire you to do something you know nothing about? What's really going on here? Look, I never asked you what you were doing that year you went away and missed my wedding. I figured you were hurt and confused and I wanted to leave you

144

alone about it but not now Ashton. I'm your best friend and I want to know what's going on!"

Ashton told her. All of it. Allison just stared at her transfixed; as though if she moved a muscle or blinked her eyes she would somehow miss some of it. She had heard of the Desmond Corporation; most people had. And what she read about Andrew Desmond in the papers appalled her. She couldn't believe that Ashton was going to be mixed up with him! She thought to herself that if only they hadn't gone to Ovals that night she never would have spoken to that bum who turned out to work for Desmond. Guilt swept over her. She should have protected Ashton, somehow. And she failed.

"Look," Ashton pleaded. "Keep this between us. This is my chance to make it. This is my chance to stand on my own two feet and let my mother be free of me. They can live their own life now. You don't know how it feels, Allison. You go home to your husband and baby every night. I go home to my parents. That's why I go to Ovals so much. The tequila dulls the pain. Please, I'm begging you, don't tell anyone else, not even Kevin."

Allison watched her friend break down into tears. She was going to do what she was going to do, period. Maybe it was better nobody else knew, especially her parents. They had been through so much heartache and pain over the years. She would stay silent, at least for now, but if this got out of control...

"Let's go get something to eat and then we can pick out some clothes," Allison smiled, steering the car towards the mall.

MARIAN WAS CURIOUS about the big bags of clothes Ashton came home with, but said nothing.

145

Better not to stir the pot, she thought. And it was true that she would need new clothes if she was going to work in an office. Anyway, she couldn't wear her jeans and sneakers.

13

Everyone was digging out now; amazed at the amount of snow dumped by the storm. Almost everyone who lived in the five boroughs of New York City and Long Island had lost power; crews were working furiously to restore it. They were making good progress though, within forty-eight hours a good portion of the areas affected had their lights on. Although generators kept the great house running smoothly in Sand's Point; Susan felt bad for those who faced the storm in the dark and freezing cold. She was glad to hear power was being restored so quickly. She remembered Hurricane Gloria in 1985 when parts of Long Island went without power for up to seven days from a storm that in actuality was so weak that you could walk outside during the height of it. There was a big investigation into the power company as to why the power even went down and since then service had improved with far fewer outages. The roads leading to the estate were already clear; snowplows had orders to be sure the extremely affluent neighborhood was one of the first areas serviced.

Being cooped up with Harold was draining to her; she could not escape to the little Cape Cod in Massapequa, so she had to put up with him alternately singing nursery rhymes at the top of his lungs and challenging Robert to a snow ball fight. Although their electricity was on the cable was down and so were the phones, so Robert was scrambling to find some blu-rays Harold could watch to keep him busy. The only one he could find was *How the West Was Won,* and Susan worried that any cowboy and Indian movies might make Harold go for the gun cabinet again, so she made sure it was locked.

As soon as the phones were working Susan called Peggy, who reported all was well at the house; power had been restored within a day. She would be going back to work on Monday; the kids had snow days Thursday and Friday; it gave them a nice long weekend. The kids in her neighborhood really enjoyed the snow; she laughed as she watched them from the big bay window in the living room. Sheena watched them too; probably wondering what that white stuff would feel like on her paws. But she was strictly an indoor cat; although Susan planned to build a sunroom on the back of the house when she moved in that would let Sheena safely see more of the outside world.

KEVIN AND MELISSA HAD BEEN FINE as well in their fourth floor co-op. Kevin had plenty of candles and a big cooler held most of the contents of the refrigerator after the power went off. The massive generators at Bellevue kicked on less than thirty seconds after Manhattan went dark; Allison was glad she had access to a hot shower and hot food in the hospital cafeteria. Although she was short staffed, there was enough of a lull in patient activity for her to take a short nap. Sure she was tired but she was dedicated to her post, and besides, she knew Melissa was in capable hands with Kevin.

On the South Shore, Bill watched the waves come dangerously close to the house and breathed a sigh of relief as the abating storm drew the waves back to the ocean. He was still disturbed by Jessica's comment about Sarah not being her real mother; but then he figured maybe she was playing some kind of fantasy game, after all, she obviously loved Sarah.

He said nothing as the family sat down to the beef stew dinner Sarah had made; she sent her housekeeper home to be with her own family in the storm so Bill helped her clean up the kitchen after supper. Jessica just continued to watch the waves crash on the snowy shore; she asked Bill if she could surf like the people she saw on *Hawaii Five-O*.

Bill laughed and told her, "Not in the snow Jessica, it's way too cold out there, but maybe in the summer we can take a trip to Hawaii." Jessica liked that; she was going to surf like the "grown-ups."

Doris was glad the storm was over and that she wouldn't have to be back at the office until Monday. Jeff was feeling good; he even took a very reluctant Sugar out to play in the snow. The dog went out only long enough to pee and then she bolted back inside, leaving Jeff standing in the thigh- high snow. "The dog has more sense than you," his father laughed good naturedly, but then went outside to have a snowball fight with his son. Sugar watched through the window, probably thinking they were all crazy.

Craig was glad he lived so close to the store. The snowplows had done their jobs clearing the streets but all that snow was now piled up on the cars parked at the curbs. It would take him forever to dig his out as his children were too small to help and even if they came outside with him Evelyn would have to be out there as well to keep an eye on them. But he knew in a few days the sun would take care of that so he bundled up and began his walk to the store; he had to admit it was tedious; normally it took him less than ten minutes but today it took almost forty-five.

When he got there Bob was already chucking cases of spoiled meat that somehow had been missed and not sold into the huge dumpster right outside the back door. Ashton was straightening shelves in the front and Marian had stayed home; she wasn't feeling well. Craig went straight back to help Bob; that's when he found out the news about Ashton leaving. He couldn't imagine where Ashton would be going; he knew of her history with other jobs and doubted she had any other skills besides working the check-out counter. But then he thought, Hey, wait a minute, wasn't she a manager of a fast food place years back, and remembered an article in the paper about her and some robbery. He wasn't going to ask Bob about that, the man clearly did not look too happy this

150

morning. Craig hoped Marian would be feeling better soon, as they would be short staffed until Ashton's replacement could be found.

SINCE THE OFFICE WAS CLOSED UNTIL MONDAY Andrew had little to do. He had few friends; his condescending nature turned most people off.

Most of his college buddies were married with families; since he had little in common with them anymore most of those friendships drifted away. And no one on his board of directors could stand him; even if one of them wanted to socialize with Andrew they were always afraid an off-the-cuff remark would be used against them somehow. It was better to just do their job and then keep their distance as long as the son of a bitch was making them money they could live with his less-than- pleasing personality.

Andrew noticed his mother called and there was a message but he deleted it without listening to it. He was focused on Monday now and making the most of Ashton's abilities. He just hoped she could hold up to all he would ask of her; she did, after all, have a conscience. But if she balked he would just remind her of her poor parents wanting to retire but never could because she couldn't take care of herself.

He would remind her of her friend. What was her name again? He looked it up quickly, oh yeah, Allison. He would remind her that she now made far more money than her best friend. He would just keep pushing her buttons to get her to comply. And when he was done with her, if she made too much of a fuss, well then, Mark Peters would take care of that. He just hoped he could squeeze in a quickie with her before Peters was called in to remedy the situation.

151

He made a quick call to Doris to let her know about Ashton.

"Get somebody in there early on Monday to clean that storage room out next to my office and get some furniture in there. I have a new assistant coming and I'm putting her in there."

Doris was perplexed but replied, "Yes sir, I'll call the maintenance supervisor now so he can get it taken care of."

When she hung up the phone she wondered what the hell he was up to now.

MARIAN SAID NOTHING about the clothes Ashton brought home from the shopping trip. She kept trying to justify it with "she needs new clothes anyway." In fact, she said very little to Ashton the whole weekend; she and Bob were busy at the store with Craig stocking shelves.

Luckily one of their suppliers delivered supplies to them the very morning they re-opened. Customers were flooding in to replace the stuff they had to throw away during the storm; all had lost electricity and ice chests only kept food cold for so long. The only ones not affected were those who had generators, and that was a rare thing in Bay Ridge. They could have used Ashton's help but she seemed so far away and distant after making her strange announcement. Who would have thought in a thousand years that she would ever have left the store.

A few people inquired about the Help Wanted sign Craig had immediately posted in the window. He jotted down some names and numbers and promised to call them next week and set up interviews. The ad he put in the newspaper wouldn't start running until Sunday, but he guessed that would bring a fair amount of inquiries as well. Since he would be in charge of hiring he wanted as strong a candidate as possible; someone he could really rely on to multi-task. Something Ashton never could do. She always seemed so easily distracted. Craig felt that with Ashton gone that Bob and Marian would not be far behind; selling the store and moving on. He'd like to buy it but knew he'd never get the financing and he could only swing a small down payment. At any rate, he hoped to stay on at least as manager when the Martins finally made their departure.

Ashton hadn't spent the whole two thousand that Andrew gave her on clothes, so she decided to make an appointment for hair and makeup. Luckily, she found a place in town that was open on Sundays; she thought a "new look" would be in order. Again she came home with a huge bag loaded with hair care products and make-up.

Marian merely smiled and continued making dinner, which they then ate in almost total silence; each of them not quite knowing what to say to Ashton. They did agree that her hair looked nice and her makeup looked very office appropriate. They were searching for words, any words to help take the awkwardness away. After dinner Ashton quickly excused herself and went to bed early; after all she had to be in the city by half past eight and ready to go. It would no longer be a ten minute walk to the store in a pair of blue jeans and hair pulled into a ponytail that took all of two minutes to do.

She rose at six from a near sleepless night. She wanted to be on the subway by seven; she knew the ride would take at least an hour. She showered and then dressed carefully in a new suit that brought out the color of her eyes. She slipped her feet into the new pair of pumps; they felt strange after so many years of wearing sneakers. Hair fixed, makeup on, and purse and notebook in hand she left just as her parents were rising; she yelled a quick good bye to them and slipped out the door before they could say anything.

The 'R' train was as she remembered it from school; crowded; and the voices flooded her brain again. Luckily she got a seat in the corner and pressed her head against her palms; trying to filter the noise out. "Funny," she thought. "All these years her mother wanted her to use her 'filters' but the people around her had none of those." She was bombarded with unwanted thoughts and impressions, and then thought of Andrew, remembering what he said about "keeping it together." She would have to make sure she did that.

This time, she switched to the right train and found herself only two blocks from the soaring tower that was the Desmond Corporation, the big "D" emblazoned on the two massive pillars that flanked the entrance. Making her way into the building she stopped at the security desk that seemed to span half the huge, marble lobby. All she said was "Ashton Lancaster," and in minutes she was riding in yet another private elevator; this one making its way to the top floor and the office of the CEO.

As the doors slid open Doris was there to greet her. Ashton sized her up immediately as a hard working, kind person who put up with her son-of-a-bitch boss because she got a big paycheck and good benefits, which helped her son who was seriously ill. Ashton felt that Doris wanted to leave for a long time now; but was caught between a rock and a hard place.

DORIS EXTENDED HER HAND to welcome Ashton and then led her to her 'office'. The boys in maintenance had done a good job with it. Despite the fact it didn't have a window everything else was

154

in place; computer, desk, chairs, file cabinets, phones and lamps with higher voltage to keep the place brighter.

Ashton put her purse and notebook down and surveyed the massive room right outside her cubbyhole. On the top floor were the various heads of the different divisions of the company; board members and their executive assistants and heads of accounting. She noticed the striking redhead poring over notes at her own desk. Moving a little closer to her, Ashton knew she slept with Andrew but, when she found out what a bastard he truly was, still decided to stay with the company and advance her career. Denise noticed Ashton out of the corner of her eye and looked up. She smiled as their eyes met. "Hello, I'm Denise," she said brightly. "I'm one of the lead accountants here."

Ashton shook her hand not really knowing quite what to say.

"I'm Ashton, and I'm Mr. Desmond's new assistant." Ashton already knew what Denise was thinking; another conquest for his bed, another notch in his bedpost.

"What kind of an assistant?" she asked nonchalantly.

"I'm here to find ways to increase employee satisfaction on the job," Ashton responded in an almost robot like fashion. That would be her pat answer each time anyone asked her. She was hoping Denise wasn't going to ask too much more or to start giving her suggestions; her head was starting to pound already as she quickly picked up on the thoughts of the others as they passed by her. Most of them were thoughts about Andrew and none of them good; they all seemed to go along the lines of, "Another Monday with that bastard boss of mine."

155

Ashton smiled slightly as she thought that those could be the words to a song; but then quickly regained her composure. The vibrations generating from the room were a mix of greed and despair, of fear and hate for their boss; some of it emanating from women Andrew had slept with; there were a few on this floor besides Denise; and she noticed they were all young and beautiful.

Unlike Denise, who had the gumption to put it behind her and make the most of her time with the company, even being promoted to lead accountant; the others were confused and hurt; but their big paychecks held them there like some kind of perverted crazy glue.

It was tough on them to see the man they had spent intimate moments with toss them aside like yesterday's newspaper. They felt used; they felt like they should never have given into him in the first place, but they all thought that they would be the one to turn him around from jumping from bed to bed into a loving, faithful partner. Then they all found out they were wrong.

Their eyes were on Ashton now; clearly the most beautiful woman in the room, wondering what her place was here and would she be the one to do what they couldn't. Ashton felt sorry for them; but was grateful in a way for their thoughts for she knew she would never get mixed up with Andrew in that way. No, she was doing this for her parents, for herself, and to prove to the world that she was not just a crazy woman who lived with the echoes of voices in her head. As she was repeating that to herself for the second time, she felt a hand on her shoulder. It was Andrew, and he motioned her to grab her notebook and join him in his office.

She followed him into his office like a puppy dog; as Doris had done a thousand times before her. As she walked behind the huge open glass doors he shut them, drawing the blinds down so no one could see. Ashton started to whisper but he quickly told her the office was soundproof, unless it was bugged; then quickly smiled at the look on her face and said, "It's a joke, Ashton; there are no bugs in here, believe me I've checked."

He then reviewed what he expected of her at her first board meeting; he would introduce her as his new "assistant in charge of employee relations," and then ask each board member to introduce themselves so that she would know who they were if anyone in their departments had any suggestions or complaints.

"Write down their names," he demanded. "Only one to a page so you can jot down your impressions from them. Be as quick as you can to get any information you need down on paper; you can always edit it later."

"But I don't know shorthand, I have no office experience," she balked.

"All the more reason to write as quickly as you can; you need to look like someone who knows what she's doing."

Ashton read his mind; he thought that if his board members saw her fumbling that they would think she was just another bimbo, and this time Andrew was getting his rocks off by bringing her into his boardroom.

Then his story about the reason she was here would fly right out the window. These people were still his board of directors, and as omnipotent as he'd like to believe he was, he still had to report to them; to assure them he was taking the company in a positive direction at all times. And bringing this obviously beautiful but dumb woman into board meetings when she had no business being there would not be considered good for the company; however, the idea of a competent person focusing on the needs of employees would be; satisfied employees made productive workers.

The intercom buzzed, startling Ashton. It was Doris reminding Andrew that it was nine o'clock. They simultaneously rose and she fell in step behind him not knowing what she would find. She kept hearing her mother's voice saying over and over, "Filters, Ashton, use your filters."

SUSAN WAS IN A HURRY; she was late for a meeting concerning the disbursement of funds for a new charity. Called "The Dancer Group," it was a charity for children with various life threatening conditions. Sarah had called her twice already. She joked that she was staving off the troops with coffee and donuts but they were almost ready to begin. Thankfully, this meeting wasn't too far from Sand's Point so it wouldn't take her long to get there.

As she exited the bathroom she was met by Harold who told her not to forget her driver. She was startled; it was something he would have told her before his senility took hold. Even his expression said *I have it all together today* and she was happy for him. But then he added, "Mommy, if you're going out can you take me to the park?"

Her heart secretly sank. Even after all these years a small part of her still loved him and it pained her to see such a great man meet such a fate—to be chiseled away at a little at a time by a demon no one could see.

"Maybe later, sweetheart," she told him and kissed his forehead. He seemed placated by that and wandered off in search of Robert.

Sarah was waiting for her by the door, but Susan was disappointed; Jessica wasn't with her today. She was going to pre-school now and thoroughly enjoyed it, although Sarah had gotten a few phone calls from the teacher telling her that Jessica seemed to be able to tell the other little children what they were thinking; she wondered if Sarah had ever noticed this herself. Not knowing quite what to say she acted as if this was the first time she was hearing it. The only thing that Sarah managed to blurt out was, "I'll talk to her about it and see what's going on."

But when she hung up the phone she realized she didn't have the slightest idea.

The meeting went quickly and orderly; funds on hand were divided among the different hospitals that serviced the children. Susan thought to herself that almost all of the women there were wealthy; but they were so different from that snotty bunch that Harold always wanted her to be friendly with back on the North Shore. Her thoughts went back to Andrew's graduation party and Marge Solis's four thousand dollar Louboutins; why would anyone want to pay that much for a pair of shoes when there were so many whose lives could be made better with that money instead?

And she glanced over at Sarah. What a turnaround she had made herself. Years ago, she would have worn those Louboutins as well, but although she could still well afford them the shoes she wore now cost far less. How Susan would have loved to have her for a daughter-in-law but that would mean she'd have to still be married to Andrew, and she wouldn't want to inflict that horror on anyone.

She had met Bill a few times and thought they were a perfect match. Kind and loving, Bill was just as comfortable talking with the average Joe as he was speaking to his board of directors. Or what would be his board of directors; as Susan had heard Jonathan was stepping down as CEO at the end of the year and was naming his son-in-law as his replacement. Susan wondered what he was stepping down from exactly though, because she knew he spent very little time at the office. Bill had been effectively running the company for years now.

As they walked to their cars Sarah invited Susan to lunch but Susan turned her down; she hadn't been out to the little Cape Cod since the storm. Sarah knew all about it and was glad that Susan could finally find some happiness somewhere. As Susan got in the car Sarah asked her how Andrew was; Susan replied that she didn't know; she assumed he was still alive because she hadn't read about his death in the papers. Although Sarah thought to herself "what a prick!" all she managed to say to Susan was that she was sorry; she knew how much that must hurt her… To have absolutely no relationship with the child you gave birth to.

Both women went their separate ways; Sarah off to do some shopping before she picked up Jessica from daycare; Susan onto Massapequa. She always felt so happy when she pulled into the driveway of the little house; like she was truly home.

Sheena was happy to see her, especially since she always brought treats and little toys, and Susan was happy to see that somehow her geraniums had survived the heavy blanket of snow that had covered them. She fiddled in the garden awhile; Sheena watching her intently from the window, then made herself a sandwich and turned the TV on. She settled on a talk show that had something to do with unhappy family relationships and thought to herself that she had the "mother" of all those. Finishing up her

160

lunch she wrote Peggy a "sorry I missed you" note, petted Sheena, and started to make her way home. It always made her sad to leave; this is where she should have stayed from the beginning.

When she got home, the big house was silent as a tomb, until that silence was broken by Harold singing at the top of his lungs "Flipper, Flipper, faster than lightning," the theme from an old TV show from the sixties. Robert was running after him, obviously flustered, yelling, "Mr. Desmond, it's time to take your medicine! You should have taken it an hour ago. Please stop singing and take your medicine, sir!"

"Poor Robert," Susan thought. "He really has earned his place in heaven."

And back in Brooklyn, it was the start of a new work week at the store and the first one without Ashton. Mondays were busy so Craig was doing double duty trying to set up interviews from the flood of people who read the ad in Sunday's paper—were there that many people looking for a job?—while simultaneously trying to run Ashton's old checkout counter.

Marian and Bob were doing the best they could as well; but it was clear to see their age was wearing on them, as well as their worry for their daughter, who was off in the city doing some kind of crazy job that she had no experience for.

Marian sighed repeatedly and Bob kept reassuring her but it looked more like he was the one who needed the reassurance. Finally about midday the pace slowed down, and Craig could start his interviews. A few showed some promise but he wanted to be sure his new hire would be able to handle all the tasks they would be asked to do. He marked off a few names for a second interview and the rest he pitched. He would interview for the first round until the end of the week, do his call backs the beginning of the following week to have a decision quickly after that. Bob was glad Craig was being selective. It would be easy to just hire somebody right away to ease their immediate burden but it was more important to get the right person for the job.

As Bob reviewed the list of names Craig noticed the concern on his face, but he knew it wasn't about the names on the list.

"She'll be alright," Craig reassured him.

"I hope so," was all Bob managed, then handed Craig his piece of paper and made his way back to the office.

14

Ashton followed obediently behind Andrew as the huge conference doors were opened. Inside was a huge oak table, with fifteen chairs around it which now each held one of the boards of directors. Each of them had either a small laptop or tablet along with a paper notebook; she noticed ten men and five women, all of them roughly about the same age group, give or take a few years; mostly forties and fifties; save for three younger looking men looking to be perhaps ten years younger. In the center of the table was a spread of coffee, tea, bagels and croissants, but Ashton noticed no one had helped themselves yet.

At the head of the table was a huge leather chair, and a big laptop. All of a sudden Doris was behind them wheeling in another chair for her and motioning for her to sit—right next to Andrew. She then trotted off and returned quickly with Andrew's expensive Kenyan coffee in a cup that looked like fine china. Doris closed the heavy doors behind her as Andrew cleared his throat.

"Good morning everyone, I'd like to introduce Ashton Lancaster; she is our new head of employee relations. I have noticed morale slipping around here and I'd like to improve on that; so it will be Ms. Lancaster's job to identify what problems our employees are facing and suggest constructive ways to address those issues."

Before Andrew could speak again a thought shot through Ashton's mind from someone seated at the table but she couldn't quite make out who; all she heard was, "Stop sleeping with the staff, you fucking prick; that would definitely improve things around here!"

That comment opened the floodgates of emotions emanating from the board; hate, disgust, fear and interestingly enough, lust. That came from one of the female board members; fantasizing about getting Andrew in bed. It was enough to make her nauseous; she felt the bile rise in her throat and her hands shook slightly. Andrew could feel her tightening up; he shot her a look; and somehow, that seemed to calm her.

Andrew went on, "If you could all please stand and introduce yourselves to her, one by one, she'd like to take some notes on each of you and what departments you manage, so it will give her a better idea of how to proceed."

164

Ashton sensed that they all thought this was crazy. They were members of the board; why should they stand to introduce themselves to her? But Ashton knew why. Having each of them stand and speak would give her a clearer idea of their emotions and thoughts; and having them there as a group she would get a better idea of how they all worked together and what their thoughts really were as Andrew spoke throughout the meeting.

Reluctantly, they did it; one by one they stood, introduced themselves and their position within the company, and the departments they headed. Ashton wrote as fast as she could; following Andrew's idea to "invent" some kind of code or scribble that she could decipher later on.

The names almost became a blur as she wrote them; and their emotions were pretty much all the same... Andrew was a genius at running this company profitably and they all benefitted greatly from it, but they couldn't stand him personally. And from more than one of them came ideas either to leave and take company secrets with them or to move up and somehow replace the chairman. That thought came from one of the younger men in the room; Steve Martell was his name. He was an executive VP of mergers and acquisitions, new to the company, having moved over from his job as president of a small investment firm that was foundering. He wanted to be the next 'Andrew'; to have that kind of money and power (not to mention the women).

Ashton studied him most of all; early thirties, intelligent and creative; and handsome enough, but he was no Andrew. Ashton felt intense jealousy emanating from him and pointing like a laser right at the chairman; this man could be real trouble.

After the introductions, they began their Monday meeting as usual, and Ashton jotted down the emotions she felt from all of them as different ideas were discussed. She found she was getting good at inventing her own symbols to make her writing faster but she knew she needed to learn to use a computer. Her mind drifted for a moment; back to her earlier days. Maybe she should have stayed in school after all. At least she would have learned some computer skills and she wouldn't be fumbling with a notepad looking like a secretary from the 1950's right now.

Finally, two hours later, the meeting was over; Ashton realized she was starving; with all those emotions and writing she hadn't even had a cup of coffee; although the rest of the board had demolished the bagels and the coffee urn was now empty.

Andrew rose and so did Ashton; she thought for a moment that it kind of looked like Mass. Andrew was the "priest" and she was congregation, dutifully rising to join her hands together in prayer. She snickered at the idea of Andrew being a priest; he'd last about five minutes before either seducing a parishioner or plotting the takeover of the Church itself. He concluded the meeting, and as the board members filed out Ashton shook hands with each one as they passed by. Steve Martell held her hand a little longer and looked right into her sea green eyes; his words welcomed her but through his mind were thoughts of seduction; it was nothing new to Ashton. But still, it upset her; but this wasn't the bar and there was no tequila here…she was cold sober and with Andrew standing next to her she was able to hold it together.

Standing tall as a statue, she met his gaze and smiled. "Very nice to meet you as well."

Andrew couldn't wait to get back to his office and get the "low down" on all that Ashton observed. But she needed time to get her notes and thoughts together first, so it was late afternoon before she was even ready to discuss any of it. And to make matters worse, the word had spread that the company now had someone that employees could discuss their grievances with, so every once and awhile there was a visitor knocking on her door asking if they could speak to her about their boss or some company policy they didn't feel was quite fair—but right now she had no time for any of them.

No, actually, she would never have time for them because that's not what she was really here for anyway. She'd have to discuss a way to get around this with Andrew; right now she just politely told whoever came in that it was only her first day here and she had preliminary work to do before she could address any of their concerns. She sat back in her chair and smiled: "Preliminary work." She'd never used that word before. Here not even one whole day and already she was smarter; she laughed to herself, but then returned to the grim task in front of her.

Doris noticed that Ashton had nothing to eat since the meeting, and now, as she seemed to be furiously working at her desk she had no lunch either. Concerned, Doris had a sandwich and some coffee brought in; Ashton was grateful; she got a good "vibe" from Doris and was pleased to have her next door. Of course, on the other side of her was the hungry lion that called itself Andrew, waiting on her results. Even through the wall she could feel the negativity emanating from him—a man never satisfied, a man never grateful for anything; a man who would not stop until he had it all. But even if he got it all, would it ever be enough? Would he ever really be happy?

167

Andrew was disappointed that Ashton wasn't ready to discuss the meeting with him until the next morning; it was past five when she finished and she and Andrew were the only ones left on the floor. Even Doris had gone; picking up Jeff from a late doctor appointment.

Andrew contemplated taking her for drinks and coaxing information from her, after all, who knew where it might lead? But he quickly pushed the thought from his mind concerned that Ashton might read it. He rode down in the private elevator with her trying to keep his thoughts neutral; and he did a pretty good job; as they exited the lobby she turned to begin her walk to the subway and he slid into the back seat of his limo. When she was halfway down the block he figured she was out of range for reading his thoughts.

He announced the name of one of his favorite hangouts to his driver, who quickly turned the huge car around. Andrew would eventually go home; but as usual he wouldn't be alone.

MARIAN AND BOB WERE SEATED at the dinner table pensively waiting for Ashton. She hadn't called them all day and they were worried. Bob thought to himself that it was a miracle that they'd made it through the day; Marian was screwing up orders left and right at the check-out and everything that Craig said to Bob had to be repeated more than once; but Craig knew their minds were on Ashton. Hopefully by the end of the week the decision would be made on who would replace her; maybe they all secretly hoped she would return but they couldn't count on that.

They were both lucky to have Craig there and they were grateful; here was a person they could leave complete control of the store to and know things would run smoothly. But Craig never told them about his autistic son; only Ashton knew about that and only because she could read his mind; they had never discussed it. But Bradley was not improving; he hadn't said his first word yet and seemed to be falling behind on even the things he was doing well with.

He and Evelyn were discussing sending him to a different school; this one more expensive and progressive than the last; but they would have to find a way to make it work. It was worse for Evelyn than for Craig; after all, she was with Bradley more and seeing him deteriorate was breaking her heart. Cooper also noticed but with his "big brother wisdom" kept silent; he saw his mother was upset and he didn't want to add to it.

He just kept saying things like, "It's okay, Bradley." Evelyn smiled; she was lucky to have such a compassionate son and at such a young age. Craig worried that he might have to take some time off to go with Evelyn to investigate and make application to this new school—that was if they really could afford it—and he didn't want to let Bob and Marian down, especially when they were short staffed and worried about their own child, albeit that child was now thirty-four years old.

It was almost seven when Ashton got home, and as she opened the door Marian leapt up to start serving the food. Ashton really didn't want to talk too much about her day but she was still hungry; it had been several hours since Doris brought her that sandwich. She put her stuff down in her room, washed her hands and sat at the table. Two seconds hadn't passed when both Bob and Marian asked how her day went. She had to be careful about what she said; after all she was supposed to be some kind of secretary trainee, so she made up some convoluted story about being in a big classroom with the other "trainees" and learning basic computer skills. She thought to herself that she probably should write all this stuff down after dinner so she wouldn't forget it when they asked again.

Bob commented that perhaps they should purchase a computer for the house; after all, both he and Marian had little computer knowledge and maybe they could all learn together.

Ashton thought it was a good idea; she definitely needed to learn; and it was better to make mistakes on her own home computer than struggling with the computer in the office where others could notice that their new "employee relations expert" could barely use even the most basic programs, although she could probably talk Andrew into getting her private lessons. But she really didn't want to "owe" him anymore than she absolutely had to; this new "job" of hers still wasn't sitting well with her.

If she had a choice, if she could go back in time she'd have stayed in school and made something of herself like Allison. She would have tried harder to block the voices in her head; she would have spent more time in the local library instead of on the bar stool at Ovals. She sighed heavily and that seemed to make Marian even more nervous; a moment ago they were talking about buying a computer and now Ashton seemed off in space somewhere.

"Honey, are you alright?" Marian asked, and that seemed to snap Ashton out of it. It was the here and the now, she thought to herself, and this is where she had to be, unless she could read the mind of a time traveler to get information on how to return to the past. Then she could get a "do-over."

"Yeah, Ma, I'm fine; let me help you with these dishes."

After the dishes Ashton settled in her room to review her notes. Everything had to be perfect for Andrew; he would expect nothing less. She wondered if he was still worrying about this morning, the board meeting, and what they all really thought of him.

But at that very moment Andrew was not wondering anything. He was too busy exploring the double D breasts of his latest conquest; found half drunk on Cristal at his favorite hangout.

Not too far away, on the south shore of Long Island, Sarah sat staring at the Atlantic; it seemed angry tonight; waves crashing hard against the jetty. For a moment she thought of Andrew and how much he was like those waves; always angry, always powerful, and always reaching for more, just like those waves were trying to inch closer and closer to the house.

Glancing over at Bill, she smiled gratefully; he was like the calm after the storm, quiet, yet confident. How wonderful her life was with him; it would have been sheer hell with Andrew; heck, it was sheer hell for those three years they were married; the only thing she regretted was not having Susan for a mother-in-law. But the Sarah she was back then never really clicked with her anyway; she grimaced at how self centered and shallow she was; just like her father, Jonathan.

He always encouraged her snooty behavior; but not nearly as much as Harold encouraged Andrew. But Jonathan still had all his marbles; now that he retired he was playing golf every morning and riding at sunset on the beach. His health was good as was his mental state; he was still welcome at his old company and Bill even asked his opinion on things from time to time, unlike Harold, who had not set foot in the Desmond building in years; partly because his senility was beginning to kick in and partly because the new CEO, Andrew, wanted no part of the old man at the company where he was the leader now. Harold's ideas might have worked when the company was in its infancy, but the suggestions he made now were mostly dismissed as "old school." And so, for the most part, was Harold himself.

And back on the north shore, in the great house, Harold Desmond looked out onto the waters of the Long Island Sound. They were not nearly as frenzied as the waters of the Atlantic; but they definitely were more agitated than usual; probably whipped up by that wicked winter wind. But Harold really saw nothing of that, anyway. His eyes might have been looking out on the water but in his head he was on Romper Room, waiting for the nice lady with the mirror to look through it and say, "I see Harold through my mirror."

Susan just looked at him and sighed; each day he seemed farther and farther away, but then suddenly he would snap back to the old Harold...sharp as a tack. But it wouldn't last long, only a day at most, until he lapsed back and began to ask her if they could go get ice cream or when Andrew was coming home from school. Most of his doctors came to the house now; Harold was far too unruly to be corralled into the limo for an appointment at an office. They tried that, once or twice, just to get him out of the house but he kept rolling down the windows, pointing at almost everything he saw in excited expectation telling Susan, "I want that!"

His poor driver didn't know quite what to do; he didn't want to disobey his boss so he kept looking back at Susan who just told him to "keep going."

He was disruptive in the waiting rooms as well; and it was embarrassing. The last time his cardiologist told Susan that he insisted on coming to the house from that point on; although he was polite; but Harold had turned his waiting room into a zoo and it was irritating the other patients.

Harold turned to her and said, "Did you see that? Did you see that Miss Cathy saw me through the mirror?"

She was stunned for a minute then remembered that old show, *Romper Room*. Yes, that lady's name was Miss Cathy.

"Yes, Harold, I think it's wonderful she saw you through her mirror. And you know what she always says at the end—that you have to be a good boy."

"I will," Harold said dutifully, and returned his gaze to the water. Maybe he was waiting for Miss Cathy to give him further instructions.

Almost on cue Robert appeared; that man had an uncanny sense of knowing when he was needed. Susan nodded to him silently and then headed out. They were installing new flooring in the little house in Massapequa and Peggy was at school; somebody had to be there to let the workmen in.

And back in Queens, Allison sat at the dinner table barely eating, in fact mostly playing with her food. Kevin remarked that she looked just like baby Melissa who was doing the exact same thing in her high chair.

"Yeah, I know, I'm just worried about Ashton. It's her first day on that new job and well, she's been with the store so long and the only thing she knows is how to work the check-out counter and…" She stopped, looking at Kevin's face, which had a perplexed look on it. She didn't want to go too far, she had promised Ashton

173

not to tell anyone what she really was doing there, not even Kevin. But she was worried. Andrew Desmond was not a man to be toyed with, and he could crush her in an instant. She saw the news. She read the papers and their stories of how Desmond easily could bring a whole town to its knees. And if he could do all that, think what he could do to one very misguided thirty-four-year-old, even if she could read minds.

Kevin smiled and said, "She's only training to be a secretary. How bad could that be?"

"Yeah," Allison wondered, "how bad could it be?"

15

Ashton set her alarm earlier than usual; she wanted to get ready and be out of the house before her parents awoke. She stopped at a local coffee shop before she got on the subway; she had plenty of time. She sat at the counter quietly munching on a blueberry muffin; she figured she might as well eat now as she didn't know what chaos would break out at the office; after all yesterday she didn't eat at all until Doris was kind enough to bring her a sandwich.

Around her the voices in the shop seemed subdued and she wasn't reading much from them; most of them were probably still half asleep. "Just as well," Ashton thought to herself; she didn't need any more turmoil right now.

Finishing up, she slid off the stool and made her way to the train. She was thankful it was still early; there would be less people riding at this time and a lot less clutter to pass through her mind.

She grabbed a magazine at the newsstand not really glancing at it before she bought it; it would be just something to keep her occupied on the long ride into the city. As she settled into a seat she flipped it over to expose the cover, and there was Andrew's face staring right at her. The headline read: Andrew Desmond, Will He Be the Next King of the World?

Ashton shuddered; he could very well be and with help from her. The thought made her nauseous; she could feel the taste of blueberry muffin rising up in her throat. She swallowed quickly and managed to compose herself. Then she snickered, "He really is a handsome son-of-a-bitch though, I'll give him that."

On the north shore in the great house, Susan and Harold were just sitting down to breakfast. Well, Susan was anyway; Harold was just playing with his Cheerios, flinging them across the huge table at Susan, who was doing her best to ignore him. After coffee was served Robert brought in the mail which included that same magazine that Ashton was reading on the train—the one with the big picture of Andrew on the front of it. Susan gasped as she saw it and the twisted headline above it.

Harold, noticing her reaction asked to see what she was looking at. She shook her head no but then he demanded, "Let me see it," in a voice that was an odd mixture of little boy and corporate officer. Reluctantly, she handed it to him.

"Andrew, that son-of-a-bitch," Harold said, clear as day. It was amazing how he could flip in and out of senility almost as easily as one could throw a switch. Most probably, it was the intense emotion he felt while looking at Andrew's picture that brought him around. "King of the world, huh? And he's getting there on the company I founded on my blood, sweat and tears."

"On our blood, sweat and tears," Susan thought to herself and then glanced over at Harold, now the picture of composure and power; mind suddenly clear as a bell. It was truly amazing to see.

"When the hell did we see him last, Susan? When was the last time he came here; wasn't it almost a year ago?"

Harold was almost exactly right; it had been about a year now. But Susan spoke quickly to subdue his rising anger. "Don't trouble yourself over it; it's just a silly magazine; a rag trying to sell lots of copies with a ridiculous headline."

But she was just trying to hide how really upset she was; no sense in getting Harold all upset over it; after all his heart was bad and in another half an hour he'd probably be singing the theme song from *The Flintstones*, having forgotten all about it.

But Susan missed her son; after all, he was her baby; the happy little boy who played at her feet laughing and giggling and being thoroughly delighted by even the smallest token.

Excusing herself from the table, she practically ran up the huge marble staircase into her bedroom. Bursting into tears, she collapsed on her bed, sobbing. And almost half an hour later, she was right, or almost right. Harold had burst into song, but now he was singing the theme from the old *Batman* show.

Ashton just flipped through the pages as the train made its way towards Manhattan; she really didn't want to read any article about the great Andrew Desmond especially now when she had to see him all day long. The train was getting more crowded at every stop; and now the voices were getting louder: "How am I going to tell my wife I'm leaving her after all these years?" "Will my boss find out I stole that money?" "Why didn't I rent an apartment closer to my office; this ride is killing me every day!"

Ashton felt like screaming for them to shut up; she had her own problems, but she stayed quiet. She thought to herself that she should have stood up with the magazine, waved it around and said something like, "How would you like to work for this bastard who has no regard for anyone or anything besides himself?!"

God, she was getting so worked up and this was only going to be her second day. "Get a hold of yourself, Ashton," she told herself, "you can do this, just breathe." Finally the train slid into her station and she bounded up the stairs as fast as her high heels could carry her. For a woman who until last week only wore sneakers, she was doing pretty well in them.

As she entered the building the security guard recognized her and immediately directed her to the private elevator. She was relieved to find only Doris in the office; and a few scattered employees getting an early start to their day. Denise Silvestri was one of them; and she smiled and waved at Ashton, who quickly waved back. Doris and Denise, two good people, she could feel it. It would be good having them around her. She was perplexed though, why Denise, an accountant, was on this floor, when most of accounting itself was ten floors below them.

Doris explained to her that when his father ran the company, especially in the beginning, there were few computers and Harold was notoriously bad at math. He always had one of his best accountants right outside his door, so he could just yell out for them to "crunch these numbers" for him.

Although Andrew changed most of the ways his father did things that was one thing he didn't. When the position became open again, human resources thought they'd score points with the chairman by sending up not only the most capable accountant, but certainly one that Andrew would find very attractive.

It was a cruel thing to do, actually, because they knew what would happen when Andrew got within ten feet of her. But Denise stood her ground. Human resources made a good choice after all. Ashton would come to see that Andrew would often call out to her to do the same thing, "crunch these numbers."

She would also see that, unlike the others that Andrew had used, Denise wasn't afraid of him anymore. She wasn't in awe of the rich, powerful and handsome man who had bedded her. She was over him. You could see and feel her confidence; she looked Andrew directly in the eye when she spoke. Ashton knew that Andrew wanted her in his bed again; he found her confidence very arousing, but he would never approach her about it.

And that was just as well, because Ashton also knew that he had no chance with her ever again. She was done with him. She saw the Desmond Corporation as a great place to work in order to advance her career. At some point, she would leave with the thought of starting her own accounting firm. That tidbit of information though; that she would be one of the ones to eventually jump ship, Ashton would never disclose to Andrew. It would be her secret.

Doris asked her if she'd like some breakfast. "Just coffee," she said, remembering the blueberry muffin still stuck in her throat. She just sat down in the chair in her office when she heard Andrew come in. He barked something unintelligible at Doris and snapped his fingers; it disgusted Ashton because he treated her like a dog.

He stuck his head in the little cubbyhole that had become her office and said, "Ashton, in my office now!" and snapped his fingers at her, too. That blueberry muffin was very close to making a reappearance at that point, but she followed him into his office with her notepad and coffee. She held the cup in mid air, unsure what to do with it at first until she heard him in her mind quite clearly…"Yeah, you can drink your coffee in here just use a coaster."

Ashton certainly didn't want to mar his beautiful and obviously outrageously expensive desk with a ring from a coffee cup. She sat, and Andrew reached into a drawer, pulled out a coaster and slid it across the desk. Doris came in right after with his expensive Kenyan coffee in a china cup. She was already carrying a coaster to place his cup on.

"He has her well trained," Ashton decided.

SHE ALREADY KNEW what he wanted to talk to her about; this would be the first of countless meetings about various people both within and outside of the corporation; in fact, he would eventually become so obsessed with this mind reading thing that he would bring her to his parents' house so she could get a read on them as well.

"Let's get right to it, shall we?" he asked her. And one by one, he read off his list of his board of directors and she read off her notes to him. She was honest; after all that was what she was here for, and she left nothing out, save for the female board member who wanted to focus on a particular area of Andrew's anatomy; she didn't want to be hurtful and quite frankly didn't see that woman as a threat; just a middle aged married lady with two kids in college having a fantasy about her very handsome boss.

But for each one he read off, save for that one woman, what she responded with was not pleasing to him. No one liked him; those who were here when his father ran the place favored Harold. They preferred his style of management; effective but more low key; he tried to keep the company out of the public eye as much as possible when it came to those hostile takeovers.

He didn't attend the closings of companies trying to stand out as much as Andrew did. He would say a few words, wish those who had lost their jobs good wishes to find new ones, and then would go on to speak about the new direction they would be going in, while Andrew would try to be as ostentatious as possible, waving at the crowd and flashing his perfect smile—especially to any good looking women nearby—and almost making light of the situation.

Though Andrew made the company more profitable than his father did, he did it in a way that few of his board members approved of. And all that sleeping around with female subordinates—that disgusted most of them. Harold had affairs as well but mostly kept them out of the office; and as he got older and closer to retiring he just seemed to stop altogether.

181

The board wanted stability; they wanted the company to be respected; they wanted to be respected; but they were not.

But even all that meant little to Andrew, until she rattled off the name "Steve Martell."

As she spoke about him, Andrew leaned forward in his chair, hanging on to her every word. She painted him a picture of a man hungry; hungry for power; who would do all he could to move up through the ranks as quickly as possible with his eye on the chair of the CEO. He made many mistakes running his own small company, which was why it closed and he was now here, but he was cocky and felt he was ready for another shot at being the top man.

But the Desmond Corporation employed over twenty thousand people and was international; Martell held court over only three hundred at his old job and the only other office besides the New York one was in Passaic, New Jersey, in a four story building next to a strip mall. Martell was only small potatoes compared to Andrew; but thinking he was so much more, that he could be so much more, would make him a dangerous man.

Andrew thought that he would watch Martell for now, and see how things unfolded; if he needed to he could always count on his old buddy, Mark Peters to straighten things out for him.

Ashton picked up on that right away and shuddered; what had she gotten herself into? Is that what he planned to do— permanently eliminate anyone who got in his way?

She stared at him while he outlined the next stage of his plan, which would include open meetings with all employees. Since she technically was his Employee Relations Specialist he could hold general meetings so he could introduce her to everyone and she could get feedback from them. Ashton urged him to make those meetings as small as possible; the idea of hundreds of thoughts coming at her would be too much to bear and she probably wouldn't get a clear "read" She suggested that he encourage employees to make an appointment with her to discuss any grievances; it would be more effective.

"Good idea," he said, "but first we have to get you computer literate. This note pad thing is just not going to work."

Before she knew it, Andrew had arranged for a computer and a tutor to be sent to her home. Ashton balked at the idea; she didn't want her parents to see too much of what was really going on here, but Andrew didn't want some tutor running in and out of Ashton's office trying to teach her basic computer skills, after all, shouldn't she have them already?

He didn't want to arouse any suspicion about her. There had been no employee hired on any level at the Desmond Corporation in the last five years who didn't have at least basic computer skills; it was a job requirement. So it would appear quite strange that this woman, hired as a "specialist" would have no idea of how to use one, save for knowing how to turn it on and off.

"It's settled," Andrew said. "What time do you get home?" he asked her.

"About six thirty," she replied.

"Okay, then the computer and the tutor will be there about seven. He'll set it up and then he'll work with you to get you up to speed. I'm going to order the same one for your office so you won't get confused."

"But there's one in there now," she balked.

"So what? It can be taken out. I think it's old anyway, and I want you to have something more up-to-date."

He arranged for the computer to be there the next evening. Marian and Bob stood with their mouths hanging open. Sure, the computer was a laptop, but it was top of the line and came with all the other bells and whistles too, like the latest printer/scanner. Bob was no expert in computer prices, but since he recently started looking around for one for the house, he knew what was being set up in his living room didn't come cheap. And a private tutor as well? What the heck was really going on here?

Ashton sensed his concern and said, "No, Bob, I'm not having an affair with my boss." She thought quickly and said, "It's part of a pilot program. They're attempting to see how productive they can make a person with little or no training become in different situations. I just happen to be one of the few in my class to get an "at home" computer. They want to see how much faster I can learn versus somebody else they will train exclusively in the office."

Ashton knew Bob didn't buy it; neither did the tutor. He took one look at this tall beauty with the sea green eyes and figured Desmond was screwing her. Ashton picked up on that too but said nothing.

For the next two hours, as Marian banged pots around in the kitchen, Ashton learned how to do more than just turn the darned thing on and off. She was glad, not only would it make her look more convincing, it would make her work easier. The tutor would come back four more times; gradually teaching her more advanced skills. She caught on quickly. And when she had built up enough knowledge and speed Andrew scheduled the first general meeting to introduce her formally.

Two weeks after her first day, she and Andrew stood before five hundred of the New York office's five thousand employees. Andrew's face was aglow introducing her to the staff and flashing his perfect white teeth. Ashton knew he was scoping out the room for "new blood" as well.

But he went on to say that he valued all his employees and wanted to be sure that working at the Desmond Corporation would be a positive experience for all of them, and that's why Ashton was here...to help insure they would be heard.

Ashton inched her way up next to Andrew and introduced herself. She parroted what he said; and then gave out her office extension for those who wished to make an appointment with her. She smiled brightly and added "Of course anything you say will be held in the strictest confidence; our goal is to improve where we can and not to chastise those that come forward with any grievance!"

Wow...she was amazed; had those words come out of *her* mouth? Pretty good, she thought. And apparently so did Andrew, not only because he nodded admiringly at her but because she heard the voice in his head: "Hey, she's not so dumb after all."

After the meeting Ashton suggested that they hold off on scheduling the next group to see how much of a response she got. If the response was overwhelming then she'd want to nail down what each one said before opening up to the thoughts of a thousand others.

Andrew agreed with her and they both headed back upstairs. She had barely been back in her office two minutes when the phone started to ring off the hook with employees wanting to make an appointment with her. She had to be careful; she didn't want to make too many appointments in any one day. She really

185

wanted to listen to what these people had to say and didn't want them to feel that they had less than five minutes to get it said, but more importantly she didn't want to burn herself out; many times feeling the intense emotions of others made her physically ill.

She would start her appointments at nine sharp the next day and schedule them at thirty minute intervals. By the end of the day she was booked solid for the next two weeks. Andrew was both amazed and dismayed at the same time; were there really that many unhappy employees here? They were all paid well and had good benefits; in fact, that was one of the things that the Desmond Corporation was known for. In a world where other companies were cutting back full-timers to part-time and making employees pay their own health benefits, the Desmond Corporation staff was over 90% full time with all benefits paid for by the company.

"There had to be something else that made all these people disgruntled," Andrew thought, as he paced back and forth in from of Ashton's desk.

Ashton heard his thoughts loud and clear and in her own mind responded with, "Yeah, and that something else is you, Andrew."

She was grateful for that computer training she got and the fact that she had the exact same computer at home as she had in her office, as she would soon be pounding away at both of them. She actually created a program to catalog the different complaints she would get, and made some colored graphs as well. She was proud of herself; it was the first time in a long while that she gave herself credit for anything. The only thing she was unhappy with was the pretense of it all. She wasn't really helping these employees but she hoped something good would come out of all this for them. She was spying for Andrew.

Andrew spent the rest of his day in his office with the big glass doors open, screaming at various people on the phone from time to time, but Ashton was so engrossed in her program that she paid him no mind. Doris stuck her head in several times to ask her if she wanted anything and Ashton asked her how she could put up with all that yelling.

"What yelling?" Doris responded. "I tuned him out years ago," and then she winked at Ashton and went back to her office. Ashton did have lunch though with Denise; she was fascinated with the whole idea of being able to voice her opinion about what was wrong with the company. She looked at Ashton, squinted her eyes and said, "I can sum it all up in one word: Andrew Desmond."

"That's two," Ashton giggled, but she didn't mention to Denise that she already knew she was going to say that.

Ashton really liked Denise; they seemed to hit it off right away. Denise was a little younger than she, just having turned thirty, and more educated with an MBA from Princeton, but the two women just found it easy to be around each other. Denise had a one bedroom apartment on York Avenue and Sixty-third street. She asked Ashton about her living arrangements.

Ashton was embarrassed to admit she still lived with her folks at thirty-four; maybe she should start to think about getting her own place. She asked Denise about her rent; it was over four thousand a month not including utilities. Ashton winched, that was pretty expensive, but with the salary she was getting from Andrew she could easily afford it. But then she thought, Who was she kidding? This job with Andrew couldn't last forever and once they parted ways she still had very little in the way of marketable skills and no college education. There would be no way she could afford an apartment in Manhattan if she had to work somewhere else. But Denise had the real credentials; she could work anywhere and still push past the hundred grand a year mark easily. Reading Denise's mind, Ashton knew she was making much more than that now.

As they rose from the table Denise said, "We should go out one night, you know, paint the town red as they used to say."

Ashton would like that. She didn't see much of Allison since Melissa was born; when she was off from work she and Kevin mostly spent time with couples with young children like themselves. Although Allison invited her over a few times, Ashton always felt like the "odd man out," single and no kids. And to be honest, watching the little kids at play was painful for her; whenever one of the kids approached her she was pleasant enough but Allison could see pain fill her pretty green eyes. After awhile Ashton just refused their invitations, always coming up with an excuse and it always revolved around the store; she seemed to always be doing inventory, but Allison knew Bob never let her do that—he and Craig took care of it. Ashton always left as soon as they closed after sweeping up.

But Allison didn't push her; she knew there was "something there" when she was around kids; something that made her sad. Funny, when they were younger Ashton seemed to always gravitate toward young children and babies; she said their minds still held the "secrets of heaven" that they would lose as they got older. But since that year she spent away her attitude towards little ones changed. She almost seemed to avoid them now. Sure, she loved little Melissa and was excited for Allison to be having her first child; but even there, Ashton seemed to pull away.

Ashton and Denise stepped off the private elevator, their heels sinking deep into the plush carpeting that blanketed most of the top floor. Ashton noticed that Denise took her shoes off when she thought no one was looking, as she did just now. "Damned carpet seems to just swallow up my shoes," she laughed. It was tough to walk in it; but Andrew liked it and this floor was his domain. Ashton found that curious as well. Having been to his apartment, she knew all his floors were marble, or almost all of them. Since when did he become a fan of carpeting that almost swallowed you up to your knees? Then a thought flashed through her head, "Maybe he thought it muffled sounds when he 'took' one of his employees. Maybe he didn't take them all to hotels or to his place. Maybe they 'did it' right on the floor there; right outside his office."

She turned bright red at the thought. Denise looked at her curiously but said nothing.

The truth was the carpeting was another throw back to when his father ran the company. Harold always had bunions and the hard floors made his feet hurt. And he, like Denise just did, would often slip his shoes off when he thought no one was looking. Andrew used to get a kick out of that; watching his father in custom made suits dart in and out of his office in just his socks. He would return to his desk and say something like, "Ahhh, I just love that carpet." So Andrew kept the carpet as a kind of nod to his father. Of course it had been changed many times over the years but it was just as plush as ever.

16

As the weeks went by, Marian and Bob saw less and less of Ashton. She seemed to be leaving earlier and coming home later each day. Most of the time she didn't even have dinner with them, having grabbed something at the office before she left for the day. They were pleased, though, that she had another friend, that Denise girl who worked in her office. Ashton had brought her to dinner one Sunday and they were impressed with her. She had an easy going manner and seemed to be interested in everything they said.

They were surprised to learn though, that Ashton was involved in employee relations; wasn't she hired as some kind of trainee in some kind of pilot program? As dinner progressed though, they said nothing of it; they didn't want to embarrass Ashton. But when Denise left they questioned her.

Ashton told them flat out that her boss recognized her ability to "read" people and to find the best way to help them get their point across thereby helping both the company be more productive and the employees happier.

"Wow, I'm really getting good at coming up with things quickly," she thought to herself.

"Ashton, he doesn't know about your "gift" does he? Marian was concerned; she had wanted that "gift" dead and buried a long time ago; using it could be dangerous.

"No, Ma," she lied. "He just thinks I'm good with people and I make them feel comfortable enough to open up about what's bothering them so he can make it better for them and the company." What she should have said was, "Yes, Ma, he knows very well what I can do and he's paying me big bucks to get all the information I can so he can eliminate anyone who gets in his way, and I mean eliminate." She thought of Mark Peters and shuddered.

"Well, has he given you a raise for all this new responsibility you have?"

Ashton mumbled something about a few dollars more but then quickly changed the subject. She didn't even remember what she told them she was making in the first place; she should have written it down.

But she had other problems. As the weeks went by there were more and more "meetings" and more and more

192

"appointments." Her workday was getting longer and longer, and that train ride was taking a big chunk out of her time each day. Besides, Andrew was getting in the habit of calling her at home to discuss matters even further; he had a few trips planned to other offices and of course she had to go. She was getting to bed later and later now as well; often retiring after two and getting up four hours later. It was time to move into the city. Andrew was on her about that now; he wanted her closer to him, and he would pay for her apartment.

Ashton was torn; how would she tell her parents that she was moving to Manhattan on her salary (whatever she said it was) Maybe she could say she was moving in with Denise? But they would surely find out that wasn't true.

Whatever… She found an apartment in Denise's building, but it was a studio compared to Denise's one bedroom. And it didn't face the East River as Denise's did. Still, the rent was twenty-eight hundred a month. Of course, Andrew had no problem with that; the lease was in his name and it sailed right through, a two year lease paid in full up front. Ashton would still be responsible for her food and utilities. It was generous of him, though, since she could well afford the rent on what he was really paying her.

It was time for her to start saving some of this money now, to make a future for herself, to have something left to be able to start over when he was done with her. But maybe now, with her being out of the house her parents would start to make that move…and retire.

Denise was glad to have her close by but also wondered how she was affording her new place. She didn't know what Ashton made but assumed it had to be less than half of what she did. Oh well, she thought, Her parents own a store so maybe they're chipping in.

She was also surprised at the quality of furniture Ashton was buying; designer stuff with exotic woods from the more expensive stores. But again, she said nothing; it was really none of her business anyway. She was glad to have her friend so close by, and the two spent more and more time together, at least for awhile. Then, it seemed, Ashton was spending more and more time at the office—with Andrew.

And then, it became trips with Andrew. At every company takeover, Ashton now accompanied Andrew, no matter where they were. Denise was puzzled; what could all that traveling have to do with employee relations? Every takeover event was now attended by both Andrew and Ashton. Was Andrew paying Ashton to counsel people who were losing their jobs as a result of a Desmond takeover? That would be kind but that wasn't Andrew. Denise knew Andrew well enough to know he didn't possess that kind of compassion; he couldn't give a fuck what happened to any of them.

She didn't know what was going on and in a way she didn't want to know; had Ashton become Andrew's mistress? She certainly was beautiful and they did work very closely together; Ashton had even remarked last week that she had to stop by his condo several times.

And Ashton was worried as well. She knew what Denise was thinking; that she was screwing Andrew, and on a regular basis, something he never wanted to do with any other woman.

Even when he was married to Sarah he was unfaithful, and on their honeymoon at that. Andrew Desmond could never be satisfied with just one woman; and he had no idea what love was, because in that twisted, cold heart there was just a void where there could have been a real connection. Sure, Andrew loved his mother, a long time ago when he was just a boy. He may have even loved his father, but even that was doubtful. No, there was only one thing, okay, make that two, that Andrew loved, and neither of those was breathing. Money and power; that was it. The real loves of the life of Andrew Desmond.

ANDREW WAS PLEASED WITH HIMSELF as he stood, admiring himself in this latest custom made suit, almost twirling around like a school girl. It was nine p.m. and the tailor was just leaving Andrew's place after an afternoon of putting up with Desmond's endless, negative comments about the quality and cut of the material the tailor had brought.

Ashton was there as well; in between they were going over the details of a visit to the Los Angeles office. Ashton wasn't pleased; the LA office was huge, just slightly smaller than New York, and Andrew wanted a meeting with all of them at one time to introduce her. Conference rooms had been booked at some luxury hotel; thankfully the rooms could be combined to hold the thirty-five hundred who could possibly attend.

Thirty-five hundred minds to deal with! The chatter in her head would be unbearable! Ashton begged Andrew to spend the week there; at least they could break up the meetings into smaller ones as they'd done in New York. But Andrew wouldn't hear of it and for a very good reason: Steve Martell.

Martell had been getting out of hand for awhile now; whispering to other board members about what he could do for the corporation. His ideas were always bigger and grander than

Andrew's; but they had no valid basis. Martell simply didn't have the "smarts" to run a company as big as the Desmond Corporation.

He thought he did; but his own small failed company was proof-in-the-pudding. And there had been other failed companies as well; and Andrew didn't even have to use Mark Peters to find that out. Martell had been hitting on Ashton regularly too, coming to her office with some made up excuse just to talk to her.

"Have dinner with me." "Let me take you dancing and show you off," were some of the old, tired lines he used. But Ashton was getting better and better at her job. She would engage him in conversation and then his thoughts would filter their way into her mind.

He'd had several failed companies, in fact. Although he did well in a corporate officer position, when he rose any higher than that it just proved to be too much for him. Bad decisions; excessive spending in the wrong places, hiring the wrong people made each venture end in disaster.

But Martell was insanely jealous of Andrew. Jealous of his looks, his money, his power, and jealous that this absolutely divine creature they called Ashton sat right in the office next to his. Martell thought what many at the company were thinking; that the two of them were having an affair.

Ashton had to keep from grinning as she picked up on that; but then had to hide her repulsion when she "saw" what he wanted to do with her. But she was a pro now; although many thoughts still caused her head to spin—like thirty-five hundred people in a conference room—she could mask her reactions to what was coming through. She smiled brightly at Steve; nodding her head in agreement with some of what he was saying; demurely rejecting his advances, batting her long eyelashes.

And then, when he was gone, a full report to Andrew.
But Andrew was getting good now, too; good at burying his thoughts so that Ashton had trouble picking up on them. And the two thoughts that he buried the deepest within his mind were that he was in love with her and that Peters would have to take care of Martell. Two reasons why he did not want to stay a week in L.A.

He made it up to Ashton by giving her a five hundred dollar a week raise; she was making almost four thousand a week now. It was decided; the L.A. trip would be scheduled next month, one day only. Andrew wanted to split the day so that Ashton could spend more time with the executives out there; they would give a courtesy one hour meeting to everyone else. Andrew really didn't give a shit about what some Suzy Secretary thought of his company, they were just going through the motions there.

Ashton and Denise left the office together that night and stopped for dinner. After a couple of glasses of wine Denise blurted out, "Are you fucking Andrew?"

After she said it she cupped her hand to her mouth and said, "I'm sorry, Ashton. It's none of my business!"

Of course, Ashton was neither surprised nor startled; she knew it was coming. She smiled graciously at Denise and told her no. She was not interested in Andrew; it was just part of her job that she had to spend so much time with him. Somehow, Denise knew she was telling the truth, although she was still embarrassed for having brought it up. "Too much wine, I guess," was her answer.

But Denise noticed how much Ashton had changed over the past months. Sure, in the beginning she had a few nice outfits but then took to wearing "ordinary clothes" from places like Macy's. Nice things, but nothing earth shattering. But then her wardrobe took a turn and became a steady diet of strictly designer fashions with labels like Prada and Chanel, even her shoes had the famous red soles indicative of high priced designers. "Red backs," they called them.

Where was she getting all this money? Denise knew Ashton's parents owned that grocery store, but having spent several Sunday dinners with her family, she also knew they didn't have all that much and they were not the type to waste it on two thousand dollar shoes for their daughter. As she recalled, her parents wanted to retire soon, so Denise was sure they were probably watching every penny. What the hell was really going on here? Denise wondered.

As they walked home from the restaurant the two women said little to each other. It had become an awkward silence. Of course, Ashton knew everything that was going through Denise's mind—all the questions about her clothes, and her apartment, and still some doubt, despite what she said earlier, about her and Andrew.

Ashton was starting to doubt as well. Maybe she did feel something for Andrew. It wasn't like it was in the beginning; that she was the scared, inexperienced young woman overwhelmed in the presence of this outrageously rich and powerful man. She was much more comfortable with him now. And the fact that she became so good at her job helped the relationship along as well. In the beginning she was struggling; struggling to learn a computer system, struggling to fit in a new environment, struggling with her conscience about using her special abilities, and struggling with explaining it all to her parents.

Now, she wasn't struggling so much anymore. She was a wiz on the computer, the office became like a second home, and it became comfortable to be around Andrew. They could work together, laugh together, and have dinner together. In fact, Ashton noticed that Andrew hadn't gone out on any dates in quite awhile; even the tabloids ran articles about it. No Andrew Desmond sightings at any of his usual hangouts.

Ashton was torn. She knew what she was doing was wrong. She knew this job wouldn't last forever. She knew Andrew would eventually dispose of her when he didn't need her anymore. She just hoped Mark Peters wouldn't be involved in her departure.

She had to stick to her original plan; save as much money as she could, learn as much as she could about office procedures so she could eventually get a "real" job, and to show her parents that they could retire and live their lives without worrying about her. But it was so tempting, all of this; could she ever really break away?

As she slept that night she dreamt of Andrew; she was in his bed, and he was slowly pulling the straps of her negligee down. She bolted upright, panicked; but then just as quickly slid back into sleep.

MARIAN AND BOB seemed to be in a state of constant anxiety. Ashton had moved out months ago, taking only her clothes and other personal belongings and leaving the bedroom furniture she had used since she was a teenager, which was the last time Marian updated the furniture in the apartment. They hadn't even been to Ashton's place, in truth she was avoiding it as she didn't want them to see where it was or how it had been decorated...professionally with high end furniture.

It would just bring more questions about how she could afford all this on her *What the hell was it that she supposed to be doing?* job. She went out of her way to visit them on Sunday for dinner, but had taken to wearing jeans and sneakers and pulling her hair back as she had done when she worked at the store. "The old Ashton," she thought, "less suspicious."

Denise still accompanied her occasionally as she enjoyed those dinners and came to think of Bob and Marian as almost family now. Her own mother and father lived in the Midwest and it had been a long time since she'd seen them but hoped to plan a trip there soon. But even she noticed Ashton was dressing down when she went to visit them and flooded them with questions about the store and their plans to retire to take the focus away from her. Their questions were dismissed with what had become her pat answer... "Oh, it's no big deal really."

The new cashier that Craig hired was working out quite well, a woman from the neighborhood with a teenage son. Her husband, like Marian's, had left her for another woman so Marian felt she was a kindred spirit. Amanda Lewis was thirty-six and had a fourteen year old son, Jeremy, in his first year of high school.

Luckily, Jeremy was a responsible kid who went straight home from school each day and did his homework and cleaned his room. Amanda was lucky; she needed this job and wanted to give her full attention to it. And also, unlike Marian, her husband and his new twenty-two year old wife lived only a short distance away, and while going there too often made Jeremy uncomfortable, seeing his dad with another woman so much younger than his mom, at least he paid his child support on time.

Yes, Amanda was working out just fine. She was doing things Ashton could never do; like inventories and ordering and Craig thought to himself that if he could ever buy the store Amanda would make a fine manager; they got along well. If things kept going the way they were Bob and Marian probably would be retiring within the next six months; Ashton was gone and apparently taking care of herself so what would hold them here?

He heard Bob on the office phone talking to a realtor in Palm Beach several times. He wondered, though, how he could swing it. He only had about five thousand in the bank; Evelyn didn't work to be with Bradley most of the time, and his credit was lousy. Bob and Marian wouldn't consider owner financing; at their age they wanted to be debt free. And Bradley... That new school they were thinking of sending him to would take a huge chunk out of his paycheck, which was generous he had to admit; unless they got some kind of subsidy. At this point, the best Craig could hope for was to stay on as the manager; he was sure Bob would put in a good word for him with the new owners.

In fact, Ashton had never met Amanda, since the store was closed on Sunday and that was the only day she ever came around. Craig had argued with Bob about that over the years; this was not twenty years ago when no store was open on that day. They should be open like everybody else. But Bob had not wavered and Craig could see it was no use. Truthfully, he could have used the overtime.

Susan spent more and more time away from the great house. Harold seemed to get worse and then rebound. It was a cycle, a vicious one at that. But his "bad" moments were really getting to her. Last week he almost fell off the landing pretending to be Superman. Poor Robert, she thought. The man who served proudly as the major domo for so many years was simply a nursemaid now. There were no more formal dinners with people to greet. And the staff was a lot smaller as well; only two housekeepers, a cook, a gardener and Robert. Why he stayed on with them Susan always wondered but she was grateful. It was never in his original job description to change the diapers of a grown man and sing nursery rhymes with him.

She was meeting Sarah and Jessica for lunch and then onto another charity event. As usual, the child was drawn to Susan; Sarah said she was always happier to see Susan than her own grandmother, who seemed bored with her preferring instead to do something really worthwhile like shopping. Only Sarah had changed over the years after marrying Bill. Her mother and father were still insufferable snobs, like Harold would still have been had he not been too busy pretending to be Superman.

Susan was secretly glad for that, as she loved Jessica as a grandchild and Sarah as a daughter. But Sarah told Susan she was becoming more and more disturbed by the things Jessica was saying. The other night, she told Bill that although he and Susan were not her real parents she would still call them Mommy and Daddy and love them with all her heart.

She also told Bill that Mommy would love a weekend in the city only seconds after he thought about taking Sarah to Manhattan for the weekend. It was disturbing, and it seemed to be happening more and more. And there was trouble in her preschool as well, now more than ever, and both Sarah and Bill were thinking of taking her out of there.

"I'm not quite sure what to do. I want her to interact with other children to have fun and learn but she's scaring them by telling them things about themselves that she couldn't possibly know," Sarah said, sadness filling her eyes.

"Maybe it's a phase," Susan said, not knowing quite what to say that would make Sarah feel better.

But the subject was dropped as Jessica ran to Sarah and put her arms around her. Instead, it turned to Andrew. Sarah read the papers and noticed the headline, that Andrew hadn't been seen around town with a different girl each night in quite awhile now. It was like he was under the radar.

But Susan sadly admitted that she knew no more about him than Sarah did, only from what she had read. Her phone messages always went unanswered. She thought of going over to his place; the Plaza management knew who she was and would let her right up to Andrew's penthouse. They had permission to do that. She could knock right on his door but she wouldn't. She wouldn't invade his privacy like that. She was actually surprised he hadn't asked for his keys back; he had given her a set when he first moved in just in case he misplaced them. But Susan felt he just probably had the locks changed.

"I don't have a clue what he could be up to," Susan told her. "It's like we're strangers now."

But their conversation was interrupted by Jessica going up to a waitress at the restaurant who seemed to have an odd look on her face, as if something were bothering her, and told her, "You knew that girdle was going to be way too tight for you when you bought it."

Mortified, the two women paid their lunch tab, grabbed Jessica and exited as fast as their feet could carry them.

In the parking lot Sarah decided to take Jessica home; Susan would go onto the charity event without her. She shoved a signed check into Susan's hands and told her to make it out for whatever amount she felt was appropriate and drove off, obviously agitated. Susan was worried as well but at least one of them had to attend.

After writing two checks for a thousand dollars each—she would call Sarah later to let her know how much her check was for—she drove to the little Cape Cod. Sheena greeted her by the door; her tail held high like a flag. After making a quick cup of tea Susan went outside to tend her flowers; it always relaxed her.

She was only there about an hour when she got a call from Robert. Harold was swimming naked in Long Island Sound, and nothing he could do would get him to come out of the water.

Sighing heavily, she put the cup in the sink, petted Sheena, wrote a note to Peggy and then swung the big Bentley back towards the north shore.

Now that Amanda was working out so well at the store Marian cut way back on her hours. Craig hired a part time cashier to pick up the slack; actually it worked out better as Marian was slowing down a little more each day. Bob toughed it out, after all, it was his store, his "baby," but even he would leave early now when he could. He came home to find Marian perusing a brochure on Beautiful Palm Beach. He sat down beside her on the couch and said, "Let's contact that realtor again. Let's fly down for a long weekend and really check out some places. We need to get this ball rolling."

"But what about Ashton?" she inquired.

"Ashton? Ashton only comes around on Sunday, remember? And as I recall, she's missed the last two at that. When did you speak to her the last time?" Bob already knew the answer to that. It was sometime last week, and a short call at that. Something about going to Los Angeles with her boss.

"She's made her life away from us now, Marian. And it's time for us to do the same."

Marian nodded as Bob made the travel arrangements. They would go next week. They had a fine crew at the store now and it would be in good hands.

As the plane took off from Kennedy Airport it climbed over the Manhattan skyline and Marian could clearly see the soaring tower of the Desmond Corporation; the big "D" emblazoned near the top of it like a badge of honor. And her thoughts turned to Ashton.

17

Ashton woke up early from that seductive dream she had about Andrew. She decided to get to the office early as well as she was in no mood for small talk. Not even Doris was in yet; as the elevator doors slid open the floor was deserted, and she took her high heels off and sank into the deep carpeting. She tossed them in her office along with her new Balenciaga handbag and made her way into the private kitchen to make some coffee. She sat, stirring the cream in wistfully as she heard the elevator door slide open. She looked at her watch. It was only eight. Who was coming in that early?

It was Andrew. As he walked into the kitchen she stood, ready to get back to her office as he approached her. "I know, I know," she said, "I have lots of work to do."

The next thing she knew he was kissing her.

"I've been dreaming about you," he said. She returned his kiss willingly; he was lighting a fire within her that was strange and unfamiliar. She had never felt that with any man, albeit most of her encounters were in bathroom stalls with both she and the guy half drunk. But this? What was this?

But suddenly she broke away from him, stepping back, and almost knocking into the table behind her. She looked into his eyes and shook her head. Then, stepping gingerly around him she bolted to her office and shut the door. He was about to go after her when he heard the elevator doors slide open; it was Doris; her arms full of reports she took home last night. She barely made it to her desk when the folders slid out of her arms, landing in a heap on the floor.

"Shit!" she yelled, and then saw Andrew standing there. She thought to herself that it was way too early for him to be here. He just looked at her; kind of looked right through her with a faraway look in his eyes and then walked off towards his own office.

Doris almost sprinted to the private kitchen to start brewing his Kenyan coffee. As she got his special china cup ready she heard movement in Ashton's office behind her closed door. Was she here early, too? Doris wondered. She wanted to beat everyone in this morning as she wanted Andrew's reports finished before he came in and on his desk ready for his review. Although she had taken much of it home with her last night Jeff wasn't feeling too well, and so little of it actually got done. The coffee ready, she poured it into the delicate cup and made her way to Andrew's office. His doors were open; she robotically entered the room and placed the coffee on the coaster that was ready to receive it. She said nothing; Andrew said nothing—he never said thank you anyway—but Doris sensed a strange vibe in the room. *Oh well,* she thought. *It's none of my business. Besides, I have my own problems to worry about.*

As Doris started picking up the folders and separating them in to piles of work she had done and what she needed to complete, more people were getting off the private elevator and making their way to their own offices. She saw Denise coming in as well; although she stopped to knock on Ashton's door. She answered it, but had a strange look on her face.

"Hey," Denise called good naturedly, "What did you do... sleep here?"

It was a joke since the two women left the office together last night, Denise wanting to stop for cocktails but Ashton insisting on rushing home. She seemed distracted so Denise didn't push the issue; instead, she stopped herself and ran into some old friends. After a glass of wine she made her way home. She thought about knocking on Ashton's door but then felt that she didn't seem to want company so she went back to her own apartment where she called her parents to tell them she'd be flying out to see them next month. They were so happy to hear from her; she knew she needed to call them more often. After reading a magazine she slid into bed and drifted off to sleep, wondering if Ashton felt a little better. She would call her in the morning and they could ride in together. They often split a cab.

But despite it being super early Ashton didn't answer her phone. She saw Denise's number on the caller ID but ignored it; she probably wanted to share a cab but Ashton was already halfway to the office, disoriented by that seductive dream. Those dreams seemed to have a life of their own; starting from the beginning when Andrew was only a shadow; become more and more well defined each time. And now this. What Ashton didn't know was that lately Andrew was having similar dreams; he knew, deep inside, that he was in love with her. But love was something Andrew Desmond never counted on ever experiencing.

Ashton smiled sheepishly at Denise, not quite knowing what to say.

"I had a lot of work to do so I wanted to get in early," was all she could offer. Denise glanced behind her to see Andrew was in early as well, did he have a lot of work to do too? Andrew looked up to see Denise standing there and barked at her to come into his office; she turned and merely stared at him; he was not going to speak to her this way, chairman or no chairman.

"Please come in Denise," he quickly corrected himself. "I'd like to go over some quarterly projections with you, since you're in early."

She nodded, winked at Ashton and made her way into his office where Ashton overheard him say, "Can I get you some coffee?"

Good for her, she thought. She really does have him by the balls. The one woman who was not intimidated by the great Andrew Desmond after sleeping with him.

But as the day wore on she could no longer avoid Andrew. They had work to do; things to review, before the LA trip. They said nothing of their interaction in the kitchen earlier; both tried to pretend it never happened. In the afternoon Ashton had some meetings set up with a few disgruntled employees; nothing Andrew would be interested in as they had little influence; lower level employees were just a necessary evil to keep his company running; if they were happy or not was of no consequence to him.

Doris sensed a weird kind of tension between them all day long; or was it just her imagination? Denise sensed it too and in her office Ashton knew exactly what both of them were thinking…"what the hell is going on here?"

Towards the end of the day she was back in Andrew's office; he shut the heavy glass doors behind her.

"Have dinner with me." He grabbed her arm and looked plaintively into her eyes. The color of the sea, he thought.

"No Andrew, I don't think it's a good idea. What happened this morning should never have happened. I'll see you tomorrow."

Denise and Ashton said little to each other in the cab ride home.

"I suppose you don't want to stop for something to eat," Denise added. Ashton shook her head and told her she'd nuke a TV dinner.

And as she drifted off to sleep, Ashton felt a sense of peace. Maybe she wouldn't have these dreams anymore. Nightmares really.

The clock read 3:07 as Ashton woke; sweating and pupils dilated. They were in Andrew's bed. Now she was naked, as was he, and he was slowly climbing on top of her…

THE REALTOR WAS WAITING for Marian and Bob's flight to land. They were lucky to have gotten a direct one so it was relatively quick; a little over two hours.

Glen Thompson had been selling real estate in this area of Florida for about ten years now. Although he sold mostly high end stuff, the average price of the homes coming in at around five million. He had taken a liking to Bob since the first time they spoke on the phone.

They both had come from Brooklyn, Glen from Bensonhurst which technically was only about twenty blocks from Bay Ridge where Bob and Marian lived. Glen knew they wouldn't be making any million dollar purchase but at least they had been qualified for a million, and he knew they were eager to leave New York for the warmer weather of Florida.

He stood with a sign by the baggage area with their names on it. He knew who they were right away, a pleasant looking older couple, smiling but obviously very tired. They looked worn down by life. Glen had made arrangements for them to stay at one of the Hilton Garden hotels. They were always neat and clean and seemed to be right in the center of things. Bob had decided not to rent a car as they would be spending the majority of their time looking at places to live, so they would need to walk to nearby restaurants. And Glen knew the Hilton served a decent breakfast as well.

He dropped them off at their hotel and looked at his watch; it was nearly four and they looked exhausted. He told them he would pick them up at eleven the next morning; it would give them plenty of time to relax and take a swim in the hotel pool. They would spend the next three days looking around; their flight back to New York wasn't until late Monday night.

As he watched Glen drive away Bob wondered if he were really doing the right thing by coming here; he worried about Ashton. He worried about this "job" she had and where all this

212

money was coming from. If Ashton had gone onto college and had her degree he could understand it. But cashier (and not a really good one at that) to an apartment in the Upper East Side of Manhattan?

They settled in their room which looked over the pool and hot tub area; they could see there was a small Tiki bar as well. After hanging up their clothes they put on their shorts and swim suits and headed down; enjoying a martini in the lounge chairs while the slowly setting sun warmed their faces. They knew there would be no spectacular sunsets; they needed the west coast for that; Sarasota, where they had originally thought of settling, but the sunrises over the Atlantic were equally magnificent. As they sipped their cocktails Bob took Marian's hand and smiled. "I love you," he cooed at her, and she replied in kind.

The next day Glen was outside at eleven sharp; he had a list of places for them to see—small condos on the beach as they requested. They wanted a place with a community pool and a balcony; and a well equipped modern kitchen was a must. Although eating out in the area was something almost everyone did on a nightly basis, Marian always loved to cook. She always wanted a kitchen with super modern appliances, but living in the old building meant that the stove or refrigerator was replaced by the landlord, and over the years, it had never been anything high end, just the "bare bones" basic. It would be nice for Marian to have a big, fancy kitchen at last.

As the day ended, Glen had taken them to five different places; all in the $250,000—$300,000 range. Marian had liked two of them; but then Bob piped up, "Can you take us to see some two bedrooms tomorrow, I think that might be better."

213

Bob again thought of Ashton, Truthfully he didn't want to spend all that much, but being pre-approved for more money than he thought they would be gave him more leeway.

Marian turned and smiled at him, pleased he was thinking of Ashton. If they saw something they would have no trouble writing a check for the down payment. They really wanted to sell the store first and then pay cash for the property, but Bob realized that would mean they'd have to pass on any place they saw they right now and they were anxious to get the wheels rolling. Nope, the mortgage would be a good idea as long as their contract did not have a pre-payment penalty clause; they could just pay the whole thing off once the store was sold.

Now back at the hotel pool Marian told Bob, "You know two bedrooms *is* a really good idea. One day, when Ashton gets married she can come to visit with her husband. That was good thinking Bob."

Yeah, good thinking for when Ashton gets married, who were they kidding? The extra room was for when Ashton fell on her face and had nowhere else to go.

He looked over at his wife again and saw the hurt and pain in her eyes.

"Maybe she will really make it on her own," he thought.

The next day Glen was back. He worked feverishly when he got back to his office the night before; they originally wanted one bedroom, now it was two. It meant looking up different listings and contacting different brokers; the only condos he had amongst his own listings were four and five bedrooms on upper floors well over the $750,000 mark. Unless, of course, they wanted that inter-coastal beauty he just listed for 4.7 million. He chuckled to himself at the thought. Even if they could afford that, they were not flashy people; that was one thing he liked about them; they reminded him of his roots. Palm Beach was beautiful to be sure, but it was so...*plastic*. It was all flash. Most of his clients were whiney and demanding.

Many of them had never worked a day in their lives. His wife liked to shop on Worth Avenue, where all the most expensive shops were, and to have dinner at The Breakers. But truthfully Glen just wanted to sit in his backyard, have a beer with his neighbors and go see a movie. He had to deal with these spoiled brats all day; he really didn't want to socialize with them too, unless it had to do with business.

It was late Sunday when Glen showed them the last place of the day; he planned a short day tomorrow with them so they would have time to relax before their plane left.

The condo was super modern; seven stories up it had an expansive view of the whitecaps whipping up the Atlantic on this windy day. The small balcony off the living room was large enough for a small table and chairs. The master bedroom had views of the ocean and a bathroom with a bidet. The other, smaller bedroom was cute and charming with a bathroom (tub and shower included) in the hallway.

But the kitchen was right out of a magazine. Marian took one look and smiled ear-to-ear. All stainless steel, high end appliances, the ones she wished she had in the apartment in Brooklyn. Bob took one look at her and knew this was the place.

"How much is it?" Bob asked, not really wanting to know. He knew this was way more than he planned for. But Marian; Marian looked transfixed. He could not let her down.

215

"Five hundred," Glen said quickly.

Without missing a beat Bob said, "Offer four fifty and let's see where it goes."

It went pretty quickly. The sellers accepted it right off; the condo belonged to their mother and she had passed not long ago. The one woman, her daughter, was living in it while her own home was being built and wasn't in all that much of a hurry to leave; construction was taking longer than planned. They were actually pleased with the one hundred twenty day escrow. It would give the daughter extra time in the condo in case the construction dragged on longer; it would give Bob and Marian more time to sell the store and get their affairs in order.

All the appliances would come with it too; like Marian, their mother loved to cook and even though she was well into her eighties just remodeled the kitchen she spent so much time in. She was strong until the end when she fell in the kitchen she loved so much, breaking her hip. After only several days in the hospital she passed away from pneumonia.

Bob quickly wrote a check for fifty thousand as a deposit and escrow was opened the next day. There was no sense looking at any more properties so Bob and Marian slept late and spent some more time by the pool until they headed to the airport.

As the plane skid to a halt on the runway at Kennedy, Bob knew he had to sell the store now. He hoped he could get it all done in the four months they had before they closed on the condo. He would offer it to Craig first after having it assessed to see what its true worth was, but he was only doing it to be polite; there was no way, barring a miracle, that Craig could swing it. And ever if he had considered holding paper on it he had just spent nearly two hundred thousand more than he'd plan to, but he couldn't deny Marian that kitchen.

ANDREW PACED UP AND DOWN in the living room. The full moon was shining eerily inside the big windows, making odd shadows on the marble floors. It was almost ghost like. Hilda and Donald were nowhere to be found; both had gone out for the evening after Andrew barked at them that he wanted to be alone.

All he could think about now was Ashton. He wanted her; he had to have her. He loved her. He knew it now. This was his dream woman. They could build a life together. They could rule the world together. They could...

He poured himself a scotch and dropped into a chair in his den. He had to devise a plan. But what would it be? He would get her to come here tomorrow night. That wouldn't be so far out of the ordinary; she came here all the time anyway; they always had some loose ends to tie up. When Donald and Hilda came in he told them to take tomorrow night off as well, and for Hilda to leave something simple on the stove for him to heat up.

Hilda didn't even know he knew how to use a microwave; she had never seen him do it in all these years. But she and Donald were perplexed anyway—there had been no women here in months. Andrew would just come home, eat his dinner quietly, get some work done and then go to bed early. There were no more late nights, no more finding women's underwear all over the place; no more drunken arguing. To them, it was like nirvana. In their rooms at night they could watch their televisions shows without all that drama and noise playing out in the background.

As Andrew drifted off to sleep he saw it plainly; he and Ashton naked in his bed, making love.

In the morning he devised a plan to get her here after work tonight; he would tell her he was extending the L.A. trip and wanted to talk to her about it. He would wait until late in the day so she wouldn't ask him to get it out of the way early so she could go home on time. He knew she didn't want to do that trip in one day; although she was really good now at reading other's thoughts and hiding her own emotions, it still was an awful lot to take in all at once.

But then he had a better idea: he would call Doris to say he wasn't feeling well! Yeah that was it, he wouldn't come in today. He'd call Doris and tell her to have Ashton come by after work; this way he wouldn't be near her all day and she couldn't read him!

Andrew Desmond would call in sick for the first time in his life.

Doris was amazed when she got the call; he had a major board meeting this morning and besides, in all the years she'd worked for him he'd never missed a day of work. Doris chuckled to herself and wondered if the world was coming to an end. Then she emailed the board members to let them know the meeting for this morning was cancelled. As Ashton got off the private elevator she told her Andrew was sick and that he wanted her to come by after work to go over some things he had wanted to cover today and felt they couldn't wait until Monday.

Ashton nodded, perplexed, and then silently walked away. As she sat at her desk she tried to get a read on him but couldn't. Last night's dream had disturbed her most of all: the two of them making love in Andrew's bed. Where was all this going? She really wondered if she bit off way more than she could chew here. Andrew was a dangerous man and now this whole relationship seemed to be taking a different turn.

About two hours later, as she typed away on her computer, she noticed someone at her door. It was Steve Martell. He knocked and asked if he could come in to talk. Ashton already knew what was on his mind. Without Andrew here he became bolder; bolder than he'd been in the past. He got right by Doris; after all, he was a board member, what could she say to him? "Get lost?" "Make an appointment?" She was going to ring Ashton but this guy moved too fast. He shut the door behind him. Ashton was cornered.

"C'mon, have dinner with me tonight," he pleaded. "Why don't you like me?" he asked her, trying to grab her hand, which she pulled away quickly.

She could read him clearly. He hated Andrew. He would take every opportunity to try to turn the board against him. He was so jealous, so vile and truth be told he couldn't run this company. It was too big, too complicated. Steve Martell was not the man he thought he was. She saw flashes of defeat in his mind. He actually thought becoming chairman would vindicate him in the eyes of the world. He would be a success. He would have what Andrew had. He would have her.

"Please leave," she told him, standing tall. "I do not want to have dinner with you so please stop asking me." She kept calm. She did not want to make a scene.

He met her gaze. "I suppose ALL of you belongs to him doesn't it?" He was angry. He was hurt.

She walked over and opened her door for him. He left quietly, walking past Doris quickly. Ashton sank back in her chair cupping her head in her hands. Doris sensed something was wrong and got up as soon as Martell was out of sight.

"You alright?" she asked Ashton, now visibly rattled.

"Yeah, thanks, that guy is really crazy, you know?"

"I don't like him," Doris said. "I've had a bad feeling about him since he first got here. He's done a lot of good in his department but I don't trust him. There's a lot of good people out there who would do just as good a job and just wouldn't be so, I don't know...creepy."

Ashton nodded; Doris had him pegged alright. He was a creep. Much worse than that even. Tonight she would let Andrew know, but in a way she was afraid. Mark Peters typically handled those people who needed to be "fired" For a moment she thought of the movie *The Shining* and of the part where the caretaker says he "corrected" his family by chopping them up with an axe. She wondered how many people Peters "corrected" at Andrew's request.

Ashton shook her head and then went back to what she was doing; or at least tried to. Denise stuck her head in at lunch and asked her to join her. Ashton welcomed the diversion; she realized she hadn't eaten since last night and it was past one now. They left the building and headed to a small café just up the block. It had outside seating so Ashton plopped herself in one of the chairs. The sun was shining brightly and she just wanted to feel its warmth on her face. It was so comforting. Denise reluctantly sat beside her; she really wanted to eat inside the restaurant but was too hungry to argue.

As they waited for their food Denise asked, "What happened to Andrew today? He never calls in sick; wasn't there a big meeting this morning?"

Truth be told, Ashton didn't know why he was out. He was too far away to read and besides, it was Doris who got the call, not her. She really didn't know anything about it.

"I don't know; I just hope he's not contagious whatever it is. I have to go over there after work; I guess he wanted to review some stuff today and it can't wait until Monday."

"Good thing you don't have a date tonight then," Denise remarked. "But it's a typical Friday and neither do I. I'll stop for a drink on the way home though, and maybe get some take out."

Then Denise laughed; she had a vision in her head of Andrew in a pair of Dr. Denton's; propped up in bed with a thermometer in his mouth, an ice bag on his head, and covered in measles.

The she asked, "What did Martell want? I don't like that guy... he's sneaky."

"No one likes him," she replied. "He asked me out. He keeps asking me out and I have zero interest in him." Ashton looked up and Denise nodded in agreement. Their lunch came right after and they both devoured it; little more was said. As they walked back to the office

Denise asked her if they were sharing a cab home then remembered she had to go up to Andrew's place; funny how she'd forgotten about that so quickly; they had just discussed it over lunch. Denise had been there—the one time Andrew fucked her and then threw her out the next morning, shortly after she started working for him.

221

She worried about Ashton getting too close to him; not that she was jealous; the thought of sex with him now turned her off completely; but she didn't want Ashton getting hurt. Denise had her doubts about this whole Andrew thing, despite Ashton's reassurances. She wondered if there wasn't something more going on here, something that ultimately Ashton wouldn't be able to handle. Of course Ashton knew exactly what was going through her mind but remained silent, thinking to herself that Denise was a good friend to worry about her like that.

Back at the Plaza, Andrew tore through his closet looking for the appropriate thing to wear for this evening, but then he thought he did not want to look that obvious. Then he thought that she could read his mind anyway and know exactly what his plan was. He sat on the huge bed and sighed heavily. Looking down at his hands he noticed his palms were sweating. He was so confused; he wanted this night to be perfect. He did not want her to reject his advances and worse than that, leave altogether, even her job. He had to have her input; it was priceless to him.

Over the previous months there had been more than a few firings due to the reports from Ashton and with each one the chairman became more secure. And the best thing about it was that no one suspected a thing. Ashton was fully booked with appointments made by employees either in New York headquarters or in other places where they would not be traveling to; smaller offices.

An email announcement as well as one put into the company newsletter let everyone know that they now had someone to talk to about their job situation. Sure, seeing these people in person was far more effective than talking on the phone, but Ashton was getting better and better at it. It seemed that all this practice was sharpening her skills; making her more able to get into people's minds no matter what type of communication was used.

For L.A. and offices in other larger cities where they intended to visit, Ashton told those employees that she would meet with them face-to-face; it made for a more effective meeting. Those employees seemed placated by that; she was getting calls and emails left and right from the L.A. office alone and they hadn't even set up a schedule for Chicago yet.

Ashton was so engrossed in her work after lunch—after all, she had been thrown off track by that unwelcome visit from Steve Martell—that she didn't notice the clock creeping up to five. Denise stuck her head in and said, "Aren't you ever leaving?" Glancing at the clock she quickly shut down the computer; slid her new laptop into her Prada briefcase and gathered everything she might need for her meeting with Andrew.

She rode down the private elevator with Doris and Denise; as Denise grabbed a cab and Doris started walking towards the subway, a company limo pulled up for Ashton. She slid in the back seat and greeted the driver, Tony, who responded with, "Good evening Ms. Lancaster. Please help yourself to a glass of champagne." She shook her head no but then quickly changed her mind. The limo was stuck in traffic and wouldn't make the trip uptown too quickly. After all, it was rush hour and Friday to boot. People were either going home or leaving the city for the weekend.

She poured herself a glass and then sunk back into the luxurious leather of the upholstery. The trip took almost fifty minutes; with no traffic it would take no more than fifteen. Ashton thought to herself that it took almost as long just to get uptown today as it used to take when she lived in Brooklyn and had to take the 'R' train every morning.

She thought of her mother and Bob; they gave her a quick call when they came back from Palm Beach but she rushed them off the phone and so had no information on how the trip went. She would be having dinner there this Sunday though and she'd wear her "uniform" of jeans and sneakers. She even left her designer pocketbooks home now and carried one that she bought at Macy's for fifty bucks. She knew the expensive clothes she was wearing upset them; even though they lived below their means and could afford more, Marian had never bought a handbag that cost her more than a few dollars; she simply wasn't that showy. Yes, Ashton always remembered that the only thing "designer" her mother really ever wanted was a designer kitchen since she loved to cook so much.

The limo pulled up to the Plaza; it shook her from her thoughts as the doorman opened the car door for her.

"Good evening Ms. Lancaster," he said, parroting Tony, who waved at her and then drove off, presumably to park the limo wherever they parked it. Funny, all this time and she didn't know. Andrew kept his personal vehicles in the Plaza garage but there were several limos and they took up a lot of space. And why was she thinking about this now, anyway? Because she was getting nervous as she glanced upwards towards the penthouse. That's why.

Andrew was dressed now, casually for him, just dress pants and a shirt. Putting a suit on was ridiculous but he did consider it at first, only to dismiss it as he was supposed to be sick all day anyway. Hilda and Donald were gone—Hilda to visit friends and

Donald to meet his son for drinks and dinner. Hilda left a pot of chicken soup on the stove; Andrew had to admit that it smelled really good; would Ashton like it? She left a couple of soup bowls on the counter next to it.

He heard the doors of the elevator slide open and just as quickly opened his front door.

"How do you feel?" she asked him.

"Oh God," he thought , "I don't want her to read me." And with all the willpower he could muster imagined a brick wall encircling his mind, keeping his thoughts locked in and safe.

"I feel better now," he said, half managing a smile. "Hilda left some chicken soup on the stove and I was just going to have some, will you join me?"

They sat at the kitchen table and ate the soup, which Andrew expertly nuked in the microwave to heat it up a bit more.

"Wow, you're quite the cook," she teased.

But she quickly got into the subject of Steve Martell, what he had said and done earlier in the day. She described the thoughts she got from him. Andrew listened intently, scrunching his brows. He was not pleased.

But he discovered he was more displeased with the idea of Martell hitting on Ashton than of the way he felt about him. Whoa…hold that thought, he didn't want her to read it. There goes that brick wall up again.

"We'll have to watch him," he said. "Let's see where he goes with this. There have been good reports about his work and he does well where he is. But more than that? Hell, his last company was a complete disaster. He just can't handle what he thinks he can."

After dinner they went into his den and reviewed the LA trip. He would make it three days and broke down the time schedule. She was glad; the calls she was getting from the west coast were overwhelming and she knew she had to have more time there. Of course, she knew it was all a farce. Andrew was only interested in the minds of upper level management but Ashton had to appear to be doing her job efficiently; otherwise she would be called to question and too many questions could lead to pressure from the board to fire her.

But as he leaned over her it happened…soon they were kissing passionately, his hands sliding all over her body and cupping her breasts, his crotch swelling. She was moaning and this time she could not stop it. It was inevitable. It played out just like in her dream and now here they were, in Andrew's big bed, making love.

In the morning he did not throw her out. He lay next to her, watching the sun's rays come through the window and dance in her auburn hair as she slept. When she awoke he had Hilda make breakfast and they ate it in bed.

"Spend the day with me," he told her. She refused, instead gathered up her clothes.

"I'll call Tony to take you home," he said, but then he changed his mind. "I'll drive you home."

She shook her head no, preferring to call a cab.

"I'll see you Monday, Andrew," was all she said as she exited his apartment as quickly as her feet could carry her.

On the cab ride home tears streamed down her face. She didn't know what to do. She didn't know what to say; truth be told she was in love in Andrew. And she knew he was in love with her.

226

How could this happen? And more importantly, what was she going to do now?

She could marry him. She was sure of that, and she'd never have to worry about money again. She could drop the pretense— okay, some of it anyway, she was sure Andrew would want her to continue working; her talent was just too valuable to him. She could buy her parents a mansion in Palm Beach; she could give Craig the money to buy the store. There was so much good she could do.

But there was the deal killer. She wanted to do good. She really wanted to help people. Andrew did not. Andrew wanted what he wanted when he wanted it and she already knew what happened to those who tried to block his path. Could she really live with a man like that? All those people, those employees she spoke with; she really wanted to help them. She really wanted to make their jobs easier. But she knew most of their requests would never be addressed. Sure, Andrew would let one "slide" here and there and give into an employee request, but he did it not to be fair but so she wouldn't lose her credibility. If she really was an "employee relations specialist" but nothing ever changed, how would it look? Pretty soon no one would want to talk with her and then Andrew couldn't get the information he so desperately wanted.

Thankfully, Denise was nowhere around when she got back to her apartment and she was also grateful that she was not accompanying her to her parents tomorrow. She begged off when Ashton told her they would be discussing the places they looked at when they were in Palm Beach; Denise felt that perhaps they would not be comfortable talking about prices or financing with her around, so she made other plans.

227

She jumped into the hot shower as soon as she got home, dropping her clothes in a heap by the bathroom door. She scrubbed until her skin was red; as if she were trying to scrub off the shame of it all. She was not ashamed because she fucked him; God knows how many times she did that with other men and often didn't remember their names the next day except for him; the lonely traveler she met at Ovals that night. She often wondered where he was and did he know? But how could he; nobody knew. And nobody would ever know.

No, she was trying to scrub off the shame of pretending to be something she was not. She was trying to scrub off the shame of prying into people's minds in the guise of helping them when the only one she was really helping was Andrew. Then she thought to herself that she had a tidy sum of money saved now; a little over fifty thousand dollars, but she would need more than that if she broke away from the Desmond Corporation. "If," she thought suddenly. "Wasn't it supposed to be when she broke away?"

He called her several times that day but she let his calls go to voicemail. She needed to think. But Andrew was like a smitten school boy now.

That night she had the dream again. But, just like what was actually unfolding in her waking life, the dream was moving forward as well.

She was in St Patrick's Cathedral, walking down the aisle in a white dress with a train that followed a full fourteen feet behind her, and up at the altar was Andrew; his gray eyes piercing her like a thousand needles; a sick and twisted smile plastered across his face. And in front of the altar was Steve Martell, stone cold dead, a knife sticking out of his chest with his blood pooling all around him.

But she could not turn to run. She seemed to be pulled by some invisible force moving her closer and closer to him. Out of the corner of her eye she saw Bob and her mother beaming with pride. As she glanced at the altar again she saw Denise was taking her place beside Allison as bridesmaids. Another glance towards Andrew and now there was Mark Peters as his best man, the dripping knife still in his hand…

She leapt from bed covered in sweat and made her way to the refrigerator for a bottle of water. She was so upset she let it slip through her hands hitting the tile floor. Thankfully it was plastic and didn't break but she left the water that spilled out of it all over the floor and tip-toed around it. She would clean it up tomorrow.

She sat down carefully on the bed and tried to imagine life as Mrs. Andrew Desmond. That's when the sobs came.

18

The sun streamed through her studio windows and hit Ashton right in the eyes waking her early. It was Sunday and it was time to go see her parents again and hear all about their trip. She got up and dragged herself into the shower and then made herself some coffee and ate a small bowl of cereal. She really kept very little food in the apartment since she and Denise were always going out and on the Sundays when she did see her parents Marian always loaded her up with food to take home.

She grabbed her Balenciaga purse and dumped the contents of it into the Macy's bag.

She grabbed her jeans and a tee shirt; fumbling in the closet for her sneakers; now buried behind what seemed to be mountains of designer shoes. Pulling her hair back into a ponytail she put little makeup on. She would do what she always did now when she returned to Shore Road—take a cab that let her off about a block from their apartment and pretend she took the subway. Since she lived over on York Avenue now, Ashton would have to take a bus to even get to the subway making the trip a good ninety minutes. A cab, especially since it was Sunday and there was very little traffic would be much faster. Of course the ride would be expensive; that would raise yet another red flag with Bob and Marian, so she would always pretend to take the subway.

As she rode in the cab towards Brooklyn she looked out the window and began to relax. Then her cell rang. It was Andrew. Reluctantly she answered it. He was asking if she was alright and why not come over for a late lunch. She told him she was on her way to see her family.

"I'll see you tomorrow at the office, Andrew." And then she hung up.

She knew she was skating on thin ice here; after all, sex or no sex, he was still her boss and no matter what he said or did, power and wealth were still what Andrew loved most in the world. He had turned his back on his parents; his mother had done nothing but love him and his father was a sick old man now but still, Andrew didn't seem to care. He might be enamored with her now but truly, over the many months she had done exactly what he wanted. She really had never challenged him. How would he be with that? How would he be with her saying, "No, I want to do things this way," or "No, I'm not going to do that?" How would it be now that they were intimate? She knew he loved her and she loved him, but how long would that last? And how were they going to work together? Would everybody else find out about them?

She signaled the cab to stop on Seventy-fifth; a block away from the old apartment and tucked a hundred dollar bill in to the cabbie's hand.

"Keep it," was all she said, closed the door and started walking.

Although she still had her key (wherever the heck she put it) she knocked on the door. Marian jumped up and rushed to open it. "Ashton, honey, how good to see you baby," she said as she hugged Ashton so tightly she thought she would burst. Bob kissed her cheek. Marian corralled her into the living room and offered her a glass of wine. She declined.

"So tell me all about your trip," Ashton said, "did you have a good time? Did you look at any properties? What do you think of them, anything stand out?"

Although Ashton genuinely wanted them to be happy she also wanted to deter them from asking her too many questions as usual, so she barraged them with questions of her own in rapid fire. It was something she had done many times and it seemed to work; she got them so confused they forgot their train of thought.

"Slow down Ashton, we'll tell you all about it."

And they went on to tell her; about Palm Beach and how they loved it and all about the condo and how perfect it was—especially the kitchen. They told her how much it was and that they'd put a deposit on it. Then they told her they'd have to close in one hundred and twenty days so they were going to put the store up for sale as soon as they could. They would arrange for an appraisal tomorrow. They wanted a cash buyer; they would not hold the note. At their age they wanted to be free of it all. Bob went onto say that he hoped Craig could buy it but doubted he could secure financing; but he would speak to whoever bought it about keeping him on. Craig had only recently disclosed that his son was special needs and might be going to a new school to both Bob and Marian, a fact that saddened them; they would have liked to be of some help to Craig, if only as a shoulder to cry on.

"But the question is, Ashton, how are you feeling about all of this? We haven't told the landlord anything so if you want to move back here now your rent would probably be a lot lower here than it is in your place, not that they'd ever seen it. It's only eight hundred a month… Are you paying more than that now? "

Since she had never taken her furniture with her, the landlord thought Ashton still lived with them, a fact they did nothing to discourage, in case she ever wanted to come back. Since she lived there originally, she still would be under rent control as her mother was now.

Whenever he asked about her; that he hadn't seen her lately, Bob and Marian just said that she'd taken a job in the city and you know how young people are; she stayed with her friends there sometimes. It was a lot more exciting than constantly being with two old folks like them. Bob and Marian knew they would lose their deposit if they left before their lease was up; but when Marian moved there years ago with her first husband David, the deposit was two month's rent—six hundred dollars. It was not an issue for them at this point.

Ashton appreciated their offer but wasn't interested in moving back to Brooklyn. She was thrilled they found what they wanted but then thought of Craig; what would become of him? She never met that new girl Amanda or that part time cashier—Ashton didn't even know her name. She hoped they could keep their jobs.

"How much do you think you can get for the store Bob?" she asked him. She really had no idea and didn't think about Bob owning the land underneath it as well. The store was free standing and not part of a shopping center strip mall.

"Probably about three million, Ashton. Of course we won't need all of it and we'd like to put some of it in a trust for you, but I do want to tell you that your mother and I are going to take full advantage of our retirement. We want to travel as well and live, well, a little high on the hog as they say." Bob was smiling ear-to-ear as he spoke.

"If someone was going to buy the store and they needed financing, I know, not from you but from a bank, how much of a down payment would they need?"

"I would imagine well over one hundred thousand, Ashton, why do you ask? Do you want it honey? If you do it's yours. Free and clear. We can live off our savings and social security. Of course, we'd have to look for a smaller place or maybe just stay here but if…"

Ashton looked at them and thought that she was well loved. This is what love is truly all about and not that maelstrom she was experiencing with Andrew. Would he do that for her? Would he be willing to live like a pauper to help someone he loved? She knew the answer. Whatever threatened his luxurious lifestyle would probably meet its end in a back alley with Mark Peters. Or maybe the altar of St. Patrick's. She winched at the thought

"No, I'm happy where I am. You sell the store and get as much as you can and then I want you to spend all of it doing whatever it is you want. I know I've been the albatross around your neck all these years and it's time this albatross set you free. You don't need to put money aside for me. I can take care of myself now."

What she really wanted to say was that there was a good chance of marrying her ultra- rich boss and helping him in his quest for world domination; now that they were on "friendlier terms." But she stayed silent. Tears streamed down Marian's face as she got up to hug her daughter once again. Then silently, she went into the antiquated kitchen to set the table for dinner.

During the meal all Marian could talk about was her new kitchen and then she sneaked it in: the place had two bedrooms, one reserved just for Ashton for when she came to visit. She left off the part about "with her husband" but Ashton read her easily. She could just see it now…she and Andrew sleeping in a spare bedroom with a bathroom down the hall and no maid to bring him his breakfast in bed.

To her parents, the new place was beautiful; the fulfillment of their heart's desires. To Andrew it would probably be a piece of shit. Ashton didn't want to be like him, abandoning his parents. Of course, he didn't think she knew about that but it occasionally flashed through his mind and she read it. The other pieces of the puzzle were filled in by Doris; she asked her about it one day when Andrew was at an appointment with his tailor. Doris asked her how she knew. Of course she couldn't tell her she read his thoughts but simply said he made some snide remark about his parents being "dead" to him. That would be something Andrew would say; definitely.

Doris told her all about Harold who founded the company, now senile and with a bad heart to boot. She spoke fondly about Andrew's mother, Susan; she was a simple woman who hated the lifestyle that was thrust upon her. As Doris spoke, Ashton knew that she kept in touch with Susan here and there, but never told Andrew; he'd have fired her on the spot.

For some reason, Ashton felt she and Susan were kindred spirits. Maybe they would meet one day.

19

Susan sped up the long driveway and screeched the big car to a halt under the porte-cochère. She ran towards the great lawn and then down to the shore of the Sound. This was no easy feat for a woman in her late sixties. Robert was walking Harold back to the great house now; wrapped around him was a thick terrycloth robe to help shield him from the chill. But Harold seemed oblivious to the fact that he had just attempted to swim halfway to Connecticut. When he saw Susan he excitedly told her he was looking for Flipper and wanted to swim with him like Bud did—he watched old reruns of the show; one of the main characters was a boy named Bud—

Susan saw poor Robert was soaked through and through; he had jumped in after Harold and pulled him to safety.

He shivered as he guided Harold towards the house. Susan was so touched by this man's devotion; when Harold was chairman he was downright mean and nasty to Robert, often condescending; now he wanted him as a playmate.

After Harold was settled into bed and the doctor called to check him out, Susan knocked on Robert's door. When he opened it she shoved something in his hand while thanking him profusely for all he did for Harold. When she left he opened his hand, staring at the crinkled object inside it. It was a check for fifty thousand dollars.

Harold was sleeping soundly as the doctor made his way down the massive marble staircase; Robert was sitting at the kitchen table now as Susan made him some hot tea. He objected at first; he should do it or at least one of the maids, but not the mistress of the house. She dismissed him with a wave of her hand and put the steaming cup in front of him.

"If you need anything else call me," she said, as she walked into the hallway to talk with the doctor. As he drank his tea, Robert felt bad for Susan; she had been so unhappy all these years married to that obnoxious, cheating son-of-a-bitch husband and dealing with that monstrous son of hers.

She deserved better than that. She deserved some peace, some happiness of her own. Robert knew about the house in Massapequa; although Susan didn't know he knew, and he was glad. He knew she wanted to leave the great house; he knew it from the moment he worked his first day as the major domo. She never fit in; at parties she was more content to stay in the kitchen chatting with the staff and trying to help them serve the food, but she was pulled away by Harold who often stormed into the kitchen and insisted she return to "her guests." But they were not her guests; they were his; snooty women showing off their expensive jewelry or their toned calf muscles made possible by private trainers in their personal gyms; men trying to one-up Harold with an expensive watch or a custom made suit made by some up and coming designer.

But Harold reveled in it; he always had the most expensive everything. And from the staircase Andrew watched; his piercing gray eyes soaking it all in. Though still only a child he thought to himself that he would have more than all of them; that he would be on top one day; the one that everyone envied...and feared.

Robert could hear some of the conversation between Susan and the doctor; the doctor saying he thought it was well past the time for Harold to be in a nursing facility; there had been many nurses at the house but none of them stayed too long because Harold only wanted Robert to take care of him. Susan tried all kinds of nurses, younger and older, men and women both. But Harold would end up screaming at them at the top of his lungs and they'd be gone in a New York minute.

There was one nurse who looked promising, a pleasant woman in her early forties with a great deal of patience and highly skilled; but she was scared away the first time Harold got hold of a gun from the gun case while playing Cowboys and Indians. Even though both Susan and Robert assured her the gun wasn't loaded the woman was scared out of her wits and was quickly gone.

Now the only nurses were the visiting ones; they'd check up on Harold three times a week but aside from that there was only Robert. But then, Harold was his only concern; there was little staff to manage now. But Susan kept the house completely up to speed; hiring people as she needed them, nothing was ever neglected. The grounds still looked like they could be on the cover of a magazine and both the indoor and outdoor pools were kept sparkling. The tennis courts looked like a major tournament could be played on them at a moment's notice, and inside something was always being remodeled.

When the time came, Susan wanted the house to fetch top dollar because that was just more to be given away to charity and her staff, especially Robert, who did not know that he would eventually become a millionaire himself, courtesy of Susan's generosity.

The doctor would come back tomorrow but it would be late; he had a full schedule of patients at his office in town.

Susan climbed back up the heavy staircase (she never used the elevator) to check on Harold who was now sound asleep; one of the maids leaving the room with his wet clothes (and the terry cloth robe) to launder them. She nodded silently at Susan as she passed her in the hallway.

As she entered the room she saw that Harold was sound asleep; knocked out by the sedative the doctor had given him. He almost looked like a lost little boy to Susan instead of the frail elderly man he had become. She wondered if he would see his son again before he passed away; then she wondered the same thing for herself.

After she got a cup of tea herself she sat down in the kitchen and called Peggy. Susan had planned to stop by after the day's events but had to cut that short because of Harold's impromptu swim. She longed for the day when she could hand the keys to the huge estate over to its new owners and leave with just a few suitcases. The new owners could have the furniture; most of it was massive and garish and wouldn't fit in the simple Cape Cod. Besides, the little house was already completely furnished; she and Peggy had gone furniture shopping just after Susan bought it. The furniture Peggy had in her rented place was old and although she was willing to keep her bedroom set so Susan wouldn't have to buy her another, they donated it all to the Salvation Army and Peggy was delighted to pick out something new.

"I'll try to stop by tomorrow," Susan said. "In the meantime water my geraniums and kiss Sheena for me." She then made herself a sandwich and climbed back up the stairs to her bedroom. Halfway through her movie on the Lifetime Channel she fell asleep, dreaming of the little Cape Cod and her geraniums.

ASHTON AGAIN SUCCESSFULLY TALKED her way out of being driven home by her mother and Bob. She didn't know how long she could stave them off, but she didn't want them to see her apartment, something they'd been trying to do. But Ashton kept putting them off.

She was making up so many stories that she could hardly keep track of them now. She negotiated the key in the lock, her other hand holding precariously onto the Pyrex dish full of rigatoni and meatballs that her mother sent home with her. As soon as she got in her cell rang again; she froze in her tracks for a moment and then realized it was Denise.

"How was dinner," she asked. "Did your mom and Bob find a place?" She knew Denise was probably hungry and that she would just love a plate of this rigatoni.

"I'm heating up the food for you now," she said, giggling, and in a flash there was a knock at her door. Denise was really hungry.

As Denise ate, Ashton told her the story of the condo. Denise was glad; they were such kind people and worked so hard. It was time that they caught a break.

"I feel bad for Craig, though. He would really love to own the store. I think he's worried he won't have a job at all when all this is over," Ashton said. But she knew Bob would try his best to convince the new owners to keep him on and that new girl, Amanda, as well. She heard they both worked well together and that Amanda helped Craig out with some of his managerial duties. Ashton saddened at the thought of that; she was never really that much of an asset at the store.

"So what did you do today that you couldn't come with me to Brooklyn," Ashton asked. Of course she already knew that Denise felt they might be discussing finances and that was none of her business. She also knew the only thing she did today was to clean her apartment.

"I cleaned my apartment, it needed it. I really didn't have plans, but I thought you might be talking about money or other personal stuff since they were looking for a new place to call home. That's none of my business."

Then she said, "How's Andrew? Is he going to live? What was wrong with him exactly? He never misses work."

Andrew… She had almost forgotten about him. Looking at her watch she calculated there was exactly twelve hours until she had to see him at the office tomorrow. And then she thought that it was a good thing that Denise couldn't read *her* mind.

"Oh, some sinus stuff, I think. He had boxes of tissues everywhere and I could have sworn I smelled Vicks Vapo~Rub." Yeah, that sounded good.

"Do they still make that stuff?" Denise asked, helping herself to another meatball. "My mother used to put that all over me if I even sneezed once when I was a kid."

"I guess they must because you could sure smell it, and I didn't even get that close to him, in case whatever he had was catching."

She thought that it was good that Denise didn't know exactly how close they had gotten.

Denise finished off the plate of rigatoni and thanking her, went back to her own place to iron some clothes.

"Share a cab tomorrow?" she asked, as she was walking out the door.

"Sure."

Closing the door behind Denise, she picked up the plate and put it in the dishwasher. She busied herself getting her clothes ready for the morning. The jeans and tee shirt went into the laundry and the contents of her Macy's pocketbook were re-dumped into one of her Chanel handbags.

She decided on a long soak in the tub instead of a shower. It relaxed her and soon she was ready for sleep. It wasn't long until sleep claimed her and then, the dream flashed in front of her like a movie, but this time she couldn't pin down the time frame. Was it before or after that horrible scene in St. Patrick's? She couldn't tell.

She and Andrew were having dinner at his parent's house seated at a massive dining room table and a heated argument erupted between Andrew and his father. She knew it was his father

245

because there were pictures of him in various places around the Desmond building, but she had never seen pictures of his parents anywhere in Andrew's office.

She couldn't make out the words; it was like one of those silent movies; with Harold rising up from his chair to bang his fists hard on the table and then clutching at his chest; Andrew standing in turn and, grabbing Ashton's arm, yanking her out of house and into a waiting limo. Glancing back she could see what she thought to be his mother, Susan, with tears in her eyes. She was like a magnet for Ashton. She looked to be as kind as her own mother, Marian; the two women would like each other if they ever had the chance to meet.

She awoke suddenly and could have sworn her arm hurt where Andrew had yanked it in her dream. It took almost an hour before she fell back into a deep, dreamless sleep.

When the sunlight began filtering through her windows, Ashton awoke with a sense of dread. Her emotions were running wild; if only Andrew was more like a "normal" person she could make a life with him. She really did love him. But he was not the type of man to go to Sunday dinner at her mom's and play gin rummy with Bob. He would not be the type to drive down to Palm Beach to visit her parents in their new place and go to dinner at one of those All You Can Eat buffets.

But actually Andrew did go to Palm Beach at least once a year, in February, for the Red Cross Ball. He didn't go because he was charitable, but he always begrudging wrote a check just to look good (after all, it WAS tax deductible) But the real reason he was there was because the wealthiest two percent of the country congregated there in the winter months and he wanted three things—one, to show off what he had like a peacock strutting with its feathers fanned out, two, to make sure there was no one who had more than he did, and three, to make sure there was no one waiting in the wings to try to take anything away from him.

Ashton didn't know that yet because they met right after the last ball, and it wasn't anything that ever crossed Andrew's mind. Andrew actually had a house in Palm Beach, oceanfront, of course, that was only about a mile away from where Bob and Marian would live.

The big house stayed empty most of the year except for the week when Andrew was there, but it had a full staff to maintain it year round. Most of the Palm Beach staff couldn't stand Andrew's arrogance or the fact that he sometimes stayed longer than a week if he found lots of young debutantes to bring home to screw. The staff prayed that each year's pickings would be lean, so he would do his fake charity thing and then head his private jet back to New York.

Lost in her thoughts, Ashton glanced at the clock and realized it was getting late. She was just grabbing her briefcase when Denise rang her cell to ask her where she was; she was already downstairs ready to grab a cab for them.

She apologized, slammed the door behind her, fumbled with her keys to lock it and then joined Denise outside. Luckily and as usual, it took all of about thirty seconds to grab a cab; one of those old checkered ones that had plenty of room. Ashton whipped out her compact and started putting the finishing touches on her makeup.

"What's wrong with you?" Denise asked. "You're always completely put together when I see you in the morning."

Ashton gave her a half nod, too busy concentrating on not stabbing herself in the eye as she put on her mascara. Thankfully, she was all finished just as the cab pulled up in front of the office. Ashton started fumbling now for her wallet but Denise tossed a twenty at the driver and told him to keep it. Turning to Ashton she told her to just get it the next time.

In very short order the two women were exiting the private elevator. Doris waved and smiled at them; she was already running around making copies of the agenda for the board meeting that was supposed to have taken place on Friday. She had to get in extra early; even though those copies were made and ready for the Friday meeting, Andrew called her over the weekend to add some extra items, so they had to be redone. Ashton tiptoed into her office and then glanced over at Andrew's office, pleased he wasn't in yet.

Maybe he would be "sick" again, she thought, smiling at the thought of working the day without seeing him. Somehow she foolishly thought that a little time would help her sort out her feelings. But that "time" lasted for only about another five minutes; the elevator doors opened and there he was, staring at her.

"I need to see you in my office right away," was all he said as he turned on his heels, Doris following behind him with his expensive Kenyan coffee, balancing it in one hand and hold onto a thick sheaf of papers with the other.

She sensed a weird kind of tension in the room. Was he going to fire Ashton? She put the cup down gingerly and placed the stack of paper neatly to his right and then got the hell out of there. She almost slammed into Ashton who was making her way into his office as she was trying to get out. Safely away, Doris sank into her chair and sighed so loudly they could have heard it in the lobby.

Ashton entered the room and stood as still as a statue, not wanting to move or speak and she certainly didn't want to read his thoughts. But when he spoke it was as if Friday never happened.

He wanted to review the changes to the rescheduled board meeting with her. He was all business; for a moment she thought that she would end up like all the rest; a "fuck and dump." But then, as his thoughts came flooding towards her, she knew that was not the case.

She knew from here on in he would not carry on like a love sick puppy in the office; he wanted no one to know…at least at this point. But she could read him clearly; he loved her and he was definitely going to pursue a relationship with her. This would be a first for him. It actually was a first for her too because, outside of her family and close friends, Ashton had loved no one.

As she looked at him she almost melted now. He wore the suit she said looked the best on him; he had asked her opinion when she came by with some paperwork and he was having it made for some out of town meeting; what city it was she could not recall. But she did remember the day; Doris popped her head in her office to let her know that Andrew called and wanted her to come by after work with some reports, when she got there the tailor was putting the finishing touches on two new custom made suits.

He asked her which looked best on him; he tried on both for her and while she said they were both nice, which pleased the tailor, she preferred one over the other. "In fact," she told him, "I like this one the best out of all of them." He remembered.

The rest of the day unfolded the way a hundred others had; the board meeting, the interrogation afterwards (always focusing mostly on Steve Martell) lunch with Denise (she paid since Denise took care of the cab fare that morning) some meetings of her own in the afternoon and then, at four thirty a call to Andrew's office.

"Have dinner with me at my place," he said, quietly.

Ashton stood, silent for a moment as if pondering her fate, then smiled and said yes. She had to see where this would go. She had to try. She told Denise she had to stop by Andrew's with some work—well it *was* kind of true, wasn't it?

But truth be told, she often had to work with Andrew after hours. It was so common, in fact, that it aroused no suspicion at all. With anyone. All Denise said was, "Cab in the morning?" And she nodded. It was only Monday and she knew she would not spend the night with him, as she'd done on Friday. It would be too obvious if she were not at her own apartment in the morning to ride in with Denise.

Andrew must have called his staff during the day because they had her favorite meal, lasagna. And then after the meal they barely made it to Andrew's big bed. Lying in his arms afterwards felt natural to her now; she was surprised she got comfortable with him so quickly. They made small talk; about the office, about Doris and then Denise. She told him she knew about him and Denise.

"I misjudged her, and I regret that. She really has turned out to be one of the best employees this company has ever had."

"She's not afraid of you, you know," Ashton said.

"I know and she was first one to stand up to me. But let me ask you this, how good a friend is she?"

She sat up and looked at him. He met her gaze and then said, "I think you know what I mean."

What he meant was, how would Denise be with knowing about the two of them? Andrew knew that Denise and Ashton went

250

almost everywhere together and on top of that they lived in the same building. He knew that although Ashton had to come up to his apartment after work on many occasions, it was never every night. He knew he couldn't go to Ashton's place—not that he ever would, the idea of even being in a studio apartment for even a short period of time was alien to him—because Denise might see him and he'd never come there before. Ashton always came to him and that was how it should be, after all, he was the boss.

Going out with her at night locally in town would be a problem as well. Although she appeared with Andrew countless times, that was always some kind of company business, though some would whisper that it wasn't. Being seen with her in fancy restaurants or in night clubs dancing meant the *Post*, that trashy New York tabloid, would have it on their front page the next morning. Neither one of them was comfortable with that kind of press this early in their relationship; Andrew would prefer if they never got any press at all. But there would be no hiding from Denise when Ashton wasn't available for after work cocktails or worse, when she would be absent from their morning cab ride.

They could hide their relationship from almost everyone, but they couldn't keep it from Denise. And Andrew worried that Denise might be jealous; that she might still be attracted to him. He pondered if he should get rid of her.

"No!" Ashton stood up now, Andrew taking in every inch of her naked body. "God, she was beautiful," he thought.

"What?" He tried to play stupid but he knew she read him.

"You're not getting rid of Denise!"

"Ashton, I was thinking about letting her go not killing her. I'll give her a good reference, in fact, I'm sure I can get her placed in another company for even more money than she's making now."

"No!"

"Okay, but it's going to be up to you to tell Denise, and I was thinking that tomorrow you could spend the night...of course we'd ride into work separately. I'd call you a cab—I couldn't have my driver pulling up early in the morning with you in the car) and I'd follow a little after you in my limo. At least for now. I'm sure you understand."

She slid back into bed and nestled back into his shoulder.

"I'd love to spend tomorrow night with you, but I need a little time to talk to Denise. It's Monday night, let's say I'll stay over on Friday. I think I need to go back to my own place until I can really sit down with her."

Ashton needed Denise to be discreet, but she also needed her to understand that Andrew was a changed man. They loved each other. They wanted to be together. She really wanted Denise to be onboard with all of this, however the relationship between she and Andrew unfolded.

"Then you'll spend the weekend with me," he said. And then they were making love but all the while Ashton was thinking to herself, "The whole weekend? What am I going to do about Sunday dinner?!"

Andrew's driver dropped her off at midnight. Ashton was pleased that Denise's apartment windows faced the East River and not York Avenue where she might have seen her coming back from Andrew's later than she had ever done before.

20

Sarah dressed quickly in an effort to get down to Jessica's preschool as fast as possible. The administrator had called her, letting her know that her little princess was scaring the crap out of the other kids in her class as well as her teacher, after Jessica told several children they still wet their beds at night and then informed the teacher that the school would eventually find out that she had submitted a phony resume; that she was not really a teacher at all. Of course the teacher left that little tidbit out when she called the administrator to let her know her class was in chaos, courtesy of

Jessica, but when they left the administrator's office Jessica disclosed that little bit of information to Sarah.

Sarah sped into the parking lot and slammed on her brakes; grateful it was mid-morning and none of the kids were outside playing. As she entered the administrator's office she saw Jessica with her head down looking quite solemn. She knew she should have kept her mouth shut, but it was as if the words had a life of their own and were forcing their way out of her mouth. But there was no going back now; she could not undo what was already done. Jessica was expelled, and this really upset her as she genuinely liked the other kids in her class. But it upset Sarah more.

When Bill got home from work they ate dinner in near silence and after the child went to bed, they began their discussion of what to do with her.

"I can take care of her, Bill, that's no problem, she's my daughter and I love her but she needs to be with other kids her own age at least some of the time."

"Alright then, at least for now let her stay home. What do you think about her seeing a counselor? Do you think that would help?"

Sarah thought that it might and agreed to do some research on who would be best to see her. In the meantime, the only other interaction Jessica would have would be at Sarah's charity events where at least she could see Susan; who she sometimes even called "grandma."

IT WAS ABOUT TWO WEEKS LATER when Sarah was sitting at the kitchen table enjoying an early cup of coffee; she loved this time of day; so peaceful, so quiet. Bill and Jessica were still asleep and she just sat in silence, until she heard Bill shuffling around; he would be down for breakfast soon. She picked up the local newspaper to browse through it while she waited for Bill to join her. As she read the headline, her eyes became as big as saucers, and she frowned. Bill was just sitting down when he glanced over at her and asked, "Honey, what's wrong?"

Sarah slid the paper across the table towards Bill; grabbing it, his mouth hung open in disbelief as he read its headline...

Local Pre-School Teacher Dismissed For Falsifying Work History

The story went on to say that she had no experience working with children; she had, in fact, been a stripper in her hometown of Buffalo. Wanting to get out, her boyfriend who owned the strip club where she worked, as well as several others, had the documents forged so she could get work elsewhere.

She wanted to get into some kind of teaching and she loved kids. But since her departure, many of the "regulars" at the club began to go elsewhere and this hurt the boyfriend's business considerably; besides, he missed her. So he "tipped" off the school several times; at that point the school had no choice but to investigate, finding it to be true. She was promptly fired. It was all as Jessica had said it would be.

Bill and Sarah stared at each other from opposite ends of the table in disbelief. They knew she had the ability to read others' thoughts; they could not deny that anymore. But now she could see the future as well.

Bob spent the morning on the phone with several real estate appraisal firms; he wanted to make an appointment to get the store

255

assessed and then get it on the market. Craig was glad they had found a place but now he was worried…the time had come. He wondered what the property would appraise out at, but then again it didn't matter, he could never afford to buy it. But he would do his best at his job as always, no matter what.

When he got home that night he told Evelyn who was visibly concerned. They had an appointment at the end of the week to check out that new school for Bradley. Even at Craig's present salary they would be stretching themselves thin if Bradley attended this new school; there would be no way they could afford it if Craig had to look for another job. Bob Martin had been generous with Craig, paying him more than he would have made elsewhere in the same position; maybe he did it because he had to put up with Ashton.

Evelyn sank in her chair, sighing heavily, as Bradley ran up to her to sit in her lap. This school could be his chance to say his first words. This school could be his chance to have a decent life. But Bradley might not get a chance to even attend this new school now.

Two days later, the appraisal came back on the store and it would be listed for 3.7 million; turnkey; it included the land it sat on. Craig knew it wouldn't be on the market very long; the store was lucrative and had an established client base. For the right person (who would even open it on Sunday and extend the hours out) it could be extremely so…but that person would not be him.

Hopefully, whoever it was, Craig prayed they would need someone to manage it and that they wouldn't cut his salary or the benefits he needed so much. Maybe Bradley could still go to that school if Evelyn got a part-time job; his sister volunteered to watch both children for a few hours each day; she had her own two little girls she had to be home for anyway.

But the action on the store was not what he'd thought it would be. There were several potential buyers, one of them looked promising, but his finances were in disarray and it was discovered that he had not even been pre-approved for financing. Bob did not want to wait around waiting for this one person to get his act together; he wanted either an all cash buyer or one solidly pre-approved by a bank. And it was doubtful that this guy would even get the financing he needed; although he did have a sizeable down payment.

In a way, Craig was relieved; both he and Evelyn visited that new school for Bradley, and they were impressed with it; this could be exactly what the child needed. They were approved for a financial subsidy, and figured they would just be able to skate by…as long as Craig stayed employed at the store as the manager and did not get either his salary or benefits cut. Otherwise, even with Evelyn working part time it just would not be enough.

Susan's nap was interrupted by the ringing of her cell phone, and for just one brief moment she thought it might be Andrew. But as she came out of her nap induced fog and grabbed her phone she realized it wasn't him. It was Sarah and she sounded upset.

"Can you meet me at the diner in town?" she asked.

The diner she was referring to wasn't very far from the great house so Susan invited her over.

"You know you're always welcome here," Susan told her. Sarah was a little uncomfortable going back there; how would Harold feel about her; his son's ex-wife? That's if he even recognized her.

She drove up the long winding private road and parked under the porte-cochère. Robert greeted her and only half- smiled; he remembered this obnoxious bitch who was married to Andrew for, what was it, about five minutes?

But he was pleasantly surprised when she shook his hand and told him it was nice to see him again. She had changed so much; no longer the nasty, whiney, rich bitch she had been when he last saw her at a cocktail party at the estate with Andrew; when she had screamed at him because one of the servants got her drink order wrong.

Susan was waiting for her in the living room, sipping on her tea, and started to pour a cup for Sarah from the heavy silver kettle.

"What's wrong, you're white as a ghost?"

Sarah looked around for a moment; the house looked as majestic as it always had, it truly was beautiful. But she also remembered how many times she'd been here with Andrew; when he was angry or upset he'd grab her arm and make a hasty exit…she rubbed her arm in the spot when he had wrenched it so many times before.

Sitting down, Sarah told Susan the whole mess about Jessica; including what she had said about the teacher.

"I don't remember reading anything about that," Susan told her, but then Sarah said it was only in their local paper.

"I don't know what to do with her. Bill and I talked about taking her to a therapist, but can anyone really help us with this? If she could only learn not to say anything to the other kids, if there was only a way of "filtering" what she says so it doesn't backfire on her. I want her to have a happy life, not one where everybody thinks she's strange."

Susan was just going to reply when Harold came into the room. He walked up to Sarah and asked her if Miss Cathy saw her in her "magic mirror." He clearly did not recognize her. Susan called for Robert to come and get him out of the room so she could talk. When he saw Robert he said "My man! Miss Cathy says she always sees you in her mirror, you're a good boy like me."

Robert ushered him out of the room apologizing to Sarah for the interruption.

Sarah was shocked to see what had become of Harold; although Susan told her, it was much more real in person. He was so different from her own father, Jonathan; even though they were about the same age Jonathan was extremely active; golfing every morning, swimming in the pool and riding one of his prized quarter horses on the private beach at sunset. He was welcome at board meetings at his old company, but he very rarely went; why should he spend more time there as a retiree than he did as its CEO?

"I'm sorry Susan, that's got to be rough on you," Sarah said, referring to Harold's condition.

"Oh, you get used to it," Susan replied. "In a way it's been a blessing, I don't know if I could have stayed with him the way he used to be. And I probably wouldn't have my house in Massapequa, and God knows if we would have even become friends. He would have tried to keep me under his thumb and probably want me to be best friends with Marge Solis."

Sarah winced. She had met Marge Solis at one of Harold's cocktail parties. At the time, both Marge and Sarah were arguing about who had the more expensive watch. How horrible that was!

259

Susan told her that, at least the last she heard about her, she was still alive and kicking and obnoxious as ever. Since Harold became more and more infirmed, that part of their lives completely drifted away. No more Marge Solis, no more talk of four thousand dollar shoes…and Susan was glad for that.

Sarah glanced down at the watch on her wrist; it cost considerably less than the ones she used to wear and she was glad for that too, and the fact that Susan had her as a best friend — almost a daughter really — and not Marge Solis. Marge would never approve of the little Cape Cod that Susan was planning to someday call "home"

Susan told Sarah that she might think about checking out some of the psychics in the area about Jessica, but when she saw the look on Sarah's face, she decided not to push it. Bill was far too conservative for anything like that, so he probably would have said no. Instead, she encouraged Sarah to interview some counselors first to see how she felt about them.

"I don't know what's going on here," Susan told her, "but I support you a hundred percent in whatever you choose to do. I'll be there for all of you if you need me."

Sarah was glad she made the trip. After their conversation they walked around the great house and its grounds. Susan showed Sarah the little patch of geraniums in the garden right next to the outrageously expensive exotic blooms. The gardener thought she was nuts to plant them next to his masterpieces but he said nothing. And Susan thought the day could not come soon enough that she wouldn't have to look at his "masterpieces" any longer and could just look out at her geraniums.

When Sarah left the great house, she shook Robert's hand again and thanked him for being there for Susan. Robert escorted her to her car, smiling brightly and said, "Come back to visit anytime." He meant it. What a fine young woman she had become, unlike her son-of-a-bitch ex-husband who just seemed to be getting meaner with the years.

Allison sat munching on an English muffin in the hospital cafeteria and her thoughts wandered… right over to Ashton. She hadn't seen her in so long; the last time was quite a few months ago; they met for lunch. Although Allison was off for the day she had a meeting at the hospital so she had to come into the city anyway. Getting done about noon she called Ashton and they met midway between her office and Bellevue.

Allison was shocked at the way she looked; like she stepped right out of a magazine. She remembered what they wore in high school; their plaid uniform skirts down to their knees with flat shoes unlike the "hottie girls" who wore high heels and skirts hiked up to their asses (she wondered whatever became of Mallory) and she remembered Ashton's store uniform…jeans, tee shirt and hair pulled back to reveal a face that never had a stitch of makeup on it.

Now she stood before Allison in clothes that must have cost thousands of dollars, makeup professionally done and God only knows what she spent on her hair; when she remarked on how pretty it was Ashton told her she got it done at Ted Gibson's salon; when Allison googled it she found out that he charged up to twelve hundred dollars just for a haircut!

All through lunch Allison stared, wide-eyed at her. Of course, Ashton knew what she was thinking, but Allison had no problem opening her mouth; after all, she knew all there was to know about her, save for that year she went away.

"What the fuck? I mean, you look great but isn't this getting a little out of hand? What do you wear when you go see your mother on Sunday? Do you dress like this?"

She noticed the Chanel bag Ashton placed on the table beside her.

"I suppose that's not a knock-off."

"I don't think Bergdorf's sells knock-offs, at least, for what I paid for it I sure hope it's not one."

"Good Lord, Ashton, what do your parents say about all this, the way you dress and all. You can't dress like this on what you earn for what they think you do for a living."

"I don't. I wear jeans and a tee shirt, just like I did when I worked at the store. And I try not to talk too much about work. I find that if I ask them a lot of questions about the store and moving to Florida, I can throw them off the track a little. I don't like doing that but I don't want to upset them. God knows what they would say if they knew what was really going on."

"And they've never been to your apartment?" Allison asked her. Come to think of it, neither had she.

"No, and I don't know how much longer I can put them off, but I really don't want them to see it. You know they'll ask me where I got all this money from."

Allison quietly chewed on her salad, taking it all in. Ashton *had* changed. Not only the fancy clothes but the way she was becoming; more put together, more confident…more, well, it seemed she was becoming more intelligent.

"Thank you," Ashton replied, having read her mind. "And no, I'm not screwing my boss." Allison blushed and then giggled.

Although they had a pleasant enough lunch, Allison hadn't heard from Ashton now in months. She was worried about her. Even Kevin remarked the other night that his wife hardly ever mentioned her best friend anymore. He actually had a friend he wanted Ashton to meet but got the feeling that she just wouldn't be interested in an average Joe living in a modest apartment in Queens. Mentioning it to Allison she confirmed what he was thinking...that Ashton had bigger fish to fry now.

But no matter what the size of the fish, Allison could wait no longer. She called Ashton, wanting to meet her, to spend time with her best friend.

As Ashton rushed up the avenue to get back to the office from lunch her cell rang. She already knew who it was... Allison. She hadn't seen her in so many months now; hadn't even called her. Now what would she say to her? Last time they were together she was telling Allison the truth about not screwing her boss; now she didn't know what to say.

They had grown apart since she took this job. And she had grown apart from her mother and Bob too; the three people in the world (save for her Aunt Madeleine who passed away three years ago) who always knew all about her...all of it, and she was drifting away from them. They were there to protect her and they loved her just as she was. They loved her when she was drunk, they loved her despite the fact that she hadn't done all that much with her life; they loved her enough no to ask her about that year she spent away from them. But Andrew, would he love that Ashton? Or only the perfectly coiffed one that stood before him each day telling him everything he wanted to know.

It didn't matter now anyway. Ignoring the call, she let it go to voice mail. Her mind was on Denise. She only had a few days to talk to her about her relationship with Andrew. She hoped Denise would be okay with it. She hoped they could still be friends. She just hoped her whole world wouldn't come crashing down around her.

WHEN SHE GOT BACK TO THE OFFICE she had to speak to Andrew about Steve Martell. He was planning on stepping up his plan to take over the Desmond Corporation. She knew he had spoken to a few board members about Andrew's wanton behavior with women—Martell just wished it were him screwing a different broad every night—but the board members were quick to point out that there had been virtually no press about Andrew being with any women for months now.

Having been shot down with that one Martell tried another one; another "barb" thrown Andrew's way…that his behavior was unacceptable at certain company events, especially company takeovers. Martell had never known Harold Desmond, but heard from the older board members that he was more low keyed.

Though Andrew stopped flashing his perfect white smile at crowds of people losing their jobs now that Ashton was at his side, he still was obnoxious and condescending. And he was still receiving bad press over it; in fact, there had been a big article about his behavior just last week at the closing of a factory near Nashville. Ashton begged him not to go; there had been talk of threats against the chairman, but Andrew insisted. In his twisted mind he thought

264

people would want to see him; to hear his insincere words telling them to take advantage of unemployment benefits.

These people did not want unemployment benefits; they wanted their jobs, their pensions and their benefits. Truthfully, it would have been better if Andrew stayed away from these things; he did not have his father's skill in placating people and in somehow putting the company in a good light through all of it.

The meeting was ended abruptly when Ashton whispered in Andrew's ear that the man standing in the third row with the navy pea coat on had a gun in his pocket and it was loaded; the "event" was abruptly halted as Andrew and Ashton hastily left the stage and hurriedly slid into the back of a waiting limo which sped off quickly for the airport. It was covered up with company PR saying Andrew had suddenly taken ill; but people found it odd, after all, only he and Ashton ever knew about the man with the gun.

But Andrew already knew some of it. While Ashton was at lunch, one of the older board members came up to see him.

Frank Delgado had been with the company almost from its inception. His was a real "rags to riches" story; starting in the mailroom and working his way up to the board of directors. He was in charge of international operations, a devoted, intelligent man who spoke several languages fluently, making him a real asset to the company.

Delgado was one of the board members approached by Martell. He was disturbed by it; what Martell was saying made no sense; sure, Andrew made a poor showing at some of these functions, but despite that, things were going quite well for the company. And all this other crap, the news about Andrew's sex life had seemingly evaporated. So why was Martell making his move now?

Delgado was a good judge of people and knew Martell was trouble. Just the way he was talking made him uneasy; it reminded him of one child telling another that he was going to put glue on the teacher's chair so when she sat down she'd stick to it. He smiled when he remembered that happening in his elementary school in Havana. But Andrew needed to know; he felt a sense of loyalty to the son of the man who gave him his start; took a poor young man newly arrived in this country and gave him a job; a real job and a new beginning.

He remembered the day he met Harold Desmond, working as a busboy in an uptown restaurant where Harold was having lunch with some of his associates. It was just before Christmas, and Harold was talking about all the things his son Andrew wanted; and he would get them all. Delgado thought of his own wife and son; living in a cold water flat near the bowery, there would be little to celebrate. That was until Harold Desmond almost cut his finger on a broken glass; Delgado was quick to notice and get it away from him. As he was leaving, Harold looked back at the young man hard at work cleaning the tables and approached him.

From that chance meeting so many years ago Frank Delgado now lived on Park Avenue with his wife Sophia, who had stopped taking in laundry years ago. Their son Miguel, who didn't get anything that Christmas, was now a resident in ophthalmology at Columbia Presbyterian Hospital.

Frank nodded as he passed Doris; she smiled brightly at him. Everyone liked Frank; he just had a way of making you feel comfortable while still getting the job done. He stopped and asked her how her son was doing; this pleased her, Andrew never asked her once in all these years. She wished she could have been Frank's assistant; but he'd had the same one for years. In Frank's office no one ever left until they retired or died. No one ever complained either; Doris had not seen one employee from Frank's office amongst the heavy traffic in and out of Ashton's office. No, this guy was a real gem.

He knocked on Andrew's open glass door and asked, "Mind if I come in for a moment?"

Andrew put aside his paperwork and motioned for Frank to enter. Frank closed the heavy doors behind him; he knew that would make the office soundproof.

"I need to talk to you about Steve Martell," he said, solemnly, and then went on to describe in detail the "meeting" that had transpired between Martell and a few others on the board. "Meeting" meant very loosely; Martell had corralled the board members and almost held them captive.

"I researched his background, Andrew, and he's certainly not CEO material. And truthfully, what he was saying was not news to us."

Andrew knew he was talking about his former sexual escapades and the arrogant way he often behaved in public. He admired Frank; he worked hard to get where he was today. Reports concerning him and his division were always sterling; profits were high and there was virtually zero turnover.

Yes, this man came from Cuba with his wife and child and just the clothes on their backs. But he learned not only to speak English but also Mandarin Chinese and French in addition to his native Spanish. He even managed a little Italian, and he was working on that. Andrew trusted Frank. He stood, thanking him and then escorted him to the door.

"I'll keep an eye out and an ear to the ground. Thanks, Frank, and my regards to Sophia."

As Frank left the office Doris was amazed; Andrew had remembered Frank's wife's name. He hardly remembered anyone's name.

Just as Frank was getting on the private elevator Ashton was getting off. Ashton liked Frank; she got nothing negative from him, well, not really. She knew he disapproved of the way Andrew behaved with women; after thirty-five years of marriage he had never strayed. He was a strict Catholic; in his book you married for life and remained faithful. Frank believed all men should be married with families of their own. But aside from that he respected Andrew and would follow where he would lead. They smiled as they past each other.

"Ah, the lovely Ashton, how are you today?"

She told him things were going great. She always enjoyed seeing him. She was about to say something else when she heard Andrew bellow. "Ashton, I need to see you right away."

"Gotta go," she said as she made a beeline for Andrew's office.

"Shut the doors behind you. Do you know what Frank was in here about?" he asked her. It was a stupid question really, she read him as soon as she walked in. She was about to say something but he cut her off.

"Okay, never mind, you already know. I can't have this, Ashton. I can't have that viper on my board of directors. He's got to go. But I need him right now."

Martell was handling the acquisition of a large software company just outside of Tucson, Arizona. Andrew wanted the new technology badly; so bad he could taste it. He had to let things slide, at least for now. But once the deal was done Martell would be history.

"What about the Tucson deal? He has to finish what he started. After that, can't you just let him go?"

Ashton looked at Andrew plaintively; she really didn't want any harm to come to him. But Andrew despised anyone who would challenge him in anything, much less his actions as the CEO. Ashton thought for a moment that he probably would have knocked off his own father had he not stepped down in time.

"Oh he'll go all right," Andrew replied. "But in the meantime Martell is your top priority. In fact, it wouldn't hurt if you came on to him a little. I know what he thinks about you, you don't need to read minds to know that. It's as plain as the nose on his ugly face."

Ashton was uncomfortable with that; she balked at the idea. She definitely did not want any kind of relationship, no matter what the reason, with Steve Martell. He was the kind of man she wouldn't even consider if there were no Andrew and no Desmond Corporation; he was just creepy…kind of like Mark Peters but better looking and with a lot more style and money.

"I don't want you to sleep with him Ashton, but a little lunch wouldn't hurt. This Tucson deal means a lot to me and a lot for the company. I don't want this guy messing it up just to make me look bad."

"I thought Denise was my top priority now," she asked him.

"Both," he responded. I need you to tell her about us this week." As she turned to leave, he grabbed her arm. "Are we having dinner tonight?"

"No, I told you I'd spend the weekend with you. Let me have a couple of days to sort this out. And now if you'll excuse me I have plenty of work to do."

As she sat down at her desk she glanced at her cell. She didn't need to listen to the message on it to know what it said. It was Allison, and she was worried about her.

"Call me," the message said. "I need to talk to you."

Ashton sighed heavily as she thought that maybe life would be a lot easier if she had never met Andrew Desmond.

21

As the days wore on, there was little action on the sale of the store. Bob was becoming concerned; almost thirty days had gone by and not one viable buyer. Another ninety and they would be closing on the condo in Palm Beach; he knew he could not give the place up, it would break Marian's heart to lose that kitchen (she had not stopped talking about it since they got back) and he didn't want to lose the escrow money. He didn't want to be an absentee owner, either. Although he trusted Craig, the twelve hundred mile distance from Palm Beach to Brooklyn was just too much.

If something happened, he couldn't be at the store in ten minutes. No, somehow the store would have to sell before the time was up. Craig and Evelyn were moving forward with Bradley and his new school; he was starting there next week. They were happy that they might soon get to hear their son say, "I love you."

Craig kept his focus on that when he and Evelyn spoke about it. He tried not to talk about the store. Every day when he came home Evelyn would ask him if there was any news about the sale. But truthfully, there was none. Their older son, Cooper, told his parents that he could watch Bradley if his mother needed to get a job. Cooper was a well meaning kid, but a seven year old could hardly be counted on to take care of his five year old sibling. They would just wait...and pray.

Marian was spending less and less time at the store now. It seemed she was either furniture shopping (which perplexed Bob as the condo came furnished; even if they decided to redecorate it they would be buying furniture in Florida and not New York) or worrying about Ashton. But at least her calls were not ignored as Allison's had been. Whenever her cell rang and it was her mother, Ashton answered it.

Now Marian was lamenting the fact that Ashton called her to say she wouldn't be coming for dinner on Sunday. She had plans. That's it, nothing more. Just "other plans." Marian asked her if they were with Denise and she told her they weren't. She asked if they were with Allison and she got the same answer. Bob, as usual, told her to let it go. It was enough that she saw them most Sundays. It was enough that they spoke once or twice (usually) during the week, and it was good that Ashton was standing on her own two feet. He always tried to hide the fact that he was just as upset as she was, but at their age they didn't need the aggravation.

Sarah had gone to see two therapists, interviewing them to see if they might be a good fit to see Jessica. She kind of "beat around the bush" as to why her little girl might need counseling; she didn't want them to think she was some kind of crazy person and then not even agree to make an appointment.

But the feeling she got from both of them made Sarah feel as though they weren't going to be of any help; she would just have to keep looking. Of course, since Jessica wasn't in school there were fewer incidents; mostly now there was just an odd comment to her or Bill, and although Jessica missed school she always looked forward to seeing her "Grandma Susan."

Bill and Sarah had dinner at her parents' house only a few days ago, her own mother almost entirely dismissing the child, preferring instead to show Sarah her latest wardrobe from Paris. Bill and Jonathan mostly talked about the company and golf. Jonathan encouraged his son-in-law to play, but Bill had little time—he was one CEO who was at the office every day, from open to close and sometimes well after. Golf with Jonathan (or his snobby friends) just was not high on his agenda. Doing the best he knew how for the company he was now the head of, was.

And Jonathan could be difficult. He missed the "old" Sarah; the whiney, demanding, obnoxious young woman who was so like her mother. He wasn't thrilled with this new version; down to earth, charitable and kind. Jonathan felt that Bill had more than enough money to keep her in four thousand dollar shoes, like his friend Marge Solis (boy, did she get around) and that he was being cheap by not indulging her as they had done for her in her younger

filters

days. Even that bastard ex-husband of hers didn't care what she spent; in fact, the more she spent the better it made him look (at least Andrew thought so).

But Sarah had changed on her own. Even though she could buy whatever she wanted they were just material things; they did not really make her happy or feel fulfilled. It was like trying to fill up a bottomless pit. But when she met Bill all that changed. She watched this man who had so much, give to others in need. Sure, he still had nice things and spent money, but not the way the Douglas family did. Why spend four thousand on a pair of shoes when four hundred would do quite nicely? It was far better to give to those less fortunate with the extra cash saved.

Bill did not force his way of thinking on Sarah; she embraced it. Her charity work made her happy. Living more simply made her happy. And the thought of raising a child of her own with this man she had come to love and admire so much, made her happy. Just look at the way her own mother barely said two words to little Jessica all night; she would have no use for the child until she was older, then she would drag her from store to store, teaching her to be selfish and self centered, just like she had done with Sarah.

And then she would revel in this miniature version of herself that she created. No, neither Sarah nor Bill wanted that. Yes she would grow up privileged; she was the child of a CEO of a major corporation, but she would not be a child of excess. Neither of them would allow it.

Bill and Sarah were glad when their visit was over. Jessica never warmed to her parents, instead asking about when she was going to see Susan next. Actually Jessica knew exactly when she would see Susan the next time, but saying things like that seem to upset her mother and father. She was still very young, but Jessica was learning when to keep her mouth shut. Not being able to go back to the school she loved so much bothered her. She would try, whenever possible, to remain silent. And within the next few minutes she would be silent; the motion of the car lulling her to sleep in her car seat.

Allison sat at the dinner table just staring at her beef stroganoff. Kevin made it for her; it was her favorite and she had worked two back-to-back shifts at the hospital, so she wasn't exactly in the mood for cooking. It has been a rough couple of days; two suicides on the ward caused plenty of commotion and plenty of paperwork.

Two young men, both under thirty, found a way to take their own lives on her watch. One had accumulated a cache of pills, the other got hold of a rope and hung himself in his room while his roommate ran around with his arms outstretched, pretending to be an airplane. Two lives snuffed out before their time. Both were schizophrenics and both said they "heard voices in their heads."

That was a common theme amongst the patients there; and sometimes, because of those voices, things didn't turn out well for them. Allison thought of another person who heard voices as well, but she wore Valentino suits and not the dingy hospital gowns of Bellevue. And "Miss Valentino" suits had not returned her phone call of the other day. Though she was not a mind reader, she knew there was something not quite right here; besides the whole convoluted story of being a secretary or whatever the hell she said she was and lying about her salary (and her lifestyle) to her parents.

No, there was something else. Allison could feel it, and she knew it had something to do with that boss of hers. Bolting upright from her chair, she almost spilled the contents of the stroganoff all over the floor, which displeased Kevin but made Melissa giggle in her high chair. As she ran into the bedroom to grab her cell Kevin yelled after her.

"Allison, are you alright? What about dinner? I made it just for you. Allison…"

She came galloping out of the bedroom holding her cell and pressing the speed dial. She should have known… Voice mail again. Would she ever answer her damned phone? She could take it no longer. No more nice messages like "just calling to see how you are." Not this time.

"Ashton Lancaster," she bellowed into her phone, "are you fucking your boss?!"

Kevin yelled at her about her language in front of the baby and then parroted, "She's fucking Andrew Desmond? Wow…"

"It's nothing to be proud of. That man is trouble. Big trouble. You've read the papers, Kevin. How many scandals has he been involved in? He's not for her. He'll just use her."

Of course, she promised Ashton she would tell no one what was really going on and besides, even after all this time she never told Kevin about her "special abilities." Kevin just thought his wife was a little stressed out right about now, and no wonder, given the last few days. And he already knew she was upset about not talking to Ashton now for months at a time. He just figured it all came to a head. There was no sense in getting her more riled up.

He poured her a shot of whiskey, and then cleaned up the dinner dishes as she sat on the living room couch, watching the tram make its way into Manhattan. He put the baby to bed; Allison was still just sitting there, although her glass was empty now. There were tears in her eyes. Kevin came over and sat next to her, putting his arms around her.

"I just want her to be happy, Kevin, that's all."

Sighing, she stood up, kissed his forehead and went to bed. She must have been dead tired, because not five minutes later Kevin heard her snoring loudly.

Now it was he who sat staring at the tram, heading towards the twinkling lights of the New York City skyline.

ASHTON LOOKED AT HER WATCH. It was creeping up to the five o'clock mark. She dreaded having a drink with Denise after work; she dreaded the whole idea of telling her about Andrew and hoped Denise could keep her mouth shut. If she didn't, the very least that would happen was that she would be fired. Or it could go another way…right into the hands of Mark Peters.

Ashton didn't kid herself. She didn't think that Andrew would give Denise a recommendation to seek employment elsewhere if she started gossiping, no matter how good a job she did or no matter how she now stood right up to him. In the grand scheme of Andrew Desmond, Denise was golden only as long as she would play by his rules; after all, good accountants were a dime a dozen. Nope, Denise would have to "play nice" if she wanted to stay, and maybe, stay alive.

She gathered her things and looked over at Andrew, who merely nodded at her and went back to his paperwork. Denise was right behind her and the two women walked towards the private elevator, nodding at Doris who was getting her stuff together as well. As they rode down to the lobby Denise asked Ashton where she'd like to go for drinks. Ashton responded that she's like some dinner and it was on her. "I need to talk to you," Ashton told her.

Having no idea what it might be about they headed to a little café on Third Avenue. Thankfully it wasn't crowded; they were able to get a seat by the window to watch the people walking by. Ashton thought to herself that she would love a shot of tequila right about now, but that wouldn't be a good idea. No, she'd stick to wine—one glass.

"Why so serious, Ashton? What do you want to talk to me about?" Denise asked, as she took a sip of the wine the waitress had just set in front of her.

"I don't know how to say this so I'm just going to come right out with it," Ashton answered her; her hands visibly shaking as she took a big gulp of her wine.

"Andrew and I are in love and we want to be together, but we want to keep it private. I had to tell you because he wants me to spend the nights with him now and I won't always be sharing a cab with you in the morning. Please don't tell anybody else, Denise!"

Ashton knew what she was thinking; that she was crazy and he was just using her. Why, she wasn't sure of that; but she felt he wasn't capable of loving anyone except himself. She wasn't jealous, she wasn't angry; she was just worried about her friend in the arms of that monster.

Denise looked out the window and watched a woman with stilettos practically trip all over herself as she walked. She then turned to Ashton.

"Look, my friend, if that's the way you want it then that's the way it will be. If you really are in love and he can give you a good life then I'm glad. But don't forget I've seen a side of him that you haven't. He threw me out of his bed the next morning the one time I slept with him. I practically had to get dressed in the hallway outside of his apartment. It was humiliating, Ashton. He was so cold…like ice. Even his eyes. There was no hint of caring. I've never been treated so badly, and I've had my share of one night stands."

"So you won't say anything?"

"No, I'll keep my mouth shut for now. But if he hurts you in any way…"

The rest of the night was off somehow, it just didn't feel the same between them. She told Denise she would be spending the weekend with Andrew and not going to see her mother on Sunday.

"I don't think Andrew would quite fit in, do you?" Ashton asked her, half grinning.

"Ashton, remember they're your parents," Denise reminded her, "and they're not getting any younger so don't blow them off for any man. I miss my parents so much. Thank God I'm flying out next month to see them. Sometimes I think I oughta chuck all this and move back home, start fresh there."

"I know, and the sad part is that I don't see them embracing Andrew. Sure, they'd be happy that I'd be set financially but then they always said that money wasn't the most important thing in a relationship," Ashton added.

"Look, just take it one step at a time. See where it goes. And more importantly, keep the relationship with your parents strong. Keep a relationship with your friends. And by the way, I haven't heard you talk about your friend Allison in a long time. Is everything okay with her?"

Allison! She hadn't even returned her phone call. But what was she going to say to her, that she was dead on; that she was now

279

screwing her boss? She had to call her, Denise was right. She couldn't throw half her life away because of Andrew Desmond, whether he was the kind of guy you could bring home to meet your parents or not.

Ashton told Denise that she already told them she wouldn't be making Sunday dinner but gave them no explanation. Denise told her to tell them she was with her anytime she couldn't make it; she liked Bob and Marian and didn't want to see them upset.

"I'll remember that for next time, and thanks, Denise."

"Hey, what are friends for?" she smiled.

They walked home from the café. It always amazed Ashton how busy the city was, even on a Monday night. Each restaurant they walked past was packed with people; she could hear a jumble of their thoughts as they passed each one. They didn't seem to bother her as much as they once did, or maybe she was just too focused on her own problems.

As they walked into the lobby Denise asked her, "Cab tomorrow?" and Ashton nodded as they each went their respective ways into their own apartments.

As she sat in bed Ashton picked up the phone to call Allison. She told her...all of it. Allison practically parroted what Denise said...to be careful. But Allison knew most of all how careful she would have to be because she knew every little detail of her employment there.

"Hey now, don't forget about me now that you have a new boyfriend," Allison teased her, trying to lighten the mood. "We're still on for lunch one day, aren't we?"

"Yes, I promise. Next week sometime. Just let me know what your schedule is, I know your shifts are always changing."

When she hung up the phone Allison turned to Kevin and simply said, "I was right."

That night Ashton slept fretfully. She kept waking up and looking at the clock. One o'clock. Two forty-five. Three thirty. And then, the dream. Mark Peters was standing over Denise's body in a back alley, wiping her blood from the blade of his knife as he called Andrew...

"Mr. Desmond, sir, it's all taken care of Mr. Desmond," in that damned whiney voice he used when he spoke to Andrew. And then a sick, twisted smile crept over Peter's face as he laughingly watched Denise bleed to death on the filthy sidewalk.

Ashton bolted upright, ran to the bathroom and promptly threw up into the sink. She then slid down the bathroom wall onto the tile floor and wept hysterically. Falling asleep there, the sound of sirens tearing up York Avenue woke her at six. And on the cab ride into the office with Denise, it was all she had just to hold it together. Every time she looked at Denise that horrible dream replayed in her head. She could feel the bile rise up in her throat; she thought she would be sick in the cab several times. Denise was concerned; she just didn't look right.

"Why don't you just take a sick day? Drop me off and then take the cab back home," she told Ashton, who looked as if she was going to hurl right there.

"No, I have work to do. I'll be all right as soon as I eat something."

Getting off the private elevator she made it to her desk and then hurled right into the garbage pail. Doris heard her and ran in. Ashton looked like death warmed over.

"Let me get you a cup of tea and some toast, you stay right there and don't move," Doris offered, and then marched into the kitchen. While she was making the tea Andrew was getting off the elevator. Sticking his head into her office he was shocked at the way she looked; mascara and eye liner now running down her face.

"Are you okay Ashton, what's wrong?"

"Come on in for a minute," she told him. "Doris will be right back. She went to make me some tea. I told Denise last night. She's okay with it; she'll keep her mouth shut."

"Is that why you're so upset?

"Who said I was upset? I just don't feel too well, that's all. Must have been something I ate."

"Oh come on Ashton. You don't have to be a mind reader to know you're upset and I'll bet it has nothing to do with anything you ate."

Ashton thought Yeah, I'm upset. I just had a premonition of what could happen to Denise if she decides to say something about us. I just saw her bloody body on the sidewalk.

Just then, she thought of another bloody body on the sidewalk, but this one was not in a dream—Phyllis Sullivan. She shivered as the thought crossed her mind.

Just then Doris returned with a steaming hot cup of tea and some plain toast. She said good morning to Andrew and placed the tray in front of Ashton. Andrew told her to eat it and then go home. She balked at the idea at first; they had a lot of work to do, but now she really was feeling worse. Andrew had his limo waiting outside for her to take her home. She barely got in the door before heading to the couch. Stretching out, she fell asleep; a deep, dreamless sleep.

282

It was nearly four o'clock when her cell rang. It was Andrew asking her if she was alright.

She felt better, actually hungry, but then remembered she had little in her refrigerator.

"Don't worry, I'll send some food over." He told her.

"Don't make a fuss, I can go out."

"I'm not making a fuss, I'll ask Denise to bring something home for you."

Andrew summoned Denise to his office. As usual now, she was the picture of composure. Walking in his office, she held her head high and then met his gaze.

"What can I do for you?"

"Ashton is sick. Are you going straight home tonight? Because if you are, would you mind picking up something for her to eat? She said her refrigerator is empty."

She nodded, and he pulled his wallet out of his trousers. Opening it, he attempted to hand her a one hundred dollar bill. She refused the money.

"I owe her a dinner, so no problem. It's on me"

"Okay, you have my number if she needs anything."

Denise was, quite frankly, amazed. Andrew Desmond was actually showing concern for someone other than himself. Maybe he really did love her. She sure hoped so, for Ashton's sake.

Ashton returned to the office bright and early Tuesday morning. After Denise brought her a big plate of lasagna from the Italian restaurant two blocks away, Ashton told her she would go in alone to catch up on some work. The place was empty; she settled in and turned her computer on. Just then the elevator doors slid open. Who the heck was that at this hour?

Steve Martell knocked on her door, a sly smile creeping over his face.

"Working hard for the man, huh? And even in so early. I hope he pays you well."

Then he sat down beside her, his hand creeping up her arm. She pulled away from him.

"You're sooooo beautiful," he told her, in a kind of low, guttural voice. "We could have a good time together, you and me..."

"Get out! Get out and stay out! And if you don't watch your step, I'll tell Andrew!"

"So tell him. He needs me to close that Tucson deal. He won't do anything to me. As long as I'm making him money I'm good, and I'm making him lots of money."

"Get out!" she hissed at him. Her voice reminded her of the movie *Amityville Horror* when the evil entity screams at the priest to get out before he can bless the house. She sounded like that evil entity now, but it worked; getting the message loud and clear Martell slinked away and back into the elevator. Where he was going Ashton had no idea but she didn't care. She just wanted him away from her, especially since the whole floor was empty; there would be no one to come to her assistance if he really got out of control.

When he was gone she got up to make herself a cup of coffee and sat in the private kitchen just staring into space. She was startled by Doris, now standing beside her.

"Are you alright Ashton? I've been saying hello to you for the past two minutes and you didn't even hear me. Are you feeling better?"

"Oh yeah, I'm sorry, Doris. I just got a visit from Steve Martell, and it wasn't welcomed."

"You need to tell Andrew about that. I'm serious, Ashton, don't fool around with that guy, he's dangerous. If you won't tell him, I will."

Ashton was touched by Doris' concern for her. She would tell Andrew. Martell needed to be fired. Let him work somewhere else. She knew Andrew wanted her to talk to him, maybe get a little more information about his motives but she knew she couldn't do that now. She read Martell's thoughts. She wasn't safe with him. He would try to force himself on her, she was sure of that. There could be no innocent flirtation while trying to get inside his head. This guy was serious. Yes, he wanted to take Andrew down but he also wanted to, well, do all kinds of kinky stuff with her. No sir. No sale.

"No, I'll talk to Andrew, Doris. But thanks for stepping up for me."

Ashton poured another cup of coffee and took it into her office. Sitting down, she began her work until she heard Doris saying 'good morning' to Andrew. He popped his head in her office; she looked up solemnly and told him, "I have to talk to you." He assumed it might be about Denise; maybe she had changed her mind about how she felt about them when she brought Ashton dinner last night. He told her to come in.

She closed the big glass doors behind her as she slid into the seat in front of his huge desk.

"I came in early to try to get caught up on all the work I missed yesterday and Steve Martell came in. He grabbed my arm, Andrew. He told me that we could have a lot of fun together. I read his thoughts. I know the kind of fun he wants to have and it's not playing Monopoly. I don't want to have anything to do with him. I'm afraid of him, Andrew."

Andrew stood up, nostrils flaring.

"That son of a bitch. Forget what I told you, I don't want you near him. That bastard. He needs to have an accident!"

"No, Andrew, please no. I don't want that and besides, you need him for the Tucson deal. Just please don't get me involved. You know what you need to know. Just fire him after Tucson closes."

The way they both were screaming it was a good idea the doors were closed. Finally Andrew calmed down. He sat back down, fiddled with his tie, and then told her that he would let things ride until after Tucson. Then he would be fired. She didn't have to be involved with him at all. As he spoke, he imagined his mind being sheltered by a big brick wall; when he did that, she seemed to have trouble getting into his mind. As he looked at her, he knew it was working; he wasn't planning on firing Martell after Tucson closed, he would have an "encounter" with Steve Martell.

As the weeks flew by they got closer, Andrew and Ashton. She spent most nights at his place, although she cut her weekends short most of the time to visit her parents, who blissfully knew nothing of Andrew. She knew deep down they would never hit it off.

Despite the fact that Andrew seemed to have done a one eighty in his love life, he would have little in common with a shop keeper and his working wife from Brooklyn. He hadn't seen his own mother and father in eons now; hadn't even spent five minutes talking on the phone to his mother, who still missed him desperately. On the weekends when Ashton didn't see her parents, they sometimes jetted to Atlantic City or Vegas where they laid in bed for hours just talking and cuddling. It was so different now for both of them; Ashton had never had a real relationship in her life, only a series of one night stands mostly, and Andrew never got past the "one night stand" stage, except for Sarah, but that whole marriage was a sham anyway.

But Andrew felt so differently now. He wanted to be with this woman, this beauty, for the rest of his life. He didn't understand the way he felt either; did he love her for what she could do for him? A woman with her skills would keep him on top. What did that article say about him that time? Oh yeah..."King of the World" that was it. He had to admit it sounded really good. Yes, he really would be the king of the world. And on a stormy Saturday afternoon in Atlantic City, on the deserted boardwalk, he knelt down on one knee and asked Ashton Lancaster to be is wife.

AS THE WIND WHIPPED THE STORM CLOUDS in and lightning flashed, he slipped the internally flawless, "D" color, five carat round brilliant diamond from Tiffany's on her left ring finger.

As she nodded her acceptance she thought to herself that the wind and lightning could be a bad omen, but at this moment, she didn't really care.

She didn't wear the ring to the office that Monday. She didn't tell anyone, not Denise or Allison and certainly not her parents, that sitting in her jewelry box in her apartment, was a ring that was double the cost of their condo in Palm Beach.

A few more weeks went by and Ashton felt it was at least time to let her friends know. Her parents were another story; they had been left out of the loop for so long that she wouldn't know where to begin. And they wouldn't be comfortable with Andrew; she just knew they wouldn't be. The few times they had actually discussed her job they always made some statement of what they had read or heard about him, and it was never positive. No, Andrew would never fit in. More than likely he would say or do something to offend her parents. Deep down, Ashton knew that a life with Andrew would most likely mean a life without them. And she didn't want to think about making that choice. Andrew had asked her about setting a date, but she just kept pushing it off.

He actually asked about meeting her parents—just to make her feel better, probably—but she pushed that off as well. Ashton was secretly hoping her parents would have moved to Palm Beach and she could just call them and say something like *Oh, by the way, I'm marrying Andrew Desmond next week and you probably can't get a flight out so I'll just send you some pictures.*

And they weren't going anywhere, her parents. For some reason the store still had not sold and the closing date on the condo was coming up in thirty days. Luckily and due to some fast footwork by their realtor they actually got an extension...an additional ninety days. It seems the daughter was still living in the place; the construction on her new home had been even more delayed. She was more than happy to give the Martins more time, although her brother wanted the sale done and over with.

But now the Martins had four months to move.

Ashton would still play her game; saying nothing about Andrew or the real details of her job. And as for her apartment, the Martins gave up on ever seeing it. It was enough that their daughter came to Sunday dinner (most Sundays anyway) and often brought that nice girl, Denise with her, the one who loved Marian's rigatoni and meatballs so much.

SARAH SAT IN A SMALL CHAIR to one side of the room as the counselor spoke to Jessica. The little girl seemed unimpressed by this latest one, in a chain of what had been four or five; each shaking their heads unable to figure out how this little girl seemed to know so much about, well, things she should have never known about in the first place. Batteries of tests showed that she was of above average intelligence as well as friendly and outgoing. Outside of this strange "ability" she was a normal child.

Sarah knew, as she walked outside into the bright sunlight that there probably was no answer. At least not in traditional sense. She thought about what Susan had said about a psychic, but then decided against it. Maybe all this would go away as she got older.

Praying by her bedside every night, she lifted her arms towards heaven and pleaded, "Dear God, let Jessica know when to hold her tongue. Let her be silent when she needs to be. Help her have a normal life; a good life."

And Jessica would hear what her mother would tell her over and over as the years marched by. "Use your filters, Jessica."

But Jessica was happy today, because after their appointment they would see "Grandma Susan." They met her at a small restaurant only a few miles away from their house on the South Shore. And Susan's smile seemed to be even bigger than usual as Sarah and Jessica walked to the table to greet her.

"Wow, somebody's really happy today," Sarah told Susan.

"Sit down," Susan said, after hugging Jessica. "I have something to tell you. I've heard from Andrew and he's getting married."

"Well I'll be darned. Do you know her?"

"No, she's a woman who works for him. They're coming to dinner next Saturday night."

"What did Harold say about it?"

"He said to have milk and cookies for Andrew when he got home from school"

Just then both women heard Jessica mutter under her breath, "No, no, no, no, be quiet."

"What did you say, Jessica?" her mother asked her.

"Nothing Mommy, I'm just practicing for when I can go back to school again, you know, being quiet and not saying things that can get me into trouble."

"Good girl," Susan told her.

But Jessica acted strangely throughout lunch, becoming sullen and withdrawn and not even wanting to hug "Grandma Susan" anymore. Sarah thought she might be coming down with something and decided to take her home.

"Call me later," Susan told her, "and let me know how's she's feeling."

Susan decided to stop by the house in Massapequa for awhile. As she sat sipping tea in the periwinkle recliner (Harold would never approve of such cheap furniture) she petted Sheena and thought about Andrew. He was coming home! With a fiancé, even. Now there just might be grandchildren and Sunday dinners and school plays and…

She nodded off in the chair dreaming about grandchildren. She could have sworn she saw Jessica in the dream saying something like, "You really will be my Grandma one day."

Susan smiled, she would like that. The child was so beautiful with those remarkable eyes, like the color of the sea…

When she got back to the great house she told Robert about Andrew and dinner Saturday night. He was happy for Susan but thought to himself that he figured he would never have to lay eyes on that son-of-a-bitch Andrew again, but he was wrong. He went inside to inform the staff to get the house ready. Then he remembered he forgot to ask Susan what the young lady preferred to eat for dinner.

"Lasagna," Susan said, "Andrew told me she loves lasagna."

"Maybe she'll be okay, after all. Lasagna…that would be his choice as well," Robert thought to himself.

As he started to make his way back into the kitchen, Robert got side tracked by Harold who told him, "C'mon, Robert, let's see if we can make a bat pole and then I can be Batman and you can be Robin."

"Oh joy," Robert sighed, "This is gonna be one very fucked up dinner," but he kept that thought to himself.

Sarah called Susan later that evening to let her know Jessica was feeling better, especially when she decided to make her favorite dinner—lasagna.

"Really? Wow, what a coincidence. Andrew's fiancé loves that as well; we're having it for dinner Saturday night."

"I NEED TO TALK TO YOU," Ashton told Denise.

"Oh Good Lord, now what?" Denise thought.

Things actually were going quite smoothly in the office. No one would know, unless they were told, that Andrew and Ashton were in a relationship. Nope, no one had inkling. And from what Ashton had told Denise, the only other person that knew was Allison. She hadn't even told her parents.

"Just as well," Denise thought. She still didn't trust Andrew a hundred percent and noticed how upset he got when that Martell guy even came near Ashton. She knew Martell was instrumental in closing the Tucson deal, but he made everyone uncomfortable, so unlike Frank Delgado, who stopped to ask her about her shoes last week.

"My wife loves shoes and I know she'd love those. May I ask you where you got them?"

Good old Frank; he put everyone at ease. He never flirted like most of the male board members, and always had something positive to say. Denise knew he had a son, a doctor she thought. She wondered if he was like his father. That would be the kind of man she'd like to marry.

As he passed by her the other day Denise asked if he got the shoes.

"Oh yes, thank you. She loves them. And I'm glad; I always want to make her happy."

"Yep," Denise thought, "if his son was like him he'd be perfect husband material."

Ashton and Denise went to that same café on Third Avenue, now referred to as "drama central" because they always seemed to go there when Ashton had something monumental to say. As they sat at the same table near the window Ashton dug into her purse. When her hand came out there was a huge diamond ring on her fourth finger.

"Holy shit!" Denise yelled, and the whole restaurant turned to look at her. "Is that from Andrew? Jesus, how much did that cost?"

"Shhhhh, let's not tell the whole world, okay? Yes, it's from Andrew and I think it cost just under a million."

"Dear God, have long have you had it?"

"About a month now."

"And when were you gonna tell me?" Denise chided. "After the honeymoon?"

"I'm just not comfortable wearing it, especially around the office. It feels weird. Andrew says I should, that it's okay, but I just don't want to. At least not yet."

"Have you told anyone else?"

"Nope, you're the first. Allison will be next."

"And your parents?"

"Maybe after the wedding."

Denise took a moment to recover. "Geez Ashton, if you love him and he loves you then what's the big deal? Listen, this should be a happy time in your life. You should be planning a wedding; walking down that big aisle in St. Patrick's, the train on your dress ten feet long."

Ashton thought of her dream; walking down the aisle in St. Patrick's with Steve Martell's bloody body lying right by the altar. She shuddered.

"I know, I know you're right. And I will tell everybody. I will plan the wedding, right after I meet his parents on Saturday night."

"Wow, I didn't think he talked to his parents anymore."

"How did you know that?"

"Everybody knows that, we just don't say anything about it," Denise admitted.

Her comment made Ashton think further about Andrew's relationship with his parents. Why *was* he bringing her to meet them? But deep down, she already knew. She was like a trophy; he wanted to show them that he could love somebody and settle down. She wasn't really comfortable with that idea; it was like there were two of him now struggling to become one; the old Andrew, manipulative and power hungry, and this new one, who loved her.

And he did love her. He really loved her. But would it be enough for him as the years went by? Would she be enough; after all, she was fast approaching thirty-five, although she looked ten years younger. Would he find more excitement in the arms of a twenty-year-old when she was forty? She knew she could see glimpses of the future sometimes but that was only the very near future. What would happen long term was as much a mystery to her as it was to anyone else.

Denise saw the look on Ashton's face; she didn't want to upset her.

"That is one damned fine ring," she said. "It's a wonder you can hold it up with your hand."

They walked back to their apartment building together. Ashton hadn't been there in quite a few days, instead, spending the night at Andrew's, where she now had most of her clothes. They talked about what life would be like with Andrew, and then Ashton remembered she hadn't even asked Denise about her trip back home to see her parents.

"It was great seeing them. I miss my hometown. I checked out a few job openings when I was there, Ashton, I'm thinking about going back. I even spoke to some people about starting up my own accounting firm. I'd like a different life, I think. Maybe even meet somebody and settle down. It gets old, this bar scene every night."

Ashton couldn't blame her. She knew she was lonely; outside of Ashton she had few friends and she dated very rarely. Yeah, she had a really good paying job but that was about it. At least Allison had a husband and a baby. She didn't sit alone in her apartment each night as Denise did.

"I think it's a good idea, Denise. I think you might be happier there."

She knew Denise sometimes consoled herself with a couple of glasses of wine but who was she to say anything; God knows how many night she spent on the barstool at Ovals drowning her sorrows in a bottle of tequila and then fucking her brains out afterwards with some stranger. She smiled when she thought of him, though...

Allison pretty much reacted as Denise did. Although she did not know Andrew Desmond; from what she read and heard about him she knew her friendship with Ashton might not survive. Could she invite Andrew and Ashton over to their apartment for a couple of beers? Would he and Kevin hit it off, the billionaire and the working class stiff who wore jeans and a tee shirt to work? Probably not. But what upset her most was the way she was leaving her parents out of the loop. They didn't even know she was seeing anyone, much less wearing a ring the size of a small skating rink. But who was she to go knock on Marian's door and tell her that her daughter was about to marry the richest man in New York? That would be up to Ashton.

But Ashton didn't even want to discuss wedding plans. Most women would be out shopping and choosing venues, especially since her budget would be unlimited. But she had done nothing, save for accepting the giant ring and telling Denise. Oh yeah, and Andrew told his parents; she remembered Ashton said that; something about going to their house for dinner. And then Allison thought to herself that their "house" was the size of Texas.

Allison could not read minds or see the future, but she had a bad feeling about all of this. Something just wasn't right here, beyond the made up job that Ashton invented. She had a feeling this whole thing was going to end in disaster.

Ashton had dinner at her parents the next Sunday, left the ring home and brought Denise, who ate two plates of rigatoni and meatballs (Where did that girl put it all—she was skinny as a rail). They talked about Denise's trip home and the delay on the closing of the condo. They talked about the store and how it was still on the market.

Ashton was careful to wear her jeans—not the five hundred dollars ones Andrew bought her last week—and a tee shirt. The flip flops she wore made Denise laugh; she was so used to seeing her in her high heel pumps. And that bag she bought in Macy's was kind of funky. But it completed the picture Ashton wanted her parents to see—the old Ashton. When they left Denise asked her if they had to do it again next Sunday but Ashton reminded her that was the weekend when she would meet Andrew's parents. Denise was relieved; she loved the rigatoni but the rest of it was starting to give her a bad case of heartburn.

22

shton raced around Andrew's condo looking for the right thing to wear. Andrew sat propped up in bed, naked, just watching her. It amused him; she was so worried about what his mother and father would think of her. His mother; Andrew was sure, would embrace her; his father, from what he had heard, was so senile he'd probably go ask her to play in the sandbox; she could probably be nude and he wouldn't notice a thing.

She settled on one of her new Valentino suits; its sage color played up the green of her eyes. She remembered to slip on her ring; most of the time it was either in her jewelry box or in her pocket.

As they slid into the limo she was visibly shaking; this made the whole engagement thing real. This was really happening. She sat snuggled next to Andrew who downed two glasses of single malt during the thirty minute ride out to the North Shore.

He wanted her to have a drink; she thought of checking to see if there was a bottle of tequila. If there was she would have drained the whole bottle. But she refused; looking out the window as the Long Island sound came into view. It was sunset and the sky was lit by streaks of orange and pink. The next thing she knew, they were turning up a long, winding drive.

Above her loomed the great house—like something right out of *The Great Gatsby*. It mesmerized her.

"How many rooms are there?" she whispered.

"I've never counted; I think about sixty," he replied.

The limo pulled underneath the porte-cochère. Robert was standing, dressed in full uniform, ready to greet them.

"Good evening, Mr. Desmond, sir" Robert said, in his most formal voice. And then turning to Ashton he said, "Good evening, Madam."

Ashton shook his hand and smiled. Andrew ignored him.

"Wow, look at those eyes," Robert thought.

His mother met him in the entry hall, embracing him with tears in her eyes. He stiffened in her arms and simply said, "Hello. Mother, nice to see you again."

She then turned to Ashton to greet her but stopped for a moment, staring at her. "Those eyes," she thought. "They look so beautiful but yet somehow so familiar."

"Welcome, my dear, it's a pleasure to meet you."

"It's an honor to meet you, Mrs. Desmond."

"Please call me Susan, Mrs. Desmond is so formal."

She hugged Ashton tightly, and Ashton could sense she was a good woman; she had a good heart. The two women liked each other immediately; Andrew was pleased about that.

Susan led them into the living room, where his father was sitting, dressed in a dinner jacket. He looked far away; Susan thought to herself that this was it, he was probably going to ask them to play Pin the Tail on the Donkey or something like that. But when he looked at Andrew something about Harold changed. The light came back into his eyes. He was focused. It was as if a switch had been thrown and now there was a light on in Harold Desmond's world. He rose and extended his hand.

"Hello son, good to see you again. And who, may I ask, is this charming young lady?"

Andrew shook his father's hand and introduced Ashton. She shook his hand but addressed him as Mr. Desmond. She sensed that he was a tortured soul; ill and in pain most of the time, feeling regret as well. Regret that his son had turned out to be so uncaring and cold. He knew he had a big hand in that, and he was sorry.

Robert arrived with a round of drinks, and they sat down to talk, enjoying their cocktails. Harold and Andrew talked about business and Susan inspected Ashton's ring.

"It's lovely my dear; have you set a date?"

"No, not yet," Ashton said, a little uneasy. "I guess I'm just not comfortable with anything too big. I don't like a lot of fuss."

"Well, it would be wonderful to have a big, bright wedding, but you have to do what you feel is right, so if you want a small

301

affair or even elope you have our blessing. Whatever makes you happy."

Susan smiled brightly at her; she couldn't help looking at her eyes. Ashton picked up on it but what she was getting was garbled; all she could take from it was that Susan knew someone else with a similar eye color, a little girl, she thought.

"Yes, I've been trying to get her to give me an idea of a date but she just hasn't yet," Andrew interjected.

The conversation actually was going well. Susan even gave Ashton a short tour of the house before dinner. Robert watched from a hallway; he liked this girl and for her sake and Susan's, he hoped the night would go well. He was shocked at how well the old man was doing; thankfully, there was no reference to Miss Cathy or her magic mirror.

The lasagna was a big hit too; everyone seemed to enjoy it although it was not the usual fare served at one of their dinner parties. Ashton told them (or mostly Susan) about her own mother and father in Bay Ridge and their grocery store. She told them of their moving to Palm Beach; but the sale of the condo being held up because they had not yet found a buyer for the store.

"Palm Beach?" Harold interjected. "Didn't Andrew tell you he has a house in Palm Beach? And directing his conversation back to Andrew, Harold asked "small place, though, isn't it? Only about ten thousand square feet as I remember."

"Yes, Ashton, it just slipped my mind. I do have a house there, oceanfront, with a small permanent staff. Your parents are welcome to stay there until the store is sold if they'd like. I only use it one or two weeks out of the year and I have no plans to be there anytime soon. Besides, although Father calls it 'small' there actually are enough bedrooms for all of us and a beautiful pool right next to the ocean," Andrew told her.

Ashton smiled shyly, not quite knowing what to say. She was surprised she didn't pick up on it, but then, he had never spoken of it before and it had never crossed his mind to read. And anyway, her parents didn't even know about them and now she was going to have them move into his Palm Beach estate? Not likely.

"Thank you, Andrew, but I think they'd be more comfortable staying here in town until the store is sold. Bob is very 'hands on' and wants to be around in case of any problems."

"Sounds like a very sensible man," Susan said. "I bet I would like him very much, and your mother, too. I miss those days of working. Did you know I used to work with children, Ashton? I taught kindergarten for many years before our situation changed. I still miss it. I love children."

That set Harold off. The old man had held it together up until now; just the idea of seeing his beloved Andrew was enough to bring him out if his stupor; to leave Miss Cathy and her magic mirror behind. The man sitting at the head of the table now was now very much again the founder of the Desmond Corporation and he was turning back into that obnoxious snob.

"Oh, stop it Susan! A kindergarten teacher! Really, I put the world at your feet and all you talk about is making minimum wage teaching some little kids who'll probably never amount to anything in this life anyway!

And then he turned to his son. "And *you*, Andrew, your girlfriend here is very pretty but where does she come from? Sarah comes from a fine family—a girl of breeding and refinement. What does this one come from, Andrew? The frozen food aisle of a grocery store? She's trash."

Susan knew that Harold wasn't in his right mind. Even totally lucid, he would never offend a dinner guest like that. He might fight with Andrew but never, in all their years together, had he ever insulted a guest at his table. He didn't even realize that he had seen Sarah just a short time ago, and she was certainly no debutante anymore. She didn't care about breeding or refinement; she was too busy helping the less fortunate.

Ashton sat there, mouth hanging open. It was playing out just as it had in her dream.

"You're one to talk, Father. I've heard you've become a useless old man, peeing in your pants and having the major domo play games with you. You're the one who's trash! People like you should be 'put down' the way they put down old animals."

And then he stood, walked over to Ashton and grabbed her arm.

"We're leaving, let's go. And we're never coming back again, ever. And don't count on a wedding invitation, either!"

Rising from the table, Ashton looked at Susan. Susan grabbed her hand and held it tightly. Ashton whispered, "I'm sorry," as Andrew yanked her arm and stormed towards the door. In a flash the limo was making its way back down the winding drive.

Harold, still sitting at the table asked his wife, "Is Andrew coming back for his milk and cookies? I know he loves them so much when he gets home from school."

Susan ran up the stairs crying. Harold got up in search of Robert; maybe he wanted to play a game. Hey, wait, he had this funny jacket on. Maybe he was already playing a game. Maybe he was supposed to be pretending to be a penguin.

In the limo Ashton sat away from Andrew, leaning her head again the window, tears streaming down her face. Andrew sat bolt upright in stone cold silence, finishing off that bottle of single malt. They said nothing to each other the whole ride home. When they went to bed, he didn't touch her or even say goodnight. Ashton just lay there in the inky silence staring at the ceiling.

Finally, she fell asleep. The dream she had made her smile. She dreamt of Susan showing her some geraniums she had planted in a little garden just outside of a pleasant little house; just like the kind of house Ashton would like to live in. She went inside and petted a little black and white cat; it reminded her that she loved animals. She sat down and had tea with Susan and they laughed and smiled.

And then the dream was over. She woke up in the big bed and glanced over at Andrew, who was still fast asleep. She rose from the bed and her feet hit the icy marble and she padded her way into the master bathroom. She drew a bath and then sank into the huge, custom made tub. She closed her eyes and hoped to get back to the little house with the geraniums, but felt movement in the water. It was Andrew, sliding in next to her.

As he reached for her she thought to herself that he just didn't care about what had transpired the night before. Okay, she could kind of understand his frustration with Harold, but his mother? Ashton had read nothing but love from her for her only child. The poor woman was devastated by what happened. Her son walked out on her for the second time. When she started to say something about it, Andrew cut her off.

"The hell with them both, who needs them anyway? My father is crazy and my mother is weak. Do you know she never made friends with all those terrific women from the club? I think she only had one friend, some other teacher, but I can't remember her name."

"Your father seems to prefer your ex-wife. She must be quite the lady."

"Used to be. From what I've heard she's remarried, adopted a kid and does charity work with my mother. In fact, she turned out to be just like my mother—shopping off the rack and doing housework. She seems to like that shit now."

Ashton got a funny feeling when she thought of Sarah, but somehow couldn't figure out why, exactly.

"Oh forget them; let's have some fun, shall we?" he said, as he grabbed Ashton and pulled her to him. He touched the place on her arm where there was now a huge bruise from where he had yanked it the night before. She winched; he didn't seem to notice.

When they were done Andrew seemed pleased with himself but Ashton felt empty inside. Was this really love? She felt as if she were marrying a cardboard replica of what a real man should be... caring and loyal and not so damned wrapped up in the almighty dollar. What was wrong with housework? What was wrong with shopping off the rack? Millions of people did that and they were happy. And kids... God, she wanted them. But would Andrew make a good father or would he fashion the child into a miniature version of himself?

"Want to go shopping? He asked her. We could have brunch and then..."

"No, Andrew, I think I'll go back to my apartment. I have some things to do. I'll see you at the office tomorrow."

When Ashton got home she dialed Susan's cell phone. She had gotten the number from Andrew's cell when he was sleeping.

"I'm so sorry," Ashton told her.

"No, Ashton, I'm the one who's sorry. I shouldn't have allowed Harold to have dinner with us. I shouldn't have mentioned to him that Andrew was coming at all. If he was in his right mind he never would have insulted you like that, believe me. In fact, right after you left he slipped right back into his senility, asking me if Andrew was coming home for his milk and cookies. I think your family is wonderful. I really hope we can meet sometime."

Ashton felt pulled towards this woman; somehow she knew Susan was going to be an integral part of her life, no matter what happened with Andrew.

Monday morning went as usual at the office. Andrew was pleased the Tucson deal was closing soon. Martell was getting more and more out of hand. His ego was being inflated because of the deal; he knew Andrew needed him more than ever now. In Martell's twisted mind, the chairman's office would be his next step.

Andrew knew all of this from Ashton, who sat beside him, as usual, rapidly taking notes on her tablet. She left out the part about Martell wondering what she would look like without her panties on; that might send Andrew over the edge.

But around the office itself things were changing. People were aware now of the relationship between Andrew and the Employee Relations Specialist, but thankfully most didn't seem to care. Maybe they thought Ashton would soften his hard edges and make him kinder. There were few women employed there now anyway that Andrew had slept with; it had been over a year now (since Ashton came) that any of that went on. Even human resources stopped picking pretty girls to fill positions that became available in the company; now they were focusing on who had real talent; some of them were middle aged men.

And curiously, even though the people within the company knew there was something going on between the chairman and Ashton, they still came in droves to discuss their issues with her. There was just something about her that they trusted; she would have their best interests in mind no matter what she was doing with Andrew. That pleased Ashton; she really wanted to help when she could, after all, these were the people who did housework and shopped "off the rack."

And Andrew asked her one more time about a date and a big wedding. She refused the wedding. She didn't want the white dress with the long train. She didn't want a reception for a thousand people. She wanted to keep things quiet. He knew what he had to do to keep her; so be it. No one would know then, if that's the way she wanted it.

"SO HOW DID IT GO?" Sarah asked Susan as they had coffee together. Jessica was home with Bill; since it was Saturday he was going to take her to see the horses at a nearby stable. Not to buy her one, but she was interested in taking lessons so they were going to check it out. His father-in-law just told him to buy her a horse. Bill wasn't going to do that until and unless he knew she would stick with it, and only when she got a little older. He didn't believe in indulging his daughter just because they had the means. He wasn't going to raise a whiney little brat. That displeased Jonathan; he thought people of power and position should do what they wanted whenever they wanted. No, even though Jonathan trusted Bill to take over his company and run it successfully, the two men never really became friends.

"It was awful," Susan told Sarah. "Harold was fine at first; I think seeing Andrew snapped him out of it, but then Ashton, that's her name, started talking about her family; just ordinary folks and they sounded like really nice people. But that set Harold off. He started talking about you, about the way you used to be anyway, and that's the kind of woman he wanted for his son: a woman of breeding and discernment. Anyway, the two of them got into it; you know how that goes, you've seen it a hundred times. He grabbed Ashton's arm and they left. He said he was never coming back again. Five minutes later, Harold was asking when Andrew was coming home from school."

Sarah touched her arm in the place where Andrew had yanked it a hundred times before. Mentally, she winced. She could see it clearly in her mind, the whole mess. And this poor girl, Ashton... Sarah felt sad and worried about her. She could only pray this woman would have a good life with Andrew, but somehow, Sarah felt doubtful about that happening. Susan seemed far away.

"What are you thinking about now? Sarah asked her.

"Oh, I was just thinking that I haven't seen my little angel in over a week and I..."

Suddenly it clicked in her mind. Those eyes... Those sea green eyes... Could it be? Sarah took one look at her and said, "You alright?"

Susan decided not to say anything about the thought that just crossed her mind.

"Oh yeah, just worried about Ashton and Andrew, and missing my little Jessica."

That night, Susan had that dream again. Jessica was telling her that someday she would be her real grandma. She sat bolt upright in bed, confused but pleased. If only it were true, she thought, and then quickly fell back to sleep.

And for the Martins, life was a mess. The store had not sold and now it really was time for escrow to close. The woman staying in the condo gladly would have extended it; that construction on her new home was still not finished, but her brother told her no. He wanted the damned thing sold and to be done with it.

He told his sister to move into a hotel or with him—he was another wealthy person who had a big oceanfront house on the beach—while she waited for her own house to be done. He was even willing to give the Martins back their deposit, as one of their family friends wanted to buy the condo; cash with a five day closing.

Reluctantly, the woman agreed, moving in with her brother. They gave the Martins back their deposit, for which Bob was grateful; they could have lost it. Marian would have to kiss her new kitchen goodbye now. She cried a little when she heard, but it was more important that she and Bob had each other. They could always find another home later on, after the store sold, even if they had to stay in the Shore Road apartment a little longer.

Craig was secretly glad, because his continued work as manager would ensure that Bradley could stay in that special school. He was so close to saying his first word now, they didn't want to take that away from him. In fact, Bob had just given him a raise. Though Bob and Marian spent as little time in the store now as possible they still did not want to be absentee owners. Craig was taking on more and more responsibility, so Bob thought it only fitting he have more money.

Bob decided to surprise Marian with a weekend away near Bear Mountain, where they had their first date so many years ago. He wanted to get his wife out of the funk she was in. Losing the condo hit her hard as was the fact that they rarely saw Ashton anymore. Her Sunday visits had dwindled to once every few weeks and they were short—Ashton staying only long enough to eat and exchange some polite banter.

They did notice that she had abandoned her jeans and tee shirts in favor of designer clothing. They said nothing, afraid to scare her off; after all, that year she was gone was the worst one of their lives and they never wanted to lose her in that way again.

Besides, she was working at the Desmond Corporation over a year now; she must be doing pretty well for herself. Ashton was sad that they lost the condo; she knew how much that kitchen meant to her mother. She was so tempted to ask Andrew if they could move into the Palm Beach house but they didn't even know she was dating. She still never told them. The Martins thought their daughter went home to that apartment on York Avenue alone each night, the one they'd never seen.

JESSICA SQUEALED WITH DELIGHT as she rode a horse for the first time, her father at her side as the horse took slow, deliberate steps. She begged her father for lessons and Bill agreed. The instructor was amazed at the way Jessica bonded with the animal; as she petted him and spoke he seemed to understand her.

"Your daughter seems to have a way with animals," the instructor told Bill. "I've never seen that horse act that way around anyone; it's as if they're talking to each other."

"Yes, my little girl is amazing in lots of ways," Bill responded, but didn't go into detail into exactly how she was so amazing. Jessica had been good for quite awhile, using her "filters" as her mother and he taught her to do.

When they got home Sarah told Bill all about Andrew and Ashton.

"Poor girl, I hope it works out for her. I've only met your ex once or twice at some business symposiums. Didn't seem like marriage material to me. It's amazing you lasted three years with him."

Sarah turned to notice Jessica ran to her room and slammed the door. Running after her, she was surprised at her mood change- she was so happy just a few minutes earlier when she was talking about riding a horse for the first time and that Daddy said she could have riding lessons. But now she was in her room, sitting on the bed, and obviously upset. She wouldn't tell her mother why. But Sarah would find out soon enough.

"Is she okay?" Bill asked. "She was so excited on the ride home. All she could talk about was the horse she rode, Oscar was his name. And now she looks angry."

Sarah didn't know what to say. She noticed that same behavior two weeks ago when they met Susan for lunch and she was telling them about her son getting married. In fact, that was the only time she saw Jessica act that way.

Susan sat in the living room, sipping on the tea Robert brought her and trying to shut out the noise Harold was making.

He was "riding" around the house on a broom singing *I am Mister Ed* at the top of his lungs. The staff learned to ignore him; the maids walked right past him now, no longer addressing him at all. The only one to pay him any mind was Robert, who was his constant companion.

Susan's thoughts kept going back to Ashton. She felt camaraderie with her almost instantly. She would really like her for a daughter-in-law. They had spoken on the phone now several times, although Andrew had no knowledge of it. She noticed Ashton shied away from any questions about the wedding so she quickly stopped asking about it; no sense upsetting her. They would get married when they wanted and the way they wanted. Susan had the feeling they would elope; just as well, as she knew she and Harold would not be guests at their wedding.

She decided this noise was just too much and headed out for the little Cape Cod and her garden. Harold followed behind her asking, "Can I come with you, Mommy?"

"Good Lord," she thought, "now he thinks I'm his mother."

Harold's parents had been gone for many years now as had her own. Neither set of parents had much; both she and Harold grew up knowing hard times. But they were likeable people; grateful for the little they did have. If they were looking down from Heaven they would be amazed at the life Harold had built for his family. *And you know what, they could have it, too,* Susan thought as she said to Harold, "If you're good and listen to Robert I'll bring you back something really nice."

Susan slipped out the door as Harold told Robert, "I'll be a good boy."

As she steered her car down the winding drive, Susan wondered how much longer Harold would live. This was getting old and wearing on her now; having to be cooped up day after day in this gold plated prison with this lunatic husband of hers.

She knew he would be better off passing away. At least on the other side he would be whole again, and not this shadow of his former self. And she would be free. Free to work with children again when they opened that daycare, and to be with her best friend.

For a moment she thought that it would be nice to have Ashton work with them as well, but then Andrew would never allow that. Susan was sure he'd insist she quit working when they married; she actually was surprised that she was still employed with the company; but then again, she had no idea of what Ashton really did for him. Andrew would never let that go.

23

The Tucson deal finally closed, giving the Desmond Corporation the technology Andrew desperately wanted and increasing the company's worth substantially. He was surprised actually that Martell pulled it off; but mergers and acquisitions was his specialty. And the fact that he "clicked" so well with the board of directors of the company they'd just acquired only made it easier; Andrew found the CEO to be irritating. But Martell almost "romanced" him; taking him to his country club for golf and boating off Newport. Andrew didn't want any part of that. But it was done now.

The closed deal inflated Martell's head even more and gave him a shot of confidence to take his boldness further. Although Ashton stopped informing Andrew every time Martell tried to put the "moves" on her, he caught him coming out of her office too many times now. Saying nothing to him or to her while they were in the office, he asked her about it as they ate dinner one night.

"What's going on with Martell, Ashton? I've seen him going in and out of your office at least a dozen times in the past few weeks, and I've heard from Frank Delgado that he's running his mouth again about taking over. But I've heard nothing from you."

Ashton took one look at him and knew he deserved the truth about Martell. He was dangerous. He was hitting on her; well, more than just that, he was being downright disgusting; telling her in intimate detail what he'd like to do to her and rallying the board to have them replace Andrew with him.

"Please, Andrew, just fire him. Let him go work somewhere else. I'm sure another company would snap him right up after that Tucson deal. He might even make chairman somewhere."

Andrew looked at her, his eyes going blank for awhile while he envisioned a brick wall encircling his brain. That seemed to keep her out as he said "If it means that much to you, I'll fire him. It won't be easy; I'll have to get the consensus of the board but I'll do it."

She leaned over and kissed him. "I love you," she told him.

"And I love you," he said in return, the image of the wall planted firmly in his mind.

It didn't take much to get rid of Martell. The whole board of directors was sick of him anyway. Ashton wasn't the only woman he was hitting on; although she would have been the crown jewel. Martell was hitting on assistants and almost anything in a skirt; it disgusted Frank Delgado especially, who asked him why he didn't find a nice woman and settle down.

"Fucking cunts! I don't want to marry them; I just want to get my rocks off. You understand, don't you, Frank. Don't you ever step out on your old lady?"

"No, I don't," Frank said. "I respect women and I love my wife." Frank walked away, disgusted by this pathetic excuse for a man.

"Stupid spic," Martell muttered under his breath, as he walked away in the opposite direction.

Andrew had not lied. He did have Martell fired, as he promised Ashton he would. But he never said that would be the end of it. No, Andrew was a man enraged. Martell tried to take away the woman he loved; or at least soil her with his filth. And he tried to snatch away the company his father built with his own two hands. No, it was too much for the vengeful Andrew. Although loving Ashton had softened him in some ways, it had little effect on others. That night, Andrew had a little conversation with his old buddy, Mark Peters.

Five days later Martell was found dead in an alley of multiple stab wounds. The press said a hooker killed him when he tried to stiff her after some quick sex in the back of his car. Maria Lansing, twenty-three; a low class prostitute who trolled for "business" from the drivers who stopped for the red light on the corner of Eighth Avenue and Forty-seventh Street. Despite protesting her innocence, Lansing was arrested and was awaiting trial at Rikers Island, unable to post bond.

Ashton gasped as she read the headline of the daily newspaper. Martell had been gone less than a month. But it was a known fact that Martell often solicited the services of "escorts" Like Andrew before he met Ashton, Martel had a voracious sexual appetite.

Ashton looked over at Andrew, her sea green eyes meeting his piercing gray ones.

"I had nothing to do with it. You knew how Martell was. He wanted to fuck anything that moved, and he wasn't exactly charming, either." And then he thought, Wall, don't fail me now.

Ashton had to agree. She knew about Martell and hookers, the whole company did. He was married once but it didn't last; and he was so offensive in so many other ways he just couldn't keep a steady girlfriend, though he was fairly good looking.

"Yeah, I guess he just pissed off the wrong person this time," Ashton responded, thinking the person Martell pissed off was a scared little prostitute sitting on a hard bench in Rikers and not the man she loved.

They said nothing more about it as they gathered their things and made their way to the office.

At lunch, Ashton had lunch with Denise where the subject of conversation was Steve Martell. His position was filled quickly by a middle aged woman who had been with the company for nearly ten years. Silvia Manning was married, one girl in college, with an apartment down the street from the Dakota. Ashton was pleased with the selection. Silvia was smart and well spoken She had come highly recommended by Frank Delgado. She was very much like him. The reign of Steve Martell was over, and every female in the company breathed a sigh of relief when Manning was named his successor.

"It's a nice change," Denise said. "That prick is finally gone. And I mean really gone. But I feel sorry for that girl, though. What a life, giving blow jobs in the back seats of cars." Ashton nodded; it was sad. And then Denise said it, "When are you getting married? You're never at your apartment anymore; all your stuff is at the Plaza. Have you even told your mother yet?"

"No."

"You know, Ashton, it's not such a bad thing, being engaged to an outrageously handsome billionaire. I think your parents would be happy. You're set Ashton; you're set for life now."

Ashton didn't want to tell Denise the reason she had not set a wedding date. And as far as her parents went, well, she was just never comfortable saying anything to them, although at some point she knew she had to.

Besides, there was something else bothering her now. As the weeks passed, she started to doubt Andrew's story about Steve Martell. She was starting to believe that it wasn't Maria Lansing who dealt his death blows, but Mark Peters. She very rarely saw him around the office when crews were there making repairs of some kind. She heard that his attendance at work as part of a maintenance crew was spotty at best; he was often late and hung over, his immediate boss Stephen Daniels, though, gave up on firing him. Andrew always blocked that move.

Daniels couldn't understand why; Peters was sloppy, nasty, unreliable and very often stewed to the gills even at work. But Daniels didn't want to challenge his powerful boss, after all, he and is crews were well compensated for the work they did. He and his men had mortgages and school tuitions to think about, and he didn't want to screw that up.

"Okay, Ashton, you look far away now. I'm sorry; it's none of my business when you get married. You know, I kind of get the feeling sometimes that you are already married."

Ashton turned bright red. "What, are you kidding me? No, I'm not married. I'm just taking my time about it all, that's all."

Denise could see she was upset; she didn't want to pry any further. She actually had gotten used to life without her friend; Ashton was never at her apartment anymore and all her clothes were gone. And it was common place for her to see Ashton and Andrew getting out of the limo together in the morning. Surprisingly though, there had been no press about it. It seems that when Andrew stopped fucking every woman in town the press lost interest in him; he had become boring to them. The only time they seemed to be around was when Andrew was preening like a peacock at one of his company's takeover. That, they liked. People losing their jobs and their livelihoods made good press, especially when they gathered en masse to protest against the Desmond Corporation and its CEO.

Ashton brushed past Doris in the hallway and slammed her office door.

"What was that about?" she thought. Ashton always stopped to chat when she came back from lunch, asking her about her son and how he was doing. But not today. Hearing the door slam Andrew came out of his office and knocked on her door; she didn't answer it.

"Open the door, Ashton…now!" he bellowed.

The whole floor turned their attention towards him; most probably thought it was a lover's quarrel. Reluctantly, Ashton opened the door; she didn't want to make a scene.

"What's wrong?" Andrew asked her. Not wanting to get into it she said Denise asked her when they were getting married.

"What did you tell her?"

"I told her I wanted a very long engagement."

"I don't know why that would upset you so much. She's your friend and that's a perfectly reasonable question. You knew this would happen. We talked about it. I let you make the decision about the way this went down."

"Are you sorry?"

"No, Ashton, I'm not sorry. But we both knew there would be questions and now we'll have to deal with it…together."

"Okay," she said, faking a smile. "You're right. I'm okay now. I have to expect these kinds of questions; after all, Denise and I are good friends."

She just wanted him out of his office. She wasn't upset with Denise or her questions about a wedding date. She was upset because she thought she was living with a killer.

THE DOCTOR WAS AT THE GREAT HOUSE for the third time this week. Harold was taking a turn for the worse; his heart was giving out. His pacemaker was almost continually shocking him; bringing his damaged heart back to life. But how long it would work, no one knew. His cardiologist told Susan that it probably would not be too long before his heart would win its battle with the device and win.

The great house was quiet. Without Harold running around pretending to be Superman or looking for Miss Cathy's magic mirror, it was almost like a tomb. Robert was relived; he could now sit in the kitchen and enjoy his cup of coffee without being interrupted every five minutes by Harold wanting to play some silly game. At least he seemed to have abandoned the Cowboys and Indian one that made him retrieve weapons from the gun cabinet. Harold seemed to forget that it even existed now. Just as well.

Although Susan was saddened by his distress, it freed her to spend more time in Massapequa. So much so, that she and Peggy purchased a building just constructed in the heart of the little town. It was almost completely finished; the original owners ran out of money and decided to chuck it all and move to Oregon. That would not be a problem for Susan. She would have the building finished and fitted out for a daycare. As she and Peggy stood outside, watching the construction process, Peggy turned to Susan.

"How would you like to call it Rising Star Learning Center?" she asked her. Of course, since Susan was paying for all of it she would have the final say —or so Peggy though— but Susan loved the idea.

"I love it. It's perfect."

When she and Sarah met for their next charity function, Susan told her the good news. Sarah even wanted to volunteer; it would be a combination daycare, preschool and have after school programs for the "bigger kids" It would be a perfect place for Jessica to go; maybe with her mother and "Grandma Susan" there this school would be a better experience for her. Jessica was elated; she loved to be with other children and to be in a place where both her mother and "Grandma Susan" would be made her very happy.

She liked that nice lady, Peggy; she had met once or twice as well. Jessica couldn't wait to get home and tell her father all about the new school she would be going to. Then Sarah asked about Ashton and Andrew.

"Heard anything more about a wedding date?"

"I've spoken to her several times; she really is a joy, you know. I think she might like working with children too."

"Andrew's not going to allow that. Is she still working at the company?"

"Yes, and that surprises me. But I think Ashton likes to work. We'll see what happens when they get married, whenever that will be, because she hasn't told me a thing."

And there it was again… Jessica, who just a moment ago was so happy at the prospect of going to a new school, now was becoming sullen and withdrawn.

"Honey, what's the matter?" Sarah asked her daughter.

"She's not safe with him," Jessica said.

"Who are you talking about Jessica? Jessica, answer me!"

But Jessica did not answer. She was merely following her mother's advice to "use her filters."

In fact, Jessica was silent the whole way home. When she walked in the door she did not tell her father about the brand new school. Instead, refusing her dinner, she went straight to her room and stayed there for the rest of the night.

"You know it's strange," Sarah told Bill as they drank their coffee in the dining room, "but it seems to me that every time either my ex-husband or his fiancé are mentioned, Jessica's whole mood changes. And she said something really weird today, Bill. I could have sworn I heard her say 'she's not safe with him' whatever that means. That's if I even heard her right."

"Oh come on honey! Jessica doesn't even know them, how could she know that Ashton, is that her name, isn't safe?"

"She knew her teacher was a stripper, honey. What about that? And anyway, look at the way she is. She just knows things. We already have absolute proof of that."

"I don't know, Sarah. I don't know what to say."

And in her room, Jessica sat upright in bed, stiff as a board. It was if she was in another world.

Finally, the little girl grew tired and sleep claimed her. Sarah watched her sleep, wishing she could unlock the secrets in her daughter's mind.

Later that night Sarah called Susan to find out how Harold was doing.

"Not well," Susan said. "I'm afraid that he's reaching the end. But whatever waits for him on the other side has got to be better than the life he has now."

Then Susan asked how Jessica was doing. Sarah told her about her silence and her refusal to eat dinner.
"Poor kid," Susan said. "It must be tough on her."

But Susan was starting to put two and two together now. Still, she didn't want to say anything to Sarah, at least not yet. Why stir the pot even more?

But there was no denying those eyes. Though Sarah had never met Ashton and could not know, the resemblance between Ashton and Jessica was striking.

ANDREW WAS WORRIED. He couldn't keep his mental "wall" up all the time. It was easier when they first met; their time together was limited. If he had something to hide from her, he could keep the mental block going, at least for awhile. Now that they were living together, it was becoming more difficult.

Which is why he sat at his desk now, regretting last night. Too many scotches; then he got drunk. Ashton, still sullen from the other day when she came back from lunch with Denise, became distant. She sat with her dinner in front of her untouched. Her favorite, lasagna. And yet she sat there openly sighing with a look on her face a million miles away. Andrew, now quite drunk, could take no more of it.

"What do you want from me," he asked her, slamming down his glass on the dining room table.

"I want the truth, Andrew. I want to know if you had anything to do with Steve Martell's death."

"Yes," he screamed at her at the top of his lungs. "Yes, okay, I couldn't let it go. None of it. The thought of his filthy hands touching you; the thought of him sitting in my chair. He had to pay for what he did!"

"With his life? Andrew, he never touched me. I didn't want him, I want you. And he was already gone. Out of the company. The board didn't want him. They were happy to get rid of him. It was fine, Andrew. But you couldn't let it rest, could you? The great Andrew Desmond was wronged. You just couldn't let it go!"

Ashton bolted from the table and ran into the bedroom, slamming the door. She flung herself on the huge, custom made bed and sobbed uncontrollably. She was living with a monster. And she had a big part in the way it turned out. If only she had kept her mouth shut about Martell, he might still be alive. Was she so stupid that she could think her love would change Andrew? That somehow he'd turn into this little teddy bear, wanting only to make nice with everyone he met? He turned on his own mother, for God's sake. She thought of Susan, so kind, and welcoming her with open arms. And even his father; Jesus, the man wasn't in his right mind, Andrew knew that. He should have let him talk about who he expected Andrew to marry. He would have forgotten all about what he said by the next morning. But no, Andrew Desmond had to have the last word.

Andrew slept in one of the guest bedrooms that night. He knew she wanted no part of him. But she would get over it. He'd call Tiffany's in the morning and order the biggest pair of diamond earrings they had. Maybe that would help her put it behind her.

Martell was gone, it was true. That Manning woman was a good choice to replace him; Frank Delgado had a good eye for people. Andrew thought that if anyone would ever replace him, it should be Frank. But Frank Delgado was too fine a gentleman to ever try to "capture" the job. He would never act the way Martell did.

As he sat in the dark, Andrew almost regretted having Steve Martell killed. He was no longer a threat. The way was clear for Andrew to garner more power once Martell turned in his key to the executive washroom. And he thought to himself that Ashton was right; that he should have let it go.

The next morning a package arrived, hand delivered from Tiffany's. The earrings in it cost nearly $750,000. Ashton opened it, smiled politely, said thank you and then putting the box down

326

grabbed her purse and headed out for a walk down Fifth Avenue. She left Andrew standing there, stunned.

Andrew thought reasoned that she was truly like his mother. All these material things were fine, they were nice, but Ashton could do without them. All she really wanted was a loving husband and a family of her own. And it was funny because as she walked down towards Thirty-fourth Street., Ashton was thinking the exact same thing—all she wanted was a loving husband and a family; but, she added "a loving husband who was not a murderer" to her equation. As the days passed, Andrew could see that Ashton was not going to get past this, even if he bought her all the jewelry inside Tiffany's.

24

Harold's condition continued to deteriorate. But at least he could die at home, in this house that meant so much to him; it showed the world that Harold Desmond had conquered it. Robert had little to do now since Harold couldn't even get out of bed, much less play games.

There were twenty-four hour nurses attending him now, and Dr Riley (Harold's cardiologist) came to the house almost every day. He told Susan that Harold wouldn't even last a month.

Thinking the news would cause Andrew to see his father one last time Susan called him. He did not answer her, nor did he return her voice mail message. Finally, she called Ashton.

"I tried to call Andrew but he doesn't return my calls. His father is dying, Ashton."

Ashton was appalled at the very idea of Andrew not wanting to see his father at least one more time before he died. She had never told him that she was in touch with his mother but this was the last straw.

"Your mother called you about your father. Aren't you going to see him before he dies, Andrew?"

"How the hell do you know that, I never told you she called?" And then he stopped for a moment and turned to her.

"You've been talking to her, haven't you? God damn you Ashton, what gives you the right? She's my mother, not yours. I haven't even met *your* mother!"

"Yes, I've been talking to her, I really like her. Andrew your father is dying. Make peace with him before he goes. You'll regret it if you don't"

"I don't regret anything! My father can go back to the hell he came from. I'm not going back to that house, and my mother can rot right along with him!"

As he brushed past her he noticed the earrings still sitting on the hall table. Picking them up he threw them across the marble floor and then he turned to Ashton.

"You are just like my mother! You don't appreciate anything. Jesus, I spent nearly a million bucks on those!"

Now it was Andrew who slammed the bedroom door behind him. He sat on the bed, thinking about his father.

"Rot in hell you selfish bastard," he thought, as he heard the front door slam.

Sarah thought that a trip to the new "family fun center" that opened not too far from their home would cheer Jessica up. Her mood had improved only slightly over the past few weeks. She still was acting strangely, even refusing to go to her horseback riding lessons and see her horsey friend, Oscar.

Susan was waiting for them. Although she spent time a good deal of time now with Harold he hardly recognized her anymore, and was getting weaker by the minute. When Robert brought up his dinner tray, though, Harold grabbed his hand.

"Thank you," he told him, "for all you've done for me, all these years, thank you."

Robert bent down and kissed his forehead; the old man smiled. Susan was glad she could see that; for a moment, Harold remembered and was grateful.

Susan was happy though, to be out of the house and to see her little Jessica. The little girl ran to her and hugged her. They sat at a table away from the crowd and had pizza and soda. They talked about the new school and about Jessica and her horseback riding lessons. When Sarah told Susan that she hadn't gone lately, Susan told Jessica that her horse was going to miss her. Jessica smiled.

Then the conversation turned to Harold. Sarah was sorry and asked if there was anything she or Bill could do.

"No, I'm just sad that Andrew never called me. I actually called Ashton and…"

"He's going to hurt my mommy, you have to help her! Please help my mommy!" Jessica began pleading with Susan, leaping off her chair and flailing her arms.

Startled, Susan then slowly knelt before the child, about to ask her a question that, deep down; she already knew the answer to.

"Jessica, who is your mommy?" Susan asked her slowly, looking right into those big, sea green eyes. There was no answer

"Jessica, please honey, tell me who your mommy is!"

Jessica looked up at Sarah, as if to ask her permission.

"Tell her!" Sarah ordered.

"Ashton. Ashton is my real mommy and Andrew's going to kill her. You don't have much time, please hurry!"

Sarah collapsed in her chair, white as a ghost. Now she knew who the mother of her child was, and she was in danger. There was no denying it. The woman had to be in real trouble if Jessica said so. Jessica was never wrong.

"Jessica, tell me what you see," Susan told her, encouraging her to open up about the "pictures" she saw in her mind.

"I see a hallway and the floor is all white and black and shiny. They are high up, in a big old building that starts with the letter 'P.' There are big windows where you can see the park."

"The Plaza," Susan thought to herself. It had to be the Plaza.

"Can you tell me what time this will happen? Is it today?"

"Today," Jessica responded, as she grabbed Susan's arm to look at her watch. The little girl then held up six fingers; opening her hand up on one and holding up her index finger on the other.

Six o'clock, Susan thought. *It's three o'clock now.* "Why is Andrew going to hurt your mommy?"

"Because my mommy wants to tell the police that Andrew is bad."

Susan was confused. Why would Ashton want to tell the police that Andrew didn't want to see his father before he died?

Jessica read her thoughts. Sarah just sat staring, in total disbelief, mouth hanging open.

"She wants to tell the policeman that Andrew killed a man. He has his hands around my mommy's neck. She'll die if you don't help her."

Susan stood up and turned to Sarah.

"Take Jessica home and don't say anything to anybody," she told her. "Not even Bill. No one."

"What are you going to do?"

"I'm going to Andrew's place."

"What if he won't let you in?"

"I have a key, he gave me one years ago, and somehow I don't think he's ever changed the locks."

"It could be dangerous, you should call the police."

"And tell them what? That this little girl told me there was going to be a murder in three hours? No, I'm going alone."

"He could hurt you as well as Ashton."

"I'll bring a pistol. If you remember, I used to be a crack shot when Harold and I used to go to the shooting range to practice. Now go!"

Sarah took Jessica's hand and led her to their car, but not before hugging Susan.

"Be careful," Sarah told her.

"I'll be fine and so will your mommy," Susan told Jessica.

Sarah and Jessica drove home slowly. Jessica turned to her and said, "I still love you even though you're not my real mommy. I still want to stay with you forever."

Sarah stopped the car and hugged her, tightly, tears cascading down her face. In the meantime, Susan sped towards the great house, being careful not to go too fast. She wouldn't want to get pulled over. She looked at her watch as she pulled up to the door. It was a little after four. She'd better hurry if she wanted to beat traffic into the city.

She hurried past Robert and opened the desk drawer. Pulling a key ring out, she used one of the keys to open the gun cabinet and reached for the .38 caliber. Using another key to unlock a second drawer, she pulled out the bullets and loaded it. Safety on, she shoved it into her purse. She looked right into Robert's eyes as he stood not far from her; he was the only one around; all the others were with Harold upstairs.

He nodded at her; he seemed to understand; she nodded back and then raced past him back to her car. She looked at her watch—four thirty.

Traffic on the LIE was unbearable; it was rush hour. Her only saving grace was that more people were leaving the city for the night and she was going into it. Finally, at five fifty, she pulled up to the front entrance to the Plaza. Now her only concern was the front desk. It was so long since she'd been to Andrew's condo that she was afraid no one would know who she was; then they certainly wouldn't allow her in the private elevator. His key was no problem; she had carried it on her own key ring all these years. It was her way of keeping Andrew close to her.

And up in the penthouse, it was playing out just as Jessica said it would. Ashton was screaming at Andrew; she was going to the police; Martell was dead and Andrew ordered his murder. If only she hadn't given him all that information about him, maybe Martell would still be alive, working somewhere else. She couldn't live with a man who had such callous disregard for life. As she

334

reached for her phone, Andrew knocked it out of her hand. He slapped her, hard, and then his hands went for her throat.

"You stupid bitch! You think I'm going to throw all this away! Not even for you, my love!"

His grip tightened. Ashton realized she shouldn't have challenged him on a night Donald and Hilda had off. Now there was no one to help her; the walls of the old building were too thick for anyone to hear her cries.

In the meantime, Susan rushed up to the front desk and prayed. Her prayers were answered. Standing in front of her was Paul Myers. He worked for the Plaza for almost thirty years now.

"Mrs. Desmond, good evening, it's so good to see you ma'am. Are you going to see Andrew? Shall I buzz him?"

"No thank you, Paul. I'm going to surprise him."

The doors of the private elevator opened, and Susan stepped in, clutching her purse tightly in front of her. And back in the penthouse whatever Andrew was saying was becoming a blur now to Ashton, as she began to go in and out of consciousness. *Dear God please let this key work,* Susan thought as she fumbled at the lock. It opened. In the hallway, Andrew had his hands around Ashton's neck. There was no stopping him now. He didn't even hear his mother come in.

"Stop Andrew, you're killing her!" Susan yelled.

Andrew turned his head, his hands still firmly affixed around Ashton's neck.

"Mother," he said coldly, "join the party; you're next, and then I'll be rid of the both of you!"

Her hand closed around the gun, taking the safety off. "Stop it, Andrew!" She pointed the gun at him; he laughed.

"Go fuck yourself," he told her, his hands never leaving Ashton's neck. She fired, winging him.

"Please stop, Andrew," she was begging him now.

The bullet did not stop him nor did her cries. He tightened his grip even further. Raising the gun, and steadying her hand so as not to injure Ashton, she fired again. The bullet found its mark. Andrew slumped to the floor. Ashton was free; shaking her head and coughing, she then grabbed the phone which slid across the floor when Andrew knocked it out of her hand.

Susan knelt by her dying son as Ashton dialed 911. Andrew's eyes softened as he gazed at his mother.

"I'm sorry, Mommy," he said, as he raised his hand to touch her face. She kissed it tenderly. After making the call, Ashton ran to him and knelt by his side.

"I'll love you always, my darling wife," he said softly.

Andrew Desmond then closed his eyes for the last time, bleeding out on his expensive black and white Italian marble floor. And before the world even knew she was married, Ashton Lancaster had become a widow.

THE REST OF IT WAS A BLUR. The ambulance came and pronounced Andrew dead. The police followed, but there was no arrest to be made. One look at Ashton's neck, with Andrew's hand marks around it clearly visible now, told the story. She refused medical treatment, though she was badly shaken up. But Susan knew she had to be the rock in all of this. She knew she had to be strong for Ashton. Funny, but she had a strange feeling that she and Andrew were already married, and now it was true. It was just like her dream; Jessica really was her granddaughter.

The police would still want to question them further; they would be out to Susan's house in a few days. Susan Desmond was a fine, upstanding citizen, had no history of any trouble with the police, and was certainly not a flight risk so there was no reason to detain her tonight. After they left Susan turned to Ashton and told her to pack a suitcase.

"You're coming home with me. I don't want you to be alone, especially if you're thinking about staying here tonight."

"But what about my parents? Surely this is going to be front page news." Ashton should have told them; she could only imagine the horror they would feel when they found out.

"Do they know you're married?"

"They didn't even know I was dating anyone."

"I'll call them in the morning and they can come over, we'll talk to them together.

Donald and Hilda were just coming back from their night off. Susan told them to go back to their families. Neither of them seemed surprised by what had transpired in the apartment; they knew Andrew had a volatile temper. Susan told them they would receive their full salaries until Ashton decided if she wanted to return to the condo. Secretly, she hoped Ashton would decide not to live in the apartment but instead move somewhere else. Maybe Susan could find her a house not far from the little Cape Cod.

As Ashton packed, Susan called Robert and asked him to come into the city to pick them up. It was late now, and traffic was light. It wouldn't take Robert long to get into the city. Less than forty-five minutes later he was waiting downstairs for them; he would make arrangements for someone to get Susan's car tomorrow.

As they sat huddled together in the back seat on the drive home Ashton looked at Susan and asked her, "How did you know? If it wasn't for you I probably would be dead, I don't think he would have stopped choking me."

"Somebody told me to come rescue you."

"Who?"

"Well, her name is Jessica, and she's almost five years old now, and she has the prettiest auburn hair and sea green eyes—just like you."

Ashton burst into tears, openly sobbing, cupping her head in her hands.

"Where is she? Is she alright?"

"Yes, Sarah and Bill adopted her when she was just a baby."

"Sarah, Andrew's ex-wife, Sarah? The one you told me about?"

"That's the one. Your daughter seems to have this unusual gift for reading people's minds and seeing the future, that's how I knew you were in trouble."

"She got it from me. That's how I met Andrew. He paid me to spy on his staff. I took the job to show my parents I could make it on my own. I never meant to hurt anyone. But as time went on, something happened. Andrew and I fell in love. Since I lied to my parents about what I was doing at the company and how much I was really making, I just never felt right telling them about Andrew and me."

"But you didn't know anything about Jessica, having this same gift?"

"I think I must have blocked it out. It was painful for me to give her up. My parents never knew about her, either. But thank

338

God Sarah has her. I know she'll have a good life; they can give her every opportunity, they have the means and from what you've told me about them, they must be wonderful parents.

"You're not so poor now yourself, Ashton," Susan said, hugging her tightly.

As the limo made its way to the north shore that fact hit Ashton right between the eyes... It was all hers now. The one thing Andrew insisted on was that his will be changed to leave her everything. She balked at that, saying that he should leave his mother in his will but Andrew just said, "Why? She already has all the money she needs and doesn't want anyway."

His lawyers were sworn to secrecy about the legal proceedings. He indulged Ashton's wish that no one know they were married, at least for now. In fact "at least for now," was something Andrew would hear Ashton say quite frequently over the last few months.

"Don't worry, Ashton, I'm here for you. We'll get through this together. Tomorrow first thing I will call your parents and invite them to the house. And then I will make one more phone call and invite a certain little girl to pay us a visit."

"What about the funeral? Please, can't we have something small? I don't think I can take all the publicity. No one even knew we were married..."

"Honey, that's up to you. We'll do whatever you want."

Inside, Susan felt like a piece of her had died. She killed her only son. Her Andrew. Her world. But she knew she had to do it. He would have killed Ashton and then turned on her had she not had that pistol in her hand. But inside, Susan felt like her whole life was coming apart at the seams.

When they got home Harold's cardiologist was there and gave Ashton something to help her sleep, after looking at her neck. Harold was already asleep for the night; the doctor was sure his time was very short. He thought of poor Susan. Her only son, dead by her own hand, and her husband soon to follow him in death. He sincerely hoped the next chapter of her life would be brighter and more hopeful.

Thankfully, the next morning, Susan's phone call came before the Martins had a chance to read the morning paper. Bob wrote down her address as Marian rushed to get dressed. When he was off the phone with Susan he called Craig to tell him they wouldn't be in at all today and to take care of anything that came up with the store. Craig just listened, he already heard it on the news, but he didn't say anything to Bob. At this point, it was better left unsaid.

Sarah and Bill heard it on the news as well. That's when Sarah told Bill all about it, honoring Susan's request to keep it to herself. Jessica came to the table all smiles; the child was positively glowing.

"Ashton's safe now, my mommy is safe," the little girl said happily.

"Andrew dead, killed by his own mother, and now Jessica is Ashton's child? You couldn't make this stuff up if you tried," Bill told her. "Of course, Jessica should meet her mother, don't you think? After all she knows who she is, and now, so do we."

"Yes, absolutely," Sarah said. "As soon as she wants to." Jessica was all smiles as she heard that.

Bob and Marian drove up the winding road leading to the great house. Marian had her mouth hanging open the whole time, amazed at the sheer size of it. Robert promptly opened the door for them and announced them to Susan, who rushed up to greet them. Ashton was sitting on the couch in the living room sipping a cup of coffee, regretting never telling her parents about any of it. And now, here they were, standing in the doorway of Susan Desmond's enormous living room.

"Ashton, are you all right?" Marian rushed to her daughter, grabbing her and hugging her tightly.

"Yeah Ma, I'm okay."

Robert brought in some coffee, while Ashton told her parents everything. All of it. All Marian could say was that if she was in love with Andrew she should have told them. She didn't need to keep it a secret. She was their daughter and they loved her, and they would support her in any decision she made.

They were grateful to Susan for saving Ashton's life. While they talked, Susan made two more phone calls; one to the funeral home; she stressed that she wanted something small for the immediate family only. She knew this was a task that Ashton didn't want to have to do. They didn't need a media circus. Then she made one more phone call—to Sarah.

It was only about an hour later when Sarah pulled her SUV under the porte-cochère. Robert opened the door and there they were: Sarah and her little daughter, Jessica.

Ashton stopped dead in her tracks. The little girl looked just like her. Bob and Marian sat with their mouths hanging open. Ashton bent down slowly and held her arms out. Jessica ran into her arms.

"Mommy, Mommy, you're all right. I knew you would be. I knew Grandma Susan would save you."

Ashton held the child tightly, tears streaming down her face. Bob and Marian looked at each other. It all made sense now; this is where she was that year she went away.

"I love you, I love you, Jessica. I'm so sorry baby that I couldn't keep you with me, and thank you for saving me."

"Oh Mommy, I love you too." Then Ashton looked at her sternly.

"Ashton, my name is Ashton, okay? That's what you'll call me. Sarah is your mommy, do you understand?"

Jessica read her thoughts. "Yes, Ashton, I understand." Then Ashton introduced Jessica to her grandparents. Marian held the little girl tightly in her arms. Bob was smiling; tears were welling up in his eyes.

After a short while, Sarah took Jessica home, but before she left she told Ashton "anytime you want to see her or take her somewhere its fine with us. We want her to get to know you; after all, you're her real mother.

"No, you're her real mother," Ashton said. "I'll just be her very good friend."

After they left Ashton turned to her parents again.

"I think you've probably figured out by now that I'm a very wealthy woman (they had but said nothing) There are two things I want to do, and I won't take 'no' for an answer. One, I want to buy the store for Craig, I want him to have it and two, I have a house right on the ocean in Palm Beach. I want you to have it. For all you've done for me this is the least I can do for you."

"But where will you go?" Bob asked her. Why not come with us, then?"

"No, I'm going to stay here. I'll sell the condo; I don't want to go back there. I'll figure it out. Right now, I have a funeral to go to. And then we have to answer some questions for the police."

Ashton was becoming a pillar of strength now, she had to be; she had the rest of her life to live, and Jessica would now be a part of it.

"We'll be with you at the service," Marian said. "Why don't you come home with us tonight? Your room is still waiting for you."

"No, Ma, I'm going to stay here with Susan. Her husband is ill upstairs and I don't want her to be alone. After all, she lost a son yesterday, and it won't be long until she's a widow as well. She needs me."

"She's a wonderful woman," Marian said. "And Jessica, oh my dear, she's so lovely."

"I'm sorry about that too. And about the ten grand I stole from you, Bob. I know you never told my mother; I appreciated that. I wanted to tell you when I found out I was pregnant, but I was so ashamed because I never amounted to anything. And I wanted to give my child a chance at a better life than the life I could give her. You'll see her a lot now, I'm sure of it. Andrew, I mean, I, have a private jet so we can fly down to Palm Beach to see you. I'm sure Sarah wouldn't mind, and she could come too, of course. From what I hear there's plenty of room for everyone."

As the day came to a close the Martins left. It was a strange day; horrible in some ways but rewarding in others. They got to meet their grandchild, the one they never knew they had. They got to meet Susan, the woman who saved their daughter's life. They were sad for the loss of her husband because it was clear Ashton loved him, but at the same time they were angry at Andrew for trying to hurt her.

They would be back in two days for Andrew's funeral. True to her word, Susan made sure it was short and sweet. There was some press around, but the security team she hired kept them at bay. There were few people there because few had been invited.

Ashton laid a single red rose on her husband's casket and kissed it; she was the last one to leave the gravesite. Afterwards, they had a small dinner at the great house.

Through all of this, Harold Desmond clung to life in his upstairs bedroom not knowing where he was or that his only son was dead. He didn't even recognize his own wife or Robert anymore. Susan thought that it was just as well; he would see Andrew again on the other side soon enough. Maybe fate was being kind to him. Soon fate would be kind to her as well when the day came that she would close the door of the great house and never look back.

Ashton stayed with her after the funeral; she started going to charity events with her and became good friends with Sarah. She saw Jessica on a regular basis and even took her to her parents for Sunday dinner. Denise and Allison were guests at the Martins as well, as was Susan.

Although Ashton had deeded the Palm Beach estate over to her parents they still stayed in the Shore Road apartment, not wanting to leave their daughter until she decided where she wanted to go. Ashton also was quick to write a check for the full asking price of the store and deed that to Craig. The man wept as he opened the envelope in his hand. The store was now his, free and clear. He wanted to somehow repay Ashton, but she didn't want his money.

"Consider it as pay back for all the times you covered my ass at the store for messing up," she told him.

It was almost two months later that Harold Desmond's heart finally gave out. His funeral was, as well, a small affair. Susan was relieved by his death; he was free now and so was she. It didn't take long before she put the great house on the market. She didn't want to stay there any longer.

"Okay, Ashton," she turned to her daughter-in-law, "what are we going to do with you? Your parents haven't gone to Palm Beach yet; they're waiting for you to decide where you want to live and what you want to do with your life. I'd love for you to come and work in the daycare; you seem to love children. I'd love for you to move near Peggy and me. But the truth is that you have to decide what's best for you. I know that I have decided to live modestly now; I never really cared for all that money and flash. But you have the means to live a very opulent life, and if that's what you want, you should do it. Travel the world; spend what you want to spend. It's not up to me to tell you how you should live. But you need to start living again. You're still young, you're beautiful and intelligent and you have a heart of gold. If you'd like, Peggy and I can get a bigger place and you can come live with us, we'd like to be near the daycare."

Ashton was touched at Susan's offer, but she knew living with Susan and Peggy was not the solution. She'd like to work at the daycare, volunteer actually; drawing a salary wasn't necessary. But living with the two women wouldn't be an option. Both Susan and Peggy were older, Peggy only recently retiring from the Nassau

County School system. Both were widows, but being older they were not interested in meeting someone new. But Ashton could have a fresh start and a family of her own. She needed her own place. She let the lease on the apartment Andrew rented for her when they first met run out; the cramped studio was just too small. She gave the expensive furniture in it to Denise; what Denise didn't want she donated to the Salvation Army. Ashton had made her decision. She called Sarah.

"Hey," Ashton asked her, "any houses on your block for sale?"

"I don't know but we can find out can't we?" Sarah teased.

The next day both women were at a local real estate office. Ashton wanted to be near Sarah because the two women had become good friends and because Ashton wanted to be near Jessica "What are you looking for," the real estate agent asked Ashton.

.Ashton looked at Sarah. It was as if she was afraid to say what she liked. For months now, she had been living with an ultra-wealthy woman who really didn't enjoy her wealth, instead preferring simpler things. And Sarah was the same. Sure, she had an expensive house and a live- in maid, but still, she wasn't over the top, either. And Ashton worried about sending the wrong message to Jessica. Sarah and Bill were teaching their daughter to appreciate the things she had the value of a dollar and that getting a good education would be the key to continued success in life, along with hard work. Ashton was pleased about that. She didn't want to appear too flashy and give Jessica the wrong impression.

But now it was Sarah who had become the mind reader.

"Ashton, tell the lady what you really want. Live the way you want to live, no one will fault you for that. We want you to be happy, Ashton."

And then Ashton said it.

"I want something contemporary, lots of glass, on the beach, three bedrooms and a pool. I don't want to spend more than seven million. All cash deal."

Sweating, she turned again to Sarah, who nodded her approval.

"See, was that so hard? That sounds great, Ashton."

Ashton moved into her new home five weeks later; a brand new construction right on the South Shore only a few miles from Sarah. Right after that, Susan moved into the little Cape Cod with Peggy and Sheena. And finally, Bob and Marian said goodbye to the apartment on Shore Rd. and headed for Palm Beach.

The kitchen in the estate put the one in the condo that Marian wanted so much to shame. As she walked around it her mouth hung open.

Bob teased her, "So are you going to make dinner now?"

Marian looked at him and then turned to Rita, the housekeeper.

"Can you make rigatoni and meatballs?" Marian asked her.

"Yes, ma'am, I can. Would you like that for dinner tonight?"

"Yes, Rita, we'll have that for dinner tonight, thank you."

Turning to Bob she said, "Cooking is overrated anyway."

As they sprawled in their poolside lounge chairs enjoying their evening cocktail and watching the waves crash against the shore, Bob took Marian's hand. "I'm glad we got this place," he joked, "it has an extra bedroom for Ashton just like we planned."

"This place has lots of extra bedrooms for Ashton," she replied, smiling back at him. It was almost a month before Marian even lifted a pot in her new kitchen. And she didn't even care.

25

Mark Peters disappeared the day after Andrew Desmond died. He knew his boss, Stephen Daniels, would have him fired now anyway; he was always a lousy worker, and he was also fairly sure that whoever the new CEO would be at the Desmond Corporation that he wouldn't require Peters' "special services."

An APB was put out as a result of Ashton's testimony surrounding the events of the night her husband died; Maria Lansing was released and cleared of all charges. She gave up her life of prostitution and moved back with her parents just outside of

Trenton, New Jersey. Spending all that time in Rikers made her see that it was time to make a big change in the way she way living.

Peters was holed up in a sleazy motel in upstate New York. He knew he was cornered; the police would track him down sooner or later. Cooped up in the dark, dirty room he began to drink heavily. When he shut his eyes he thought he could see old Phyllis Sullivan coming towards him, anger burning in her tired, old eyes. He became convinced she was coming to kill him but he beat her to it, hanging himself from the overhead light. He was dead for three days before the police found him. He had no next of kin; no one claimed his body which was then unceremoniously cremated.

A month after Andrew died Frank Delgado was named the new CEO of the Desmond Corporation. As he moved into Andrew's old office, he passed a pensive Doris. Pausing, he asked her, "Do you know how to make Cuban coffee?"

"Yes, I do," Doris replied, puzzled.

"Good, I like a cup when I get here, make yourself a cup too, I never drink alone," he joked.

Doris was thrilled; she was sure Frank would have brought his own assistant with him and she would either be terminated or placed in another office. The assistant of the chairman was the highest paid job of that kind in the company, and she needed the extra money it brought for her son's medical bills. And working for Frank was like a dream come true. He shook her hand warmly; adding that any time she needed off to care for her son Jeff was fine with him. So unlike Andrew, she thought, who didn't even know her son's name.

Denise decided to stay with the company; she too, liked Frank Delgado. It was as if the windows were opened and a lovely spring breeze wafted in. There would be no theatrics; no grand standing. There would be no more screaming and yelling; no more icy stares from those piercing gray eyes. Frank was always polite and smiling when she was called to his office, and he always offered her a cup of coffee, which he drank out of a mug from the dollar store. And the fact that she was now dating a handsome patent attorney made her decision to stay in New York a lot easier.

Allison was expecting her second child, another girl, who they would name Chloe Roxanne, Roxanne being the name of Kevin's late grandmother. Melissa always enjoyed the ride out to Ashton's house to play by the pool or with her bucket at the private beach which was just steps from Ashton's door. And she loved to follow Jessica around the house when she was there, looking up to her like a big sister.

Before she left the great house for the last time, Susan gave each staff member six month's severance pay and sterling recommendations. All of them found work within a few weeks, except for Robert. In the envelope Susan gave him there was no six months' severance pay. Instead, there was a check for two million dollars. Robert retired and moved just north of Atlantic City, where he bought a small house and went fishing every day. Now, when he went into the water it was to enjoy a swim, and not chasing after a senile old man trying to find Flipper.

The great house was sold for an undisclosed amount of money to a couple from London who bought it fully furnished. They brought their own staff over with them. Susan heard the wife got along famously with Marge Solis, until she showed up at some party wearing a more expensive pair of shoes than Marge was. That seemed to cool their friendship off considerably.

RISING STAR DAYCARE AND PRESCHOOL was operating at full capacity, almost from the day it first opened its doors. There were five full time teachers, in addition to Susan and Peggy who, as owners, were there every day and Ashton, who ran the afterschool programs. Sarah volunteered on a regular basis and brought Jessica, who seemed to fit right in and had very little trouble with the other kids, since she now had both Sarah and Ashton giving her that "filters" look. The only time Ashton took off was when her parents flew up from Palm Beach to stay with her and visit their granddaughter. Jessica called them "Grandma" and "Grandpa" but followed Ashton's strict instructions to call her real mother "Ashton." Sarah often let Jessica stay overnight so Bob and Marian would have more time with her.

Ashton was settling into her life quite well now; though she still missed Andrew, working with the children gave her a great deal of satisfaction as did seeing her daughter almost every day. She had been to the office several times to have lunch with Denise; although Frank Delgado asked if she'd like to stay on as the Employee Relations Specialist she declined. Frank did like the idea though, and HR hired another woman to replace her. From what Ashton heard from Denise she was doing very well, although under Frank's command there were few complaints from staff. People were now happy to work at the Desmond Corporation.

"So how are you doing, really? Denise asked Ashton.

"What can I say?" I miss Andrew, I loved him despite the fact he tried to kill me. But I love working with the kids. They are so open, so happy; their life is just beginning and the joy on their faces is just... I don't know, wonderful! And to see Jessica all the time and to know that she has a good mother and father to raise her, that's great too. And my parents are happy. Did you know Bob told me my mother hardly ever goes into her new kitchen? He says Rita makes a mean rigatoni and meatballs. They're happy and they're living the life they deserve to live."

"How's the guy you gave the store to, what's his name? Craig, isn't it?"

"He's doing great. The store is open seven days now and he's hired two assistant managers. His little boy is doing well in that new school he's going to; I understand he's started to speak."

"But what about you and Larry? How's that going?" Larry was the patent attorney Denise was dating.

"It's going good, you know; one step at a time and we'll see where it takes us. It feels good, though, not to be trolling the bars at night anymore," Denise told her. "The lease on my apartment will be up in a few months though so let's just say I might not be renewing it. I will take all that gorgeous furniture you gave me though when I leave."

"I'm glad, Denise, you deserve it."

"And you deserve to find someone too, Ashton."

"It's not so easy. I'm like my mother-in-law; I want to live well but not crazy. Most of the guys I meet now just want me for my money. Sure, they may pay for the first date when we go out but then they ask me 'where's my jet' or 'I want to see your house' or 'let's go to the Bahamas for the weekend'. I want to find someone who'll like me for me and not for what I can give them."

"You'll find him, Ashton, I know you will, but in the meantime, can I come to your house this weekend? I want to work on my tan," Denise winked.

"Sure, we'll both work on our tans."

As Ashton drove home, though, she was saddened by the thought that she was alone. She longed to find someone she could really love and tell the world about it. She looked down at her hand; she still wore that outrageously expensive engagement ring Andrew gave her.

She had never gotten a wedding band; Andrew wanted her to have one but since she didn't want anyone to know she was married she refused. It was funny; one of the reasons she didn't want anyone to know was because of all his money. How would they react to all of it? In reality, now it seemed to be no big deal. Her parents got used to their Palm Beach house and the servants it came with very quickly; she laughed at the thought of her mother being waited on hand and foot.

Her father called only the other day and asked her to send the jet to pick them up next week as they wanted to spend the weekend with her and see Jessica. She was pleased to do all that for them; she felt she was no longer a failure in their eyes. As she pulled into her driveway her housekeeper came out to greet her.

"What would you like for dinner, Miss Ashton?" Ashton never liked being called "Mrs. Desmond." She felt that title belonged to Susan. She actually wanted her housekeeper, Donna, to call her Ashton but Donna felt that would be disrespectful, and so they settled on "Miss Ashton."

"How about rigatoni and meatballs, Donna," Ashton said as she made her way to her pool deck to mix herself a cocktail.

Okay, life was good, Ashton thought, but it would be better if she had someone to share it with.

Susan was pleased the school was doing so well; it was her dream to work with kids and to live in a little clapboard house as she did in the days when Andrew was a baby. Those years were the happiest of her life. She missed Andrew terribly. She often went to his gravesite and just sat there, talking to him as if he were still living, telling him about Ashton.

"You know she really is a wonderful girl, Andrew, you picked a good one. But she's lonely; she needs someone to love her. I don't want her to be alone for the rest of her life."

That night, as Susan slept, she had another dream. Andrew came to her and he was smiling. There seemed to be a glow all around him as he told her "Mother, Ashton will find love. And this time it will be forever. I love you, Mother and I'm sorry for the way I treated you. One day we will meet again."

Susan awoke the next morning wondering if it was real or just a dream, but then she remembered another dream she had—the one about Jessica being her granddaughter. That dream became fact the day Ashton married Andrew.

Saying nothing about her dream to Ashton, Susan went about her day. It was a pleasant day but warm, and now the air conditioning was on the fritz again. As she passed Ashton in the hallway she told her she had to call someone about the air conditioning. Ashton told her some of the lights seemed to be flickering; perhaps they needed to call an electrician instead. One of the teachers had some problems in her own home and just had her own wiring fixed.

She recommended a local company; one whose office was not far from the school. In fact, she still had their business card in her wallet. She brought the card to Susan who promptly dialed the number.

"Scott Davis Electrical," the pleasant voice answered. Susan set up an appointment for the next afternoon. She would not be able to be there; she promised Peggy they would go to some art exhibit that just opened, but Ashton could handle it.

The next day, promptly at two thirty as promised, the white panel truck bearing the name Scott Davis & Company pulled up in front of the school. It was the first time Scott Davis would lay eyes on Ashton Lancaster Desmond.

He couldn't keep his eyes off her; he was like a school kid with his first crush.

Those eyes, they're like the color of the sea, he thought, but he tried to be cool and business-like.

"What seems to be the problem, Miss? He glanced down and saw the enormous ring on her finger, he didn't know quite what to say; was that thing real? It couldn't be…

As he struggled to take his eyes from her left hand, Ashton went on to tell him about the problems with the flickering lights and the a/c going out. As she spoke, she noticed his bright blue eyes and sandy blond hair. He looked to be about the same age as she was; she wondered if he were married at first, but reading his mind quickly, found he wasn't. She directed him to the fuse boxes.

"Looks like we need to do some rewiring here, which is odd, because this building is brand new. My office is not far from here and I pass here often. I watched it being built."

"Yes, but the people who built it ran out of money and hightailed it to Oregon," Ashton said. "Maybe they started to cut corners on its construction when they realized they might not be able to finish it."

"You could be right about that—Miss…?"

"Ashton, my name is Ashton. You must be Scott."

"Yes," he said, acting like a schoolboy again, as he shook her hand.

"So what do we need to do to fix it?"

"We'll have to do some rewiring. Shouldn't take more than a week or so."

"What about the children? Do we have to close the building?" Ashton asked.

"No, we can actually work around it so you'll be fine," he said. "How's Monday morning? I can give you an idea of the cost right now."

Ashton knew it didn't matter how much it cost, but she let him talk. He gave her his estimate; she accepted it, and wrote a check for the entire amount.

When he got back to his office he gave his secretary the work order. One of the men who worked for him asked him where he was. Scott told him and said he met this incredible woman named Ashton. As he handed Ashton's check to his secretary she noticed the name on it…

"Ashton Lancaster Desmond." She spoke up quickly, "Scott, don't you know who this is? This is the wife of that super rich guy who got shot by his mother last year. She's worth like a trillion bucks!"

Scott never heard of her, but then he didn't watch the news much. So that honker on her finger must be real, then. He thought to himself that she was the most beautiful woman he'd ever seen, but he'd bet she'd never go out with him.

As Ashton drove home from school, she thought about Scott. There was just something about him; he was so friendly, so genuine. In the short time they spoke she felt so comfortable with him.

When Monday came Ashton dressed extra carefully, making sure her makeup was just so. Before she grabbed her briefcase she slid her ring off her finger and put it in the safe.

AS THE WEEK WENT BY ASHTON found herself stopping to talk with Scott; they sat outside on one of the benches having coffee. Scott told her all about himself: that he owned the company, which ~~was~~ consisted of a secretary and ten electricians like himself. He never married but was engaged once when he was twenty-three, but his fiancé decided they were too young to get married after all; at thirty-eight he was still single. He liked the beach, was an avid surfer and rented a small apartment about a block away from it.

It would be more difficult for Ashton to tell him her story. What could she say? That she could read minds; that the adorable little girl sitting over there with the auburn hair was her real daughter now adopted by her husband's ex-wife and she could read minds as well? And that she, Ashton, had a net worth of a little over 750 million dollars? How exactly do you explain all that while drinking coffee out of Styrofoam cups—she thought of Andrew for a moment and the fancy cups he used to drink his expensive Kenyan coffee from.

What she did say was that she was married and her husband died; she loved children and that's why she took a job working with Susan, who was her mother-in-law. She said she too lived on the beach. She didn't say that her house cost seven million dollars and that she had two full time housekeepers. While she spoke she could see Jessica looking at her, smiling brightly and giving her the thumbs up.

"He's the one, Mommy! He's the one!" Ashton heard her daughter's voice clearly in her mind. And then he asked her out. To a diner. In town. For hamburgers. She was thrilled.

THE SCHOOL NOW PROPERLY WIRED, Scott's work there was done. But his relationship with Ashton was just getting started. She eventually told him almost everything about her but left out the part about the mind reading. And it seemed that everyone around her felt just the way little Jessica did; that he was "the one."

No matter who she talked to, they all said the same. In the morning Susan would ask "Seeing Scott tonight?" and smile so wide Ashton wondered if she would split her lips. Sarah did the same. In fact, Ashton and Scott double dated with Sarah and Bill. Scott also got along great with Kevin and Allison.

And Ashton was on Cloud Nine. It was never like this with Andrew. Okay, she had to admit that some of it was her fault, after all, she told very few people about him; but then Andrew just wasn't the kind of guy to enjoy a barbeque at the beach after a game of volleyball. Ashton knew a life with him would be exactly that…a life with him, and practically no one else. He couldn't even get along with his own mother, something Ashton especially never understood. She loved Susan so much now. They worked together. They socialized together. They genuinely enjoyed each other's company. So many people couldn't stand their in-laws, but not Ashton; Susan was even close to Bob and Marian now, seeing them every time they flew up to see their daughter.

The only problem in the relationship between Ashton and Scott was Ashton's money. Although they didn't speak of it often, Ashton could easily read his thoughts. She knew he loved her, she knew he was thinking of asking her to marry him, but the money was a stumbling block. Scott did fairly well; he would have been able to make a good life for a family, and he was proud of that. He knew that modern women had careers, unlike his mother, who had been a stay-at-home until he went to college, and then only worked to have something to do. But he wanted his wife to take it easy if she wanted to, and not have to put in a forty hour work week. But with Ashton...

He remembered when he first went to her house. As he pulled in the driveway he knew, how could you not, that she had a very large bank account. He never asked her how much she had; that would be rude and besides, he was no gold digger. The secretary in his office thought she was worth a billion; Mike, one if the electricians who worked for him, and one of his best friends, said he thought it was more like five hundred million. Whatever it was, when he walked into her house he could have caught flies his mouth was open so wide.

But still, the feelings he had for her were so natural that her money ultimately didn't matter. He reasoned to himself that, despite all that wealth, she still worked every day; he was sure she wouldn't try to stop him from doing the same.

Ashton knew it was coming: Scott was going to ask her to marry him. She asked her parents to come up to meet him; they were pleased. When Ashton told them about him she sounded so happy. She would call and tell her mother Scott said this and Scott said that, and Marian was glad. They had never met Andrew.

Ashton hid the relationship from them in much the same way as she hid Jessica from them as well. Marian wondered if Andrew hadn't died that night if they even would have known about their daughter's marriage. Maybe she just would have taken off one day with him to some foreign city never to return.

And it was on a sunny Saturday afternoon, surrounded by her family and friends that Scott Davis got down on one knee and asked Ashton Lancaster to be his wife. He presented her with a two carat marquis shaped diamond that was not internally flawless and not colorless, and had been purchased from a local jeweler in town. It did not cost almost a million or look like someone could ice skate on it. But to Ashton Lancaster Desmond, it was the most beautiful ring she had ever seen. As she looked around at the smiling faces of her family and friends, Ashton thought this was a very good sign.

THEY WERE MARRIED IN ST PATRICK'S CATHEDRAL. Ashton's gown had a ten foot train trailing behind it. As she walked up the aisle, she could see Scott and his best man, Mike, waiting at the altar. Allison and Denise were just taking their places at the railing as well. And just for a moment, standing right ahead of her as she slowly put one foot in front of the other was Andrew, and he was smiling; his gray eyes as soft as a gentle mist. When she blinked her eyes, he was gone. In front of only about seventy-five people, Ashton Lancaster became Mrs. Scott Davis. Her parents insisted on paying for the wedding, which they held at the Waldorf Astoria.

ASHTON WAS WORKING ON A new schedule for the after school program. Jessica was playing at her feet, constantly looking up at her and asking if it was time to go to the hospital. But it would be another two months before Matthew Scott would make his entrance into the world.

"You know it's not time yet, Jessica, you ask me that every day."

But Ashton couldn't blame her, so did her mother. Marian called her every day asking her if she thought Matthew would make an early entrance into the world.

"No, Ma, I'm sure I'll go nine months just like everybody else." Ashton repeated those same words over and over to her anxious mother. The only thing that got Marian off the phone was Bob yelling in the background for her to get off the phone and leave her daughter alone. And Susan couldn't be happier for Ashton.

She remembered her dream, the one where Andrew came to her and told her that Ashton would find love forever. As she stood besides Andrew's grave she told him how much she missed him. She told him all about Ashton and her having a baby. But somehow, Susan thought he already knew. It was amazing; sometimes, when she was walking in a crowd she thought she could see him. But now, those piercing gray eyes were soft, loving, caring, as if Andrew had found peace at last. Wherever he was, there were no deals to close, no companies to take over, and no fights to get to the top.

On a cloudy September afternoon, Peggy was sitting behind the desk finishing up some paperwork. Susan had gone home early; she wanted to try a new recipe one of the mothers had told her about. As she worked, a young woman entered the office with her little boy, wanting to inquire about placing him in one of the afterschool programs. She told Peggy that she lived in Queens but had moved to the Midwest to be with her parents when her son was born. But she found it difficult to find work in the small town that her parents lived in, and besides, now that her son was nearly six years old, she felt she had imposed on her parents long enough; they were getting on in years and her little boy could be quite a handful. She was determined to make it on her own.

Peggy looked up and smiled. Extending her hand, she asked the woman her name. "Nicole Marshall, and this is my son, Daniel."

As the woman filled out the paperwork, Peggy made small talk with her.

"So, you used to live in Queens? What part? I'm from Forest Hills," Peggy told her.

"Long Island City. I just got a job not too far from here. I'm glad I don't have to work in the city anymore. I used to before I moved back home."

"Oh really, what did you do?" Peggy asked.

"I was an administrative assistant for a little while. I worked at that big building downtown, the one with the big "D" on the top that everyone always remarks about. The Desmond Corporation."

Peggy reviewed her completed paperwork and smiled at Daniel. "So how do you like Long Island?" she asked him.

"It's okay. There's a lot more people here than where my grandma and grandpa live," the little boy reported. Peggy told her that the woman who runs the afterschool programs was still in the building. She buzzed Ashton.

"Tell her to wait, I'll be right there. I want to tell her about the different programs we have and find out which one she feels will be best for her," Ashton said.

As usual, Jessica was sitting by her feet, asking again when they would go to the hospital. Wanting to give her something to do

Ashton told her, "Hey, there's going to be a new student in the afterschool program. Want to go meet him?"

"Okay."

Grabbing her hand, they walked to the administration office. Opening the door, Ashton stopped dead in her tracks, watching as her little girl with the auburn hair and sea green eyes came face-to-face with the little boy with the raven black hair and the piercing gray eyes.

ABOUT THE AUTHOR

Originally from the New York City area, Deborah Ailman now resides near Tampa, Florida. A Positive Thought Counselor, she can be reached through her website, **optimistforever.com** .

Made in the USA
Charleston, SC
11 March 2015